PRA...
the North America...

"The Gears have written an epic novel that combines the cultural history of Cahokia with the fast-paced narrative of a thriller to explore the all-too-human and universal dangers of greed and overweening ambition."

—*New York Journal of Books*
on *People of the Morning Star*

"A magnificent, sweeping world—America, circa 7300 B.C.—that is so real you can almost breathe in the air of it. It tells a bighearted story of war and peace, love and violence, with a cast of richly drawn characters. This is a novel that will stay with you for years—I guarantee it."

—Douglas Preston,
New York Times bestselling author,
on *People of the Raven*

"An exciting tale about the age-old quest for power . . . An exciting, skillfully crafted, and fast-paced story that also serves as an engrossing look at ancient culture . . . The authors lavish passion and rich detail on this fine addition to their fascinating series." —*Publishers Weekly*
on *People of the Silence*

"A novel of suspense as well as a book to give you joy and goose bumps . . . A great adventure tale, throbbing with life and death . . . The most convincing reconstruction of prehistory I have yet read." —Morgan Llywelyn,
author of *Lion of Ireland,* on *People of the Earth*

"A first-rate murder mystery, anthropological information on pre-European Native America, a slight dash of sex (mostly innocent), and plenty of politics. Whew! The amazing thing is that it is all done so well."

—*Booklist* (starred review) on *People of the Mist*

By W. Michael Gear and Kathleen O'Neal Gear
from Tom Doherty Associates

NORTH AMERICA'S
FORGOTTEN PAST SERIES

People of the Wolf

People of the Fire

People of the Earth

People of the River

People of the Sea

People of the Lakes

People of the Lightning

People of the Silence

People of the Mist

People of the Masks

People of the Owl

People of the Raven

People of the Moon

People of the Nightland

People of the Weeping Eye

People of the Thunder

People of the Longhouse

*The Dawn Country: A People
  of the Longhouse Novel*

*The Broken Land: A People
  of the Longhouse Novel*

*The Black Sun: A People of
  the Longhouse Novel*

People of the Songtrail

THE MORNING STAR SERIES

People of the Morning Star

Morning Star: Sun Born

Morning Star: Moon Hunt

THE ANASAZI MYSTERY
SERIES

The Visitant

The Summoning God

Bone Walker

BY KATHLEEN O'NEAL GEAR

Thin Moon and Cold Mist

Sand in the Wind

This Widowed Land

It Sleeps in Me

It Wakes in Me

It Dreams in Me

BY W. MICHAEL GEAR

Long Ride Home

Big Horn Legacy

The Athena Factor

The Morning River

Coyote Summer

This Scorched Earth
  (forthcoming)

OTHER TITLES BY
KATHLEEN O'NEAL GEAR
AND W. MICHAEL GEAR

The Betrayal

Dark Inheritance

Raising Abel

Children of the Dawnland

Coming of the Storm

Fire in the Sky

A Searing Wind

www.Gear-Gear.com | www.gear-books.com

MORNING STAR

Sun Born

W. Michael Gear and
Kathleen O'Neal Gear

FORGE®

A TOM DOHERTY ASSOCIATES BOOK
NEW YORK

To

Tom Doherty

An old and dear friend

Have we really been at it this long?

NOTE: If you purchased this book without a cover, you should be aware that this book is stolen property. It was reported as "unsold and destroyed" to the publisher, and neither the authors nor the publisher has received any payment for this "stripped book."

This is a work of fiction. All of the characters, organizations, and events portrayed in this novel are either products of the authors' imaginations or are used fictitiously.

SUN BORN

Copyright © 2016 by W. Michael Gear and Kathleen O'Neal Gear

Excerpt from *Moon Hunt* copyright © 2017 by W. Michael Gear and Kathleen O'Neal Gear

All rights reserved.

Illustrations by Ellisa Mitchell

A Forge Book
Published by Tom Doherty Associates
175 Fifth Avenue
New York, NY 10010

www.tor-forge.com

Forge® is a registered trademark of Macmillan Publishing Group, LLC.

ISBN 978-0-7653-8062-3

Our books may be purchased in bulk for promotional, educational, or business use. Please contact your local bookseller or the Macmillan Corporate and Premium Sales Department at 1-800-221-7945, extension 5442, or by e-mail at MacmillanSpecialMarkets@macmillan.com.

First Edition: October 2016
First Mass Market Edition: September 2017

Printed in the United States of America

0 9 8 7 6 5 4 3 2 1

Acknowledgments

A fan recently stated that the PEOPLE books are doing for Native America what Homer did for Iron Age Greece. If our work has made a contribution to the understanding of our nation's prehistory, it is because of Tom Doherty's dedication, faith, and encouragement over the years.

Additional thanks go to Linda Quinton, our associate publisher. No stranger to our acknowledgments page, Linda gave us just the shot in the arm we needed—and at the moment we needed it. Linda, a thousand thanks.

To Claire Eddy and Bess Cozby we extend our most sincere appreciation for their editorial dedication in helping us to make this the best book possible, and for catching most of our errors. We're responsible for the rest of them.

To Theresa Hulongbayan, we offer our gratitude. Her Gear books fan club on Facebook (https://www.facebook.com/groups/54987233824/) is a special gathering place for those interested in American archaeology. Someone should give her an honorary Ph.D. for her expertise on our books. She establishes the criteria for the term "a most remarkable woman."

Finally, we wish to acknowledge the staff at Cahokia Mounds State Historic Site, including Mark Esary, Bill Iseminger, Matt Migalla, Marilyn Harvey, and Linda Krieg. Our gratitude is also extended to the Cahokia Mounds Museum Society for their incessant labor and constant dedication to the recovery, preservation, and interpretation of Cahokia's heritage. For more information—or to make a donation to help preserve this World Heritage Site—contact them at www.cahokiamounds.org.

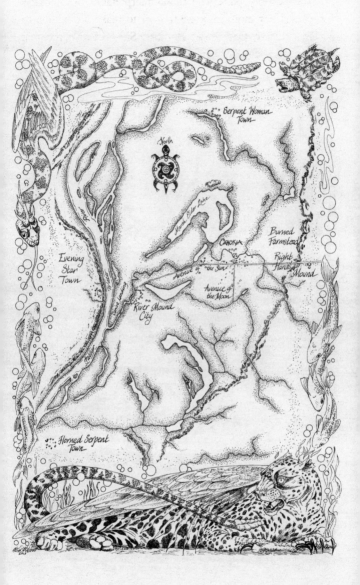

Serpent Woman Town

North

Morning Star Lake

Cahokia

Burned Farmstead

Right Hand Mound

Evening Star Town

Avenue of the Sun

Avenue of the Moon

River Mound City

Horned Serpent Town

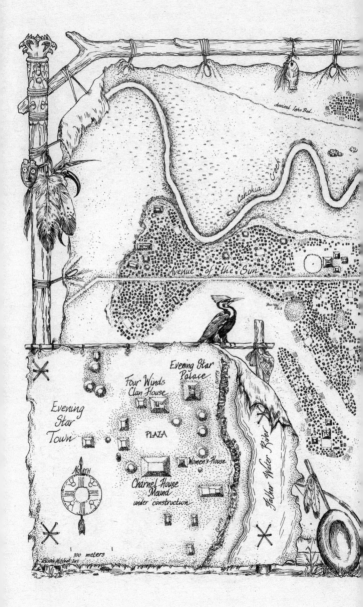

Ancient Lake Bed.

Cahokia Creek

Avenue of the Sun

Borrow Pits

Evening Star Palace

Four Winds Clan House

Evening Star Town

PLAZA

Women's House

NORTH

Charnel House Mound under construction

Father Water River

100 meters

Elliott Mitchell 2011

1 Morning Star's Great Mound
2 Night Shadow Star's Palace
3 Tonka'tzi's Palace
4 Four Winds Clan Palace
5 Rides-the-Lightning's Temple
6 Record Keeper's Temple
7 Four Winds Burial Mound

Cahokia Creek

Avenue of the Sun

Avenue of the Moon

CAHOKIA

NORTH

B.C.

13,000	10,000	6,000	3,000	1,500

PEOPLE *of the* WOLF
Alaska & Canadian
Northwest

PEOPLE *of the* EARTH
Northern Plains & Basins

PEOPLE *of the* NIGHTLAND
Ontario & New York &
Pennsylvania

PEOPLE *of*
the OWL

Lower
Mississippi
Valley

PEOPLE *of the* SEA
Pacific Coast & Arizona

PEOPLE *of the* RAVEN
Pacific Northwest &
British Columbia

PEOPLE *of the* LIGHTNING
Florida

PEOPLE *of the* FIRE
Central Rockies &
Great Plains

A.D.

0	200	1,000	1,100	1,300	1,400

PEOPLE *of the* LAKES
East-Central Woodlands
& Great Lakes

PEOPLE *of the*
WEEPING EYE

Mississippi Valley
& Tennessee

PEOPLE *of the* MASKS
Ontario & Upstate New York

PEOPLE *of the*
THUNDER

Alabama & Mississippi

PEOPLE *of the* RIVER
Mississippi Valley

PEOPLE *of the*
LONGHOUSE

New York
& New England

PEOPLE *of the* MORNING STAR
Central Mississippi Valley

PEOPLE *of the* SILENCE
Southwest Anasazi

The
DAWN
COUNTRY

The
BROKEN
LAND

PEOPLE *of the* MOON
Northwest New Mexico
& Southwest Colorado

PEOPLE
of the
BLACK
SUN

PEOPLE *of the* MIST
Chesapeake Bay

Prologue

Night Shadow Star walked through shining darkness. Roots clung to the roof and walls of the cave. Knotted and twisted like an old woman's joints they curled out from the limestone walls. Her feet barely dimpled the soft mud. The occasional crawfish or turtle scurried away, surprised by such an unusual and otherwordly visitor.

As she passed, the current stirred, lifting and feathering her long black hair until it floated behind her in an undulating wave.

"Why have you brought me here?" she asked the beastly Piasa, the Spirit creature that stalked silently beside her.

"You have been summoned."

Piasa stared sidelong at her, its yellow eyes surrounded by the three-forked-eye pattern of the Underworld; the creature's pupils might have been wells descending into a stygian eternity. The mysterious beast's head was that of a cougar, its nose pink, the wiry whiskers spread as if seeking prey. From the beast's back, mighty wings rose, the feathers patterned in rainbow colors that alternated with black bars and charcoal-dark circles. Rather than paws, Piasa's cat legs ended in eagle's feet: yellow and scaled with black talons. They barely stirred the mud as he paced beside her. The creature's tail resembled that of a serpent: scaled, diamond-hatched, and tipped with parallel rows of squash-sized rattles.

She said, "You already whisper to my souls and stalk my dreams. Why summon me to the Underworld?"

"I was ordered."

Fear sent its cold filaments along Night Shadow Star's spine. She instinctively clenched her hands to fight an urge to shiver.

The cavern through which they walked had darkened. The roots winding down through the stalwart rock had a tortured appearance. From dark crevasses in the stone, she could sense eyes watching her, and the presence of wounded and hungry souls desperate to devour anyone who passed. Here, in this place, death and birth were locked in a mutual and terrifying Dance.

"She wishes to speak with you."

"Why?" Night Shadow Star's voice tightened. "What have I done?"

"I serve. I do not explain."

The cavern narrowed and twisted as the muddy floor rose and fell. Piasa dropped behind until his warm breath tangled in her current-borne hair. Prickling unease worked its way into her bones.

In the weird half-light of the Underworld, she could see images carved and painted on the water-gray limestone: spirals, renditions of vulvas and phallic images—some combined in intercourse—flowers and seeds, skulls, hand and footprints, and zigzagging serpents.

A new sensation traced patterns across her skin: that of immense Power. The water around her had grown heavy from the crushing depth.

Rounding a bend, she discovered the way blocked by a tangle of roots. Before her eyes, the mass began to stir, bending and flowing out of her way as it created an opening through which a golden light poured.

Night Shadow Star stepped through and into a womb-like gallery. The roof consisted of writhing roots; the floor might have been a pool of old blood hardened into red granite. Along the walls, glistening images of spirals, sacred portals, vulvas, and phalluses were interspersed with skulls and bones: Birth and Death intertwined.

A lone figure, an impossibly ancient woman, sat upon a cushioning mound of green moss. Twelve brightly colored serpents—the Power-filled Tie Snakes—had woven themselves into and through the moss. Callers of rain and masters of water, springs, and rivers, the Tie Snakes now seemed to flex and bunch beneath the old woman.

Night Shadow Star stopped short, subtly aware that Piasa had advanced no closer than the grotto's root-crowded entrance.

The old woman rested on her knees, a single thick-bodied Tie Snake coiled protectively around her. The serpent fixed its unwavering gaze on Night Shadow Star; its tongue flicked in and out.

Clutched in the old woman's hands was a simple gray-chert hoe. She raised it, chopping down. The keen blade cut deeply into the serpent's back. From the cut, a green sprout arose to join others that grew from the creature's tortured flesh until squash vines and cornstalks curled around the old woman's withered and bony legs. Her breasts hung like empty leather bags, the enlarged nipples as hard and round as walnuts. What white hair remained had been pulled into a bun at the top of a time-wizened skull. A basket brimming with corn and squash had been slung over one shoulder. Age had wasted the woman's arms until the thinnest parchment of skin outlined the underlying bones and joints.

When Night Shadow Star met the old woman's eyes, her balance wavered. Time and space stretched beneath that eternal gaze the way buffalo wool thinned as it was pulled through a tiny hole.

Emotion surged in Night Shadow Star's breast, encompassing her with its remarkable purity: grief, loss, and tragedy. Hollowed to the core, she gasped in the emptiness.

Only to tremble as incredible joy burned a radiant path through her veins.

A heartbeat later, despair, like a tangible blackness, sucked away even the faintest glimmer of hope.

Then, with the intensity of slaps to the face, emotions cascaded through her one after another, mixing, twisting. Seething rage knotted her muscles as an orgasmic climax pulsed in her pelvis. Fear's brittle ice paralyzed her bones, and simultaneously vibrant triumph blazed a searing flame in her heart.

The next instant ecstasy exploded in her chest.

And as quickly, it was gone.

She staggered, dropping to the stone floor, gasping and reeling in the spinning aftereffects.

"I . . . What happened to me?"

"I shared the tiniest fraction of my being with you. A mere hint . . . the barest essence. The Power of Creation and Chaos. Everything that wisdom, order, and peace are not."

"Why?"

"So you should understand."

"I understand nothing."

"Then you understand everything."

Night Shadow Star blinked, confused. "Your words—"

"Are everything. The One, the Dance, the Spiral, the blinding darkness, the thunderous silence. Everything and . . . nothing." She paused. "Look at me."

The instant Night Shadow Star met the old woman's gaze, the chaos of conflicting emotions blew through her again, exploding like a thousand stars.

When her wits returned, she lay gasping and exhausted, the cavern whirling around her until it slowed and she could draw a breath.

"Do you understand now?" the old woman asked flatly.

"Why are you doing this to me?"

"So that you understand what is at risk."

"I . . . don't . . ."

'Not since young Lichen pleaded for my help have I given much thought to Cahokia or what it has become. Your brother Walking Smoke brought you to my attention. He would have caused me a great deal of trouble, but for you. Thankfully, your presence balances the influences of the Sky World. Therefore you've earned this warning."

"Warning?"

"Reality is a shifting thing. It changes with time and the direction from which it is viewed. Everything you hold dear— your Cahokia, your very world—dangles from a thread. A man is traveling to Cahokia who understands the stakes. His goal is to change your world, redirect its reality."

"Who?"

"An Itza lord from the distant south. A man of unbridled ambition and charisma."

"You wish me to defeat him for you?"

"I care not, Night Shadow Star. You know me as Old-Woman-Who-Never-Dies, or as First Woman. In his world I am known as B'a Yal Na, which you would translate as First Mother. Because of his offerings, I have given him my protection. He thinks his divine mission is to return Cahokia to the True Belief. Therefore, if you would thwart him, it will require your cunning and skill. It is my order that neither you, nor your allies, take his life."

"But if he—"

"Those are my terms, Night Shadow Star. He serves me, as do you. The battle for Cahokia is between the two of you. Beyond that, I shall not interfere."

An instant later, as if the world had been jerked sideways and her souls had been squeezed by a mighty fist, Night Shadow Star found herself in the narrow passage outside Old-Woman-Who-Never-Dies' root-choked grotto.

"You have heard." Piasa's whiskers bristled, and his yellow eyes were baleful. "But I will tell you this: the path to ultimate victory over the Itza will require that you surrender yourself to him, and that your Red Wing must be invincible in battle and sport."

Exhausted, every muscle aching, Night Shadow Star blinked awake. She lay in her familiar bed, a blanket twisted around her. In the faint light cast by a hickory-oil lamp, she made out the furnishings of her private quarters: her storage boxes, folded blankets and robes, the altar, her beautifully engraved pole bed where it was built into the back wall.

In the silence she could hear her captive war chief, Fire Cat, breathing where he slept just outside her door.

She rubbed her eyes. Every muscle in her body ached as if from some terrible exertion. The Dream had been so real: Piasa, Old-Woman-Who-Never-Dies, the watery Underworld tunnel with its roots and limestone walls.

She shook her head in disbelief and sat up. As she did, the cold and heavy weight of her long hair fell over her shoulders. She grasped it and twisted. So soaked was her hair that water pattered on her floor like rain.

One

A thousand fires lit the darkness; the great city of Cahokia pulsed and throbbed as if it were a bizarre and disparate organism—a sort of mindless being. Its avenues and arteries overflowed with celebrating people. So many people: from the exalted members of the ruling Four Winds Clan; the subordinate Earth clans with their chiefs and matrons; the myriads of priests, shamans, and Traders; and, of course, the tens of thousands of immigrants. Known as "dirt farmers," they'd picked up entire towns and flocked to the burgeoning city.

Despite the numbers and vast diversity of Cahokia's population, the burly man known as Seven Skull Shield considered himself to have few—if any—equals.

He glanced at the Anilco Trader who walked beside him. A case in point.

Like all river Traders, the man, whose name translated as "Water Bird," was all shoulders and arms, and little else—though he dressed in finery. Of medium stature, he wore his hair up, had a thin straight nose, and fleshy lips. He spoke Trade pidgin and supplemented his words with sign language.

The Anilco—a Nation several weeks south of Cahokia by

fast canoe—had established themselves in the eastern flood-plain at the confluence of the great Western River where it flowed into the Father Water. Their swamp-surrounded town occupied a strategic position, controlling access to Western River and its upstream Nations, including the Caddo.

Two days back, at the canoe landing outside River Mounds City, Water Bird had Traded with Seven Skull Shield for his services as a guide. In return for two fabric bags filled with salt, Seven Skull Shield had committed to show Water Bird the highlights of Cahokia's Green Corn celebration, or Busk as it was locally known.

As they strolled north along the dark, crowd-packed margins of Cahokia's Great Plaza, Water Bird kept gasping his amazement. Within twenty paces he could hear a dozen languages, most of them incomprehensible. Every manner of dress, hairstyle, body adornment, and peculiar facial tattoos from a hundred different peoples were on display. Like a whirlpool, Cahokia had sucked in pilgrims from a half-year's journey in all directions.

"Just how many people live in Cahokia?" the Anilco wondered. Hundreds of fires burned within sight of the plaza, and hundreds more covered the uplands in the distance. The orange glare was so bright only the largest stars could be seen in the night sky.

"Tens of tens of thousands," Seven Skull Shield replied. "In the last two days, you've only seen a piece of the city stretching from the canoe landing and River Mounds City, to the Avenue of the Sun, and the Great Plaza. There's just as much to the south, north, and east. It would take you weeks to see it all."

"I'd heard . . . but never believed." Wonder gleamed in Water Bird's eyes.

Seven Skull Shield pointed to the high palace atop the magnificent mound on the plaza's northern side. "That's where the living god dwells."

"Right there?" Awe filled his voice.

"Absolutely."

Water Bird fingered his receding chin, eyes speculative. "Then . . . it is true? The storied hero from the Beginning Times, the Morning Star, has been resurrected into a living human body?" The Anilco shook his head. "It is so hard to believe. Some say that your Morning Star is not a living god but just a man playing a role."

Seven Skull Shield shrugged. "I've been up there in that palace. Sat face-to-face with him. If that's Chunkey Boy, the young man whose body was used as host for the resurrected god's souls, he's pretty convincing."

"So . . . what do you believe?"

Seven Skull Shield rubbed the back of his neck. "I don't believe in much, good Trader, but I've seen some pretty amazing things happen around the Morning Star. I might scoff at the priests and some of their sleights, but I've been in the center of Power. And let me tell you, by Piasa's swinging balls, it's scary."

When it came to guile, craftiness, and the ability to lure adventurous young women into his bed—all the most pragmatic of skills—Seven Skull Shield considered himself a man without peer.

Power, however, was a whole different critter.

Hard experience had taught him that a wise man didn't underestimate the living god. The resurrected hero was just as cunning and capable as Seven Skull Shield, though in a different sphere. After all, how hard did a living god have to work when it came to filling his bed with women? He just had to point, saying, "I want that one."

On the other hand, the Morning Star had never had to steal so much as a loaf of bread, avoid a jealous husband, or hold his own in a knock-down, eye-gouging brawl down at the canoe landing.

Those kinds of skills weren't just granted to everyone.

"Why are you scowling at the Morning Star's high palace?

Is it that you yourself really don't believe he's a reincarnated god?"

"No. Just wondering who's the craftier. Him or me?" After all, Seven Skull Shield was still alive—clanless and unprotected by privilege as he was—which proved he was the consummate survivor in this great city.

Which, of course, meant the world.

"Come, Water Bird. I'll show you where the high and mighty live. Let you stare up the great staircase to the Council Terrace Gate. Point out Lady Night Shadow Star's palace. She's something, she is. A real beauty—and possessed by your Piasa, too. Scoff all you like, but I've seen her under the beast's spell."

"Then she is a dangerous woman of great and unusual Power." Water Bird gave him a disbelieving glance.

"Indeed, she is," Seven Skull Shield replied as his stomach growled. "You hungry? Don't move a step, or you'll get lost in this crowd and I'll never find you. Be right back."

He slipped sideways in the press and prowled the crowd. For some reason he couldn't shake a sudden foreboding. The feeling that something was about to go wrong clung to his souls like a morning-spun cobweb.

This was the final night of the Busk ceremony. Tonight's feast was the joyous celebration after four days of fasting, ritual prayer, cleansing and purging, and sexual abstention— the biggest, grandest festival in the Cahokian world. It celebrated the resurrection of Morning Star. This evening's festival began when the first ears of this year's green corn were consumed by the Morning Star.

Seven Skull Shield should have been as jovial as the ebbing and flowing crowd. And, pus and blood, Water Bird was certainly paying him enough. Instead, his thoughts, unaccountably, were plagued with notions of murder and mayhem.

Seven Skull Shield located his target: a Deer Clan Trader who stood behind a raised table on which roasted turkey legs were displayed. The stall beside him was manned by an old Panther Clan woman selling pigments and dyes, the colors filling assorted clay bowls on her blanket.

"How's business?" Seven Skull Shield asked the old woman.

"Slow," she told him as the crowd jostled past.

"You've got a good location." He pointed at the white-clay-capped mound behind her where the frame of a huge new building loomed in the firelit night. "That's the Four Winds *Tonka'tzi*'s new palace going up."

"I thought it would give me a little more prestige," she told him. "I'm only asking what's reasonable. Look at these yellow clay dyes. Have you ever seen such bright colors?"

Which was when Seven Skull Shield's opportunity came. Three little boys, giggling and pushing each other, ran behind the turkey vendor's booth, squealing as they tore past.

"Hey! You boys!" Seven Skull Shield roared and pointed. "Bring that turkey leg back you little scoundrels!"

The boys stopped, blinking in surprise.

"How'd they do that?" Seven Skull Shield asked the Deer Clan man in wonder. "Grab that leg right out from under you, and you never saw?"

The turkey vendor swung around to stare at the boys, who, suddenly terrified—and accused of something they hadn't done—whirled and ran for their lives. The Deer Clan turkey vendor let out a bellow of rage and pelted off after them.

"Vile little thieves," Seven Skull Shield told the Panther Clan woman, and paused only long enough to snare two turkey legs before stepping into the crowd.

Stealing was simple. Killing other human beings, by contrast, was such a complicated thing. He considered it as he slipped through the throngs packing the plaza margins. In one set of circumstances men and women lauded each other, singing, feasting, and calling upon Spirit Power to aid their mutual quest to dispatch other human beings, often in the most hideous manner; clubbing, slicing, bashing, burning, suffocating, and crushing among them. Doing so was not only justified, but encouraged in the pursuit of territory, loot, or as a remedy for some real or perceived insult.

At other times, the "good of society" required that a person sneak up behind a relative who had transgressed, stolen, or committed an outrage, and bash his or her un-suspecting brains out with a heavy club. Families were responsible for the actions of their own. Such elimination of a miscreant for the betterment and peace of mind for all was considered a distasteful but necessary duty. Again, it took place with the full sanction of the community.

Everyone understood that hanging a war captive or politi-cal prisoner in a wooden square and burning, cutting, and beating him for days until he finally succumbed was not only just, it was a measure of the victim's courage—which pro-vided his miserable afterlife soul with a path to redemption. More, it served as a religious observance, one that helped balance the red Power of chaos and blood with the white Power's order and tranquility.

But change the circumstances, even a little, and what the community once gleefully sanctioned became taboo and evil. Should a kinsman goad his relative into a sudden rage and a lethal blow be delivered? Such a killing crossed the line into murder. It was all a matter of rules.

Picky little subtle rules.

Seven Skull Shield had always had trouble with rules.

Mostly because they were made by people who expected him to obey them.

Water Bird, true to his instructions, stood exactly where Seven Skull Shield had left him. The man was watching the Dancers in the stickball field and gratefully took his turkey leg.

As Seven Skull Shield sank his teeth into the juicy

flesh, he wondered why these perplexing notions of murder and mayhem were popping into his head on this of all nights.

"Have you ever seen anything like this, Water Bird? They're celebrating this most important of rituals—the renewal and rebirth of the entire world."

"It is more than I can believe," the Anilco replied with a full mouth.

Seven Skull Shield pointed with his turkey. "The sacred fire up there in the Morning Star's temple was extinguished and relit by the Morning Star himself. That was the moment of rebirth."

Water Bird shook his head, eyes still on the lines of Dancers out in the plaza. "For the last three days I thought you were all head-struck crazy. I can't believe you strip your houses and temples down to the walls and replace perfectly good furnishings."

"They call it ritual cleansing." Yesterday in River Mounds City, he'd watched Water Bird's awed expression as last year's matting was committed to monstrous bonfires and new matting laid across the packed-dirt floors.

"Well, Water Bird, you can go back and tell your Anilco that you survived days of deprivation. That the purging, prayers, sacrifices, and acts of atonement didn't kill you. You've seen miscreants pardoned for their deeds. Exiles, whose petitions were granted, will be allowed to return home to the embrace of families and friends. Happy times all around. Just like the Morning Star himself, the world is risen from death. Everything made whole. Even the new corn crop."

"It's so much grander than our First Fire celebrations held at the solstice and equinox," Water Bird lamented.

The feasting going on around them included people gorging on new corn and roasting entire carcasses of deer, turkeys, ducks, geese, and swans. Basket-loads of fish, turtles, cattail roots, coontie-root bread, and nuts and berries of every kind were everywhere.

Yet here Seven Skull Shield was, chewing on a succulent turkey leg and unable to think of anything but murder as he led Water Bird through the smoke-filled night.

Crowds of brightly dressed people thronged around them, laughing, chattering happily, and clapping their hands in the warm summer air. An eerie illumination filled the night sky as tens of thousands of fires reflected orange over the sprawling city.

The sound of flutes and drums rose and fell, coupled with the rhythmic thumping of feet in the great plaza. Thousands Danced in honor of Corn Maiden, Old-Woman-Who-Never-Dies' daughter, from whose vagina had come the gift of corn back in the Beginning Times.

Lines of men, their arms linked, shuffled and stomped as they faced similar lines of women. Bodies illuminated by leaping fires, the Dancers moved in a sinuous and beautiful unison, swaying and singing on grass trampled by four days of frantic stickball games.

The plaza margins, where Seven Skull Shield led his Anilco charge, were packed elbow-to-elbow with vendors. Food, pottery, textiles, carvings, and trinkets were laid out on blankets or offered from portable stands. Throngs of passersby looked on or stopped long enough to dicker for a necklace or feathered cloak.

Seven Skull Shield barely grabbed Water Bird out of the way as a flock of screaming children tore through the throng. A sudden break in the crowd gave him an unrestricted view of Morning Star's mound.

"There, Water Bird. Look. This is the best view you can get."

The massive mound dominated the northern side of the Great Plaza like some hulking monster. On the heights, the Morning Star's soaring temple rose behind its palisade and seemed to glow in the fluttering orange gleam.

"The palace is huge!"

"As befits a living god. You see that terrace that juts out on the south? That's the Council Terrace where the *tonka'tzi* receives embassies from every Nation, including the Anilco. And there, at the top of the stairs, do you see those people standing in the Council Terrace Gate? You wanted to see the Morning Star? There he is."

Even over the distance the colorful and feathered costumes stood out, dominated by the Morning Star's magnificent red feather cape.

"The people around him? Those are the high-born rulers of the Four Winds Clan and their retinues. Come on, let's get closer and I'll point them out."

Like all things pertaining to the Morning Star, the spectacle was magnificently orchestrated. The living god of Cahokia and his servants were suitably displayed for the masses to see and marvel over.

The thunderstruck Water Bird appeared to be getting his value in Trade, his eyes wide, mouth hanging open to expose half-chewed turkey.

While the southern half of the Great Plaza hosted the thousands Dancing in honor of Corn Maiden and her gift of the sacred plant, the northern half was dedicated to the noble born. Unlike the inclusive Corn Maiden Dance where anyone could participate, in the plaza below the great mound only elite individuals Danced in honor of the Morning Star.

Each of the Four Winds Clan "Houses" was represented, of course, but so, too, were the Earth Clans and the representatives of foreign Nations like the Pacaha, Casqui, Yuchi, Muskogee, Albaamaha, and Caddo.

With the exception of the long strips of manicured clay dedicated to the chunkey courts, the whole grassy area north of the World Tree pole was filled with costumed Dancers and their musicians.

To Seven Skull Shield, it appeared a chaos and cacophony

as feathered and painted Dancers wheeled and leaped, each seeking to outdo his competition.

All that for the living god who stood above with his arms raised in blessing.

The Morning Star cut an imposing figure. His polished-copper headdress glinted in the gaudy light; exotic feathers rose from shoulder splays. His remarkable feathered cloak gave his spread arms the appearance of mighty crimson wings. A snowy white apron—a representation of a scalp lock—hung before his hips, its tip dangling between his knees.

"He looks like a Spirit Being from the Beginning Times," Water Bird marveled.

"You can barely make it out from here, but the living god painted his face white with black forked-eye designs. The forked eye? That's the sign of the Sky World. His soul was recalled from the sky during the resurrection."

"And the costumed woman to his left?"

"That's the *tonka'tzi*, which means the 'Great Sky' in Cahokian. She's the ruler of the Four Winds Clan. The Four Winds normally trace descent through the males, but upon her brother Red Warrior's death last spring, Matron Wind ascended to the *tonka'tzi*'s position."

"I heard that generated some animosity among the other Houses in the Four Winds Clan."

Seven Skull Shield grinned. "The only people the Four Winds Clan love to scrap with more than themselves is anybody else. See to the *tonka'tzi*'s left? That's my good friend Clan Keeper Blue Heron. She's the one who sniffs out the plots against the Morning Star and cracks heads. Her spies have ears in every Four Winds House, every Earth Clan chief's palace, and just about everywhere else."

Water Bird gave him a sidelong glance. "Your good friend, huh? I heard you're one of her spies."

Seven Skull Shield grimaced. "*Spy* is an unkind term."

To change the subject, he said, "The people you see clustered behind the Morning Star are the lords and matrons of the other Houses that rule the city. My excellent friend, War Duck, he's High Chief at River Mounds City. The fat guy? He's Green Chunkey of Horned Serpent House down south. You can see the woman? That's Columella, from Evening Star House. I was the man who pulled her children out of her burning temple last spring."

He waved. "The rest are high-ranking chiefs from the subordinate Earth Clans who've been lucky enough to wrangle an invitation for this most august of nights."

"Look at how they're dressed!" Water Bird said through a worshipful smile.

"And there, to the right? That's Lady Night Shadow Star, eldest daughter of the late *tonka'tzi* Red Warrior, sister to Chunkey Boy whose body the Morning Star now inhabits. You ask me, she's the second most Powerful person in Cahokia after the living god."

"And her souls are really possessed by Piasa?"

"No question about it. She often sends her souls to the Underworld."

Water Bird tilted his head skeptically. "I'm not sure I believe it. Anyone possessed by the Underwater Panther's Power would go mad. Humans aren't meant to contain such Power."

"You may be right, my friend." Seven Skull Shield's lips thinned. "She's one scary woman when Piasa's whispering in her souls. Eerie, dark, reeking of the watery smells and ways of the Underworld. And maybe more than a bit insane."

"She's beautiful!"

"Ah, yes. There's that, too. Part of the lady's charm. The moment she steps into a room, any normal man is going to start dreaming about ways to fit his body against hers. And just about the time he's imagining himself slipping his hard shaft into her, Night Shadow Star's eyes go vacant, her voice changes into Piasa's, and horrifying revelations pass those full lips. Revelations that terrify a man's souls and shrivel his rod into a nubbin."

He tossed his gnawed turkey bone to a slinking cur—a bear-looking thing with odd blue-and-brown eyes. The dog studied him thoughtfully, then snapped up the treat and vanished into the crowd.

They rounded the plaza onto the Avenue of the Sun—the renowned east-west thoroughfare that passed below the Morning Star's mound and transected Cahokia.

"You see that man kneeling behind Night Shadow Star? The one dressed in full armor? That's Fire Cat."

"No! Really? The famous war chief of Red Wing Town who defeated three Cahokian armies? That's him? Why is he still alive?"

"Because after Cahokia finally conquered Red Wing Town last spring, they took him prisoner. Fire Cat was supposed to die in agony on a square, but Night Shadow Star, on Piasa's orders, cut him down and bound him to her. For such supposed enemies, they have a curious friendship."

Seven Skull Shield grinned as he turned his attention back to Clan Keeper Blue Heron. The old woman had a pinched look on her face; bits of shell and mica sewn to her skirt winked in the light. Her throat sported a wealth of shell-bead necklaces, no doubt hiding the scar that Seven Skull Shield knew so well. His life, and hers, had changed the night an assassin came within a whisker of severing her throat.

"And who are these Dancers?" Water Bird asked.

Seven Skull Shield turned his attention to the spectacle on the plaza. In the forefront were Dancers representing the Four Winds Clan Houses. Behind them Dancers from the Earth Clans whirled and leaped. And finally came the representatives from the other Nations.

"They Dance in honor of the Morning Star and seek his recognition. In the end, Morning Star will pick one for special honor based on the Dancer's skill and costume."

Among them Seven Skull Shield could pick out the Caddo, dressed in traditional Dance garb, and to the east, a whole contingent representing different Muskogee Nations. They Danced and whirled among a flurry of feathers and shell bells. The Pacaha—costumed to represent Piasa—held a position in the center rear.

But dominating the demonstration was the Quigualtam Dancer, a young man, brother to the Great Sun, or lord of the Natchez confederacy in the south. Dressed in a snake costume covered with reflective mica disks to represent scales, he whirled and pirouetted. Light from the bonfires glittered like a thousand eyes on his costume. Deer antlers were fixed to the headdress, and quartz-crystal eyes seemed to gleam with an inner light. Eagle wings sprouted from the serpent's back, spread as if to bear the creature into the sky. Behind the man's pattering feet, a rattlesnake's tail with gourd rattles whipped back and forth with remarkable similarity to a living snake's. The young man looked out through the beast's mouth, as if he were a soul devoured by the winged snake.

"It's Horned Serpent!" Water Bird cried, pointing with delight.

Oral tradition was filled with stories of those who'd been devoured by Horned Serpent. The great winged snake spent its winters in the Underworld but flew into the southern night sky during the summer moons to guard the pathway of the dead.

"There you are," a familiar voice said in Cahokian. "Been looking for you."

Seven Skull Shield turned, crying, "Crazy Frog? You're a bit far afield tonight. What brings you all the way from River Mounds City?"

Water Bird, unable to understand their language, smiled and nodded politely before turning his attention back to the Dancers.

If there were ever a nondescript Cahokian, it was Crazy

Frog. Nothing about the man, including his smudged and unrecognizable tattoos, stood out. Average of height and body build, he wore a formless brown breechcloth; a simple hemp-fiber cloak hung from his shoulders. His hair was wound into a round bun and pinned with wooden skewers.

One would never guess he was one of the wealthiest and most influential men in Cahokia. Crazy Frog liked it that way. The less the Four Winds Clan knew about his activities, the better, though he had recently come to Clan Keeper Blue Heron's attention. She, however, was smart enough to turn a blind eye to his more nefarious activities.

"I'm here on a hunch." Crazy Frog glanced up at where Morning Star and his minions watched the Dancers performing in his honor. "You still tight with her?"

"The Clan Keeper? We, uh, get along."

Crazy Frog kept his expression bland. "Her reputation is that she's never had good taste in men."

"We *don't* have that sort of relations. It's a . . . a sort of . . ."

"Working relationship?"

"Good choice of words." Seven Skull Shield jammed his thumbs into his belt. "Which brings me back to my original question: What brings you here, on this, of all nights? You should be watching the celebrations in River Mounds City and fingering your winnings after four days of betting on chunkey matches."

"Which is where I'd rather be," Crazy Frog admitted. "I think someone important is going to be murdered tonight."

Seven Skull Shield glanced sidelong at the clueless Water Bird and used a thumbnail to pick at a bit of turkey stuck in his teeth. "Who?" he mumbled past his thumb. "A Four Winds lord?"

"That, I don't know. One of my people told me that he overheard two Traders who overheard something at the canoe landing. Something big and secret. Knowing that you and the Keeper like to know these things, I sent a man to learn more. When he got there, one of the Traders was dead, the other packing to leave and scared out of his wits. Said it wasn't worth his life, or his future on the river, to say anything else. My man tried to pry more out of him, but all the Trader would say was that he depended on his Trade in the south."

"The south?"

"Make what you will out of that. Those were the Trader's last words before he pushed his canoe out and headed downriver himself."

"That's not much."

Crazy Frog gave him a sidelong glance. "Call it a gut feeling. The last time people were being murdered, it was Four Winds Clan nobles. The city almost came apart." He indicated Clan Keeper Blue Heron where she stood next to the Morning Star. "If that sort of thing is about to break loose again, I want her to know that I took it seriously. Gave you everything I had. She rewards her friends well."

"You think someone's moving on the Four Winds Clan again? Maybe one of the other Houses? Some of them are resentful of *Tonka'tzi* Wind and how leadership is concentrated."

"Maybe." Crazy Frog made a face. "I don't know. 'Trade in the south' takes in a lot of territory from the Caddo to the Muskogee and everyone in between." He slapped Seven Skull Shield on the shoulder. "So, there it is. You're warned. Now I'm having my litter carry me back to River Mounds City and my winnings. I'll give my wife your love . . . since Otter will never give you any of hers back."

"Oh, you never know. Eventually Mother Otter's curiosity might get the better of her. I think every woman wonders what it would be like to have a real man bed her."

Crazy Frog's smile thinned in pity. "Well, I guess if you ever become a 'real man,' I'll have to worry, won't I?"

Crazy Frog chuckled, turned on his heel, and vanished into the crowd.

Seven Skull Shield shot a worried look at the Council Terrace landing above. The living god seemed oblivious, his gaze on the Dancers, but as if she sensed him, Blue Heron turned her eyes his way.

The last time a murderer had stalked important people in Cahokia, the city had barely survived. Only through patience and sense had calm prevailed in the days since the Morning Star's one-time brother Walking Smoke had reportedly met his doom.

As Seven Skull Shield watched, the Morning Star raised his arms high, the feathered cloak spreading like a giant bird's scarlet wings.

A sudden silence descended on the Dancers. The musicians stilled their instruments. The crowd around Seven Skull Shield went quiet.

A young warrior, his face painted, hips girdled in a red sash, emerged from the gate and bowed before the Morning Star. Seven Skull Shield could see the Morning Star speaking, though the sound didn't carry.

The young warrior nodded, rose, and received the intricately feathered cloak as the Morning Star removed it from his shoulders.

Holding the cloak, the warrior almost skipped down the grand staircase, passed the guards who stood in ranks at the bottom, and trotted out among the Dancers.

As every eye followed, the warrior stopped before the Quigualtam Dancer in his Horned Serpent costume. The warrior dropped to one knee, and shouted, "It is the will of the Morning Star that this man, Nine Strikes, Little Sun of the Natchez Confederacy, brother to the Great Sun, or high chief, and nephew to the Natchez matron known as the White Woman, doing honor to both Horned Serpent and his people, receive this gift of appreciation in the name of the people of Cahokia, the Morning Star, and the Powers of the Sky World!"

A thunderous cry went up as the Quigualtam Dancer extended his arms from inside the costume and took the stunning feathered cloak. He dropped to his knees as he lifted his prize toward the Morning Star.

"Enough of Dancers and celebration," Seven Skull Shield muttered to himself. All evening, his thoughts had been consumed with murder. And now Crazy Frog, of all people, comes to warn him?

He was turning to leave when he saw the man. Young, his face sported distinctive tattoos reminiscent of the Natchez. The fellow was well-muscled, maybe twenty-five summers, with a leather pack over his left shoulder. His hair was done in a unique style: split in the middle into braids that had been curled around separate buns as if to mimic horn buds. His only clothing consisted of a breechcloth that hung from his waist.

The problem was that if he were from the Natchez confederacy, he should have looked delighted. A representative of his people had just won the grandest of the Morning Star's gifts and recognition. Instead, a cold rage seemed to brew behind the young man's eyes, and his fist was so tight where it clutched the pack that his knuckles had gone white.

"Hey. Water Bird. You're from the south. This man over here. He's Natchez, right?"

"Sun Born," Water Bird agreed. "Only those in the Great Sun's lineage may wear their hair in that fashion."

As Water Bird spoke, the Natchez ground his teeth and turned to a man on his right. Older, maybe fifty summers, and wearing a fine hemp war shirt, the older man listened carefully and nodded. In the light of the fires, Seven Skull Shield could just make out the man's tattoos, smudged as they were with charcoal.

Four Winds Clan.

"Water Bird? Have you seen everything I promised?"

"Yes, and then some. I am most delighted."

"Good, 'cause I've got to go. Something's come up."

And then the crowd began to jostle, the celebration over. By the time Seven Skull Shield shifted to catch another look, the Natchez and the furtive Four Winds man were gone.

Two

Standing at the head of the stairs, Night Shadow Star watched the Horned Serpent Dancer as Morning Star's warrior awarded him the eagle-wing cloak. She glanced sidelong at the living god who inhabited her brother's body. In his splendid feathers and face paint, he looked every bit the resurrected hero from the Beginning Times. Bedecked with a polished copper headpiece in the shape of Hunga Ahuito, the two-headed eagle, he wore beautifully dyed fabrics and a spotless white leather apron with its soul bundle tied to the front.

When his gaze met hers, his dark eyes caught the reflected firelight and glinted in the black forked-eye design on his white-painted face. The Morning Star's Power came from the Sky World, celestial, born of the wind, sun, clouds, moon, and stars.

Night Shadow Star's Power had once been of the Sky, born as she was, into the Four Winds Clan. But that had been before she'd made a paste from Sister Datura's sacred seeds and rubbed it into her temples. As the Datura's Power had wrapped around her souls, she had sent them through a sacred well pot and into the Underworld to search the watery passages for her dead husband. Lost in those perilous depths, her souls had been ambushed and devoured by Piasa.

The beast had sunk his fangs into her skull. Night Shadow Star jerked, forcing the terrible images from her memory. Shivering in the aftermath, she took a breath.

"Lady?" Fire Cat asked from behind her.

"I'm fine," she whispered unsteadily.

As if reading her thoughts, the Morning Star nodded slightly, acknowledging that they were adversaries. He served the Sky World and Hunga Ahuito, the mottled, two-headed eagle who perched at the heights of Creation. She served Piasa and the Powers of the Underworld, dominated by Old-Woman-Who-Never-Dies.

The symmetry didn't escape her. Her brother had surrendered his body to be consumed by the Morning Star's Spiritual essence. She had been devoured by the Lord of the Underworld. Brother and sister. Vessels for two different Powers. Balance. Every act—all of existence—was an attempt to maintain Spiritual equilibrium.

"Once again, we teeter on the precipice," Piasa whispered, as if the Spirit Beast hovered behind her right ear.

In recent days, she had been catching more glimpses of Piasa than usual. Sometimes it was only a flicker at the edge of her vision, a shifting of shadows. Other times it was a yellow flash of the great water panther's eyes, the momentary gleam of a fang, or the lightning-quick whip of the creature's snake-like tail. While on second glance, nothing seemed amiss, she could feel his heavy presence, like the electric crackling of rubbed fox fur.

Now she sensed the great beast as he hovered at her shoulder.

"Grant me some peace," she growled under her breath as she watched the Quigualtam noble raise the eagle cape in honor of the Morning Star.

"Lady?" Fire Cat asked again from his position behind her. The man knelt on one knee, guarding her back as always.

He had been the heretic war chief of Red Wing Town, her sworn enemy. Her husband Makes Three had died at Fire Cat's hand. Her desperate hope had been to torture the Red Wing to death. Slowly. Painfully. To repay him for the grief and suffering he'd caused her.

One of the hardest things she'd ever done was order Fire Cat's shivering, half-dead body cut loose from the square. Her skin had crawled at the realization that she'd have to take her most-hated enemy into her household and watch him breathe her air, eat her food, and share her hearth.

Proof that Power had a wicked sense of humor.

"It's nothing," she told him, and steeled herself, knotting her fists; the premonition of chaos filtered through her souls.

"Power is shifting," Piasa whispered. *"Feel it? Just there, barely over the horizon of the future. Soon, now, it will begin."*

"We just managed to bring everything back into balance," she muttered. "Now you tell me it's all starting over again?"

Night Shadow Star was aware that the *tonka'tzi,* her Aunt Wind, was watching her warily. Since Night Shadow Star had fallen under the Piasa's control, she and the Great Sky hadn't managed to quite define their relationship. Once Night Shadow Star would have followed her aunt into the position of Clan Matron and finally ascended to the Great Sky's chair. But, possessed as she was by the Piasa's Power, Night Shadow Star's life had taken a different path.

Nor could Night Shadow Star blame her aunt, or any of the kinsmen around her. For devotees of the Sky World, having a relative possessed by the Lord of the Underworld had to be like living in the shadow of a dark and terrible storm where lightning and chaos might strike at any moment.

Only the Morning Star seemed to accept her transformation without reservation, but then the resurrected god inhabiting her brother's body was a creature very like herself.

"Who is he?" she asked aloud. "The Natchez Dancer?"

"His name is Nine Strikes," Blue Heron called back. "He

is the Quigualtam Great Sun's younger brother, one of the 'Little Suns' sent here as an emissary to represent the interests of Natchez confederacy."

"His costume is remarkably accurate. He even moves like the Horned Serpent."

"And you know this, how?" the *tonka'tzi* asked dryly.

"Horned Serpent was among those who passed judgment on my souls in the Underworld."

She ignored the uncomfortable stares that all but the Morning Star sent her way.

"You can feel it coming, can't you?" The Morning Star's words were meant for her alone.

"Of course. Odd, isn't it? That beauty and terror can mix in such a deadly fashion. Which side do you play for this time? Or like usual, are your motives hidden under layers upon layers, Sky Lord?"

Refusing to answer, the Morning Star raised his arms once again, eliciting a roar of approbation from the thousands in the milling crowd. As though an afterthought, he shot a sidelong glance at Blue Heron, saying, "Keeper? I've pardoned an exile. Someone we hadn't discussed. I know you will do your duty."

"What? Who?" Blue Heron asked, clearly unsettled. Her eyes were wary, the starburst tattoos on her old cheeks looking smudged in the gaudy red glow from the night.

An enigmatic smile on his lips, Morning Star turned on his heel and strode through the palisade gate to indicate that the final ceremony marking this year's Busk was over.

Three

Normally the ride down the grand staircase would have worried Clan Keeper Blue Heron. She perched atop her litter, borne as it was, step by step, by her porters. While the lower stairs were nowhere as scary as the high staircase that led to the heights of the Morning Star's great mound-top palace, a fall and tumble here would still break her old bones, not to mention her neck.

After four days of feasting, ritual, and the affairs of state, she felt so exhausted she could barely keep her eyes open, let alone worry. Not even the Morning Star's cryptic mention of another pardon during the Busk seemed important.

"I know you will do your duty." Of course she would. As if the Morning Star had any doubt, since his will was literally life or death. She'd barely avoided hanging in the square herself during Walking Smoke's reign of terror last spring.

She was the Four Winds Clan Keeper—the person who kept and ensured the clan's order and discipline. She'd heard herself referred to as "the poisonous old spider that lurked in the Morning Star's shadow." A description that delighted her. The other Houses and the subordinate Earth Clans both feared and respected her.

More than anything she wanted to sleep.

For the last quarter moon, from the moment she'd awakened, to the last instants before she'd been carried home to fall into bed, her days had been consumed with one ritual event, council, or reception after another.

And through it all, her spies had been reporting to her trusted house manager, Smooth Pebble, who in turn had relayed the information to her. It had absorbed her attention. Politically, the Four Winds Clan remained fragile in the wake of Walking Smoke's murderous rampage. Even with the monster's death, distrust among the major houses was at an all-time high. Columella, Clan Matron of the Evening Star House, had barely managed to maintain her authority over the western bank of the river.

Now, with the conclusion of the New Fire ceremonies and the cooking of the green corn, Blue Heron could finally relax. The dancing, feasting, and rekindling of the sacred fires had gone without a hitch. Her own palace had been cleaned and swept. The floor sported a new mat covering. Her central fire had been extinguished and relit by a brand carried from the Morning Star's personal fire.

The Powers had been appeased. The world made right.

He pardoned another exile? Who?

They'd reached the ground now, her bearers stepping past the warriors who guarded the stairs and out onto the Avenue of the Sun. Blue Heron closed her eyes as her porters bore her through the slow-moving throng toward her mound-top palace.

"Make way!" the warrior in charge of her guard called. "Make way for Clan Keeper Blue Heron!"

She cracked an eye open, wondering at the crowd who, even at this late hour, clogged the great avenue. Rot take them, didn't they have homes and families? What were they all doing this late at night? And after four days of ceremonies, games, fasting, and sweating?

Why wouldn't he have brought the name up with all the others?

Her litter proceeded slowly, turning north past Lady Night Shadow Star's mound-top edifice. In the darkness she could barely make out her own palace where it stood on the northwestern corner of the Four Winds plaza.

We've exiled thousands to the colonies. Why did he mention this particular one?

She barely felt her bearers carry her up her own stairs, past the eagle guardian posts, and to her veranda porch. If she just . . .

"Keeper?" Smooth Pebble's voice came softly, as if through a haze.

Blue Heron blinked awake. When had she dozed off? She hadn't even felt her porters set her litter down. She grunted and allowed her aide to help her to her feet.

On tottering legs, she made her way into her palace, glancing about at the tidy interior with its wall-mounted sleeping benches. All in order, the storage boxes and pots were neatly stowed beneath; the newly woven cane floor was bright yellow and unstained with mud, food, or ash.

"Pus and blood, I'm tired."

Smooth Pebble asked, "Would you like anything? Mint tea? Perhaps something to eat?"

"Piasa take me, berdache, I've been feasting since sunset. If I eat another bite my belly will split open like an over-packed old sack." She waved Smooth Pebble down. "I'm going to bed. If any damn fool tries to wake me, tie him in a square and burn him to death for stupidity."

"Yes, Elder." Smooth Pebble barely managed to stifle a smile. She was berdache, a female soul inhabiting a male body. For two tens of winters, Smooth Pebble had been an able lieutenant in the discharge of Blue Heron's affairs.

Old Notched Cane was the other aide she depended upon. He watched over the house and made sure that the fires were kept burning, that food was cooked, waste carted out, and water brought in.

Walking past the central hearth to the rear of the great room, she stepped through the door into her dimly lit personal quarters. Her attention fixed on her bed where it was attached to the back wall. Her blankets looked good.

She dropped her cloak on the floor and had just slipped her skirt off her hips when a familiar voice said, "I appreciate the gesture, Keeper, but you're a little old for my tastes."

Heart hammering, she blinked in the gloom, locating the dark form seated on one of her storage boxes. "Thief? Is that you?"

"As if anyone else could be?" He cocked his head as he studied her naked body. "I think we've got a problem."

Blue Heron placed a hand to her startled heart, taking a deep breath. "How, by Piasa's swinging balls, did you get in here?"

"Wouldn't be much of a thief if I couldn't," he told her with a grin. "But don't take it out on Smooth Pebble. She's had enough on her shoulders these last days." He gestured toward the main room. "I approve of what she's done with the place. If only the real world could be cleaned up so easily."

"Your irreverent tongue is going to get you hung in a square one of these days." She raised a hand. "I'm asleep on my feet. Tell me what I need to know and get your pus-dripping body out of my sleeping quarters."

"You know Crazy Frog?"

"That weasel who gambles on chunkey and cons innocent Traders out of their wares over in River Mounds City? What about him?"

"He came to find me tonight."

"Thought he didn't like leaving River Mounds City."

"He doesn't." Seven Skull Shield crossed his muscle-thick arms, his block-like face grim. "He said that someone important is going to be killed tonight. He didn't know who, or why, or where, just that it was going to happen. Something two Traders overheard. Something important enough that it got one of them killed and the second ran. Something about the south and what's happening there."

She tried to blink the fatigue from her eyes. "You lost me."

Seven Skull Shield ran a hand over his craggy face as if he, too, were tired. "It might be nothing, Keeper. Crazy Frog said he just had a feeling in his guts that it was important. Important enough that if it went wrong, he wanted you to know that he'd made a special trip to warn you."

She sighed, dropping to her bed. "But no idea who?"

"None. Just someone important."

She yawned, rocked her jaw, and shrugged. "Take whoever you want, warn the war chiefs, especially Five Fists and War Claw, that something's afoot. Maybe I'll have an idea after I get some sleep."

He nodded, rising to his feet. "I'll see to it."

He started for the door, stopped, and glanced back, an eyebrow arched speculatively. "You know, Keeper, for a woman your age? You're not without your physical charms. Even for a discerning man like me who has an in-depth appreciation of the fine female form."

He ducked the black ceramic cup she threw at his head and was out the door.

"Ought to have you hung in a square to teach you some respect," she growled as she flopped onto her wooden-frame bed.

Nevertheless a faint smile crossed her lips as she fell into exhausted slumber.

Four

Nine Strikes had won his name in battle against the fierce Pacaha, a Nation north of the Natchez territory and on the Father Water's west bank above the confluence with the great Western River. On his first battle walk it had taken him nine strikes with his war club to dispatch an imposing Pacaha warrior.

His entire life had been spent in preparation for the responsibility of rule. His maternal aunt was the White Woman, the matron in charge of the Natchez Nation. His older brother served as the Great Sun, the hereditary high chief of the Quigualtam lineage of the Sun Born, the chosen rulers of the Natchez confederacy who were directly descended from the original first Great Sun. Since he was a child, Nine Strikes had made offerings to the Stone, the actual remains of that first Great Sun. Power had turned the hero's body into stone in order that it would never corrupt or decay. To this day it sat in the center of the Natchez Nation's most sacred space, a reminder of the virtues and courage necessary for a ruler of his people.

As Nine Strikes, followed by his slaves and musicians, entered his house it was with a feeling of great satisfaction. Tomorrow he would dispatch a messenger—along with the

Morning Star's cloak—to his brother and aunt, informing them of the great honor he had won for the Natchez people.

Out of respect for his ancestor, Nine Strikes had created a small altar—a raised clay platform with a stone carried from his homeland. Still dressed in his Horned Serpent costume, and carrying the magnificent feathered cloak, he faced west, toward the altar, bowed, and called, in the traditional greeting of his people, *"Hau. Hau. Hau."*

Only then did he rise and place the cloak atop the intricately carved wooden trunk that held his personal effects.

"Do you need anything else, Sun Born?" asked his commoner servant.

"That will be all. My most sincere appreciation to all of you. Your music tonight was an inspiration. I could not have Danced so well without it. Get a good night's sleep. I'll see you all in the morning."

He watched them bow and touch their foreheads in the faint light cast by his smoldering fire. Then, yawning, but still feeling euphoric, he turned and stepped through the cane-mat doorway and into his personal sleeping quarters.

In the gloom he stopped short, wishing he'd waited to dismiss his servants until after he'd had their help removing the heavy and cumbersome costume. He wasn't thinking well. Tired. Exhausted from the exertions of the Dance.

He smiled as he began tugging on the laces that bound the costume to his body. He had Danced well, as if the Power of Horned Serpent had flowed into his blood and bones.

"I wouldn't take it off," a soft voice said out of the darkness.

"What? Who's there?" Nine Strikes turned, the costume tail catching under the bedposts and almost tripping him.

"There are worse fates than being devoured by the Horned Serpent," the voice continued. "At least it's a glorious end."

"I don't—"

The shadowy form lunged.

Nine Strikes, his vision restricted by the fanged serpent's mouth, never saw the lance that thrust between the costume ties and sliced deeply beneath the hollow of his ribs.

Then, somehow, he was on the floor, the heavy costume supporting his weight, the pole of the spear propping his body as it cut and pulled at his innards.

"Tell the White Woman I . . ." The words seemed to vanish in an endless gray haze. . . .

Five

Once he had been known as Fire Cat Twelvekiller, high war chief of the Red Wing Nation. He, his mother, and two sisters—who were now slaves of Clan Keeper Blue Heron—were all that remained of the Red Wing Clan of the Moon Moiety. Years back his ancestors had fled Cahokia. They had been supporters of Chief Petaga and the priestess Lichen during the great civil war that had rocked Cahokia in the days before the first supposed resurrection of the Morning Star.

Fire Cat's people hadn't believed the mythical hero from the Beginning Times could be incarnated into a human body, and Fire Cat still didn't. To him the Morning Star was, and would forever remain, Chunkey Boy, the oldest of the old *tonka'tzi* Red Warrior Tenkiller's sons, brother to Night Shadow Star. Maybe not the worst of the lot—Walking Smoke had taken that distinction during his violent rampage—but still a bitter and rotten piece of fruit fallen from a diseased family tree.

Granted, Chunkey Boy played the fraud for all it was worth. Maybe some part of his sick souls had actually come to believe the masquerade. The teeming thousands who inhabited Cahokia—from the nobles down to the immigrant dirt farmers—had swallowed the hoax whole and unchewed.

In the gray light of predawn, Fire Cat grasped a finely crafted black chunkey stone. Just large enough to fit into the cup of his hand, the disc-shaped stone had been concavely ground on both sides. The piece had once belonged to Night Shadow Star's husband Makes Three. That she had "gifted" it to Fire Cat after he saved her life still amazed him.

His left hand gripped a perfectly balanced javelin, lovingly crafted of white ash. It, too, had once belonged to Night Shadow Star's husband. Perhaps it was a measure of Fire Cat's heresy that he could use them without a second thought. A man's chunkey gear was painstakingly imbued with a Spiritual essence—a bit of the player's soul. If the pieces had any resentment that their previous owner's killer now wielded them, it surely hadn't surfaced in the performance of the pieces. The stone rolled true; at his cast the javelin flew like a thing alive, seeking the fleeing stone.

Fire Cat took his position, hefting the stone as he looked down the narrow chunkey court. The Four Winds plaza courts faced away from the Morning Star's hulking mound with its high palace. It was bad enough living in the abomination's shadow without having to see it while he practiced.

Fire Cat took a deep breath. Imagining the throw, Fire Cat started forward at a run, his right arm dropping back. In perfect stride, he bowled the chunkey stone. The round disc kissed the ground in a smooth release.

In the next stride, he transferred the lance, arm back, and with a mighty lunge, launched it after the rolling stone. The lance arced through the sky, spinning just fast enough to stabilize itself as it dropped toward the slowing stone.

The point drove into the clay no more than an arm's length from where the stone finally toppled onto its side.

Not a perfect cast—one had to hit the stone, which automatically won the game—but good enough to beat most of the opponents he might face. Were he ever to play the Morning Star, however? Well, he'd have to be a lot better than this.

He walked down, retrieving his lance and the black stone.

"Not bad, Red Wing," a voice called.

Fire Cat glanced over to see the miserable thief, Seven Skull Shield, as he appeared out of the misty morning. Burly arms bare, a smirk on his ugly face, the miscreant wore only a brown fabric hunting shirt and breechcloth.

"What are you doing up at this hour, thief? Running from some jealous husband? Or did they catch you trying to steal corn from the altar in Old-Woman-Who-Never-Dies' temple?"

Seven Skull Shield gave him a dismissive look. "Sorry. Actually, I thought I'd come over early, watch Night Shadow Star take her time getting dressed. She's what? Almost twenty now? The notion of a ripe body like hers not having a man on top of it just seems like a violation of the laws of Creation. Since there's no other man around, I might even volunteer to fill in."

Fire Cat fingered his chunkey lance, eyes narrowing. "Do you know why you're still alive?"

Seven Skull Shield's expression looked deceptively mild. "Because I'm smarter, craftier, and meaner than most of the clod-headed dolts I have to deal with? Or maybe because Power is saving me for the moment I get to share Night Shadow Star's bed? If someone hadn't killed her late husband, it wouldn't be an issue but . . . Wait! Wasn't it *you* who killed her husband?"

Fire Cat ground his teeth. "On the day I split your skull open and dump your guts out on the ground, I will laugh and sing with joy. Why are you here, thief?"

"Did the warriors the Keeper ordered out show up last night?"

"They did." Fire Cat continued to nurse his rage. "They wouldn't say why they were sent, just that there might be a threat to Night Shadow Star. I took extra precautions, sleeping at her door."

"Might be nothing." Seven Skull Shield glanced speculatively up at Night Shadow Star's slope-sided mound with its opulent palace. "Just a warning. Better to be safe, especially after what that two-footed maggot Walking Smoke put us—"

"Thief!" a worried voice called.

Fire Cat turned to see Smooth Pebble, the Keeper's berdache, approaching in the growing light. She came at a half run, waving her hand.

"Greetings, Smooth Pebble!" Seven Skull Shield called back. "What's your hurry?"

"I'm instructed to find you!" She pulled up, panting, though it hadn't been that much of a run down from the Keeper's palace. "There's been a murder."

The thief seemed to tense, his expression curiously strained. "Who, Smooth Pebble? Someone important?"

"Depends on who you consider to be important. It's a foreigner. Some Natchez noble."

Seven Skull Shield's blocky face turned pensive. "Well, that's certainly in the south."

"What's going on?" Fire Cat demanded, propping his lance as he hefted the stone and wondered what it would feel like to use it to crack Seven Skull Shield's head open.

"Murder," the thief told him with an evil grin. "But, for once, it wasn't directed at her." He pointed with a knobby finger.

Fire Cat turned to see Night Shadow Star as she appeared between the two magnificently carved guardian posts: Horned Serpent on the right, Piasa on the left. They stared down from the mound top at either side of the stairs, as if watching her descend through their shell-inlaid eyes.

At sight of Night Shadow Star, Fire Cat's heart skipped a beat. She seemed to float down the stairs, an apparition not of this world. Her long black hair hung down over her shoulders like a glistening black mantle. A form-fitting dress clung to her perfect body. The fine features of her face seemed pinched, her large eyes dark and possessed of other-worldly Dreams.

"Glad you dislike her so," the thief muttered under his breath, a sidelong glance fixed on Fire Cat.

"I can't help who Power has bound me to serve," Fire Cat gritted back reflexively. "I'm the last of the Red Wing. I take my vows seriously."

Smooth Pebble was watching the interchange through wary eyes.

Fire Cat chafed under their stares.

"The story is that you were dying in the square when Night Shadow Star appeared out of the night and asked if you'd bind yourself to her. I heard you thought she was a vision: First Woman come from the Underworld to collect your souls for the journey to the afterlife."

Fire Cat winced. She'd appeared out of the predawn drizzle, naked and ethereal. A creature of unbelievable beauty, with water beading on her smooth brown skin, her dark hair falling about her broad shoulders in wet strands.

"Do you swear to follow my orders, no matter the consequences?"

"I swear on the graves of my ancestors," he'd rasped through his misery.

To Seven Skull Shield, he said, "Thief, let's tie you up, beat you black and blue for days, starve you, let you thirst, and hang you in a square for a couple of days and see just how clever you remain."

He straightened as Night Shadow Star walked up, feeling oddly uncomfortable that he held the chunkey stone.

"It's begun," Night Shadow Star said simply. "Thief, the Keeper requires you."

"But I don't know where—"

"The Natchez embassy along the Avenue of the Sun. Go." She extended a slender arm.

Seven Skull Shield shot her an uncertain glance, then turned on his heel and left at a trot.

Smooth Pebble asked, "How did you know, Lady?"

Fire Cat saw the faintest change in Night Shadow Star's expression—the one she got when Piasa was whispering in her ear. This morning it sent gooseflesh along his skin.

"He wants to change the Power," Night Shadow Star replied as if it made perfect sense. "He wants to change everything."

Six

Nine Strikes' body was hunched in the cramped space between his storage boxes and the elevated frame of his bed. Still wearing the Horned Serpent costume, his torso was partially supported by the lance. Its butt had wedged against the wall. The point had apparently stuck in the man's back ribs. Blood pooled on the woven rugs covering the floor and had dried to a dark black that fed a column of flies.

Blue Heron waved them away and made a face. Death would be so much cleaner without flies, let alone the maggots that inevitably followed. What could Hunga Ahuito have been thinking during the Creation? Even an old woman like her could have devised a less messy way to deal with corpses. Perhaps a Spirit Beast that arrived out of the night mists, swallowed the body, and quietly slithered away?

"Keeper?" a winded Seven Skull Shield asked as he appeared in the doorway. Then he glanced down at the corpse. "A Natchez, huh? Wait. Isn't that . . . ?"

"The Dancer honored by the Morning Star last night," she finished. "Yes. Still in costume."

"Who was he?"

"The younger brother of the Natchez Great Sun, nephew of the White Woman. I met him several times, talked with him. An impressive young man. Very competent. He's been here for a couple of years now, learned our language. Would have become the next Great Sun had anything happened to his brother."

"Who'd want to kill him?" Seven Skull Shield batted at a pesky fly.

"Don't know." She fingered the wattle of skin below her chin. "His servants found him this way. I've already questioned them. They all tell the same story: After the Dance the Little Sun was congratulated by some of the other Dancers. Everyone seemed to be awed by his award.

"Then they made their way down the Avenue of the Sun to the Natchez embassy house." She gestured to indicate the building in which they stood. "Nine Strikes thanked his household for their help and music and dismissed them for the evening. Everyone went to their beds in the main room, and Nine Strikes retreated to his private quarters."

"And no one heard a thing?"

"That's their story." She stared down at the body. "I'd say he was killed immediately. That costume wasn't the sort of thing a man would want to wear longer than he had to."

"Makes you wonder why he wore it home from the Dance."

She shrugged. "Living in the afterglory? Savoring the moment? That we may never know. Odd that his people didn't hear anything. The rooms are just separated by this flimsy split-cane wall."

Seven Skull Shield bent down to inspect the body. "We'll know more when we pull him out of here, but my guess is that spear sliced through his diaphragm and lung. Maybe got some of the heart as well. It would have been quiet."

"I suppose." She stepped to the door, turning her gaze to the huddled servants who clustered in the main room. "So, which one of them do you think is the culprit?"

"What's this?" Seven Skull Shield was staring into the dark recesses of the Horned Serpent mask's fang-lined mouth.

Extending his fingers between the teeth, he pulled a long black feather from the dead man's mouth and held it up to the light.

"A black feather?" Blue Heron wondered. "He had that in his mouth?"

"Someone stuck it in after he was dead. Look, they broke this tooth in the process." Even as he indicated the loose fang in the snake mask, it fell from its socket. "A black feather in the mouth? Does that mean anything to you, Keeper?"

"No," she mused, racking her brain as she took the feather and inspected it. "Looks like a crow feather. Black. The color of death. Crow. A trickster bird. Sky World Power. Crows, along with vultures, are associated with mortuary rituals where corpses are left on elevated platforms for carrion birds to carry away the flesh."

"Maybe it means something to the Natchez?" He inclined his head to indicate the huddled servants.

"Let's go ask." Blue Heron led the way into the main room, the feather held high. She picked out the translator, an older man, perhaps forty years of age and wearing a brown smock. His face was tattooed in Natchez designs, the meaning of which eluded her.

"This was in his mouth. Looks like a crow feather. What . . . ?"

The man's eyes widened. He made a warding with his fingers, and whispered something in Natchez. The others, horrified gazes fixed on the tacky feather, seemed to shrink in on themselves as they, too, made warding signs.

Blue Heron knelt down before the translator. "What does this mean?"

The man seemed to collect himself. "The black witch," he whispered. "She's back."

"So," Seven Skull Shield growled, looking intimidating as he crossed his muscular arms, "which one of these women is the black witch?"

The translator repeated his words in Natchez, and to Blue Heron's surprise, the whole rotted bunch of them seemed to wilt, staring uneasily at each other, shrinking back from their fellows in horror.

Blue Heron studied them one by one. No one seemed any less appalled than the others. Not a single face betrayed anything but abject panic. She didn't detect so much as a flicker of an eye, the gloating turn of a lip—nothing that would have betrayed a witch exulting in a triumphant murder.

Assuming she knew anything about Natchez witches.

The translator finally swallowed hard, shaking his head. "It is not one of us, Keeper. We would know. We've served the Little Sun for two years now. We expected to die with him, accompany him to the land of the ancestors and continue to serve him. Each of us, we have loved and respected him. It's bad enough that one of the Sun Born would die of violence. But by the hand of the black witch? She is Powerful, strong. We all know each other here, like a small family. If it is the black witch, she flew in from the night, killed the Sun Born, and flew back out again. Nor does she always appear as a woman. She can take a man's form at will."

As he repeated his words for the benefit of the others, they seemed to relax, moderately reassured.

"Some witch," Seven Skull Shield muttered. "She had to use a spear to kill your lord."

"The spear just killed the body," the translator replied, as if things were beginning to make sense to him. "The feather was the real weapon. The witch used it to soak up the Little Sun's souls."

"You mean your master's souls are in this?" Blue Heron asked skeptically, giving the matted feather a sidelong glance.

"Not that one," the translator insisted. "That's just the one she left behind. The second, or message feather, if you will. She would have used a different feather to absorb the Sun Born's souls as they were exhaled from the dying body."

"A two-feather killer?" Seven Skull Shield asked irritably.

"Do not mock!" the translator cried, his terror rising again. Then he pointed at Blue Heron. "And you, Keeper, you've touched the darkness! You're holding it now. She'll come for you. You've marked yourself. Given her evil a rope line to follow, hand over hand, to your own souls!"

She arched a disbelieving eyebrow as she glanced distastefully at the feather. The skin in her thumb and finger began to crawl, and it was all she could do to keep from flicking it away.

Silly Natchez superstition. She willed the sudden fear from her souls.

Seven Skull Shield's lips twitched as he fought a smile. He stood, glancing around the room with its wall benches, Natchez artwork, trophies, and the stone altar against the west wall.

"We're missing something," he noted.

"What would that be?" She straightened.

"Not counting what the Natchez, here, might believe, what would be the most valuable item in the Sun Born's possession?"

"I don't follow you."

"No, you don't," Night Shadow Star called as she stepped into the main room followed by Fire Cat. Her dark eyes glanced this way and that, taking in the cowering servants, the stone on its altar. Then she fixed on the opening that led to the Little Sun's private quarters.

Fire Cat, a war club in his hands, reflexively placed himself between Night Shadow Star and the cowering Natchez.

"What are you doing here, Niece?" Blue Heron asked.

"My master sent me." Night Shadow Star hesitated. "Can't you feel it, Aunt?" Her gaze fixed on the feather. "It's right there. In your hand. Like a moonless and midnight death."

The crawling feeling returned with a vengeance. Blue Heron tried to grasp the feather's quill with only the tips of her thumb and forefinger.

"It's a feather," Seven Skull Shield growled, his apprecia-tive gaze, like usual, fixed on Night Shadow Star's provoca-tive body.

"A feather to you, thief." She shot him a mocking smile, apparently unaware of his male interest. "A warning to the rest of us."

"What warning?" Blue Heron asked warily. Night Shadow Star had come at the bidding of Piasa? Why?

"Deception comes in layers, Aunt." Night Shadow Star moved with a sinuous grace as she walked to the back room and glanced in at the corpse. One hand on the doorframe, she turned, saying, "The Father Water flows relentlessly south, as a golden darkness floats north along its course."

"You're talking in riddles."

"The killer didn't just murder the Natchez; he has enraged Horned Serpent. What sort of person would dare . . ." Night Shadow Star blinked, as if at something off to the side. "But of course. It makes so much sense, doesn't it, Lord?"

Blood and pus, she's talking to Piasa again.

Blue Heron glanced warily at the empty space Night Shadow Star seemed to address.

Seven Skull Shield appeared amused, but then he was one of the most irreverent men she'd ever known.

"Tell it to me straight, Niece. What does Underworld Power see in this outrage?"

Night Shadow Star turned eerie eyes on hers. "It's all tied together, Aunt. This murder, all part of a much more intri-cate plot. One meant to confuse us, distract us, when all along, the threat is so much more insidious."

"Rot take it, what's so insidious? He's a Natchez. Proba-bly killed by one of his own. This black witch everyone's so scared of."

"Tell me, if you wanted to weaken Spirit Power, how would you do it?"

The question caught Blue Heron completely off guard. "Weaken Spirit Power? I don't understand."

Night Shadow Star approached the stone on its altar, her fingers absently caressing its surface. "That's exactly the point, isn't it?"

And with that, she crossed the room and out into the morning light, her long black hair hanging down her back in a blue-black wave. Fire Cat shot Seven Skull Shield one last look of disgust and followed her.

Blue Heron shook her head. "Did you understand any of that?"

"No." Seven Skull Shield stared thoughtfully after Night Shadow Star. "But the young woman's charm has never been in what she says."

"What were you saying before she arrived?"

"I was about to point out that we've forgotten the most important thing about the Little Sun's murder."

"What's that? The black feather?"

"No, Keeper. I was referring to the man's most valuable possession, at least from the standpoint of Cahokia."

"And that is?"

Seven Skull Shield arched a scarred eyebrow. "Where's that marvelous cloak the Morning Star bestowed upon Nine Strikes? It's not in his room. I don't see it out here."

She turned, calling, "Translator? Where did the Little Sun put the Morning Star's gift? The cloak?"

The man, still looking like a panicked rabbit, pointed to one of the large, intricately engraved wooden chests against the back wall. "Right there on the . . ."

He swallowed hard, struggled to his feet, and walked over to the box. Reverently he lifted the lid, looked inside, and then around the floor lest it had fallen.

"It should have been right here, Keeper." He turned, calling to the others, all of whom shook their heads in negation.

"None of us would have touched it, Keeper," the translator protested. "Not on our lives!"

Seven Skull Shield, for the first time that morning, looked

pleased. "Solving this isn't going to be as difficult as Lady Night Shadow Star seems to think. Find the cloak, find the murderer."

Blue Heron narrowed her eyes. "Bold words, thief. I hope you don't live to regret them."

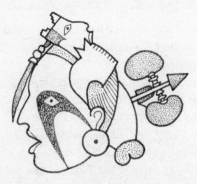

Seven

Quite a crowd you've managed to draw." Horn Lance cradled his chin between thumb and forefinger. He stood at the edge of the Avenue of the Sun and surveyed the people who'd stopped to gawk at the Natchez embassy. The structure was a simple four-sided, trench-wall building, its thatch roof grayed by the passing of seasons. A single guardian post topped with a sun emblem stood out front by a recently reroofed ramada. An elevated storehouse, in the southern style, rested on four posts at the southwest corner. A latrine screen was just visible behind the building.

A small squad of warriors kept the curious at bay.

"Word travels fast," his younger companion replied. In Cahokia, with its teeming and varied peoples, the young man's hairstyle didn't draw attention, parted in the middle as it was, braided, and drawn into separate buns like blunt horns.

At that moment, an older woman—gray haired, wearing a fine red skirt, her shoulders covered with a light fabric cloak—stepped out of the door. The ancient sunburst tattoos on her face looked faded, partially obscured by the wrinkles lining her cheeks.

"Ah, now there she is." Horn Lance crossed his arms, feeling the twinge of joint ache in his left.

"Who is she?"

"Clan Keeper Blue Heron. Look at her, Swirling Cloud. Study her. If there's anyone who can bring this all crashing down around us, it will be her."

Swirling Cloud shifted the pack on his back, head cocked. "She's an old woman."

"So was your storied White Woman. And you know how canny and clever she was."

"She wasn't quite clever enough. Against Thirteen Sacred Jaguar? She never suspected a thing. Her body, along with Nine Strikes' brother's, is rotting in the blessed earth of the great mound, surrounded by the strangled bodies of her guards and servants."

"Which allowed your mother to become the White Woman, and your brother the Great Sun. Your people are about to remake the lower river into a Nation to rival Cahokia." Horned Lance shared a victorious smile with the younger man. "Think grandly, Little Sun. Played correctly, you can become one of the most influential men in the world. Great Sun in place of your brother? That could be only the beginning."

Swirling Cloud's lips bent into a smirk as he watched Clan Keeper Blue Heron walk to a litter and seat herself. As her porters lifted her, and a couple of warriors cleared a path through the crowd, the woman's head was bent, a pinched expression on her face. She was inspecting a crow feather with a displeased expression.

"Ah, they've found the feather."

"May it lead them on a merry chase. Meanwhile, you're free to take the next steps in your assent to the pinnacle of Natchez society."

"You're assuming I want to remain stuck in the Great Sun's temple, settling petty squabbles, marrying commoner women, and begetting futureless children. Thirteen Sacred

Jaguar wants to remake our world." He turned to the east, where Morning Star's palace rose like a wedge against the sky. "The real Power, unbeknownst to my silly brother, lies here. At Cahokia." He paused. "The four messengers should arrive any day now to pave the way for Thirteen Sacred Jaguar's arrival. Then the fun really starts."

"That's assuming that Thirteen Sacred Jaguar can prevail." Horn Lance rubbed his scarred chin as he watched Blue Heron's litter vanish down the crowded Avenue of the Sun. "And to do that, we cannot underestimate either the Morning Star or Blue Heron."

"How do you know so much about her?"

"She was the one who had me exiled."

"For what?"

"Oh, before we started to hate each other, she was my wife."

Eight

In preparation for the Morning Star's summons to council, Fire Cat had donned armor over his red war shirt. The chest piece consisted of hardwood slats sewn front and rear onto a cured leather cuirass. He had then strapped a thick leather helmet to his head and painted his face white with red wings on the cheeks. White, the sacred color denoting peace, harmony, and wisdom, the red wings in denotation of his clan.

As he had followed Night Shadow Star out of her palace, he'd slung a bow and quiver over his shoulder and plucked up a copper-bitted war club.

He'd caught the barest smile of amusement on Night Shadow Star's full lips. They were going into the Morning Star's lair. His appearance was a subtle reminder that while this was only a council, she remained a force unto herself. Someone to be reckoned with.

And why do I care?

These were not his people, but enemies. Less than a year ago the Morning Star had dispatched High War Chief Spotted Wrist in a fourth, and finally successful, attempt to destroy Red Wing Town. The greatest humiliation was that the canny Spotted Wrist had done through deceit and guile what no previous Cahokian army had been able to by force of arms: He had taken the town in the middle of the night and in complete surprise.

The first Fire Cat had known of the attack was when Cahokian warriors had ripped him from his second wife's side as he slept. Her name was False Dawn—named for the soft light of the coming day. His first wife, Fall New Moon, had been sleeping with their infant children that night. He'd never heard what befell either of his wives. Nor had he sought such knowledge. The fate of a conquered chief's wives was to be taken as trophies, made slaves, and perhaps passed from man to man.

And his children?

That he knew: Their mutilated corpses had been tossed into the cool green depths of the Father Water—an offering to the Spirits of the Underworld.

Sometimes he wondered if that act of insult hadn't backfired on the Four Winds. Had Piasa taken the souls of his children as offerings? Was that why the underwater panther had ordered Night Shadow Star to bind Fire Cat to her through oath?

Serve Night Shadow Star he might, but at the same time the world would be reminded that a Red Wing war chief—slave though he might be—still lived and walked fearlessly among them.

"Your thoughts?" Night Shadow Star asked as they passed through the Council Terrace courtyard and began the long climb up the stairway that led to the high palisade and the Morning Star's soaring palace.

"On my family, Lady."

She nodded slightly as she preceded him. A gust of wind fluttered the fine white fabric of her skirt and molded it to her toned legs. He tried not to notice.

"Power has been unkind to the two of us." Her head bowed; the breeze teased her glossy black hair. "Difficult as the past has been, what's coming will be no easier."

"And what is that, Lady?"

"A desperate trial." She stopped a step short from the head of the stairs where two warriors stood guard. Turning, she fixed him with her dark eyes and said, "We will do what we must. You understand that, don't you?"

"I gave you my oath."

She nodded, sadness behind her gaze. Then, taking a breath, she hurried up the last step. At the top the two warriors touched their foreheads in respect as she passed. For Fire Cat, however, they had only hard glares and smirks of disdain.

He marched proudly past them as only a blooded and tested chief could. In the recent fighting against Walking Smoke's Tula warriors, he'd killed five. Were he still a war chief, his name would have been changed to Fire Cat Seventeenkiller—an honor without peer among his once-unconquered people.

Take that, maggots.

Passing through the gates and into the courtyard, he narrowed an eye at the stunning Eagle guardian posts. Night Shadow Star passed them without so much as a gesture. They were Sky Power, after all.

At the soaring World Tree pole, however, Night Shadow Star paused, glancing up at it. Carved from a giant bald cypress towed upriver from the south, it rose into the sky like a mighty lance. Lightning scars had nearly obliterated the intricately carved reliefs that told Morning Star's story: his birth, life, and his mighty battles with the monsters and giants, from the Beginning Times.

Night Shadow Star laid a delicate hand on the wood, then hurried toward the palace. The steeply pitched roof seemed to cleave the pale blue sky; carved effigies of Hunga Ahuito rose from the high ridge pole. The thatch—freshly repaired for the Busk—had a yellow-and-gray mottled appearance. High as it was, wind and weather took their toll.

More warriors stood before the palace door, bowing and touching their foreheads as Night Shadow Star passed. Fire

Cat kept his expression blank, fighting the urge to smile wickedly as they fretted over an armed warrior setting foot in the sacred space.

Once past the beautifully carved doors, murmurs arose as he followed Night Shadow Star past *Tonka'tzi* Wind, Blue Heron, and the great central fire and into the Morning Star's forbidden personal space. Gasps arose when she did so.

Night Shadow Star stopped short, slightly to the left of the imposter's raised dais. Fire Cat took his place at her back, drawing himself to attention, fully aware of the gravity of Night Shadow Star's violation.

The grizzled war chief called Five Fists, a man in his forties, took a half step in their direction, a war club in his scarred right hand. His face, arms, and entire torso were tattooed in honor of his many victories. Some mishap, either from battle or a stickball injury, had left his jaw crooked on his face. His graying hair had been pulled back in a bun, and he wore the Morning Star's Bird Man insignia on the front flap of the apron that hung from his belt.

Five Fists served as the Morning Star's trusted personal war chief. Piasa take him, he surely wasn't about to challenge Night Shadow Star's transgression, was he?

After a moment's self-debate, Five Fists stepped forward, addressing Night Shadow Star. "Lady, with respect, might I suggest that the Red Wing wait outside with the rest of the servants?"

Very well, he wasn't going to challenge Night Shadow Star's impudence, only her servant's. Fire Cat couldn't help but swell with rising satisfaction.

Come on, Lady. Tell him I'm staying. Let him push it. I'll gleefully knock his jaw crooked in the other direction.

"You may suggest, Five Fists." She fixed the old warrior with her eerie stare. He swallowed hard, taking an involuntary step back. "But that is all you may do."

"Lady, it is customary for the Morning Star's safety—"

"My understanding was that we have been summoned

here to discuss the murder of the Natchez Little Sun. And nothing more."

"But, he's a Red Wing!"

"He is *my* Red Wing," she almost hissed. "He serves me, and I serve Piasa."

Five Fists wet his lips, nodded. It seemed a heroic act of will to take a step back.

Fire Cat remained expressionless, letting his eyes adjust after the midday sun. The great room's opulence never ceased to amaze him. The newly replaced floor matting had been woven in intricate designs. Select women labored on the project for an entire year. The wall benches, serving double duty as seats for audiences and beds for the Morning Star's household, were covered with fine furs and blankets. The frames had been carved by the finest woodworkers in the world. The upright posts had been finished to represent Spirit Beasts: sinuous tie snakes, snarling panthers, graceful swans, leaping fish, elegant ducks, fierce screaming eagles, and keen-eyed falcons.

Above the benches the plastered walls were hung with carved and brightly painted wooden reliefs of the Thunderbirds, the Bird Man image of the Morning Star, the Cahokian sun symbol, and scenes depicting the Morning Star's exploits in the Beginning Times. Inlaid with various woods, shell, stone, and copper, they dazzled the eye. Fine fabrics, dyed every color, were hung between trophy skulls that stared down at the room through empty sockets. Shields taken from defeated enemies, occasional leg and arm bones, and copper plate added to the wealth.

Around the peripheries sat the recorders with their assorted boxes of colored and shaped beads. If asked, they would create a record of the proceedings. Along with Blue Heron and *Tonka'tzi* Wind, who sat behind and to the right of the fire, a half dozen warriors, a bevy of servants, and a collection of the Earth Clan chiefs waited in the rear.

Fire Cat shot the Keeper a curious look. She'd given Fire Cat's mother and sister—also captives—sanctuary in her house. For that, he owed the woman. The few times he'd caught glimpses of them, his only remaining family had seemed well treated.

If only there were a way . . .

At that moment the Morning Star emerged from his private quarters in the rear. His face was painted red on the left, white on the right, with black forked-eye patterns surrounding his eyes and running down his cheeks. A beautiful copper headpiece in the shape of the bi-lobed arrow rose above a small wooden Bundle box at the top of his head. An eagle-feather cloak draped about his shoulders; his waist sported an immaculate white apron that dropped to a point between his knees. Thick strands of white shell beads hung at his throat.

Fire Cat barely kept his lips from twitching. Chunkey Boy, playing the living god. He always dressed the part.

The room rustled as the people dropped to their knees, touching their heads to the floor.

All but he and Night Shadow Star.

Chunkey Boy carefully seated himself on the litter chair atop the raised clay dais behind the fire. The thing had been covered with cougar furs. A steaming bowl of black drink had been placed easily at hand.

Arranging himself, Chunkey Boy turned piercing black eyes on Night Shadow Star where she and Fire Cat stood no more than three paces from the dais. Only the insane would venture so close were he or she not invited by the Morning Star. For anyone but Night Shadow Star it would have been considered an affront worthy of a quick death.

That knowledge sent a warm spear through Fire Cat's heart.

Chunkey Boy had always given his sister too much latitude, even before he adopted the sham of playing god. The relationship between them was complicated, no matter at which level of assumed authority it was played.

"Rise," Chunkey Boy said to the rest of the room.

People lifted their heads warily.

Fire Cat could feel the tension as wary glances were cast their direction.

"I would hear the Keeper's report," Chunkey Boy began. "Has the Little Sun's murderer been apprehended? Do we know the reason behind such a foul deed?"

Clan Keeper Blue Heron spread her hands wide. "We do not, Great Lord. I have personally inspected the scene. Last night, after the Little Sun returned to his quarters, someone thrust a spear through his body. He still wore his Dance costume. I have spoken with his servants, and they report hearing nothing. One of them discovered the body only this morning. Our inspection of the lance used to kill him has determined that it was one of his own."

Blue Heron lifted a black feather. "This was thrust into the dead man's mouth. The Natchez attributed it to some woman they call the black witch. My inquiries suggest that the killer was someone from outside the household. This feather? Perhaps a distraction to mislead our investigation and lure us down a false path."

"Did the Natchez offer any motive for the Little Sun's murder?"

"They did not, Great Lord. They claim that he was beloved by all. Worse, you know how the Natchez will take this. They consider it a terrible calamity when a member of the Sun Born dies violently." She paused, narrowing an eye. "Unless handled very carefully, and with the greatest discretion, the Little Sun's murder could seriously complicate our relations with the entire Natchez Nation and our Trade and travel on the lower river."

Chunkey Boy, with a serene glance at the recorders waiting off to the side, asked, "Master recorder, could you refresh our memories of the Natchez?"

The old white-haired man bowed, touching his forehead. "Yes, Great Lord. The Natchez live on the eastern bank of the Father Water and dominate the lower river. They are ruled by the influential Quigualtam alliance of closely related Sun Born, all descended from the first Great Sun. Lowered to earth from the sun itself, the first Great Sun instructed the Natchez on rules of behavior and how to order their society. Upon his death, he turned to stone in order that his body might never suffer the indignities of decay.

"Their society is divided into an elite composed of Sun Clan and a class of commoners sometimes unkindly referred to as 'stinkards.' Oddly, perhaps, Sun Born can only marry stinkards, never their own kind, which would be considered incest. Their lineages, like so many, run through the female. Thus, though a woman of the Sun Clan must marry a stinkard man, her children will be Sun Clan and automatically eligible to all benefits of status and position. The Great Sun's children, through his stinkard wife, have no more standing than any other commoner and essentially blend into the community."

Tonka'tzi Wind asked, "Correct me if I'm wrong, but isn't the White Woman the Little Sun's aunt?"

"*Tonka'tzi,* she is." The recorder turned his attention back to his beaded mat, running his fingers over the patterns and colors of beads to discern their meaning. "The White Woman is so called because, as is common in so many societies, white is the holy color of wisdom and knowledge. She is believed to be the most direct living descendant of the original White Woman in what serves as the Natchez Beginning Times. Her eldest sister's son is the current sitting Great Sun. Our murdered Little Sun was the sister's second-eldest boy, the last of his particular Quigualtam lineage. He would become Great Sun should his older brother pass."

Tonka'tzi Wind was frowning. "Sent here as a measure of

the Great Sun's high regard and respect for the Morning Star, as I recall."

"And with an ulterior motive," Blue Heron added. "The Natchez are ambitious and through the Quigualtam alliance, have the military might to back it up. Their high bluffs above the river give them a defensive advantage as well as a good view of who is traveling past. One of the Little Sun's purposes here was to evaluate and learn our strengths before returning to advise his brother."

"Learn our strengths? To what purpose?" the *tonka'tzi* wondered.

Blue Heron shrugged. "We are the greatest Nation in the world. The Morning Star has guaranteed free Trade on the river. The river runs past the Natchez. In addition, our colonies worry a great many foreign Nations. We have moved east, west, and north. Do we have designs on the south? What are the chances of a Cahokian colony being established in lands claimed by the Natchez?"

Fire Cat tensed, a sour taste in his mouth. His beloved Red Wing Town, once a bastion of freedom in the north, now suffered under the Cahokian blasphemy.

"We have no aspirations to move on the south," Chunkey Boy said as he listened. "We are better served through Trade with those Nations."

And, Fire Cat thought to himself, they'd be a much tougher military nut to crack, let alone hold. As Red Wing Town had proven until taken by stealth. Cahokian colonies tended to be placed in the lands of poorly organized chiefdoms that could only rally hunters and part-time warriors. The kind who had no chance against trained Cahokian formations.

Tonka'tzi Wind took a deep breath. "Be that as it may, a murdered Little Sun is going to complicate things with the Natchez." She glanced at Blue Heron. "What steps do you recommend?"

The Keeper replied, "The body is being given special treatment in the Earth Clans charnel house. The Healer Rides-the-Lightning is caring for it. I suggest that we send a special embassy downriver with the bones. It will cost us. We'll need to send sufficient gifts and offerings to ensure—"

"You won't have the chance," Night Shadow Star interrupted.

"How's that, Niece?" the *tonka'tzi* asked.

Night Shadow Star smiled as if at some internal thought. "The storm comes from the south like a midsummer torrent. Tremors run though the Underworld. A new Power is sending its first tendrils into our world. Like a newly germinated seed, only the finest filament of root is extended at first. If nurtured it will slowly thicken and twist into a mighty root capable of sundering the stone upon which our world is built."

"Pus and blood, girl," Blue Heron muttered. "Can't you talk in plain words?"

Night Shadow Star turned to fix Chunkey Boy with her knowing gaze. "Once again we play a deep game, don't we, Great Lord? The filament is already here. Its fine thread has found the first crack in the stone that is Cahokia. The problem with a root is that once it gains a foothold, pulling it out can be a difficult and troublesome task."

Chunkey Boy's eyes flashed behind his painted face. "It is far easier to kill a noxious tree, Lady, when it begins to grow in one's own garden. The task is much more difficult when it flourishes in a distant neighbor's plot, and a thousand seeds are cast onto the wind."

"I hope the few fruits you seek to harvest don't turn out to be poison, Great Lord."

With that, she turned on her heel, stalking past Fire Cat in a languid stride.

Fire Cat allowed himself one last hard look at the imposter

before wheeling, his war club held purposefully. Matching Night Shadow Star's long-legged stride he stalked along behind. Confusion and worry reflected in the Keeper's and *tonka'tzi*'s eyes.

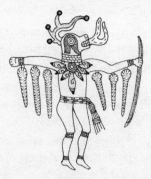

Nine

After leaving the dead Natchez in Blue Heron's capable
hands, Seven Skull Shield had headed west on the Avenue
of the Sun, winding through the confusion of people, porters, and load-bearing parties that surged against and through
each other. The busy thoroughfare served as the artery over
which most of Cahokia's lifeblood flowed.

Goods from all over arrived at the long canoe landing below River Mounds City: logs and timber from the north,
corn, squash, cured buffalo hides, textiles, exotics from the
south, cane, thatch, ceramics, copper from the distant north,
sheets of mica from the far-off eastern mountains, tobacco
and black drink tea from the gulf, the finest cherts and
hardest sandstones, immense loads of both fresh water
and more-prized saltwater shell. While some went to Horned
Serpent Mounds or to Evening Star Town, the rest was
carted up to River Mounds City, then along the Avenue of
the Sun to central Cahokia, or up to North Star Mounds a
half day's walk above Cahokia.

The route—hemmed on the north by Marsh Elder Lake
and on the south by swampy lowlands—was marked by the
Black Tail's great tumulus mound, which included Petaga's
grave. The monument was bordered by countless temples,

charnel and clan houses, and served the clusters of farm-steads that occupied every spare bit of arable soil between the Avenue of the Sun and the marshy lowlands.

He might have heard thirty different languages, seen people dressed in all manners of style, their hair done in what he would have thought peculiar fashions. These were the "dirt farmers," the immigrants that had crowded into Cahokia from every direction to share the miracle of the resurrected Morning Star.

Each of the closely spaced dwellings had a small garden plot, ramada, pestle, and log mortar. They clustered around an associated council house and chunkey court, usually overseen by one of the Earth Clans. Nearby were temples dedicated to Old-Woman-Who-Never-Dies and to the Morning Star, a charnel house, sweat lodge, and low conical burial mound.

Having arrived at River Mounds City, Seven Skull Shield wandered among the warren of stalls and workshops, striking up conversations with the craftsmen and Traders. Anyone seeking to rid himself of a valuable cloak—especially one gifted from the shoulders of the Morning Star himself—had only a limited number of places to dispose of it for profit. Most of them were in River Mounds City or its associated canoe landing, where a thousand vessels a day might land or depart for the vast river system that linked the Cahokian world.

The individuals who might traffic in a stolen cloak thrived in the underbelly of Cahokia's narrow passages. And there, Seven Skull Shield was most at home.

He was wondering what to do about his empty stomach when a fortuitous shouting match broke out between two rival potters vying for space to display their wares. When a young woman with a sack full of goosefoot bread stopped to watch, he was able to pluck one of the loaves from the top of her open pack.

Slipping between two warehouses, he munched appreciatively as he made his way to the ramshackle abode occupied by Mud Foot. A scrawny Deer Clan man with a twitchy left eye, Mud Foot had been disgraced by some indiscretion his clan had considered intolerable. He had ended up providing various "services" to the stream of Traders who flowed through the canoe landing. Neither Mud Foot's appearance nor his dwelling reflected his true wealth or influence among the footloose adventurers who'd flocked to Cahokia. He'd learned long ago that camouflage was a necessary survival skill.

To Seven Skull Shield's delight, Mud Foot was seated in the shade of his ratty ramada, counting out shell beads to two young undernourished women.

"That's all," Mud Foot told them. "But if you want more, come back tonight. I can find you more work."

Both of the women nodded, smiled, and rose to hurry away.

Seven Skull Shield took another bite of his bread as Mud Foot glanced up. At the sight of him, Mud Foot's left eye really began to twitch. "Oh, it's you."

"That's a fine greeting," Seven Skull Shield muttered through his mouthful. He ambled over, glancing around to see who was near. Stuck as it was in the narrow confines between a weaver's workshop and two warehouses, Mud Foot's house always had privacy. "You're hiring scrawny dirt farmers these days? And barely more than girls?"

Mud Foot shrugged, looking oddly uncomfortable. "A handful of beads can be traded for a couple of loaves of bread. They'll have full bellies tonight, and the Traders whose beds they warmed didn't care if they were fat or not. After four days of sacred chastity, demand was high last night." His eye twitched again as he added, "Not just everyone gets to sleep in the Keeper's high palace."

"Do I detect sarcasm?"

"Detect what you want."

"A cloak was stolen last night. A beautiful thing, gifted from the Morning Star to a Natchez lord at the conclusion of the Busk. Someone killed the Natchez to get it."

"Sorry. I was here. Like I said, business was good. You can ask around if you want. And I don't know any Natchez lords."

"Whoever took the cloak might want to dispose of it without having to answer any embarrassing questions, like how he happened to have it in his possession. Traded to the right person . . ."

"Ah, I see." Mud Foot sighed, relaxing slightly. "Thanks for the warning. I won't touch it if it shows up."

"I just need to know who—"

"No."

"Huh?"

Mud Foot gave him a humorless smile. "You're not one of us anymore. No one trusts you."

"I saved your life. Remember that time when that couple of nasty Caddo Traders were going to slit your belly open? They'd figured out that you'd stolen—"

"Let's call that debt even. You're dangerous. Anyone dealing with you? Look what happened to Black Swallow. You got his fingers broken."

"He was compensated. And there's a reward—"

"Maybe you've forgotten. Most of us down here, we survive by not being noticed by the Four Winds Clan. You are a Four Winds spy. If you never cast your shadow across my path again, I'll consider it a blessing."

"And there was the time when you had to hide from—"

"Go. Now. And don't come back." He paused. "And just so you know, word's out. No one wants to deal with you. Just being close to you can get a person killed in the most unpleasant of ways."

"If you so much as hear of this cloak—"

"You're as dumb as you're dangerous. Get your accursed carcass out of my sight!"

At the stinging betrayal, Seven Skull Shield raised his hands in surrender and backed away.

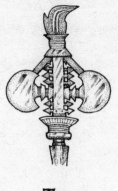

Ten

Blue Heron paused halfway down the long staircase from the Morning Star's high palace. She hated stairs. Now, however, she took a moment to study the vista. In any direction she looked, the great city spread in a patchwork of buildings, fields, marshes, and sinuous lakes. Between her and the eastern bluffs, the floodplain was filled with mound-top structures alternating with conical burial mounds. Every square of dry ground was covered with farmsteads, clan houses, society houses, granaries, and a maze-work of small fields. The sprawl crowded up against the eastern bluffs; and could she but see beyond the heights, it continued for a hard day's run in the direction of the distant Moon Temple and mound complex at the Avenue of the Sun's eastern terminus.

To the south, the Great Plaza spread before her with its chunkey courts, World Tree pole, and the stickball grounds. Lining the plaza were mound-top palaces and temples, society houses, and at the southern end, the twin mounds where Rides-the-Lightning and his Earth Clan priests communed with the dead. From there the Avenue of the Moon ran due south on its elevated causeway to the High Sun Temple complex with its imposing Rattlesnake Mound just visible in the hazy distance.

Beyond that, the road turned southwest toward the Horned Serpent mounds, invisible in the smoky haze. That route, too, was lined with dwellings, as if wherever the city spread its tentacles, settlement followed.

Looking west, her eye followed the Avenue of the Sun as it demarcated the equinox line that ran through Cahokia, past the observatory's circle of posts and through endless houses to the distant Sunset Temple and Black Tail's tomb. There the avenue bent west-southwest along the southern edge of Marsh Lake to River Mounds City and the canoe landing. Across the river, and atop the distant western bluffs, Blue Heron could barely make out Evening Star Town where it dominated the mighty river's bluffs. And beyond that, the endless farmsteads and temple groups continued.

People. Countless people. Farther than the eye could see.

No one could count them. Tens of tens of thousands, from all over the known world.

So great was the city that the various Four Winds Clan Houses had been given authority to govern specific areas. They in turn had granted subdivisions of their territory to individual Earth Clans who administered districts teeming with immigrants who spoke a polyglot of languages and practiced a myriad of odd behaviors.

Despite the differences—and often age-old enmities— worship of the Morning Star tied the chaos of peoples, clans, and Houses together. Disputes were generally settled through sanctioned games of chunkey overseen by Earth Clan subchiefs or their representatives.

Now a Natchez lord was murdered. The Morning Star and Night Shadow Star were apparently locked in another incomprehensible Power struggle. If Blue Heron could believe the warnings, some unperceived threat was coming from the south.

And I'm the one charged with keeping it all from exploding?

Sometimes, on days like today, she wondered where she got the strength.

She minced her way down the rest of the staircase to the Council Terrace where it extended from the great mound's southern slope. The area was palisaded, the logs encased in a thick coat of clay. In the western half stood the great Council House—essentially Cahokia's political center. The heart of Cahokia's cutthroat politics beat within these walls, all overseen by the *tonka'tzi,* and monitored by the Morning Star's picked representatives. Here the business of empire was conducted. Embassies from distant Nations were received.

Beside the council house a generous thatch-covered ramada allowed business to be conducted outside when the weather allowed. In its shade stood three daises, the middle slightly taller than its sisters on either side. Perched in the middle, *Tonka'tzi* Wind sat on her litter. Several of the representatives from the various Four Winds Houses had already gathered.

Blue Heron didn't need the young runner waiting at the bottom of the steps to redirect her course.

She ran her tongue over the few teeth remaining in her jaws as she walked over and nodded to the assembled nobles.

"What was that business about trees and roots?" the *tonka'tzi* demanded without preamble. "Did you understand any of it?"

Blue Heron settled herself on the dais to the Great Sky's right, nodding to the various nobles as she did so.

"Sister, I have no idea at all." Blue Heron rubbed her thighs, feeling muscles gone tight from the climb and descent.

She gave the others crowding around—curiosity brimming in their eyes—a wave of the hand. "The *tonka'tzi* and I need to discuss something. If you wouldn't mind."

The others touched their chins respectfully and melted away, carefully distancing themselves just far enough for propriety but close enough that they might hear something if either the *tonka'tzi* or Keeper happened to raise their voices.

Blue Heron gave the closest a narrow-eyed scowl and watched High Chief War Duck's cousin Ties Wood back up an additional couple of steps. Then she turned to her sister. "Wind, the last time the Morning Star and Night Shadow Star played this cryptic game, half of our family was murdered, and the Powers of the Underworld were almost let loose into this one."

"You think we're about to be caught in the middle again?"

"Let's put it in context: At the height of the Busk, the thief gets a warning from Crazy Frog that someone's going to be murdered. Something about trouble in the south. The Morning Star gifts the Natchez Little Sun with a cloak. The Little Sun goes back to his quarters. He's mysteriously murdered and left with a feather in his mouth. Supposedly the sign of a terrible Natchez witch. The cloak is missing."

"You didn't mention that up there." She indicated the palace looming above them.

"I never got the chance." Blue Heron fingered the wattle on her chin. "Nor did I mention that Night Shadow Star showed up at the Natchez embassy, wandered in with that look she gets when Piasa is whispering in her ear. She glances at the body, says something irritatingly vague about Power and golden darkness, then floats out in that odd walk of hers."

"Golden darkness? Is that something Piasa told her?"

"I don't know." She paused. "Sometimes she scares the piss out of me."

Wind rubbed a hand over her age-worn face. "We've barely managed to tie the city back together after the last time. Blood and dung, why can't Power leave us alone for a couple of seasons?" She shot Blue Heron a bleak look. "Power's touched all of our nieces and nephews. Among the ones who've survived, one hosts the resurrected god, another's become a creature of the Underworld, and young Lace is a soul-broken wreck. Thank the spirits my children weren't chosen for such terrible fates. What is it about our family?"

"You might ask the Red Wing?" Blue Heron said, her thoughts on the whimpering ruin Walking Smoke had made of Lace.

Wind shook her head. "I still think the Red Wing is going to cut Star's throat some night. And bringing him, armed for war, into the Morning Star's palace? Did you see that look he gave the living god? He *hates* us."

"You didn't see him when he charged into Columella's burning palace. He mowed through those Tula warriors like they were dry cornstalks. And then he disappeared into the flames to save Night Shadow Star." She cocked her jaw. "They both claim they detest each other. But I think Power had its reasons for throwing them together. I thought it was punishment at first. Now? The looks they give each other when they think no one's watching?"

"That will never happen. He killed the only man she ever loved. And you've got his mother and sister hostage." Wind shot Blue Heron a sidelong glance. "At least we've got that much leverage to keep Fire Cat in line. But get back to this murder. What was Night Shadow Star's reason for going to see the dead Natchez?"

"It's a hunch, but I think she was trying to tell me it's a distraction."

"Some distraction. When the Natchez hear—and you know that some Trader is already breaking his back paddling headlong down the river to tell them—the whole south could go up in flames."

"My people tell me it's being talked about all over the city." Blue Heron could sense something, as if she was missing a subtle clue. "I've got the thief out looking for the missing cloak."

"And that's another thing." Wind pointed a bony finger in

her direction. "You and that loathsome, woman-hopping thief. How can you stand to have him in the same room? Makes less sense than Night Shadow Star and the Red Wing. At least they're highborn."

"Me and the thief?" How did she put this into words? "He's—"

"Keeper!" A runner—one of the warriors she'd left at the Natchez embassy—came bolting through the gate, caught sight of her, and headed her way. The young man's face looked stricken. He dropped to his knees, touching his forehead to the matting in obeisance. He was panting, sweat beading on his brown skin.

"What?"

The runner looked up, expression horrified. "The Natchez, Keeper."

"Don't tell me a war party just landed at River Mounds."

"No. It's . . ." He swallowed hard. "The Little Sun's servants. *They're all dead!*"

Eleven

Night, like a hot and damp blanket, lay over the city. The sky was overcast; a haze of smoke pressed low to mix with the mist rising from the marshy swamps and stagnant ox-bow lakes. Occasionally dogs could be heard barking in the distance, the sound of it carrying on the thick and pungent air.

The figure moved with athletic grace as it left the Avenue of the Sun, following the beaten path north around the eastern side of Black Tail's imposing ridge mound. Draped in spectral black from head to knee, the hooded figure strode with familiar ease through the darkness, passing the temples, council houses, and low burial mounds that crowded the area.

On the northern edge of the clustered buildings, isolated atop the low terrace overlooking Cahokia Creek, rose a grassy, rectangular platform mound. Weeds now grew around the long-abandoned protruding and charred timbers that still littered the flat top, evidence of an ancient fire from which there had been no recovery. Offerings including cornhusk dolls, small balls of tobacco bound in colored fabric, painted sticks, and beaded feathers had been laid around the mound's sides.

That such offerings continued to mysteriously appear along the flanks of the forbidden mound was a subtle reminder that the ancient beliefs stubbornly burned in the hearts of the city's oldest inhabitants.

The figure in black paused, a darker shadow in the night, and stared at the ghostly hump of earth. Then it turned, following a trail through the grass to a small trench-wall house with a weathered split-cane roof.

While it, too, might have appeared abandoned given the flaking clay on the walls and unkempt surroundings, a faint red glow could be seen around the burlap fabric hanging in the doorway.

The figure paused and considered the offerings that had been placed around the building's walls. Little bundles, crude figurines, offerings of food, and both tobacco and kinnikinnick to be smoked. Here, too, the old believers made their offerings.

"Some things die slowly," a reedy voice called from inside. "Yes, they still offer their devotions. How curious that you're surprised."

A hand extended from the black fabric and pulled the door hanging to one side. Then the figure entered. The room was small; a bed of coals glowed in the puddled-clay hearth dug into the dirt floor. A single sleeping bench was built into the back wall. Bags upon bags of herbs and dried plants hung from the ceiling poles and walls. A couple of battered wooden storage boxes and a mismatched collection of chipped and cracked brownware pots and seed jars lined the walls. Large utilitarian baskets filled one corner.

The solitary occupant sat before the low fire; a round bundle of brown cloth the size of a cow bison's heart was clutched in her lap. Wrinkles upon wrinkles lined her age-ravaged face, her jaw undershot. White hair, thin and loose, seemed to float on the hot and steamy air. A threadbare brown smock hung from skeletal shoulders where fragile skin sank around her stick-like bones.

But the eyes shining in the red light were anything but feeble, almost burning in their dark intensity.

"I didn't think you'd come yourself. Though it is fitting that you'd do it in the dark of the moon on a cloud-black night."

"In all things there are beginnings and endings."

She smiled, exposing toothless pink gums. "But which is it? The Natchez is dead. The gaming pieces are cast. Now we wait to see how the players will move. An ending for you and yours, or a beginning for yet another twist of the Spiral?"

"That answer lies in the wind, and in the inherent character of the human heart."

"What if you have misplaced your trust in hearts and Power?"

"Then in every ending there is a new beginning. A truth you discovered so long ago. Devoured and reborn. You survived wounds, wars, and foaming-mad chiefs. Every move the Four Winds Clan made against you. You are finally failing, Priestess. What then for the Bundle?"

She studied him, the Power of her gaze reflecting the passion in her soul. "Not only do you make alliances with the Underworld, but with me as well?"

"Endings and beginnings. The Four Winds Clan has forgotten you. Nor do I have any intention of reminding them. I know your time is limited. An inevitable ending. For a beginning, I would ensure that the Bundle goes to someone responsible. Someone who understands its Power and sanctity."

"And if I choose differently?"

"This threat from the south? This foreign and different Power? The ending of which we speak could be for all the Spirits, Dancing, and Dreaming. Cahokia's Spirits, ways, and practices can be replaced as easily as Petaga's were. Different gods, new names for Power, and oblivion for your Spiral and the knowledge of our ancestors. In the coming struggle, the Bundle may make the difference."

She closed her eyes, thin chest expanding as she inhaled. "Endings and beginnings. Full circle. Once again the Spiral brings you to my door. Very well. Assuming we defeat this rogue god and its minions, when the time comes for me to hand the Bundle over, I shall bring it to your palace."

The black-clad figure inclined his head, touching fingertips to the hidden forehead. "My deepest respects . . . Priestess."

"And to you." A flicker of a smile played at her lips. "Hard to believe we would have come to this, you and I."

The black-hooded figure turned then, slipping out into the night.

In the wavering light of the embers, the old woman played her bone-thin fingers over the fabric, closed her eyes, and sighed.

Twelve

Seven Skull Shield was prowling the canoe landing that morning, seeking any word of the stolen cape. His reception by old and supposedly good friends left him devastated. Most avoided his eyes, offered evasions, and slipped away with an excuse. Some wouldn't even talk to him.

Seven Skull Shield might have considered himself a loner, but he'd never *felt* so alone before. Along with the hurt came a curious desperation, a confused urge to either laugh hysterically or weep.

Why are they doing this to me?

He was asking himself that question when the Natchez arrived. They came from the south, four large canoes, each filled with strapping, tattooed warriors who stroked rhythmically. Their pointed paddles rose and fell, dipping into the Father Water's turgid surface. Like all travelers headed upriver, they paralleled the banks, where the current swirled in slow, tepid patterns.

The high-prowed canoes, hewn from giant red cedars, were inlaid and painted. The warriors, their skulls shaved of all but a topknot, sported full-body tattoos indicative of their many feats in battle. In each vessel's bow stood an athletic young man who wore a cloak of a different sacred color: red, white, black, or yellow. A similarly dyed apron hung from a breechcloth and fell to each man's knees. In their hands were the sacred staffs of office, again colored to match the bearer's ensemble.

Paralleling the crowded canoe landing, they chose the center for their landfall, partially clogged as it was with heavy Trade canoes.

As they drove onto the charcoal-dark sand, the warriors clambered out, hoisting each of the heavy craft and carrying them up onto the beach.

Seven Skull Shield—perplexed, hurt, and slightly stunned after his meetings with supposed old friends—watched the whole thing from where he wandered among the Trade ramadas above the landing. Packed as the place was with goods, people, grilled foods, and hawkers, he had never felt more alone.

Mud Foot, Bear Fat, Slick Rock. After all I've done for them.

His old friends had shunned him as if he were a soul-sick and foaming-mouthed skunk. They might have jabbed a forked stick into his belly and twisted it, given the way he felt.

As the crowd began to encroach on the newly landed canoes, the warriors reached for their weapons, forming a ring around the vessels. The newcomers remained mute as questions were called from all sides: "Where from?" "Come to Trade?" "What do you carry?" "Fresh venison here!" "Do you need a guide?" "Service for Trade!"

The hawkers, with their trinkets raised, crowded as close as they dared, seeking to tempt the line of warriors with souvenir pots in the shape of Old-Woman-Who-Never-Dies, carved wooden statues of the Morning Star, Cahokian cups, clay chunkey stones, reliefs of the Morning Star in various poses, and every other memento that might interest a foreigner.

At the same time old women and children ran forward bearing platters of roasted meats, ears of boiled corn, baked rabbit on a stick, sweets made of berries and currants, loaves of coontie, corn, and lotus root breads.

All of which the steadfast warriors ignored, only to lift their shields and war clubs should one of the swarming horde press too close.

Seven Skull Shield caught sight of Black Swallow where he stood in the shade of a rope vendor's ramada. Coils of cord, basswood rope, and plaited rawhide were always in demand for netting, binding, and canoe line.

He approached cautiously, still stung and wondering if this friend, too, was about to add to the wound.

"Now, who do you think they are?" Seven Skull Shield sidled up next to the man. Waiting for Black Swallow's reaction, his heart had begun to pound as if he were sneaking into a forbidden temple.

Black Swallow gave him a sidelong glance before returning his attention to the throng around the canoes.

"You've been around long enough to recognize a delegation of foreign nobles when you see one. Given your current associates, you'd know better than I would."

At least he hadn't been told to scat.

Seven Skull Shield tried to ignore his friend's incessant massaging of the irregularly healed fingers. That, ultimately, had been Seven Skull Shield's fault, though the wily and unscrupulous Black Swallow had been compensated handsomely for the damage.

"Some embassy from the south." Seven Skull Shield stroked his chin, desperate to appear at ease. "Can't see the designs through the crowd. Four of them, each with his own color, must be important."

"Your knot is pulled tight with the Keeper. Generally these things are negotiated in advance so both parties know who they're going to meet." Black Swallow's voice turned snide. "Or didn't she tell you?"

"She doesn't share the trivia of her day with me, old friend. I just get called for the dirty work." He could be just as snide. "I realize that Morning Star House works at a constant disadvantage when they don't bring me in for consultations on the intricacies of running the empire, but they've got to do something on their own."

Black Swallow smacked him impudently on the shoulder, an act that filled Seven Skull Shield with relief. "Well, you're not making a lot of progress on finding that cloak. Maybe I ought to go throw myself on the Keeper's floor mat and offer my services. Get her some competent help for once."

He's already heard about the cloak.

But that shouldn't have been surprising as quickly as information flowed along the waterfront.

"Thought you didn't especially care for her."

Black Swallow stared sullenly at his fingers. "She didn't *have* to break my hands, you know."

"Haven't heard you complain since you started providing information on things she's interested in."

"You ask me, you're dancing foot to foot with disaster, working with her. But then, you've never been any too smart."

"No one's hung me in a square."

"Yet."

A stern voice called out in a language Seven Skull Shield didn't know, and the crowd drew back. But something about the words, the accent, nagged at the edges of his souls.

The warriors had re-formed around the four messengers with their colored staffs. The formation started up the beach, though not without some effort as they tried to make their way past beached canoes and around the clutter of ramadas and vendors stands.

"Excuse me," Seven Skull Shield said, rising. "If you hear anything about that cloak, send a runner. I'll make it worth your time."

"Sure, just be sure it's something I can Trade for a small fortune will you?" His gaze darkened. "And don't come around me again. You're poison these days. You and your high-and-mighty friends."

The venom in Black Swallow's voice burned through Seven Skull Shield's veins.

But just as discomforting, he knew who the emissaries were, and his stomach had an empty feeling that had nothing to do with the despair caused by supposed old friends.

Thirteen

Blue Heron studied the youth—more of an urchin, actually—who crouched on the newly laid mat floor. If he tried to bow his head any lower, he'd leave a dent in the matting. Maybe just into his teens, he was mostly bones.

"And what brings you to my palace?" she asked.

"I . . . I . . . ," he croaked, shivering in terror.

"Speak, boy. Nothing here will hurt you." Which, depending on what he said, might be an out-and-out lie.

"S-Seven S-Skull Shield says to tell you that a Natchez delegation has arrived at the canoe landing!" The youth, his body still streaked with clay from the workshop where he made pots, was nearly breathless. "He made me remember this: four canoes; each with twenty warriors; four emissaries, each carrying a staff of office, one red, one white, one black, one yellow. They should be on the way here now."

The miracle was that Smooth Pebble had allowed the urchin inside the palace. In the old days, that would never have happened. Now the Deer Clan youth raised his head and was staring around with eyes so big they could have fit into a buffalo's skull.

"Why did he send you?"

"I . . ." He swallowed hard. "I'm the fastest runner he knows."

Four canoes of Natchez warriors? Just out of the blue?

Makes me wonder where the rest of my spies are.

No doubt they'd come trickling in moments after the Natchez delegation appeared at the base of the Morning Star's mound and demanded a conference in the Council House.

Pus and blood! Tell me the Natchez haven't heard about the Little Sun's murder.

"Feed this boy and send him on his way with a blanket or something." She stood, clapping her hands. "Smooth Pebble! Send word to the *Tonka'tzi*. I need a squad of warriors. I want them dressed and formal, and in perfect formation at the foot of the stairs. I want that done yesterday. Now move!"

Her entire household exploded into activity.

A finger of time later she thought she could have done a better job with her hair and dress, but rushed as she was, it would have to do. Her porters were carrying her posthaste onto the Avenue of the Sun, almost beating the crowd of pilgrims out of the way before they deposited her at the base of the stairs.

To her disgust, no warriors were present except the small guard that kept the gawkers from trying to climb up to the Council Terrace or from leaning on the great mound's base. The usual throng of petitioners, messengers from distant colonies, Earth Clan chiefs, and sycophants were waiting for their turn to ascend and plague *Tonka'tzi* Wind with whatever petty grievance they might have.

She could hear the whispered comments as she spryly leaped from her litter and hurried up the stairs.

At the top, the two guards bowed and touched their foreheads. Then she was through the gate, wheezing and blowing from the climb as she hurried on trembling legs to where Wind sat on her litter beneath the ramada. Her sister was discussing something with representatives from North Star and Horned Serpent Houses. It couldn't be too important since the recorders, with their strings and pots of beads, sat idle among the collection of advisors behind the *Tonka'tzi*.

"Leave us," Blue Heron ordered as she puffed her way up to the *tonka'tzi*'s elevated seat. The shade provided a hint of relief after the blazing heat of the sun.

She barely allowed the bowing and scraping nobles to escape before blurting, "Natchez are coming. Four canoes of them."

"They couldn't know about the Little Sun this quickly." Wind straightened in her seat.

"Sister, I don't think we can call this a coincidence." Blue Heron gestured toward the line of servants and recorders who sat in the shady overhang of the Council House a stone's toss away. "You! We need a feast prepared. Black drink boiled."

To the Morning Star's representative she called, "Three Echoes, inform the Morning Star that a Natchez delegation is on the way. Four canoes of them, bearing staffs of office."

"Not a coincidence," Wind mused as she leaned her chin on a propped arm. Her eyes slitted as she considered it. "No, I'd think not."

Blue Heron settled her weary bones on the pedestal to Wind's right. "Casts the Little Sun's murder in a whole new light, doesn't it? Someone's playing a deep game. The question is, did whoever murdered the Little Sun do it to put us off balance and give the Natchez embassy an advantage in negotiations, or was he killed to upset their plans?"

"Wouldn't be the first time some Nation's local politics were played out here," Wind agreed thoughtfully. "Something tells me that we'll have a better idea based on what they say when they get here. Righteous indignation, accusations, and demands for redress means they knew and were involved. Worry or dismay with sidelong glances and sudden insecurity tells us something else."

"Or there's a third party."

"Always a possibility." Wind shifted. "Nothing new on

the murder? Anything to explain why the Natchez servants all killed themselves?"

"I could speculate all day, but so far I've nothing solid." Blue Heron sighed. "We've been carting a stream of bodies to the charnel house. It's quite the sensation. Murder and mass suicide? Proves the black witch wasn't one of the servants. Witches don't kill themselves."

"The last thing we want is to be drawn into some internal squabble among the Natchez. They might be half a world away, but they could shut down the entire lower river if they wanted, and some of our colonies on the Tenasee are within striking distance of their war parties."

Blue Heron closed her eyes, picturing the Father Water as it ran south to the gulf. A multitude of Nations, like beads on a string, clung to the great river's banks: Michigamea, Casqui, Quiz Quiz, Pacaha, Nodena, Paski, Chactah, Quiguate, Anilco, Guachoya, and so many more. In the usual fractious political dynamic, if one of the southern river Nations began to dominate, the others inevitably overcame their dislike for each other and allied to knock the aggressor down a peg or two until equilibrium was restored. Like snarling dogs, the lower river Nations would fight amongst each other, but the moment a wolf appeared they'd form a pack and all pounce at once.

That distasteful tendency had always dissuaded Cahokia from trying to extend its political authority into the region.

"Something else is worrying you."

Blue Heron pulled at her chin. "What really scares me is the Morning Star's angle in all of this. He gave that cloak to the Little Sun, as if he knew it would upset the entire basket of corn. He's in this, I swear to the ancestors. And so is Night Shadow Star and her soul-whispering Piasa. This is more than politics, Sister. This is Power, and once again, we're like little gaming pieces right in the middle of it."

Wind pursed her thin lips over pink gums. "Last time that happened, we barely survived."

Blue Heron fingered the scar on her throat. "You don't have to remind me."

She turned as one of the Morning Star's runners came pelting down the long stairs from the palace. She placed him as one of Matron Soft Bread's sons, of the Hawk Clan. He held one of the staffs of office, indicating official business.

He trotted up, and dropped to one knee, bowing and touching his forehead. Then he glanced up, his dark eyes meeting the *tonka'tzi*'s as he said, "The Morning Star informs you that he will see the Natchez delegation in the palace and requires your presence." He glanced at Blue Heron. "The Keeper is requested as well."

Tonka'tzi Wind dismissed him with a gesture, and after he'd gone, added, "So, the Morning Star knows the Natchez have arrived? And we have just found out?"

"Feels like we're treading in deep water, doesn't it, Sister?"

"And the currents below our feet are most sinister." She smiled bitterly. "You ready for a climb?"

"Did I ever tell you how much I hate those stairs?"

Fourteen

Horn Lance had dressed impeccably. He'd darkened his graying hair with charcoal-laden grease and wound it into a tight bun over which he placed a leather helmet onto which scarlet macaw feathers had been fixed to stand straight up in a vertical cylinder. On his waist he wore a fine red Itza war kilt embroidered with an attacking eagle. His forearms were wrapped with thick leather guards to which bands of eagle down had been glued. An Itza breastplate covered his chest: a butterfly-shaped piece that protected his heart and lungs. He'd painted his face carefully with a white foundation and drawn black spirals over his age-faded Four Winds tattoos.

I am ready. He took up a war club and shield, then walked out of the Four Winds Clan House where he'd been staying. His feet almost skipped down the stairs and into the crowded plaza.

As he'd expected, people stopped short, gaping, having never seen the likes of his dress and ornamentation. The scarlet macaw feathers rising from his head had no match, not even compared to spoonbill feathers from the south. Nor could the finest of Cahokia's weavers duplicate the intricate Itza cotton fabrics.

He lifted the round Itzan shield with its red ring around a black circle, and despite the light weight, arthritis burned in his shoulder and elbow.

Hearing calls of amazement, he made his way to the Avenue of the Sun, where a larger-than-usual crowd had gathered. He immediately noted that Lady Night Shadow Star stood at the southeastern corner of her great mound. She seemed oblivious to the crowd that slowed on the road below her, some pointing in awe, others calling greetings up to her.

Her long black hair glistened in the sunlight, and she'd dressed in a stunning green skirt, her shoulders covered with a matching hemp-fiber cape.

As if she'd been waiting in anticipation, she fixed her dark eyes on him. He met her gaze, and an odd prickling sensation ran along his nerves. No change of expression crossed her face, but he could sense her hostile interest, as though she was taking the measure of a despised adversary.

Horn Lance shook off the eerie premonition and forced his way through the crowd, winding around vendors' booths with their little clay statues of Old-Woman-Who-Never-Dies and wooden cutouts of Morning Star bowling a chunkey stone. The smells of grilled food, hominy, and cooked fish alternated with the stink of unwashed bodies sweating in the hot sun.

"I see you received my message." Swirling Cloud appeared at Horn Lance's elbow. He had his hair in the stylistic twin buns on either side of his head. The part down the middle was painted a bright red. He, too, had dressed in his finest as befitted a Little Sun of the Natchez confederacy. The characteristic tattoos that ran across his nose and over his cheeks had been carefully outlined in black.

Horn Lance thought Swirling Cloud would have been a handsome young man had he not had that crazy burning anger behind his eyes. Sometimes the young Natchez gave way to his darker moods, unleashing them on women, children, or should none of the former be available, upon the occasional unlucky dog. What was it about the noble classes that soul sickness just seemed to leak out of so many lineages?

He glanced back through the crowd, catching a glimpse of Night Shadow Star's great palace atop its mound. She'd vanished from her point of vantage on the southeastern corner.

She couldn't know what we have planned. The thought seemed to insert itself in Horn Lance's souls.

"Ah, well, the mighty will take what they will." He smiled at that. He'd never really cared for Morning Star House. Let alone for Red Warrior Mankiller. Nor had it turned out that the dead *tonka'tzi*'s children were particularly tasteful, either. That vicious little Chunkey Boy might claim to be the living god these days and inhabit the Morning Star's palace, but word was that Lady Night Shadow Star herself was possessed. That it was by Underworld Power either added spice to the story, or proved that the young woman was insane. Maybe the latter since one person's insanity was another's miracle.

Whatever claim to Power she might have, in the end it wouldn't save her. Not when Thirteen Sacred Jaguar arrived.

You will learn the real meaning of "possession," Cousin.

"Here they come," Swirling Cloud said, nudging Horn Lance's elbow.

He turned, seeing the crowd part as if it were water pushed aside by the prow of a mighty Trade canoe. Then the lead Natchez warriors appeared, the forefront holding shields bearing the Quigualtam insignia that marked them as "Honored Men" in service of the Great Sun.

"Ready?" Swirling Cloud asked with a smile. As the entourage passed, he slipped between two of the warriors and took a position behind the four staff bearers and ahead of the warriors carrying engraved and polished wooden trunks filled with gifts for the Morning Star.

Horn Lance was a skip and step behind him, falling into the ranks.

"Glad to see you made it," called Wet Bobcat, the squadron first, where he marched in the rear. "Thought you might be hanging from a square, and we'd have to tear a hole through Cahokia to get you out."

Horn Lance shot Wet Bobcat a victorious smile. "All is unfolding according to plan."

He turned forward as the formation marched up to a line of Cahokian warriors in full regalia, adding under his breath, "They haven't the first notion of what's about to be unleashed on them."

As Wet Bobcat bellowed, "Squadron, halt!" Horn Lance stepped forward, and called, "Warriors of Cahokia! Messengers of the Great Sun, born of the White Woman, of the Sun Born lineage of the Quigualtam, descended from the First Sun and rulers of the Natchez confederacy, seek council with the Morning Star House and the representatives of the reincarnated miracle. We come, our souls white with peace and wisdom, order and harmony, bearing gifts and offerings as a measure of the Great Sun's high regard for the Morning Star, and submit them in order that he be pleased and accept this delegation."

An older war chief stepped out in advance of the Cahokian guard. He was dressed in fine armor. Beads of sweat were trickling from under his leather helmet and falcon feathers. His age-gnarled face looked off balance from a dislocated jaw. "The Morning Star House welcomes the Great Sun's delegation and sends greetings to the representatives of the Sun Born, of the Quigualtam, and the Natchez confederacy. We receive you under the white color of peace and wisdom, and offer you safe passage. Food and refreshment have been prepared."

The war chief pointed with his own staff, adding, "The valiant warriors who accompany you are asked to find refreshment and food at the Morning Star's Men's House." He indicated the building on the eastern side of the Great Plaza. "Come and be welcome!"

Horn Lance touched his forehead respectfully, his heart beginning to hammer in his chest. The arrow of destiny had been shot. There was no calling it back now.

Even as the four staff bearers started forward through the ranks, he glanced at Swirling Cloud. "You notice anything odd about this?"

"They were ready for us."

"I told you not to underestimate Blue Heron."

"But . . . how?"

"Doesn't matter. Oh, and remember, we've a few surprises of our own remaining to be sprung." He smiled in anticipation.

Fifteen

Night Shadow Star watched the Natchez delegation vanish into the throng at the foot of the Morning Star's great mound. She turned, walking thoughtfully past the Piasa and Horned Serpent guardian posts at the top of her steps.

She could feel the tendrils of Power, as if they were filaments of spider silk settling around her. Invisible, deadly, and binding.

"Should you be up there?" Fire Cat asked as he came trotting up her long staircase. From the glisten on his skin, his chunkey practice had been spirited. With the lance he gestured toward the Council House, its roof just visible behind the clay-coated palisade.

She studied him for a moment—this man who'd killed her beloved husband and lied about the manner of his death. Fire Cat had assured her that Makes Three had died well. She had hated him with all of her heart. Had anticipated slowly burning him alive in the square.

As he stopped before her, perspiration gave his skin a glow, accenting his black Red Wing tattoos along with those marking his military successes. Muscle packed his arms and shoulders, his belly rippling down to where a loincloth snugged around his thin waist. Trickles of sweat followed the contours of his pectorals and ribs. She experienced the oddest urge to reach out with a fingertip and trace one of the glistening beads as it slipped down his hard body.

His gaze had turned wary, as if he could sense her disquieting interest.

He. Is. My. Enemy. She forced the words down between her souls where they could not become dislodged, and cocked her head as she heard Piasa's faint laughter, as if it mocked her from a distance.

Her gaze shifted to the Council House roof where it rose behind its palisade. "My presence would change nothing. The struggle will have to be waged." In the place of fear came an inexorable weariness and distaste.

"How was your game?" She changed the subject, indicating the lance and stone he carried. The sight of Makes Three's prized stone in the Red Wing's hands no longer incited rage.

He was still watching her through cautious eyes. "I won by three. I shouldn't have. Your cousin wasn't on his game. He made mistakes. But even though I won it's as if . . ."

"Yes?"

He shook his head, tossing the stone up and letting it slap into his hand as he cast another anxious look across to the Council House. "As if part of me is numb and blunt, Lady. The part of my souls and Power that should be sharp and skilled."

She nodded, feeling the same of herself. "My master tells me you must find it, Red Wing. He . . ." The words eluded her, unsure herself about what the whispered warnings spun of the air actually meant.

She hadn't yet found herself—her Spirit-possessed souls shiftless inside the new woman she'd become. A part of her remained shattered by revelations called up from deep within her hidden memories.

My brother raped me. And some sickness in my souls hid it.

She'd learned, no, rediscovered, that truth last spring while her souls were being judged in the Underworld. The terror, pain, and betrayal had been too great to bear.

I am insane and polluted. No wonder Power twists me about like a knotted rope.

She tightened her fists until the nails cut into her palms, the unclean taint of incest tickling her skin like wind-borne soot.

"It would help," Fire Cat said gently, "if you could give me some sense of what's to come. The last time? I was a half a breath away from being too late."

Did she really remember his hand reaching down, fixing in her hair and lifting, drawing her from the river's depths? Or was that some made-up memory she'd pieced together from his description of when he pulled her soul-dead flesh from the water?

Her first true memory was of his breath forcing its way into her lungs. His frantic hands on her breasts as he pressed water from her drowned body. Only when she'd coughed and shivered had he lain his warm body atop hers and collapsed in relief. Her heart skipped as she relived that instant of amazed realization that she was alive.

She shot him a wary glance. *And breathing life into me? Did he also breathe some of his souls into mine?*

The thought carried too many implications. She forced it away.

"Piasa hasn't told me all of it." She returned her gaze to the Council House. "Only that the Spirit World is threatened."

"I'll look for the lightning ahead of time."

"This isn't a battle between Sky and Underworld." She shook her head, trying to quiet her roiling thoughts. Memories of the river's dark depths stirred, tried to possess her. Walking Smoke had gripped her by the throat until lightning blasted the river. She banished the image, concentrating on the here and now. "But something different. We're . . . gaming pieces. Bet upon by Power."

"Piasa told you that?"

"A hunch, Red Wing."

He took a deep breath, swelling his chest. A woman could admire a chest like that. Dream about it.

But not her. Not with this man.

She turned, the sense of unease creeping through her souls like a winter mist.

"He must play like the heroes of the Beginning Times," Piasa's voice seemed to hiss from the air.

"Then call upon the Morning Star," she retorted.

"He has already abandoned you."

"Lady?" Fire Cat asked as he hurried along behind her. "You want me to call upon the Morning Star? I don't understand."

"Not you, Red Wing. And understanding isn't required. Just chunkey. Perfect, flawless chunkey. As if our lives depended upon it."

But why? What goaded Piasa's insistence?

She didn't look back as she stepped onto the veranda of her palace. All she'd see in Fire Cat's face was confusion, and she already had enough of that for the two of them.

"Lady?"

At Fire Cat's call she turned, following his gaze.

She could see the Natchez delegation, four messengers, two men dressed in finery, and warriors bearing heavy boxes as they climbed the high staircase to the Morning Star's palace.

"It begins." Piasa flickered at the edge of her vision, his sibilant voice chilling her souls.

Sixteen

Face it. People just don't trust you anymore." The words echoed between Seven Skull Shield's souls as he pondered his new status among the thieves and con men along the waterfront. Gone was his fame as the ribald seducer of young married women. The joking familiarity among equals had been replaced by dissembling double-talk. Old friends now watched him through wary eyes filled with distrust.

Saddled with a sense of disquiet, he drifted through the shops and warehouses on the outskirts of Chief War Duck's long plaza at River Mounds. On the day after the Busk, the normally vibrant passages between the buildings remained subdued, people having feasted, frolicked, Danced, and sung through most of the night.

When he arrived at Wooden Doll's immaculate dwelling, he wasn't surprised to find her servant, a young woman called Newe, sitting outside the door. Of all the slaves Wooden Doll had taken in Trade for her services, she'd kept this one. A barbarian girl, Newe had been captured far up the River of the Northwest at the foot of the distant Shining Mountains.

"She busy," the girl said, not bothering to rise from the mat before Wooden Doll's closed door.

Of course she'd be busy. The Busk was the most sacred ceremony practiced in Cahokia. For four days prior to the cooking of the green corn and the relighting of the sacred fire, men and women segregated themselves, fasting and purging, spending hours in the sweat lodge, and abstaining from the simplest of pleasures. During those four days of ritual purification, the most heinous of taboos included so much as a covetous glance at someone of the opposite sex.

A line would have formed at Wooden Doll's door the moment the first ear of boiled corn was pulled from the Morning Star's pot.

Seven Skull Shield glanced in the direction of the slanting sun, obscured as it was by peak-roofed storage buildings.

"I'll wait."

He plunked himself down in the shade of Wooden Doll's ramada, his back to one of the support poles. Newe wasn't known for being chatty. Perhaps that was the reason she hadn't been Traded off with all the rest.

By the time Wooden Doll's door opened and a Pacaha Trader stepped out, the evening had turned to gloom.

Seven Skull Shield rose, dusted off his butt, and was told by the slave girl, "You wait," before she vanished into the house.

A moment later, Wooden Doll herself appeared, leaning against the door frame. She wore only a white fabric wrap that did little to hide her high breasts or narrow waist, and left her long legs exposed. "So, Skull, what brings you to my door this time?"

He gave her his best grin. She was beautiful, her long black hair hanging down below her shapely bottom. The wry smile on her soft lips sent a pang through his heart. He wanted to reach out and run the backs of his fingers along the line of her triangular jaw. Her knowing eyes locked with his.

"I could tell you it was a stolen cloak, but that would only be the excuse."

She gave him a weary smile. "Come on in."

Her house was neat as always, ample wood piled beside the door. A low fire burned in the central hearth, sufficient to fill the high roof with enough smoke to deter the mosquitoes while providing enough light to illuminate her possessions, all of which were remarkable and worth a small fortune. Her storage boxes were intricately carved and inlaid. Ceramic jars, vessels, and storage pots echoed the skilled hands of the finest potters in the known world. The floor mat—new and masterfully woven of cane slats—had been replaced during the Busk. In the rear, her bedding was plush and thick with bear and beaver hides, the blankets dyed with the brightest of colors.

Seven Skull Shield seated himself on the edge of her bed, trying not to think of the Pacaha Trader who'd just left. Trying harder not to think of his once-secure world—the one whose demise left him feeling looted.

Wooden Doll crouched by the fire. The wrap stretched to expose the rounded curves of her buttocks. She lifted a red-and-white Nodena bottle and poured two cups of mint tea before rising and walking over to hand him one.

With a sensual movement she flipped her hair back and seated herself next to him. He thought he could drown in her soft gaze.

"A Natchez chief was murdered."

"I've heard." Her voice might have been like a caress. "Heard your Keeper was hot in pursuit of the murderer."

"I've been talking to people." He sipped the tea. Sighed hard. "It's not the same. They think I'm different. Changed."

"Are you?"

"Pus and rot! I'm still me."

Her delicate laughter sent a shiver down his bones. "Skull, you're mixed up with the Four Winds Clan. After that business last spring? What do you expect people to think? You're one of the Keeper's spies."

"I am not." He rubbed his muscular arm and scowled.

"Then what are you?"

He took a deep breath. "She's . . ."

"Yes?"

"A friend."

Her laughter was deeper this time. "It is said the Keeper has no friends, only those she uses as tools and those destined to hang in the square."

He studied the cup he held. "So, they think I'm a tool?"

"That, or destined for an early and most disagreeable death. Most are betting on that last part. You're no longer one of them. They think you're nothing. A clanless fool. A clever thief that the Four Winds will discard as soon as his usefulness is at an end."

He set the cup on the floor and stood. "Then I'll be on my—"

"That's what they say," she corrected, patting the bed. "Here. Sit. Talk to me."

Grudgingly, he lowered himself to the soft bedding.

"Tell me, Skull, what's this really about?"

"What do you think of me?"

No guile lay behind her dark eyes as she said, "I think the Keeper is an incredibly clever and dangerous woman, and I think she sees through that clownish act you wear like an old basswood fiber shirt. You saved her life over in Evening Star Town, didn't you? You were the one who located the Tula, kept the city from war and chaos."

He shrugged uncomfortably.

"I know you, Skull. Better than anyone alive. From the top of your head to the bottom of your toes."

"Then, why do I feel so . . . ?" He shook his head, trying to find the words.

"Betrayed?" Seeing it hit home she nodded. "People are who they are. You must be who you cannot help but be. But for the moment let it go. Tell me about this Natchez and his mysterious cloak."

He gave her a fleeting smile. "Crazy Frog had himself

carried all the way to the Great Plaza to find me, warn me. Didn't know it was going to be the Natchez. But this morning? Lady Night Shadow Star knew. Then she showed up to see the body."

He paused, remembering the way she'd moved through the room.

"Ah, I know that look. Is she that enchanting? Forgive me, but you go sticking your rod into that one, I'm changing my bet on how soon you end up hanging from a square while Four Winds warriors burn your body into a cinder."

"Trust me, she's the kind to be enjoyed from a distance. As soon as you start to lose yourself in fantasy explorations of that body of hers, she fixes you with those crazy eyes, and your rod shrivels like a persimmon in the fall." He frowned, changing the subject. "Trouble is coming. The Natchez was just the beginning. I . . ."

"What?"

The words came unbidden from his mouth. "Pack everything you own. We can hire a canoe. Go somewhere far away. Maybe among the Caddo. Winters are warm there. We could live well for the rest of our lives, be exalted and honored people. We could—"

She was shaking her head, a wistful smile on her lips. "No, my old love. Once, maybe. If you'd been different. And I had been someone I'm not. But that day is long past. And, like I said, I know who you are. And who you will forever be."

"Who is that?"

"You said that trouble is coming. And if there's trouble, you're going to be right in the middle of it. Your greatest strength, and most dangerous failing, is that you can't turn down a challenge. A skunk can't rid itself of its stripe."

He tossed down the last of his tea and rose. "Then I'd better be about finding that Spirit-cursed cloak."

"It's dark out there."

"I'll find a place down by the—"

"Stay with me."

"I didn't bring Trade."

She rose and let the white fabric fall from her shoulders, the curves of her muscular body illuminated in the firelight. Her slender fingers untied the belt at his waist before she slipped his shirt over his head.

In her sensual way, she molded herself against him. Breasts soft against his chest, hips pressing into him, she wrapped her arms around his neck.

As his loins began to tingle she stared into his eyes and said, "We can pretend, Skull. Just for one night. We can imagine what it would have been like if we could have run away all those years ago."

Seventeen

Blue Heron might have been adrift in a dark sea. The sensation of floundering, of unseen currents reaching out for her, had every nerve in her body on edge. A lifetime of ferreting out plots, of intrigue and danger, filled her with the premonition that they were all teetering on heartbreak and disaster.

She studied the Natchez delegation standing under Five Fist's wary gaze. They packed the rear of the great palace, all but two of them gaping at the room's wealth and splendor.

The Morning Star's playing us. Playing me.

And that knowledge scared the spit out of her. She'd barely escaped with her life when Walking Smoke had come within a hair's breadth of murdering the Morning Star in his bed. Not only was the scar on her neck a constant reminder of the assassin's knife, but only Night Shadow Star's last-minute arrival and intervention with the Morning Star had kept Blue Heron from hanging in a square herself.

As if they held the key, she fixed on the two men who stood behind the four staff bearers. The young one, his hair in two coiled braids at either side of his head, wore the clothing of a Sun Born Natchez. The other, older, some-how familiar, wore odd clothing: a cylindrical-shaped red-feather headdress, and curious armbands. The breastplate on his deep chest was like nothing she'd ever seen. His face was oddly painted in a design that smacked of the exotic and foreign.

She fixed on his face. Something about him. His stance, the way he shot a curious glance her way, sent a familiar twinge through her. As if recognition lay just at the edge of memory.

The Morning Star appeared from his private quarters in the rear of the building. She and the rest dropped to the floor; her forehead pressed into the new matting.

She waited until the Morning Star had seated himself on the panther-hide-covered chair atop its dais before she lifted her head.

The Morning Star was resplendent, his copper headpiece gleaming in the light of the eternal fire. His face was painted white, the two black forked-eye designs in contrast. White shell ear ornaments in the shape of human heads covered his ears. Strings of beads hung at his neck, and a copper turkey-tailed mace lay in his hands atop the white apron that fell between his knees. Splays of eagle feathers were tied behind each shoulder.

He fixed the Natchez with his knowing dark eyes, a faint smile upon his lips. "I welcome you in peace and wisdom. Come forward and declare yourselves."

The oddly dressed Four Winds man said something in Natchez, and the entourage approached as if coached, stop-ping short of the fire.

Blue Heron got a good look at the man.

No! It can't be!

As priests brought forth black drink in polished whelk shell cups and the sacred pipe was ritually prepared, she stared in a mixture of rage and disbelief.

He's banished!

As if he could hear her thoughts, Horn Lance shot her a knowing gaze, a triumphant smile curling his lips. He understood that she had to remain mute for the moment, but that look he gave her? As if he *dared* her to shout out.

Through the long greeting ritual, she sat engulfed in a mixture of smoldering anger tempered by warmer memories of his smile, of how his naked body had felt as he timed his climax to her own. How it all had gone wrong as she tired of his caress and self-serving ambition. Interest in another had taken his place.

Blood and dung, I've made a wreck of my life.

The smoking, prayers, and ritual drinking of black drink finally came to an end, the Morning Star asking, "Who comes this day in peace?"

At a signal from Horn Lance, the Natchez noble stepped forward and introduced himself in a barbarically accented voice. "I am Swirling Cloud, direct descendant of the first Great Sun, of the Quigualtam, son of White Woman Sacred Oak, first brother to the Great Sun."

Blue Heron lost the rest. The White Woman was called High Pine. She'd had the recorders check after the Little Sun was murdered. And hadn't Nine Strikes been the first brother?

Picking up her thoughts, she listened as the Natchez added, "We come with the news of great misfortune and great joy. Power has called my aunt, the White Woman you once knew, to the blessings of the afterlife. At the same time it also took our Great Sun. Sacred Oak has taken the name of White Woman for as long as her service shall please the Sun from whom we are descended."

Ah, so there's been a change of leadership! And a new Great Sun has been named?

Suddenly it all made sense. Of course Nine Strikes had to die. According to the rules of Natchez succession, he'd have been the new Great Sun. She thinned her eyes as the Natchez messengers continued.

"The joyous news we bear is that a mighty lord is on his way to Cahokia." The Natchez smiled as he spread his arms. "I have been given the glorious mission to announce his coming to the Morning Star and all of Cahokia."

"Who is this great lord?" the Morning Star asked, the words coming as if rote from his mouth.

"His name is Thirteen Sacred Jaguar, son of the *yitah* Four Fire Shield, one of the *multepal*, the ruling brothers of the mighty empire of Chichen Itza. Word has traveled, Great Lord, of your resurrection in the body of a man. At the order of the sacred *multepal*, the lord Thirteen Sacred Jaguar has been sent to offer his congratulations and see for himself the miracle of your return that he might report the glorious news to the *multepal*.

"In advance of his arrival, we are sent, bearing the gifts of Thirteen Sacred Jaguar and the White Woman as tokens that you might receive him with the honor and respect due his lordship."

A stunned silence filled the room.

Stories had drifted up the river for years. Remarkable yarns about great cities of stone, of terrible gods, bloody human sacrifices, and remarkable lords. Even the occasional rare Trader who claimed to have Traded with seaworthy canoes manned by Yucatec, vassal people of the Itza, had passed through Cahokia.

But they'd been stories. The wild and impossible things told about distant frontiers.

Now one was coming here?

"It is true, Great Lord." Horn Lance stepped up beside the Natchez, his deep tenor a relief after the Natchez accent. "I am Horn Lance, of the Horned Serpent House of the Four Winds Clan, cousin to High Chief Green Chunkey." He smiled faintly, stealing a glance Blue Heron's way. "After a misunderstanding, I have traveled far and wide. Hearing the rumors about the great Itza, I ventured south to see if such wild tales could be true."

He gestured in humility. "The fantastic stories told of the Itza? The Yucatec? Or the Toltec in their capital of Tula? Upon my blood and breath, upon the honor of my ancestors, they are true." He paused. "And of greater magnificence than the yarns passed from lip to lip can ever suggest."

Whispers of disbelief passed among the onlookers. Blue Heron smiled in vindication. Horn Lance's wild assertions were going to destroy him again.

The Morning Star's eyes had a pensive look, and Blue Heron just knew he was about to break out in laughter. With grim satisfaction, she wondered if Horn Lance's body would be hanging in a square by sundown.

The Morning Star shocked her when he said, "We are delighted to await Thirteen Sacred Jaguar's arrival, and do so with joy and anticipation. We thank the White Woman and Great Sun for their role in facilitating the Itza lord's arrival here. Your gifts are received with appreciation and gratitude and in the spirit with which they are offered."

Horn Lance glanced again at Blue Heron. "With the Morning Star's kind pardon during the recent Busk, my exile is ended. Upon my happy return to my clan, city, and great lord, I am honored to be of service."

He's pardoned? Her belly tightened. *So that's who the Morning Star meant.*

She stilled the first tendrils of outrage. Rot it all, Horn Lance had been too ambitious for his own good years ago. What made the Morning Star think he'd be any less of a disruption now? And with a suddenly not-so-mythical Itza lord in tow?

She cast a glance at Wind. From her sister's expression, similar thoughts lay behind her worried eyes.

If even half the stories told about the Itza and their cities of stone were true, what kind of chaos was this going let loose among the rival Four Winds Houses? A Powerful foreign lord? His presence could be like a smoldering ember tossed into tall dry grass.

The Itza, he's only one man, she reminded herself.

Horned Lance was watching her through narrowed eyes, that familiar triumphant smile of his barely hidden. In that instant she saw the bottled hatred, nursed and grown more Powerful through the years. She could only imagine what he had planned for her . . . and Horned Lance had always enjoyed his revenge.

The man she'd once known would bring Cahokia down in ruins for the chance to pay her back.

"We shall await the arrival of the Itza lord with anticipation, and thank you and the White Woman for apprising us of his proximity. We must unfortunately inform you of a tragedy," the Morning Star replied. "At the conclusion of the Busk, your representative here, known as the Little Sun, was murdered in order to obtain a cloak once worn upon my own shoulders. As a consequence, we have employed every means at our disposal to apprehend the perpetrator of this vile deed."

Blue Heron fixed her gaze on the Natchez, seeing consternation among the warriors. The supposedly new Little Sun, the one called Swirling Cloud, seemed to tense, his jaws tightening in outrage.

Swirling Cloud extended his hands. "I am charged with informing the Little Sun of our . . . let us call it, change in circumstances among the Quigualtam. This news, however, may have the most severe consequences." He seemed to search for words. "Great Lord, among our people, the violent death of one of the Sun Born . . . It *must* be rectified! To do otherwise might irreparably impact our relations with Cahokia."

The Morning Star's mouth quivered. Blue Heron couldn't tell if it was in anger, or amusement, but when he spoke the words were measured. "A great deal hangs in the balance,

Little Sun. I, too, take this as a personal affront. But even as we speak, Clan Keeper Blue Heron has agents running down the miscreant."

His voice hardened. "Within the next couple of days I expect her to deliver the murderer to justice."

He fixed her with a cold smile, no give in his eyes.

Eighteen

Outside Night Shadow Star's palace, Fire Cat practiced with his war club. Dressed in full armor, shield on his left arm, he leaped forward, using momentum to swing the club in a deadly arc. Skipping to one side, he dropped to a defensive crouch, shield up to block an imaginary blow.

His muscles ached, but he launched himself out of the crouch with a reminder that in battle no one stopped to rest. Gasping for breath, he continued his drills, forcing himself to the edge of endurance.

As the sun had set, he'd watched a procession of Earth Clan chiefs as they climbed the high steps to the Morning Star's palace. Across the smoky night, he could hear drumming and flute music mingled with the sounds of laughter.

Which spurred him to continue until his legs trembled under him and he staggered. Despite the cool evening, sweat beaded and ran down his body.

Finally exhausted, he pulled the leather helmet from his head, having slain a thousand imaginary Four Winds Clan warriors. He could almost feel the smiles of his ancestors.

Head back, eyes on the cloud-puffed sky, he slowly ambled toward the veranda and stepped inside.

Night Shadow Star's palace was lit by a low fire, its smoke

pooling under the high roof to deter mosquitoes. Inside the door, he shucked off his armor and laid the club and shield to one side by the wall bench.

In the rear corner, Green Stick and Clay String tossed a cup full of gaming pieces onto a cloth, counting up points. Winter Leaf sat to their right, pushing a bone awl through fabric as she fastened freshwater pearls to one of Night Shadow Star's skirts.

Fire Cat found one of the water bottles and stepped outside to sluice the sweat from his body. Relishing the cold water, he poured it over his hot skin.

Reentering, he took stock. Firewood was piled neatly on the other side of the door, the cooking pots cleaned from the night meal. Bedding lay folded and ready, everything in order. A far cry from the day he'd finally taken control of the household. The place had been a shambles, Night Shadow Star having sent herself on a soul journey to the Underworld.

To his relief, since then she'd refrained from rubbing datura paste onto her temples and attempting a repeat of such dangerous Spiritual excursions. She'd barely survived the last one.

"Did you slay them all?" Clay String asked, looking up from the game.

"All but the ones who turned and ran." Fire Cat stripped off his wet breechcloth and pulled a hemp-fiber hunting shirt from the box beneath his bed. He and Night Shadow Star's household servants had come to a sort of understanding, though it remained tenuous at best.

"How's she doing?" He gestured to Night Shadow Star's door.

"I think she's asleep." Winter Leaf looked up from her sewing, her voice dropping. "You saw the way she looked at supper?"

He nodded. Night Shadow Star had been preoccupied, worried. It had taken all of his wiles to get her eat. When she had, it had been in silence, her eyes vacant, the muscles bunching under her smooth cheeks as she chewed.

"Trouble's coming," Clay String said. "Piasa's told her something." He glanced at Fire Cat as if in hopes that he knew.

"She didn't tell me." He walked over, staring down at the gaming pieces. Each was a polished flat of bone, hash marks cut into either side to denote value. "Who's winning?"

Green Stick indicated Clay String. "If we were playing for stakes he'd own everything I possess down to the clothes I'm wearing."

Taking the moment, Fire Cat seated himself on the bench to watch as Clay String dropped the gaming pieces into a cup, shook them, and cast.

"Fifteen. I win again."

Fire Cat eased a knee up. "Was she ever happy?"

Clay String paused, glanced uncertainly at Night Shadow Star's door, and in a low voice said, "After the last resurrection of the Morning Star. When she married her husband"—he wouldn't say a dead man's name—"the living god had this palace built for her. What was it? Two years before you . . . um, he was killed up north. They were young and very much in love. Some said too much so for a political marriage. No one who knew her before her first woman's moon would have believed it, but after she married, she changed. Became responsible in the ways a lady should. She was taking her place in the Council House. People expected she'd become the next matron when Wind either passed on or took the Great Sky's mace. She'd just turned eighteen when the news came of the disaster up north."

He avoided Fire Cat's eyes. "It was like part of her died with him. She just . . . well, changed. Like all the life had run out of her souls."

"That's when she started hearing things, seeing things that weren't there." Winter Leaf shooed a pesky fly. "For days she'd be excited, almost frantic—do this, do that—

and she'd rarely sleep. Then for a moon following, it was like deflating a fish bladder. She'd barely have energy enough to get out of bed. Everything was black and depressing. We never knew what to expect. And Matron Wind and the *tonka'tzi*, they were half frantic."

"She started using the datura," Green Stick added. "Rides-the-Lighting gave it to her. For at least a little while it seemed to help. And then, just before your arrival, she threw us out. Told us that no one was to enter, and she retreated to that altar she'd built back there. That's where the Keeper found her, her souls lost in the Underworld." She shrugged. "You know the rest."

"Was she always drawn to the Underworld Powers?"

Clay String looked appalled. "On my ancestors, no! She's Four Winds Clan! Her brother's body is the home of the incarnated god. No, this started after her husband's death, when she decided she was going to send her souls to the Underworld to find his afterlife soul."

Which, of course, was where she would have expected to find it. Fire Cat had ordered Makes Three's body chopped up and tossed into the Father Water outside Red Wing Town as a gift to Piasa and an insult to Cahokia.

He grunted at the bitter irony. Not only had he ended up serving her and those selfsame Powers, but after the sacking of Red Wing Town, his own relatives had been dismembered and tossed into the river by War Chief Spotted Wrist.

"You've been good for her," Winter Leaf said softly. "You know that, don't you?"

"Power, for its own twisted reasons, has thrown us together for the time being. The only thing keeping me here is my oath. And I wouldn't have given that had I known who I was talking to that night." He gestured toward her door. "As for her? If Piasa would let her, she'd like nothing better than to hang me back in a square and repay me for every minute she's suffered."

And with that, he rose, angered at the hollow sensation in his gut. Of course she'd torture him to death. Only by the barest act of will had she once stopped herself from driving a blade into his heart.

"We're both prisoners," he muttered as he walked to his bed beside her door and crawled under the covers.

He'd barely closed his eyes when memories swam up from the depths of his souls. Rain pounded on his back and head, stippling the lead-gray surface of the Father Water as lightning cracked and banged around him. His fingers were entwined in Night Shadow Star's wet hair as he hauled her naked body from the river. His heart began to pound as he laid her in the canoe. Straddling her, he stared at her slack face, the eyes slitted and vacant, her lips parted. The long swirl of her hair shifted with the water sloshing in the canoe bottom.

How cold she'd been as he laid his trembling hands on her chest and pushed down. Water had burbled from her mouth. Again and again, in rising desperation, he kept pushing.

And then, as panic filled him, he was leaning over her, pressing his mouth against her slack lips. Breath by breath, he exhaled his life and souls into her, willing her to take a part of him and live.

And she'd taken a breath, coughed, and breathed again.

Delirious with relief, he'd thrown himself onto her, seeking to share his warmth as they drifted aimlessly with the current.

She was looking up now, her marvelous dark eyes drinking his life soul. Her supple arms rose, wrapping around him and pulling him down onto her soft body. Her breasts pressed into his chest, her legs twining themselves around his waist . . .

He jerked awake, intimately aware of his erection.

What possessed him? It hadn't ended that way. When she'd recovered enough to sit up and hug herself into a shivering ball, he'd paddled to shore. Led her to a farmstead where he'd ordered the dirt farmers out of their house and thrown all of their wood onto the fire.

He'd bundled her in blankets, raided their store of corn-meal, and fed her a hot soup.

"Blood and fire," he muttered as he waited for his erection to fade. "What's wrong with me?"

He heard a soft mewing, the sort of sound a newborn puppy made when deprived of its mother.

Rising, he stepped to her door hanging, parting it to peer into her dim quarters. She lay on her bed, the dark wealth of her hair atop one arm.

"Please, don't make me do this," she whimpered through sleep slurred speech. "Not . . . to him . . ."

His heart like a cold rock in his chest, Fire Cat pinched his eyes shut. Refusing to meet the servants' eyes where they sat in their corner, he flopped back on his bed and clamped a forearm over his ear in the futile search for silence.

Sometime in the night he came awake again. Night Shadow Star's dream pleadings were just loud enough to mingle with the continuing celebration atop the Morning Star's mound. And both were like torture.

Nineteen

Blue Heron circled the outside of the crowd that had gathered around the great fire in the Morning Star's courtyard. Firelight illuminated the towering World Tree pole with its lightning-scarred reliefs depicting the Morning Star's exploits in the Beginning Times. It cast people's shadows on the clay-coated palisade walls.

She carried on desultory conversations with Kills Four, chief of the Snapping Turtle Clan, and joked amiably with the Bear Clan chief, Eight Scars. The Earth Moiety chiefs treated her, as always, with reserved respect. She may have known them for most of their lives—even been married to some for a while—but their relationship remained a wary thing. Over the years she'd exiled too many of their relatives to the colonies.

To her surprise she caught sight of the dwarf, and walked up behind him. "How'd you get in here?"

Flat Stone Pipe turned, grinning up at her. "I don't take up much room, Keeper." He waved a small hand with its stubby fingers. "A live Itza? Who would have thought? My matron will want a full report."

"But how did you get in?"

He pointed. "Our new high chief, Burned Bone. I just happened to be in this part of the city when news came."

She glanced at Matron Columella's youngest brother. The young man had been recalled from a Trading expedition to fill the high chief's position at Evening Star House.

"How's he doing?"

"I think he'll do, Keeper."

"Give your matron my regards."

"Of course. If there's anything you need, please don't hesitate to ask." He bowed his head, touching his forehead respectfully.

She kept throwing glances at the knot around Horn Lance and his Natchez companion where they stood before the entrance to the Morning Star's palace. Everyone wanted to hear about the Itza lord. Yes, the Itza were really a people, and yes, one was coming here to see Cahokia for himself. The excitement was palpable.

For her part, Blue Heron had always assumed both the Maya and Toltec existed. That many stories didn't just pop out of thin air. But the stunning reality that she was about to lay eyes on a living Itza was unsettling enough. That he was coming through the machinations of an ex-husband? A man whose honor and reputation she'd destroyed, and she'd had banished? That cast the entire affair into a darker and more sinister light.

The Horn Lance she remembered—with greater clarity after an evening of avoiding him—had been a man with clever ambitions.

Which husband had she just divorced back then? Red Mask? No, that had been a couple of years earlier. And how many had come and gone between Red Mask and Horn Lance? Did it even matter anymore? She'd been young, hot-blooded, and always ready for a man to slip his shaft into her seemingly insatiable sheath.

Lost in her thoughts, hands behind her back, she paced the beaten grass.

"What? No greeting and hug?" the subject of her concerns asked as he appeared beside her.

She glanced at him, heart leaping. "You shouldn't sneak up on a person like that."

"Or you shouldn't lock yourself in your head so deeply a man can just walk right up to you."

"So, he pardoned you? It's been what, almost twenty years?"

"And how Cahokia has changed in the meantime. A new, young Morning Star, and so much new construction! When I left the Great Plaza was still being leveled, filled, and graded. Today I find a grand plaza, huge new mounds and palaces, and people. People everywhere. And from all over." He smiled condescendingly. "Maybe I had to come back. Just to see if the wild stories were true."

"Cahokia has become the grandest city in the world."

"Hardly," he snorted. "Compared to the places I've seen, I find rude wooden buildings on piles of dirt. But it's not worth discussing. You'd never believe the Itza, Putun, or Yucatec cities. The marvels they've constructed, and have been constructing, while our ancestors were living in huts."

To change the subject, he said, "So, you've become Clan Keeper now? One of the most important women in Cahokia. I always thought you'd end up as matron."

She gave him a slitted glare, seething at the condescension in his tone. "Was that why you sought me out way back then? Sniffing an opportunity, a tool to elevate yourself?"

Horn Lance had appeared ready, willing, and eager. He had been a good match, coming as he did from Horned Serpent House, and of impeccable Four Winds lineage, but separated far enough to avoid even the hint of incest.

"You had your enchantments." He cocked his head, tilting the curious headdress.

Not only had he been charming, but he'd made a study of

the female body and used that knowledge with remarkable skill the first night she had dragged him into her bed. The experience had been so exhilarating she hadn't turned loose of him until past high sun the next day.

"And you, it turned out, had your faults," she shot back. "We had only a moon or so of wedded bliss before I began to notice you were using your newfound preeminence for your own gain."

He had started asking her for favors, particularly those that would advance his personal prospects and those of Horned Serpent House.

His mouth thinned, eyes hardening. "Let's say you were in my position—a mere cousin with no chance for a chieftainship. Ambitious and crafty as you are, would you have been any different?"

"I was." She gestured toward the city. "Look around you. See what we've built. After generations of squabbling feuds, after the mayhem of Tharon and Petaga's civil wars, we've had decades of peace. And you know why? It's because we've constantly weeded ourselves of troublemakers. People like you who would have brought the whole thing tumbling down into chaos for their own aggrandizement."

He pursed his lips, fists knotting. "And what has that made you, Keeper? A worn-out old hag with an exalted position and a scattering of husbands left behind like beads from a broken string. Oh, I watched you just now. Joking and laughing with the Earth Clan chiefs and matrons? They put on a good show, don't they? But you can see it in their eyes. They treat you like a water moccasin, a Powerful and deadly creature they must appease, but forever fear lest you strike out."

He paused. "So, tell me, do you have any real friends? Anyone you can truly share yourself with? Or are you just a bitter old woman whose sole purpose is to ferret out plots?"

At his words, her heart skipped, a chill in her gut. Could she call anyone a friend? Her sister, perhaps. But even then they never talked of the commonplace, only the matters of state.

Smooth Pebble? Definitely not a confidant of the soul.

"Ah," he said, watching his words hit home. "I see."

"What of you, banished man? What great success have you made of your life? Come crawling home, dressed in fancy feathers, wearing an exotic breastplate. I assume you bought your pardon from the Morning Star, but you're still wheedling your way into the presence of authority, still longing to be more than you are."

He tapped the butterfly-shaped breastplate with a thumb. "This is the insignia of a warrior, presented to me by the *Kukulkan*. He's a sort of priest and holy advisor to the Brotherhood Council. And while it may not mean anything to you, I have advised the sacred Brothers of the *multepal*. I have stood on the heights of ancient Tikal, walked the elevated stone causeways they call *sacbe*, followed in the steps of great lords the likes of which you cannot imagine."

"And I serve a living miracle, the reincarnated Morning Star," she replied.

"Is that what he is?"

"Meaning?"

Horn Lance bit off a knowing smile. "You cannot understand."

"Try me."

"Perhaps some other time. After Thirteen Sacred Jaguar arrives." He paused. "You do know what a jaguar is, don't you?"

"A big spotted cat. Like a cougar. They kill them occasionally in the south. My grandfather had a hide."

"A cat," he agreed. "And so much more."

"Whatever you're up to, I will stop you."

"I expect nothing less. But then, given your charge to find the Little Sun's murderer, it seems to me that you have enough to occupy yourself. Or are you immune from the wrath of your living god?"

Immune? She'd barely escaped the square as it was.

As if reading her thoughts, Horn Lance added, "Perhaps your position is more tenuous than you think. Don't make a single mistake, Heron, because I'll be waiting to give you that last shove that pushes you over the edge."

Twenty

Seven Skull Shield climbed the wooden steps to the Keeper's palace. A weariness weighted his legs, his heart like a rotten log in his chest. Normally, he'd have noticed everything, always searching for an opportunity to take advantage of one of the inattentive persons thronging the Avenue of the Sun. Today, as if in a daze, he could barely remember the trip. Only some comments about a lot of dead Natchez and an Itza, whatever that was.

As if he walked beneath a cloud, his thoughts centered on Wooden Doll, and the feel of her body against his. How she'd looked into his eyes. Of the ways that things might have been different if he'd known what he was losing all those years ago.

I'm alone.

The thought stunned and wounded him.

His touch of the forehead might have been mocking as he passed the eagle guardian posts on either side of the Keeper's walk.

A collection of people waited on the Keeper's veranda, most of them spies come to report on the doings among the other Four Winds Houses, or the Earth Clans under their thumbs.

Unfazed, he passed through them and stepped into the Keeper's palace. Uncharacteristically, he didn't cast a single covetous glance at the fine fabrics, the perfectly rendered sculptures, or the embossed copper plates that lined the walls.

Smooth Pebble stood by the fire, giving instructions to Notched Cane. The berdache glanced up, a sudden hope in her eyes. Hurrying forward, she asked, "Any news on the cloak?"

"Nothing."

Smooth Pebble's expression fell.

He asked, "Where's the Keeper?"

"Out back. But you'll have to wait your—"

He grabbed a loaf of bread and a bottle of water from the platter by the fire, turned, and started for the door.

"She demanded to be left alone," Smooth Pebble insisted as she hurried after him.

"It's not an 'alone' day," he returned over his shoulder as he stepped out into the sunshine. Odd, he'd thought it a cloudy day on his walk back.

Heedless, he forced his way through the press on the veranda and followed the mound top around the south side of the Keeper's palace. He had some vague awareness that the palace walls had recently been replastered.

He found her sitting on the southwest corner, her back to the wall, feet propped, a bowl of embers beside her as she puffed on her old stone pipe. Her gaze was fixed on the crowded Avenue of the Sun where it ran off to the west on the other side of the Four Winds Plaza.

Without looking up, she growled, "I said I wanted to be left alone."

He passed in front of her and lowered himself to prop his back against the wall beside her.

She shot him an evil glance. "Is your hearing as bad as your manners? You rotted well better have that cloak, and better yet, the two-footed bit of dirt that killed the Natchez."

He ripped a piece from the bread and stuffed it into his mouth, giving it a couple of chews before he washed it down with water from the burnished brownware bottle. "No one has seen so much as a feather off that accursed cloak."

"Then why are you here?"

"Because I've got nowhere else to go." The words surprised him.

She took a pull on her pipe. "That's the last thing I needed to hear, thief."

"That makes two of us."

Her chuckle was devoid of humor. "I thought there was always a young wife waiting to give you a place. And what about all of your thieving friends?"

He ripped off another piece of goosefoot bread. "Suddenly, they prefer to keep their distance. Seems I'm too close to the hated Four Winds Clan."

She grunted, her eyes on the flow of goods and people on the Avenue across the way. "Doesn't matter. The cloak's not going to show up among your conniving comrades."

"It's not?" He gazed out to the west, past the temples and society houses, beyond the observatory, to where a smoky haze obscured the distant Marsh Elder Lake and the stippled pattern of buildings along the Avenue of the Sun.

"That Natchez delegation you warned me about yesterday? Seems they had a spate of mysterious deaths down south among the Quigualtam chiefs. There's a new Great Sun and White Woman. Nine Strikes would have taken his brother's place as the Great Sun. No one seems to find it odd that the Natchez arrived here, having *already* replaced him with someone from a different lineage."

"Convenient." He munched the bread thoughtfully.

"More than that." She knocked the dottle from her pipe before repacking it with tobacco. "Your Natchez delegation is outraged. Seeking every advantage it gives them. And better yet, they came to announce that an Itza lord is coming to Cahokia."

"What's an Itza lord?"

She threw him an irritated look. "They're a very Powerful and distant people who live across the gulf. If you believe the stories, their Chichen Itza is bigger and grander than Cahokia."

"Then why have I never heard of them?"

"Maybe it's a bigger world than you thought, thief." She used two sticks to pick up an ember and light her pipe. "So the Morning Star orders me to find the murderer—and to do it pus-licking quick. In case you haven't noticed, the Morning Star likes his orders to be carried out. If they are not, there are consequences. And who knows what the arrival of this Itza really means, or what its implications are? I'm in the middle of a deep game. Morning Star and Sky World Power are playing for goals I don't understand. And then there's Night Shadow Star and Piasa. Each with an agenda."

She paused. "Maybe the sacrifice of an aging Keeper is an acceptable loss compared to what might be gained."

"I see."

"And worst of all? Horn Lance is right at the bottom of it, working behind the scenes like a clever fox."

"Who's Horn Lance?"

"An old husband I had banished for skullduggery once upon a time. Piasa alone knows what he gifted to the Morning Star to be pardoned during the Busk."

Seven Skull Shield washed down the last of his bread as Blue Heron puffed on her pipe. He said, "Sounds like this Horn Lance pushed a stinging thorn under your skin."

"Accused me of being a dried-up old hag without friends. I've got friends. People who don't care that I'm the Keeper."

He smiled at the way she said it, as if convincing herself. "I thought I did, too. According to them, I'm nothing more than your tool. Headed for a square before the next full moon. You'd think I was sick with foaming mouth disease the way they couldn't wait to get away from me. Men whose lives I've saved. Even Black Swallow."

"I did have his fingers broken for taking those stolen statues." Her expression turned bitter. "Maybe I am too dangerous for people to be around. In that case, you'd better run, thief."

"Hand me your pipe, and I'll consider it."

"You know how I feel about my pipe. Just because I did it once doesn't mean . . . Oh, pus and rot!"

He took the pipe she offered and pulled on the sweet tobacco. Being Keeper had its advantages. She got the best of everything, not the rude mixture Traded at the canoe landing.

He exhaled with contentment as the Power of Sister Tobacco eased his tension. "I heard something about a bunch of dead Natchez."

She grunted, taking her pipe back. "I did some asking around. Seems it's an honor to go to the afterlife and serve the Little Sun. One of them strangled the others, and then hung himself. On top of everything else, Rides-the-Lightning and his priests are up to their chins in dead Natchez. He's trying to prepare the bodies according to Natchez ritual so that we 'don't give offense.'"

"It's the talk of the city," he agreed. "Do you think that's what the Little Sun's murderer was counting on? That in addition to the murder, a mass suicide would create a sensation? Distract us even more?"

"Could be. Their lord is suddenly dead. They're alone in a foreign city surrounded by strangers. It's their custom to die with their lord. What else would they be expected to do? By Piasa's swinging balls, that's brilliant."

She turned, meeting Seven Skull Shield's eyes with desperation. "So far, they've boxed us in at every turn. If I don't figure a way out of this . . ." She smiled wearily. "Well, I make you this promise, thief: If there's any way, I'll give you enough warning so you can get away. I don't want you dying in a square beside me."

"That bad, huh?" So, he did have at least one friend in the world. Who would have thought it would be the Keeper?

"Worse," she muttered.

Twenty-one

A series of runners had apprised Horn Lance of Thirteen Sacred Jaguar's progress as the flotilla of five canoes approached. Now he waited at the canoe landing, aware of the curiosity the entourage he'd assembled was drawing.

The moment had finally come. He watched in appreciation as Thirteen Sacred Jaguar's lead canoe angled in toward shore, paddles dipping in unison. The Natchez warriors kept the growing crowd from swarming the beach.

Everything had been perfectly orchestrated. Horn Lance had seen to it. Porters had been hired, along with a magnificent litter. Gifts of food and drink were prepared. He'd hired local men to carry the inlaid boxes of gifts and the Itza lord's personal possessions. Musicians waited with drums and flutes. His Natchez warriors were dressed in full regalia and stood in formation to escort the procession.

Even the weather seemed to cooperate, a morning rain having cooled the air before departing to the east.

Thirteen Sacred Jaguar's standard bearer, Burning Ant, stood in the bow, the lord's *kukul* standard elevated on its pole. Carved in the form of a feathered snake and painted in bright yellow, black, blue, and green, the standard pulsed with *ch'ulel*: the living Spirit of the War Serpent,

Waxaklahun Kan. More than Thirteen Sacred Jaguar's most prized possession, the *kukul* contained the war god's presence in this world. The jadeite eyes seemed to burn with a fire of their own. The *kukul* had carried the Itza lord this far, and in the end, its Power would grant him Cahokia.

Seated behind the standard bearer, Thirteen Sacred Jaguar looked regal.

True to form, the Itza had donned his finest raiment, an *ahau nak,* or lord's mask, encased his head. The opulent headdress was intricately carved, painted in bright green, yellow, red, and black; an iridescent green plume of splendid quetzal tail feathers rose from the top and fell to the rear. Giant ear spools covered his ears. A gleaming green quetzal-and-parrot-feather cloak draped down from his shoulders. The kilt he wore had been woven into a masterful checked design from dyed threads. Each crossing of the pattern sported a drilled obsidian disk. In his hand Thirteen Sacred Jaguar held a magnificent fan of splayed scarlet macaw feathers.

Behind him sat his four warriors—all that remained of the party of forty that had left Chichen Itza so long ago on the quest for Cahokia. They, too, wore feathers, armor, and paint, their hard eyes bright with excitement.

After Thirteen Sacred Jaguar's canoe speared the sand, the standard bearer leaped to the bank, the *kukul* raised high. A new Power had come to Cahokia. Horn Lance swallowed hard, awed and humbled. Waxaklahun Kan stared out at Cahokia with glittering jade eyes.

He could feel the god's Power. From this moment forward, nothing would ever be the same. He would talk of this day for the rest of his life, and his souls would be honored in the afterlife.

Two of the Natchez paddlers stepped out, prostrating themselves in the shallow water so that the Itza lord might disembark onto their backs and walk ashore without wetting his feet.

Horn Lance advanced, then dropped to one knee, head bowed as he called, "*Ahau Oxlajun Chul B'alam, Cahokia cham aj payal!*" Then he translated for the crowd: "Lord Thirteen Sacred Jaguar, Cahokia receives he who leads!"

As he rose, the musicians started to play, and the Natchez warriors rhythmically banged war clubs on their wooden shields. The Itza warriors were grinning at each other as they retrieved their *yaotlatquitl,* or war equipment, including their shields, atlatls, and the long, bark-sheathed *macuahuitl* swords. With eager eyes and rapacious smiles they trooped ashore.

As Horn Lance had expected, the crowd cheered.

"How has it gone, *Ch'ak Payal*?" Thirteen Sacred Jaguar asked, taking in the crowd. He kept his head carefully erect. The mask and headdress might have been stunning, but it severely restricted the wearer's movements.

"All according to plan, Lord. The city is buzzing about your arrival. Our potential enemies are distracted."

"*This* is mighty Cahokia?" He was looking around in dismay.

"River Mounds City, Lord. Cahokia's main port. We have a distance yet to go before we reach the city center. If you will seat yourself, we'll be on our way." Horn Lance indicated the litter; the porters knelt in the sand beside it, their heads bowed.

Burning Ant took his place in front and raised the *kukul*. Thirteen Sacred Jaguar seated himself regally in the litter, and at a gesture from Horn Lance, the porters lifted him high.

Another shout broke from the crowd. Many, as Horn Lance had predicted, were dancing in step, clapping their hands to the music and the hollow clacking of the warriors' shields.

Even as they started, the Natchez paddlers were hauling the craft onto shore and shouting orders as the bearers began shouldering boxes, bags, and bedding to follow in line.

The musicians fell in behind, their music adding to the

majesty of the proceedings as the entourage wound through the narrow tracks between buildings.

"Do these people not have architects?" Thirteen Sacred Jaguar queried incredulously. "A *sacbe,* built of proper stone and elevated above the muck, will be one of my first orders of business."

"Cahokians do have elevated causeways. Their versions of the *sacbe* are made of earth. The Avenue of the Moon south of the Great Plaza is one such, and many run through marshy areas." Horn Lance then added, "The task before us, I fear, will be daunting. These people will need to be taught how to quarry and square stone for the construction. Among so many other things."

"Then we shall be worthy of the challenge the Lords of Sky and Earth have given us."

"As you order, Lord."

In fits and starts the warriors beat their way through the confusion of densely packed buildings and out onto the thoroughfare. "This, Lord, is called the Avenue of the Sun. It is the main road leading through Cahokia from the east to the west."

"Another *sacbe* to be built. This wouldn't pass for a farmer's trail. Though it is an improvement compared to those wretched Natchez."

"You will find many disappointments, Lord." Horn Lance smiled as he added, "And, of course, incredible opportunities for one as bold as you."

"I have always cherished the historic Yucatec lords and envied their divine authority. The *multepal* council has its advantages, but being on my own, I shall found my dynasty and rule as an *ahau*. From what you have told me, the Cahokians are used to having a supreme lord to rule them. Have you found a suitable woman for me? One the people and nobles will accept?"

"I have, Lord. And, to your honor, she is young, beautiful, and revered by the Cahokians."

"I trust her family will be amenable."

"You can buy her for what would pass as a trifle in Chichen Itza. She is the false god's sister and antagonistic toward him. He's of the Sky World; she's aligned with what you would know as Xibalba, the Lower World. I've told you of the similarities in their corrupt myths. Her Spirit Creature is called Piasa here, analogous to jaguar, lord of Xibalba."

"And her name?"

"Night Shadow Star, Lord."

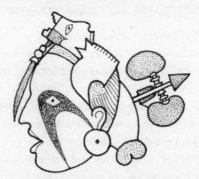

Twenty-two

Night Shadow Star's preparations had taken longer than usual. She'd tried on several of her finer garments, finally settling on a midnight-black skirt that clung to her hips and accented her athletic legs toned by stickball. In the end she chose a lightweight black fabric cloak adorned with jagged white lightning bolts. Copper, pearl, and shell necklaces hung to the tops of her breasts. Polished copper pins secured her hair in the bun she had wound tightly atop her head.

On the way out the door she added a final accoutrement that brought a smile to Fire Cat's lips: She picked up a slender-handled war club fitted with a copper ax head just above a vicious copper spike.

She'd ordered Fire Cat to wear his usual armor, to sling his bow and quiver over his shoulder, and take his best war club.

"Going as the dark Spirit of death?" he asked after they touched their foreheads in respect to the guardian posts and trotted down her stairs. Green Stick and a small squad of Panther Clan warriors waited.

The warriors cleared the way, calling, "Make way for Lady Night Shadow Star!"

The crowd was thicker than normal where it lined the Avenue of the Sun in preparation for the arrival of the Itza. It seemed odd to see the thoroughfare kept clear of its usual traffic.

"Death?" Something stirred in the dark depths of her eyes. "There are many kinds of death, Red Wing. I fear we may rue this day for many years to come."

At the foot of the great mound's stairway, she paused. "Whatever happens, do not act unless I order you. You can do that, can't you?"

"That's my vow."

She arched a narrow eyebrow, a curiously warm smile on her lips. "Your honor is exactly what worries me."

He didn't have time to question her further as she started up, taking the steps two at a time, as if driven by some internal conflict.

At the Council Terrace Gate, *Tonka'tzi* Wind waited along with a collection of Earth Clan chiefs and matrons.

"A war club, Niece?" *Tonka'tzi* Wind scowled at her weapon.

"On this day symbols are important, Aunt."

Wind's eyes narrowed at Night Shadow Star's black dress—the color of death and the Underworld—but she said nothing more.

Fire Cat took his place at Night Shadow Star's back, aware of the effect his armed appearance had on the Earth Clan chiefs.

"Look, here he comes," the Panther Clan chief, Kills Four, said, pointing.

Fire Cat turned his eyes to the west, looking out beyond the observatory's circle of upright posts. After the morning storm, the air was unusually clear, allowing the eye to follow the concentration of buildings and mounds clear to the jog where the Avenue of the Sun bent southwest at Black Tail's tomb. He could even make out the tiny skyline of Evening Star Town on the Father Water's western bluff a half day's travel to the west. No stranger to Cahokia's immensity, the sight still awed him.

The Itza's approach reminded him of a snake: the Itza on his litter at the head, the body that of the crowd as they followed in procession down the avenue.

He's just one man, he reminded himself.

But so was the pretend Morning Star, and look at the incredible transformation he'd inspired. Before his supposed resurrection, what was now Cahokia had been a series of scattered, warring towns.

While the others chatted in excited anticipation, Fire Cat could sense Night Shadow Star's growing apprehension. In the time since he'd bound himself to her, he'd learned to read her subtle signals: the tensing of her back and set of her shoulders, the slight pinching of the eyes.

Today he knew that Piasa's Spirit was whispering in her ear, as it always did after she'd had a tortured night's sleep.

His thoughts turned to that day when he had saved her life on the river, to her cold body as he crouched over her, pressing the water from her lungs. How her mouth felt on his as he breathed life and soul into her slack body. If only he could find a way to—

Fool! She's your enemy. Sister to that misbegotten thing sitting up in the palace.

He forced himself to think of his wives, now condemned to endure who knew what kind of indignities. He tried to imagine his murdered children and kin, bits of their corpses mired in mud at the bottom of the Father Water.

Yes, that's it. Hate. Nourish that sense of injustice.

The procession was passing the Four Winds Plaza, and he could see the litter with its single occupant following some sort of feathered snake standard.

Night Shadow Star turned to him. "Follow me."

"Where are you going?" *Tonka'tzi* Wind asked, shooting her niece a suspicious look.

"To take my proper place," Night Shadow Star answered as she walked through the Council Terrace Gate.

"The Morning Star ordered that you greet the Itza here."

"Yes," Night Shadow Star called over her shoulder. "I suppose he did."

Fire Cat couldn't help the wry smile that bent his lips as he followed his lady.

Twenty-three

It's impressive," Thirteen Sacred Jaguar admitted from atop his litter, "if a bit rustic." He had his eyes fixed on the high, palisaded mound with its peak-roofed palace. "And the tall pole? I've seen so many of them. What does that represent?"

"The World Tree, Lord. What you call the *Yax Cheel Kab*." Horn Lance walked beside the litter. The entire trip had been filled with questions. And, not to his surprise, he hadn't been able to answer all of them competently. So many changes had been made to his old home.

"They share that with us as well?"

"Yes, Lord."

"But they only represent the *Yax Cheel Kab* with a pole? Where are the branches? It should have the two sacred branches!"

"I cannot answer that, except to say the custom here is to represent it with a single tall pole."

"How have the gods allowed these people to become so corrupt in their beliefs?"

"You have come to correct that, Lord."

"And that observatory? Just a circle of carved poles set in the ground?"

Thirteen Sacred Jaguar would make that comparison, of

course. As a noble youth in Chichen Itza he'd served the priests in the Temple of the Wind, a mighty stone tower atop a limestone pyramid whose elevated observatory was reached by an internal circular stairway.

"The palace to your left, Lord, is the dwelling place of Lady Night Shadow Star."

Mindful of the limitations imposed by his mask, Thirteen Sacred Jaguar barely turned his head as he gazed at the thatch-and-plaster structure atop its platform mound. He seemed to fix particularly on the guardian posts that dominated the head of the stairs.

"Those effigies? Kukulkan and Jaguar?"

"Here they are called Horned Serpent and Piasa. Unlike Kukulkan, Horned Serpent lives most of the year in the Underworld, only flying into the summer sky to guard the entrance to the Spirit Road before retreating to the Underworld again in early fall. Thus, he is different from the plumed serpent you know. Kukulkan is a sky god, and not to be confused with White Bone Snake who dwells in Xibalba."

Thirteen Sacred Jaguar noted, "Do you truly believe that Piasa and First Jaguar are the same? That this woman and I venerate the same gods?"

"I am no priest, Lord. People tell me that Piasa consumed the woman's souls in Xibalba, and that the god still whispers secrets into her ear. Cahokians consider her to be a most Powerful person."

"All the better," Thirteen Sacred Jaguar said softly. "And you say the city continues? How far?"

"To the east, along the Avenue of the Sun for at least as far as we've traveled. The same to the north and south. And still farther west past Evening Star Town."

"Larger than Chichen Itza," he mused. "I would not have believed it. But such a shabby place."

"I would not mention that, Lord. Cahokians think their city the greatest in the world."

"They haven't seen much, have they?"

"If you permit, I would warn you against belittling them. Cunning will enable what truth is sure to defeat."

"I hear your words with open ears, Councilor." Thirteen Sacred Jaguar turned his head slightly to look up at the great mound. As the procession stopped before the grand staircase, he added, "Stairs of wood. A pyramid of dirt. Well, let us see what else the barbarians have in store for us."

"Do you wish to be carried up the stairs, Lord? It is custom here for nobility."

"As you wish."

Horn Lance gave the orders, and the porters wheeled, skillfully altering their hold on the litter poles to begin the ascent in the *kukul* bearer's wake. As they climbed to the Council Terrace, the bearers of boxes and packs followed.

At the head of the stairs, *Tonka'tzi* Wind and her small contingent nodded, turned, and led the way through the gate.

"At least their wood carving is the equal of ours," Thirteen Sacred Jaguar noted as they passed through the carved wooden doors bearing the likeness of the Morning Star, his wings spread, a mace in his hands.

During the final climb, Horn Lance held his breath. If a porter so much as stumbled under the load . . . No, he dare not even imagine it. Though but a matter of breaths, the climb seemed to take an eternity before they passed through the palace gate and into the courtyard.

As Thirteen Sacred Jaguar was carried into the palace great room, Horn Lance ordered, "Place the Itza before the fire."

Thirteen Sacred Jaguar, in all of his splendor, was lowered, and Burning Ant set the *kukul* at the lord's right. Horn Lance took a stance to the litter's left, while the four Itza warriors with their shields and cased *macuahuitl* positioned themselves immediately behind. The rest of the entourage crowded into the rear. The *tonka'tzi*, Blue Heron, and a host of nobles filed down the sides, all prostrating themselves on the matting.

The fire snapped and popped, casting the room with flickering yellow light.

Horn Lance noticed that Lady Night Shadow Star was standing with her slave in the forbidden space at the Morning Star's right. What did that mean?

The Morning Star himself, face painted a light blue with black forked-eye designs, wore a dazzling copper headdress depicting a soul-arrow splitting clouds. A soul bundle was tied before it, and a beaded forelock hung over his forehead.

"His face is painted *blue*!" Thirteen Sacred Jaguar barely whispered. "Does he mean that?"

"It's different here," Horn Lance breathed back just loud enough for Thirteen Sacred Jaguar to hear. Among the Itza, blue was the color of priests, and most of all, of those about to be sacrificed and have their hearts cut from their chests and their sacred *itz*, or blood, offered to the Gods of Life or Death.

He turned his attention back to the Morning Star. Spread eagle wings rose from the man's back, and his neck was draped in polished white beads that mirrored the shell masks of long-nosed human heads covering his ears. Among other names, the Morning Star had been known in the Beginning Times as "He-Who-Wears-Human-Heads."

When it came to comparisons, there were none. Thirteen Sacred Jaguar's ostentatious and colorful display left the Morning Star imposter looking inferior.

For long moments, Thirteen Sacred Jaguar and the Morning Star stared at each other. The silence—heavy and stifling—was only broken by the crackle of the fire.

Thirteen Sacred Jaguar spoke first, asking in Itza, and then repeating himself in Yucatec, "Are you truly Hun Ahau brought to earth in human form?"

A slow smile spread on Horn Lance's lips as the Morning Star's expression remained blank. Thirteen Sacred Jaguar's words were meaningless to the Cahokian imposter.

"If he really were Hun Ahau he would know the sacred

tongues. He is a fraud," Thirteen Sacred Jaguar whispered under his breath. "We may do with these people as we wish, *Ch'ak Payal*."

"I told you so, *Ahau.*"

A hardening of the Morning Star's eyes was his only reaction to their soft exchange. He lifted the copper mace he clutched in his lap. "Welcome. Who speaks for these revered guests?"

The prostrate people lifted their heads, settling into seated positions.

"I do, Great Lord," Horn Lance called. "Lord Thirteen Sacred Jaguar—known as Oxlajun Chul B'alam among his people—son of the *yitah* Four Fire Shield, of the Itza *multepal*, the Brotherhood Council, rulers of the great city of Chichen Itza and the Itza empire offers his greetings to the Morning Star and empire of Cahokia. In the name of the *multepal* and the brotherhood council, he comes from a great distance, bearing the white Power of peace in his heart."

"By my order, all of Cahokia receives the great lord in welcome, the white Power of peace in our hearts." The Morning Star remained erect, no change of expression on his face. "It is my wish that Cahokia may enter into a fruitful and prosperous relationship with the Itza, and that this is but the first of many such meetings. As a gesture, I offer black drink and the sacred pipe as a symbol of Cahokia's friendship and sincerity."

Horn Lance translated.

"What does this mean?" Thirteen Sacred Jaguar asked.

"As among the Natchez, Lord. The ritual is the same."

"Tell the imposter what you will. This is your world."

Horn Lance spread his hands wide. "*Ahau* Oxlajun Chul B'alam is most honored and accepts the Morning Star's kind offer in the spirit in which it is offered. He shares the Morning Star's noble aspirations for the initiation of friendship between our two peoples and thanks you for your kind welcome."

Two young men appeared, one carrying a large stone pipe to which a long stem in the shape of a serpent had been affixed, the other bearing a steaming whelk shell filled with foaming black drink brewed to an opacity like squid ink. It was offered first to the Morning Star, and he took the cup, drinking deeply.

When the youth brought it to Thirteen Sacred Jaguar, he carefully lifted it from the youth's hands and sipped.

"I know you'd prefer cacao, but drink fully, Lord," Horn Lance advised.

Thirteen Sacred Jaguar sucked down the rest of the cup.

The second youth was busy with the pipe, its bowl carved in the shape of an eagle. Shaking out the tobacco, he used a wooden rod to tamp the leaves tight. When finished he carefully offered the pipe to the four directions, then earth and sky. He lit a punky stick in the fire. Holding the bowl, he offered the long stem to the Morning Star. As the living god pulled, the youth held the flame over the tobacco.

Morning Star drew deeply, tilting his head back to blow smoke toward the roof. Then he raised his hands and prayed, "In the name of Hunga Ahuito I greet the Itza lord in peace and friendship, extending my hand in brotherhood that we might have a long and beneficial relationship."

The youth carried the pipe around the fire to Thirteen Sacred Jaguar, who took the stem in his mouth and drew smoke into his expanding lungs. Exhaling through his nostrils, he prayed, "Great Kukulkan, let me prevail among these savages. Chac, give me the strength and cunning to bring this place and people back to the true faith. Tlaloc, through blood, pain, and sacrifice, let me rid the world of Cahokia's corrupt worship."

Then he took a second pull on the pipe, exhaling in the direction of his standard. "Waxaklahun Kan, mighty War Serpent, I may have no army, but the war to which I commit myself is no less dangerous, though it will be fought on a different battlefield. Give me strength and courage, for which I shall offer you my blood and pain."

During the entirety of the prayer, Horn Lance remained mute, fully aware that the Cahokians—awed by the lord's incomprehensible language, but obvious conviction—interpreted Thirteen Sacred Jaguar's words in a most different light.

The Morning Star remained expressionless, his painted face inscrutable. Blue Heron's expression was sour, her crafty gaze shifting back and forth between Thirteen Sacred Jaguar and Horn Lance. But the rest of the room seemed entranced, their eyes glowing in awe and excitement.

Then he glanced at Night Shadow Star, dressed in black, holding a copper-bitted war club. A deadly smile curled her lips, her eyes half-slitted as she studied Thirteen Sacred Jaguar. Behind her, her armored slave looked just as grim, a promise of mayhem on his face.

Twenty-four

He does make a grand figure," *Tonka'tzi* Wind noted as she watched the Itza being offered succulent bison calf, deep-pit roasted and served with walnut bread and sweetened squash. Ample black drink, currant jams, varieties of steaming paddlefish, baked crappie, beeweed-seasoned squirrel, turkey with mint, coontie root breads, hickory and acorn mash, greens, and other delights had been offered to the Itza one by one.

After each, Thirteen Sacred Jaguar had said something to Horn Lance, who proclaimed, "Marvelous," "Exquisite," "Delightful to the tongue," or some other appropriate remark.

Blue Heron paused from giving a baked duck leg a working over with her remaining teeth. "I'm not sure what he's saying." She gestured with the greasy bone. "You'll notice that the Itza's voice doesn't quite carry the conviction Horn Lance imbues it with. That overdressed foreigner could be saying it tastes like dog shit for all we know."

Wind gave her a dismissive glance. "You judge too much by the company he keeps. Were his translator anyone but Horn Lance, you'd at least give him the benefit of a doubt. And so what? He's no threat. His Chichen Itza is a world away. What if these supposed cities of stone are real? They're as harmless to us as we are to them. Or do you really think they could paddle an army around the gulf shores, and then up the Father Water?"

"That doesn't worry me."

"What then?"

Blue Heron glanced at the Morning Star, seated on his panther litter and licking bear grease from his fingers after finishing a piece of nut bread. The living god's evaluative gaze had remained on the Itza the entire night, at least when he wasn't casting furtive glances Night Shadow Star's way.

The tension between the three of them almost crackled. Nor had Night Shadow Star partaken of the feast—an insult to the living god had it been anyone else. Though she and the Red Wing had seated themselves, they still clutched their weapons.

To Blue Heron's way of thinking, when Night Shadow Star turned her eyes on the Itza, she might have been watching a coiled water moccasin rather than a foreign lord armed with no more than his gaudy outfit and feathered-snake standard.

"Why does my back begin to prickle when the living god and Night Shadow Star are at odds over Power?" Wind muttered as she used a splinter to pick at the venison stuck between her teeth.

"Because you're a smart woman." Blue Heron glanced at the Natchez Little Sun, seated back with his warriors, laughing and stuffing his face with cornbread.

Wind followed her gaze. "No sign of the cloak? What's wrong with your thief these days?"

"Neither he nor I believe the cloak is going to turn up in any of the usual places. After he and I talked this morning, I listened to what my spies had to report. If one of the Four Winds Houses had it, there'd be at least a hint. The Earth Clans wouldn't touch it on a dare."

"Those Natchez back there hadn't even arrived when Nine Strikes was killed. Your thief saw them come ashore."

"All of them? Do you have a count I don't know about? And so what if Swirling Cloud and Horn Lance arrived the same time as the Natchez delegation? A thousand Natchez agents could have come ashore within the week prior to their arrival, and we wouldn't have a clue."

"Then where's the cloak?"

"Somewhere we can't possibly find it."

"Destroyed?"

Blue Heron shook her head. "I don't think he's that pragmatic. No, indeed. I smell arrogance and vanity behind this. They think we're blind, dumb, and stupid."

"I thought you said you'd been frustrated at every turn?"

"I have been. And they know it."

"So?"

"That's their mistake. The one that's going to bring them down."

"Excuse me, if they're that much ahead of us—"

"They're smug enough to make a mistake . . . like keeping Nine Strikes' cloak as a trophy when they shouldn't have."

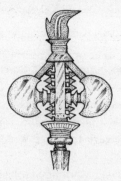

Twenty-five

The warm night air had a muggy feel. The humming of a thousand mosquitoes added to the heavy atmosphere. Clouds had moved in from the south, their bellies reflecting a dirty orange from Cahokia's thousands of cook fires.

Seven Skull Shield glanced up, hearing the chitter of bats ducking and darting through the swarm of mosquitoes that hovered in a column over his head. Bats loved Cahokia. The high-thatch roofs were a haven for the creatures, and the city bred pesky bat food in hoards: flies, moths, mosquitoes, and every other sort of insect a hungry bat might crave.

Seven Skull Shield scratched under his belt. Too bad Hunga Ahuito hadn't created a predator for lice and fleas as well as for mosquitoes. The warrens of packed humanity not only hosted such crawling discomforts, but the dirt farmers were often riddled with intestinal parasites. On occasion he'd seen them crap out more worms than feces in their open latrines.

"Come on, concentrate," he muttered under his breath as he slipped along the plastered wall of the Four Winds Men's House. The building fronted the eastern side of the Great Plaza, about midway between the Morning Star's palace and Rides-the-Lightning's twin mounds. Normally it served

Four Winds warriors when they congregated and conducted their rituals. It was here that the most sacred Four Winds War Medicine was normally kept. Seven Skull Shield had seen it paraded on special occasions. The sacred bundle consisted of a box large enough to be worn as a pack. Fantastically carved and inlaid, the box contained the sacred Power items that gave the Four Winds Clan victory in combat.

For the time being, Morning Star had ordered the Four Winds warriors to remove all of their accoutrements and sacred objects and "loan" the building to the Itza lord and his Natchez escort.

To say that the Four Winds warriors had been displeased with the forced relocation of their social center would be a mild understatement. But who in their right mind argued with a god incarnate?

Seven Skull Shield wondered if it wasn't the living god's way of putting the warriors in their place, given their recent strutting and increased influence in the wake of Red Wing Town's bloodless defeat.

Seven Skull Shield glanced up at the Morning Star's high palace. The feast had to be in full swing given the amount of firelight reflecting from the World Tree pole and the palace front. Over the chirring of crickets, the faint voices calling in the distance, and barking dogs that served as Cahokia's nightly background noise, he could hear the revelry.

Seven Skull Shield peered around the corner of the Men's House. War totems overlooked the empty avenue that lined the plaza. Ivory Billed Woodpecker, Panther, Falcon, and Snapping Turtle were equally spaced, each looking fierce as they guarded the Men's House.

Ah, and there, crouched by the door, was the lone guard.

Seven Skull Shield rubbed his jaw thoughtfully. One man, just as he'd figured. The rest of the Natchez warriors were either up in the palace courtyard or arrayed at the bottom of the great staircase awaiting the eventual descent of their lords.

The single guard had no doubt been left as a precaution in the event any of the Four Winds warriors might have missed hearing that their society house had been loaned out. After all, absolutely no one would have the temerity to slip into such a place uninvited. Not under the Morning Star's very nose. It would be unthinkable!

Seven Skull Shield batted at the mosquitoes, grinned, and stepped around the corner, a long-necked bottle in his hand.

"Greetings, Natchez lord," he called.

The man leaped to his feet, shaking himself, and presenting his war club as if in the vain attempt to look alert. He barked out a challenge in the Natchez tongue that Seven Skull Shield thought sounded like something a sick turkey would cluck.

"Here," he said in Trade pidgin and offered the bottle. "My master sent this. You understand 'master'? Gift?"

The Natchez stared at the bottle Seven Skull Shield held in his hand, muttering something incomprehensible.

"Gift," Seven Skull Shield repeated, and made the hand sign universally employed by Traders up and down the river.

"Ah!" The Natchez guard nodded, repeating some word in Natchez, then mimicking "Gift" in a tortured accent.

"Blueberry and raspberry juice," Seven Skull Shield told him. "Good! Welcome to Cahokia."

The Natchez lowered his war club, took the bottle, and sniffed. In the darkness Seven Skull Shield could barely make out the man's smile before he lifted it to his lips and sipped. Nodding, he took an even deeper draft.

"Yes, you just drink that and enjoy," Seven Skull Shield told him as he bowed at the waist and walked off.

If Smooth Pebble had measured the proportions correctly, there was just enough datura juice in the syrupy mix to have the man nodding off to sleep in no time.

Twenty-six

As soon as the feast was concluded and the servants had removed the plates, bowls, and jars, Thirteen Sacred Jaguar gestured that the first of the ornate boxes be brought forward.

After being granted permission, Horn Lance carried the first offering and laid it before the Morning Star, saying, "Great Lord, we present a remarkable Putun cotton shawl dyed in yellow, green, red, and blue." The colors, more vivid than anything previously seen in Cahokia, had their desired effect: The onlookers oohed and awed.

Then he brought forth his next offering: "This fine basket made by masters in the city of Yaxchilan contains copal, or *pom,* the heady and sacred Mayan incense. It is to be burned on sacred occasions as an offering to the Sky World. Next I offer a rubber ball. This ball contains the *ch'ulel* or soul known as *jom sak,* which translates to 'White Destroys.' Used in the sacred ball games, the peoples in the Itza world consider it as valuable as you do a prized chunkey stone."

The Morning Star took the heavy orb and curiously pressed his fingers against the soft surface to see it dimple. A shadow of a smile bent his lips.

"We offer cacao," Horn Lance said as he proffered yet

another intricately woven basket. "Cacao is the sacred drink of the Maya and Itza lords, and is presented in a treasured basket said to have been woven by the ancient rulers of the great city of Tikal."

As each of the treasures was revealed, the awestruck spectators whispered excitedly to each other.

The Morning Star, however, watched through calculating dark eyes, his gaze going first to the item, and then to Horn Lance, as if to read the value and motive behind the offering.

At Horn Lance's gesture, a fantastically carved box was brought forward. Opening it, Horn Lance demonstrated the contents. "This, Great Lord, is *juna*, upon which the Itza and Yucatec record words, much as you do with your beaded strings and mats. The difference being that the Itza draw their words, each symbol having meaning. Among other uses, once *juna* is written upon, it can be burned, the rising smoke carrying messages to the Sky World much as you do with tobacco."

The Morning Star may have smiled ever so faintly.

Next a small textile bag, remarkably embroidered, was brought forward. This Horn Lance laid at the Morning Star's feet. "This bag, Great Lord, contains dried sea snails from the Western Ocean. Properly soaked and boiled, they will produce the most vibrant purple dye, the likes of which you have never seen."

Morning Star barely lifted an eyebrow.

Horn Lance continued to lay out fabrics; spices including achiote, pequin, vanilla, chili; and other treats. These were followed by coca leaves and other hallucinogens, including dried and powdered frogs, thinly sliced mushrooms, and ololiuhqui seed.

"And finally, Thirteen Sacred Jaguar and the Itza *multepal* bestow this last gift. The hide of the illusive black jaguar, an animal of special Power who hunts the night and communes with the Lords of Xibalba, which you know as the Underworld."

With a flourish, Horn Lance snapped it open, the glistening black hair reflecting the firelight.

A gasp of amazement rose from the audience.

The Morning Star glanced at the midnight cat's hide, nodded slightly, and said, "I thank the Itza lord for his wonderful and priceless gifts. In the coming days, I hope to reciprocate and double his kind generosity. Is there anything in particular that he might have already admired?"

Horn Lance dropped to his knee, head lowered as he touched his forehead. Straightening, he doffed his scarlet macaw helmet, and in a supplicant's pose, said, "Great Lord, the Itza council has sent one of its most noble sons, an *ahau* of great renown, to open and establish relations with Cahokia, its Morning Star, and peoples. It is a symbol of the respect and reverence they have for the resurrection of your Spirit Being into a living body that a high lord of such status and prestige as Thirteen Sacred Jaguar has been dispatched to represent the *multepal*. The Itza Council, therefore, would humbly request a token of alliance between our two great Nations and your sacred presence on earth."

"What might that be?" Morning Star's lips thinned, as if in amusement.

"Thirteen Sacred Jaguar is the son of *Yitah* Four Fire Shield, perhaps the most noble and respected advisor to the *multepal*. They seek an alliance at the highest level, Great Lord. A joining of Chichen Itza and Cahokia's greatest lineages."

"Ah, a marriage." Morning Star smiled in satisfaction. Raising his voice, he asked, "*Tonka'tzi*? As the titular head of the Morning Star House of the Four Winds Clan, would you have any objection to the marriage of a suitable woman to an esteemed Itza lord?"

Horn Lance turned on his heel, seeing the surprise on Wind's age-lined face. She wet her lips, arms rising helplessly. "I—I suppose not, Great Lord. I would need to—"

"And who might the honored Thirteen Sacred Jaguar have

in mind?" the Morning Star interrupted, his keen gaze on Horn Lance.

"It has come to our attention, Great Lord, that Lady Night Shadow Star has been recently widowed. Should you be amenable, such a union would be favorably received by the lords of the *multepal*."

Horn Lance heard the sudden intakes of breath from those in the room. Willing himself to remain calm, he held the Morning Star's level gaze. In his peripheral vision, Night Shadow Star's grip on her war club tightened. She didn't, however, seem startled in the slightest. Why?

"Night Shadow Star," the living god finally said, "is one of our most exalted of ladies."

"Her brother's body now hosts your souls, Great Lord. That her family is so honored by Power indicates that she would be a suitable match for a *yitah*'s son. A marriage between equals, Great Lord."

For the first time, he dared to glance fully at Night Shadow Star, expecting to see her expressing astonishment and confusion. Instead she watched the Morning Star with half-slitted eyes, her jaw set, muscles tense. Behind her, the armed slave was the one who looked shocked and appalled. The man's eyes were flashing, his jaws knotted like over-strained rope.

"Great Lord?" Clan Keeper Blue Heron had dared to stand, her face thoughtful as she touched her forehead.

"Clan Keeper?"

"Marriage between the Itza and Morning Star House is by no means a frivolous undertaking. A period of reflection whereby both parties might—"

"Agreed, Clan Keeper." The Morning Star gestured with his mace. "For the moment let us consider Lady Night Shadow Star and the noble Thirteen Sacred Jaguar to be formally betrothed. The traditional feasting has occurred, and the suitor has certainly offered the most unique if not customary gifts. Four days should be sufficient time for both parties to ensure agreement and to allow Morning Star House to make preparations for the appropriate celebrations."

Horn Lance bowed, backing to his position beside Thirteen Sacred Jaguar.

"What has happened?" the Itza asked.

"You are betrothed to Night Shadow Star. They want four days to prepare."

"Is that bad?"

"Not at all, Great Lord. It allows the word to spread, pressure to build, and time for you to add to your prestige among the Cahokians. Taking Night Shadow Star to your bed will be a foregone conclusion."

"And what did she say?"

"Not a word." Horn Lance frowned, again glancing at where Night Shadow Star had now turned her burning black gaze on Thirteen Sacred Jaguar. "Which I find most curious."

Even as he said it, Night Shadow Star stalked from the room, her pet dog of a warrior following.

"She doesn't look happy, does she?"

"Her happiness isn't required." Thirteen Sacred Jaguar thinned his lips. "But she is such an ugly woman. She looks so common and lowborn with that high forehead and pointed chin. Nor do her front teeth protrude like a true lady's. Her lips are so small. And yes, they are woman's muscles, but her body reminds me of a field worker's. Not soft and round the way a proper—"

"*Ahau*, neither her looks nor form is at issue. All we care about is that she submissively spreads her legs so that you can plant your child in her womb."

Twenty-seven

Y ou seriously aren't going to go through with this, are you?" Fire Cat cried as soon as he and Night Shadow Star passed beyond hearing and into the palace courtyard. Overhead the night sky had a dull and oppressive look, the smell of rain mixing with the city odors of smoke, stagnant water, and too many humans. Lightning flashed in the clouds to the southeast.

Night Shadow Star slowed and tilted her head back to gaze up at the darkness. Yellow flickers from the courtyard's central fire illuminated her tortured face. "It is required of me."

"Blood and dung! Tell them no! You're a noble woman. It's your right to refuse."

She chuckled humorlessly. "The Morning Star? The *tonka'tzi*? My family? Them, I could refuse."

"Piasa?" he guessed warily.

She nodded, starting for the gate, her fists knotted around the handle of her war club.

"Tell him no."

"One doesn't tell one's master no. As you are to me, I am to him: bound." She shot him a weary smile as she stepped through the gate. "Nor do I know who has the more capricious and heartless master, you or me?"

"Though it amazes me to hear such words pass my lips, Lady, I believe you do."

She started down the dark stairs, head bowed.

"Here, take my hand." He reached out. "It's treacherous in the dark. Your master might hold it against me if you fell because of a simple misstep."

"Gallantry, Red Wing?"

"Self-preservation, Lady."

To his surprise, she shifted the war club to place her right hand on his arm. "Thank you."

Her touch sent a jolt through him, his heart skipping.

A curious dread and dismay simmered in his breast, vying with the need to strike out, to charge back up the stairs and beat the overdressed Itza in his shimmering green feathers. Beat him to a bloody pulp.

He gave voice to his growing disquiet. "There's got to be a way out of this. Even if I have to knock a couple of heads."

"As I must, you, too, will obey. You have continually told me that your oath is your bond. I hold you to that." Her tone lightened slightly. "Though the notion of you knocking a few heads does have its appeal."

"When it comes to head-bashing, I am at your command, Lady."

"Be patient, Red Wing. First we must endure, learn. Then, perhaps, we shall be given our chance to act."

"I don't understand."

"Neither do I." She pursed her lips. "The Itza has Old-Woman-Who-Never-Dies' protection, so I am ordered not to kill him."

"Piasa told you this?" he asked somewhat incredulously.

"No, Red Wing. She did."

He shot her a suspicious sidelong glance, but the woman appeared dead serious.

"You saw Old-Woman-Who-Never-Dies? When? I haven't seen you touch the datura for—"

"A Spirit Dream. During the Busk. I was exhausted after

a solid day of stickball games. Piasa summoned me in the middle of the night."

What was he supposed to make of that? Old-Woman-Who-Never-Dies? Ruler of the Underworld? The second-most Powerful deity in the cosmos after Hunga Ahuito, the Creator? She *talked* to Night Shadow Star? Summoned her in a dream to the Underworld?

They crossed the Council Terrace, and Night Shadow Star acknowledged the guards at the gate before descending to the foot of the stairs.

"Make way for Lady Night Shadow Star," Fire Cat ordered, alerting her escort in the process. Her warriors separated themselves from the knot of retainers, guards, and household staff waiting on the avenue. Beyond them, a huge crowd swelled, all hoping to catch sight of the near-mythical Itza.

"So, we have four days? Are you sure I can't sneak in and assassinate him in the middle of the night?"

The fleeting smile had returned to her lips. "Just follow my orders, Red Wing. No matter how preposterous they may sound at the moment."

"Yes, Lady."

Twenty-eight

Blue Heron blinked in an effort to stay awake. Body exhausted. Souls drifting. Her thoughts seemed to spin as aimlessly as a spindle whorl on a hardwood plank.

What is Horn Lance's end game?

Crack that one puzzle and she would know exactly how to handle the situation.

Instead of clarity, her fatigued souls kept replaying scenes from the day's events. Most were dominated by the Itza in his incredible iridescent-green feathered cape, the eye-popping colors, the remarkable soaring headdress with its plumes. The stunning fabrics.

Through the entire evening, the man had sat as if he were enduring the most boring night of his life. His face had been expressionless, the black eyes dismissively studying the room from behind half lids. All that had been missing was the occasional yawn.

Only when he looked at Morning Star did the man's visage change, keening the way a falcon's did when in the presence of a hapless rodent.

Not even the hopelessly blind would have missed the tension between the two.

Blue Heron considered that as she stepped off her litter

and nodded to Smooth Pebble. Crossing her veranda, she reached up and began pulling out the skewers that held her hair in its bun. Shaking her graying locks loose, she entered her palace, walked past her fire, and into her personal quarters.

It's Horn Lance's game. Not the Itza's. The foreign fool doesn't know he's being played just as—

She started at the shadowy shape of a man sitting on her trunk.

"Easy there, Keeper," Seven Skull Shield called in reassurance.

"Thief? By Piasa's swinging balls, so help me, if you don't start waiting outside like everyone else . . ." She gave up, shaking her head.

"You look like you're about to fall over. Long night up at the palace?"

"Let us just say the Itza was greeted with style." She stumbled over to her bed and sank onto the blankets with relief. "Make it quick. I want to sleep for a couple of moons."

"What, exactly, does this Itza's arrival mean?" Seven Skull Shield shrugged his thick shoulders. "Why is he so special? Foreign lords show up here all the time. As I understand it, he's just from someplace a little farther away and therefore a bit more exotic. Why all the commotion over him and not some Timucua chief from down in the peninsula?"

She rubbed her gritty eyes. "Timucua *utina*s . . . that's their word for chiefs . . . don't build huge cities of stone the size of Cahokia. They don't raise stone mounds halfway to the sky. Nor do Timucua *utina*s field armies of thousands as the Yucatec, Mixtec, Putun, and Itza are reputed to do. At least if we can believe the stories Traders tell."

"Can we?"

"Apparently. You should have seen the gifts he presented to the Morning Star. Goods the likes of which I've never seen, but only heard about. So, if cacao, quetzal feathers, prayer paper, the rubber ball and the other things are real, does that mean the stone sky palaces, ball games, massive armies, and the ceremonial sacrifice of thousands of human beings are real as well?"

"Maybe. Just how far away is this Chichen Itza?"

"Think of it as being on the other side of the world."

"Then why are we worried about one man and a handful of Natchez?"

She blinked, willing herself to think. "For the moment, it's the excitement over what it could potentially mean for us. Especially Trade. The obstacle is the distance, the danger of crossing a huge open ocean, and a host of hostile and barbaric peoples between here and there."

"So, is this Itza a Trader? Come to check out the local wares before heading back to the far distant, or is he thinking about staying for a while?"

She shot him a sidelong glance. "He's marrying Night Shadow Star in four days. What's that tell you?"

Seven Skull Shield crossed his arms, muscles bulging. "That's quick."

"Yes, it is."

"And what did Night Shadow Star say about it?"

"Not a word. She and the Red Wing came dressed for war. But when the time came, she didn't so much as open her mouth. In the end, she just stalked out."

"What if she says no tomorrow or the next day?"

"She can't. The Morning Star gave her up without so much as a flicker of his eye. It took me by such surprise that I risked my fool neck and asked for some time for the parties to consider. Bought us four days."

"The Red Wing might kill him first."

"What would he care who Night Shadow Star marries? He hates her. Something about being his captor and enemy."

"Sure he does." Sarcasm. "And I'll bet when he heard he looked as red and choked up as if he'd stuck a plum pit halfway down his throat."

"So you think he's actually grown fond of her?"

"Keeper, I can drive the man half mad just by licking my lips in Night Shadow Star's presence. Baiting the Red Wing is more fun than teasing a scorpion with a twig."

"Does she feel the same way about him?"

"If I'm any judge of a woman? Which, of course I am. She'd bundle him off to her bed in a minute if he were anyone but the Red Wing. Never seen two people drawn to each other work so hard to convince themselves that they're both forbidden."

"Poor fool. He'd have better luck falling in love with a cougar."

Seven Skull Shield shrugged. "So? If the Red Wing kills this Thirteen Sacred Jaguar, what of it? The Morning Star orders him hung in a square, and it's all over. It's not like the Itza will show up next spring with an army to avenge the murder if they're as far away as you say. Meanwhile, Morning Star gets all the goods."

"Maybe that's why Morning Star gave Night Shadow Star up so easily. He's planning on just that. But it doesn't explain Horn Lance and the Natchez." She pulled at the wattle under her chin. "That's the part I don't understand yet."

"Well, you might want to give that some thought." Seven Skull Shield shifted, reaching behind him. He tossed her a tightly bound, cylindrically rolled bundle of something.

She barely managed to catch it before it hit her in the chest. In the gloom, she fingered the bundle, recognizing the texture of a feather cape. "You found it? Where?"

"In a storage box among the things the Natchez piled into the Four Winds Men's House. I decided we needed it more than the Natchez did, along with some other things to reimburse me for my time and effort."

"So the Natchez are indeed behind Nine Strikes' death."

"Apparently so."

She fingered the eagle-wing cloak, remembering how it was offered to the Little Sun.

"I can't wait to see Swirling Cloud's reaction when you

hand him that." Seven Skull Shield touched his chin in mock subservience.

"All in good time, thief." She patted the rolled cloak. "Before we play the game, we need to figure out the rules and objectives."

"And exactly who's playing for which side," Seven Skull Shield amended.

"For the moment, we don't even know how many sides there are."

As she ran her fingers over the cloak, she wondered if once again the thief had saved her life, or if, in some perverted way, the cloak would place her one step closer to disaster.

"Come. You and I, thief. We're going back up that mound to tell the Morning Star."

"What? Me?" he protested. "Why me?"

"Maybe I want you there to catch me if I fall."

Twenty-nine

Lightning, twisting like knotted threads of tortured silver, throbbed in the clouds to the south. Batting gusts of breeze buffeted Seven Skull Shield as he helped the Keeper make her tired way up the steps—as if the very air itself were fleeing the white flashes of light that illuminated the squared logs sunk into the steep stairway.

In Seven Skull Shield's grasp, Keeper Blue Heron's arm felt oddly delicate for as tough a lady as he knew her to be. She almost tottered, yawning despite the panting effort she expended on the climb.

Another of the eerie white flashes illuminated the great city in a contrast of colorless highlight and opaque shadow. Temples, clan houses, circular council houses, and mound-top edifices all cast in actinic miniature, as if the great city were the construct of a warped and fevered imagination.

At the top, the two guards passed Blue Heron on sight, reserving their suspicious and hard-eyed stares for Seven Skull Shield. He shot them a vacuous smile, lit by a distant strobe of lightning, and followed the Keeper into the palace courtyard. The high palisade gave them a little relief from the wind.

At the Morning Star's carved-plank door, another guard

saw them inside. He gestured for them to stay before stepping over to Five Fist's bed, where he murmured to the old warrior and retreated back outside.

Five Fists pulled on a breechcloth, yawned with his crooked jaw, blinked, and padded over, asking, "Keeper? What brings you at this time of night? And what are you doing with this two-legged maggot?"

Seven Skull Shield met the man's distasteful glance with an exaggerated smile that exposed his teeth. The mocking rictus either hit home—given the old warrior's slight wince—or something gruesome was stuck between his incisors.

Blue Heron tapped the rolled cape under Seven Skull Shield's arm. "We've got the cape."

"And the Little Sun's murderer?"

"That gets a bit more complicated. We need to see the Morning Star."

Five Fists rubbed a scarred knuckle down the long-faded tattoos on his misaligned cheek. "I'll see. Wait here."

"As if we'd go anywhere else," Seven Skull Shield muttered, the prickly sensation of unease starting to claw its way along his bones. Had he really been so gullible as to boast to the Anilco Trader that he enjoyed the Morning Star's company? Just being in the palace pulled the slipknot in his pucker string tight.

A particularly virulent gust of wind made a hissing sound in the high thatch overhead.

The great central fire, burned down to coals, left the room and its splendid furnishings ruddy and shadowed. Taking stock, Seven Skull Shield figured that maybe half of the sleeping benches were occupied by the Morning Star's staff and servants.

Five Fists emerged from the rear door, beckoning.

Blue Heron led the way back into the living god's forbidden space. Seven Skull Shield cast one final longing glance at the double doors that led out to freedom and safety.

"He'll see you in his quarters," Five Fists said with obvious reluctance. Then, his eyes boring into Seven Skull Shield's, he added pointedly, "I'll be right outside."

Blue Heron, her body gone tense, swallowed hard, nodded, and hesitantly stepped through the door.

In spite of his trepidation, Seven Skull Shield looked around the Morning Star's bedroom with no little curiosity. Three hickory-oil lamps placed on wooden chests illuminated the room. The bed built into the back wall was covered with the finest blankets and furs, most of them rolled up against the back wall given the midsummer heat.

The usual storage boxes and ceramic jars were stowed beneath the bed. An elaborate paint palette, paints, and a collection of jewelry, headdresses, feather splays, cloaks, maces, and other exotica were laid ready to hand on a series of magnificently carved boxes, each as high as Seven Skull Shield's hip. To one side of the door stood the Morning Star's copper chunkey lances and a wooden rack with his variously colored stones.

The living god himself sat on the edge of his bed, a white cloth wrap around his narrow waist. His muscular arms were propped, his hair falling down his back in a black wave.

Seven Skull Shield had never seen him without facial paint, his face-shaped ear covering, or headdress. In the glow of the hickory lamps, he looked remarkably human. A handsome young man with a strong face, the Four Winds Clan tattoos looking pristine on his smooth cheeks.

Chunkey Boy's face.

The resemblance to his sister Night Shadow Star couldn't be missed.

"What news, Keeper?" he asked, his cautious gaze going to Seven Skull Shield, though he didn't offer him so much as a nod in recognition.

"The cloak," she said softly, taking it from Seven Skull Shield's grasp and unrolling it so the brilliant red-dyed eagle feathers could be seen. "The thief recovered it from the Natchez called Swirling Cloud. It was hidden in the man's possessions. It appears that Nine Strikes' murder was political, a means of keeping him from assuming his brother's place as Great Sun."

"Of course." The Morning Star barely shifted, his dark eyes fixed on Blue Heron's.

"How do you wish to handle this?"

Morning Star's face remained expressionless. "Let them proceed."

Seven Skull Shield noticed the bunching of muscles in the Keeper's jaw, watched her shoulders rise in confusion. "Let them proceed? We've got the proof! They killed the Little Sun. They're either playing the Itza, or he's playing them. Whatever they're here for, it's not for our benefit. And this marriage to Night Shadow Star? We're cradling a nest of water moccasins to our breast and pretending that they won't bite us."

"I failed the Itza's test."

"What test?"

He smiled enigmatically. "I expect you to continue doing what you do so well."

"I don't understand."

"Of course not. Thank you, Keeper. I suggest you get your rest. The coming days will prove most trying. You will need all of your resources. Sleep well."

He barely lifted a hand in dismissal.

"What about the cloak?" she asked.

"You know what it means . . . and how to use it best." His smile wasn't pleasant. "No need to send Five Fists in. Oh, and do be careful on the stairs. For the moment I'm not sure we could do without you."

It wasn't until they were outside, buffeted by the balmy air swirling over the palisades that Seven Skull Shield asked, "What just happened in there? I mean, did any of that make sense?"

Blue Heron stopped short, glancing back at the dark palace. "Phlegm and spit. I'm cursed if I know."

Lightning flashed overhead as the first drops of rain, large and cold, spattered the ground.

"This Itza and the Natchez are plotting right under our noses. He doesn't even seem concerned, does he?"

She looked up at him through night-shadowed eyes. "That sends a colder chill down my back than that caused by the Natchez."

The rain began with a vengeance, slashing down from the lightning-riven sky as if the fury of the Thunderbirds could not be contained.

Thirty

Horn Lance crouched on his heels, a cup of steaming mint tea held by the cup's horn-like handle. He watched the sun's first rays shoot across a cloud-mottled sky. Sometime after midnight it had started to rain and lasted long enough to not only leave puddles but to scrub the sky of smoke and haze.

His back to the Men's House wall, he watched the first people as they trooped across the Great Plaza to lay offerings at the foot of the great World Tree pole where it rose like a mighty spear. On the other side of the grassy expanse, the east-facing palaces and temples gleamed in the fresh light. The colorful guardian poles and standards in front of them contrasted to the cloud-backed horizon.

At the twin mounds on the plaza's southern boundary, the Earth Clans priest Rides-the-Lightning was leading his acolytes in the ritual greeting prayer on the eastern side of the temple. People stopped to watch and join the prayer as they emerged from the Avenue of the Moon's northern terminus.

Despite the hour, the first of the vendors and Traders were arriving, setting up their small stalls or laying out goods on blankets along the plaza margins. From outlying areas and other districts, many had been walking most of the night to arrive early enough to claim the best locations.

"We have a problem," Swirling Cloud said as he stepped out and crouched beside Horn Lance. The Natchez hadn't even taken the time to braid his hair and wrap it in the traditional Sun Born's coils at either side of his head.

"Only one?"

"The cloak is gone. Someone went through our boxes last night. Some jewelry and sacred ornaments are missing along with a box of hallucinogens." The young man's jaws knotted, a seething rage behind his eyes. "The Morning Star is going to hear about this. We're going to turn this place upside down until the culprit is turned over to hang in a square. If it means bringing half of this city down in—"

"No. We won't."

"What do you mean? I just told you, we were robbed last night! Someone *took* the eagle cloak! Stole objects sacred to the Great Sun! Defiled our—"

"What about Spearing Beak? Wasn't he the warrior on guard last night?"

"Two Throws had to kick him awake when we got back. I'll deal with him in a moment. First thing, we have to tell the Morning Star—"

"Tell him what? That we were so lax and incompetent we only posted one warrior on guard? That we can't see to our own security?"

"Don't you *care*?"

"Of course. And it's my own fault."

"*Your* fault?"

"I should have expected this. Laid a trap."

"When I tell the Morning Star—"

"He'll smile behind his face paint, say something soothing, and order the miscreant to be produced. Which, of course, Blue Heron will work assiduously to accomplish. In the end, I suspect she will come up with some slave or other poor person who's managed to raise her ire. We'll be distracted while we torture the poor maggot to death, all the while listening to his pleadings that he knows nothing about the stolen items."

"Blue Heron? You think she's behind this?"

"Of course." Horn Lance sipped his tea. "Which is why we will say nothing."

"Are you head struck? *She has the cloak*!"

Horn Lance stared placidly into Swirling Cloud's burning eyes. "Now, think, my friend. Use the wits the Sun supposedly imparted to your Natchez souls. Blue Heron is counting on your rage."

"Then I'm going to give her a full dose of it! I'm—"

"What happens when we charge up to the Morning Star's palace, demanding the return of our stolen property? Blue Heron may even be waiting up there with the cloak, with your sacred Natchez items, and an eager smile on her face.

" 'Yes, Morning Star,' she says, 'a Trader reported to me that a slave had tried to relieve himself of stolen goods. When we investigated, we found not only the stolen Natchez goods, but the cloak! The very one Nine Strikes' murderer took from his dead body! How could it have ended up among Thirteen Sacred Jaguar's noble Natchez?' "

Swirling Cloud paused, the heat of his rage draining away. "I see. So, what do we do?"

"Well . . . maybe beat Spearing Beak to within a whisker of his life, but no one says anything to anyone. And if asked, we all declare that we had no theft. Nothing of ours is missing. That being the case, and since Keeper Blue Heron claims to have found the cloak, she must have Nine Strikes' murderer as well, correct? And if she doesn't? How can she have one and not the other?"

"Then, do you think she's done that? Taken the cloak and our sacred artifacts to the Morning Star?"

"I dearly hope so. She didn't get to be Keeper for all these years by being stupid."

Swirling Cloud curled his fingers, as if raking the air. "I tell you, I'll make her pay for this."

"Not if you insist on falling into a rage every time she plays you. Do that, and we'll lose it all."

"Very well. What do you suggest? Just sit here? Let her get away with it?"

"No, my young friend. It's just that when a bobcat hunts a badger, he must do it very carefully." Horn Lance smiled. "And employ distractions of his own."

"And when are you going to employ these distractions?"

At that moment a litter appeared out of the morning, borne by eight muscular young men.

"Just as soon as I've eaten."

Thirty-one

Homecoming. The thought dominated Horn Lance's souls as his litter was carried past the two large Horned Serpent guardian posts that rose on either side of the Avenue of the Moon.

So much had changed since the day he'd last set foot in Horned Serpent Town. Even the huge guardians were new. Hewn from mighty red cedars, the guardians had been carved in the image of the winged and antlered serpent who flew up from the Underworld and into the southern summer sky to guard the entrance to the Spirit Road of the Dead—the great band of frosty light that crossed the night sky. To mark Horned Serpent's duality, the serpent on the west side of the road had the three-forked eye design of the Underworld, while the one on the east had the two-forked design indicative of the Sky World.

From some dusty corner of Horn Lance's souls came the reflexive impulse to reach up and touch his forehead.

Then his litter was borne past the guardians and into Horned Serpent Town proper.

Horn Lance's porters carried him through an unfamiliar maze of houses with their little garden plots, past temples dedicated to Old-Woman-Who-Never-Dies, granaries, society and charnel houses, ramadas and workshops. The structures grew larger and more ornate, as well as more closely packed, as they neared the central plaza. So, too, did the number of people who had to scurry out of the way as Horn Lance's porters bulled forward along the narrow path between the buildings. Someone kicked a dog who wasn't quick enough, eliciting a yip as the beast shot away.

And then they passed around the base of the Horned Serpent House palace mound, past the Four Winds Clan House, and into the spacious central plaza.

At the foot of the stairs leading up to High Chief Green Chunkey's mound-top palace, Horn Lance's litter was lowered. The porters, sweating and panting softly, bowed in respect as Horn Lance rose.

He took a moment to let his gaze roam the plaza. Before him two chunkey courts had been laid out, province of the Horned Serpent House and available only to Four Winds Clan members and their guests. Around the plaza's periphery a collection of vendors and hawkers displayed their wares, but nothing like he had seen in the Great Plaza.

The lightning-riven World Tree pole stood in the center of the plaza, directly in line with an elongated mound on the east that marked the spring and fall equinoxes. A stickball field, now occupied by a practice skirmish, filled the southern half of the open square. Beyond the Four Winds charnel house on the west side were three conical burial mounds. A men's house dominated the southeast corner, and various Earth Clan council houses filled in on the sides, each subordinate to High Chief Green Chunkey and Horned Serpent House.

Turning his attention to the palace, Horn Lance nodded to the warriors standing guard at the foot of the stairs. Here, too, were a collection of individuals who had, or thought they had, business with Green Chunkey. Deer Clan, Panther Clan, Fish Clan, Hawk and Bear Clan, they waited for their chance at an audience.

Horn Lance strode forward, fully aware that he cut quite a figure in his formal Itza dress with its remarkable textiles, parrot, macaw, and toucan feather splays, all accented by the exotic wrist and ankle bands.

"Who comes?" the commander of the guard asked, fully aware of Horn Lance's identity.

"Please inform High Chief Green Chunkey that his cousin Horn Lance is returned from the distant south and would brief the high chief on the arrival of the Itza Lord Thirteen Sacred Jaguar and its implications for the Horned Serpent House."

"The high chief is expecting you, honored lord."

Horn Lance barely stifled a grin as the onlookers oohed and awed, their eyes gone large. He added a bit of spring to his steps as he started up the stairs in the commander's wake.

At the top, he reflexively bowed and touched his forehead as he passed the Horned Serpent guardian posts. Then he followed the commander across the courtyard and into the plaster-sided palace with its high thatch roof.

The interior was shabbier than he remembered, but then, so was much of Cahokia. In his youth he had thought this the second most splendid palace in the world after the Morning Star's. Now the carvings and trophies hanging on the walls, the interlinked Four Winds spirals behind the dais on the back wall, the carved bed frames and coverings, the storage pots and boxes beneath them all seemed rustic and crude.

Green Chunkey sat on the raised dais, his fingers ruffling the cougar hide covering beneath his litter. A line of nobles, most of them Horn Lance's relatives, stood behind. Green Chunkey himself looked but vaguely familiar with his faded serpent tattoos on his cheeks, the same blocky, if sagging face. Along with the jowls, Green Chunkey had developed a corpulent belly that hung over his apron. The eyes, however, hadn't changed. Horn Lance would have known those keen and crafty orbs anywhere.

"Hello, Cousin." Horn Lance gave the slightest of bows, the touch to his forehead fleeting, the gesture that of an equal meeting his peer.

"So, Horn Lance is returned from exile. Pardoned by the Morning Star himself. You look hale and hearty, old friend. And what, in the name of Piasa's balls, are you wearing?"

"This, Cousin, is the dress of an elite Itza warrior. The mark of an honored man among the distant lords. While it is rare for a vulgar barbarian—which is what the Itza considered me in the beginning—I managed to distinguish myself in the command of warriors in battle."

He paused, knowing he had a rapt audience. "The people in the far south—the Itza, Yucateca, Putun, and Ch'ol—believe that their warfare is an extension of the conflict of the gods. That they are participating in ritual battles between Tlaloc, Chac, Waxaklahun Kan, and the other deities. They think conflict in this world is a mirror image of an eternal battle being fought in the Spirit World—a sacred parallel to the realm of the gods. Their actions in this world influence the outcome, and vice versa, of combat between the gods. The link between the worlds lies in the Power of the *kukul.*"

He paused for effect. "I took a more pragmatic view, one less bounded by ritual and oriented toward destroying my enemies with the greatest efficiency. It's a delicate Dance, winning without offending ritual tradition."

Green Chunkey smiled thinly. "Perhaps the Morning Star was correct to banish you all those years ago. Better that you distinguish your ambition among foreign Nations than here."

"Indeed!" Horn Lance tapped his Itza breastplate. "But fate and the ways of Power have brought me back."

"Why?"

Horn Lance glanced at the line of nobles behind Green Chunkey. They were hanging on his every word. By nightfall his pronouncements would be all over Cahokia.

"The miracle of a resurrected god knows no borders. Word of the Morning Star's resurrection travels out from

Cahokia like a great wave, washing upon distant shores. In both Maya and Itza beliefs the Morning Star is called Hun Ahau, and his wild brother is Yax Balam, who we know as 'Thrown-Away' boy, or the 'Wild One.' Together they travel to the Underworld, which the Maya call Xibalba, and play a ball game with the Lords of Death. Winning it, they bring their father back to life."

He spread his hands wide. "Sound familiar? Essentially, they believe the same things we do. And then, out of the north comes this story about Hun Ahau's essence being reincarnated in a human. But he hasn't come back among the Yucatec, the Putun, the Ch'ol or Itza. Not even among the Mixtec or Mexica. No indeed, he's said to be reincarnated somewhere in the hazy and barbaric north among the wild men in a benighted land."

Horn Lance waved his finger back and forth. "This, Cousin, has their priests, sorcerers, lords, and astronomers in a tizzy. If the stories are true, this is a theological dilemma. Why far-off Cahokia and not Chichen Itza, or the ruins of Tikal, or Copan, or even Teotihuacan?

"The Itza *multepal*, their ruling council, has sent Thirteen Sacred Jaguar to see if it's true that Hun Ahau has been resurrected at Cahokia."

"And now that Thirteen Sacred Jaguar has seen the Morning Star?" Green Chunkey leaned forward, chin braced on his palm.

Time to lie. "He needs to prove to himself that Morning Star really is, or is not, the reincarnated Hun Ahau. In the process of doing so, he will stay for a while as a representative of the *multepal*. His aspirations are to open relations between Cahokia and Chichen Itza. The first step is his marriage to Lady Night Shadow Star, which forges a bond between the two peoples."

As Green Chunkey thought, his fingers tapped his cheek. Finally he said to the others, "Leave us, please. I would speak to my cousin alone."

After everyone had filed out, Green Chunkey gestured intimately. "Now, Cousin, tell me what this really means . . . and who you really serve."

"What it really means? Morning Star House has admitted a water moccasin into its midst, and I am that serpent." Horn Lance smiled. "Let's call it sacred justice, Cousin. A new future is about to unfold, one in which Horned Serpent House will play a new and more exalted role. But first, a few potential problems must be dealt with. Now, tell me about my old wife Blue Heron. I want to know all about her."

Thirty-two

Seven Skull Shield wouldn't have used the term *skulking* to describe what he was doing. He would have called it watching. He hovered around the Traders who had displayed their wares on the eastern side of the Great Plaza.

Most attention, however, was on the stickball match being played in the southern half of the Great Plaza. Today it was two women's teams. Night Shadow Star's team, wearing black, was dedicated to Old-Woman-Who-Never-Dies. Her opponents, dressed in blue, played for the Thunderbirds, the giant ivory-billed woodpeckers who lived at the four corners of the world and whose mighty wings drove the various winds.

The two teams consisted of nearly a hundred women per side, each carrying two racquets made of willow splits, or other suitable wood, bent double to create a netted hoop in the far end. The challenge was to toss a small deerhide ball through the opposing team's goalposts. The rules were simple: A player could only catch or propel the ball with a racquet. No hands. Head-butting and holding of any kind were illegal. The play continued until one side scored twenty.

Two old men, both limping from a litany of long-ago injuries, toddled along the sidelines as referees. Each held a feather-topped stick that he could throw into the play to stop the action if he observed a penalty. If a score was made, one of the elders would carry the ball to center field, where he'd toss it between the two teams to resume play.

As Seven Skull Shield watched, the blue team had just scored and were now two ahead. The old white-haired referee waited, ball in hand, at the side of the field. With his feathered stick, he kept pointing at over-eager women as they panted and crouched, seeking to edge forward for advantage.

"Back! Back, I say."

Catcalls erupted from the blues, saying that the blacks were delaying the game and cowards. Night Shadow Star stepped forward, ordering her teammates, "Give them room."

With irritated sidelong looks, her teammates barely stepped back, racquets rising and falling as they tested their grips.

The elder tossed the ball, clearly favoring the blues, which brought howls of dismay from the blacks and their fans on the sidelines.

"Foul throw!" Seven Skull Shield himself bellowed.

One of the blues used her racquet to snatch the ball, pivot, and sling it to the far side of the field. A teammate neatly caught the ball and raced forward. Leading a mass of blue-clad players, she tried to flank the swarm of blacks that surged after her.

The resulting impact of bodies drove the blues out of bounds, scattering spectators like minnows before a trout.

The far-side referee tossed his staff into the melee, stopping action and demanding the ball, which, to the dismay of the blues and their proponents, he tossed to a black player.

"Center!" Night Shadow Star's cry carried, and the ball was successfully relayed to a young woman who in turn passed it to Night Shadow Star. By means of a feint, she handed it off. The woman who received it was immediately tripped by a blue. A knot of women collided, each fishing for the loose ball.

The thumps and smacks of bodies, grunts of pain, and hoarse screams of rage brought a smile to Seven Skull Shield's lips. Didn't matter if it was men or women playing. Stickball was not for the weak of heart.

One of the blacks, a hefty middle-aged woman, hammered an opening in the press that allowed her to fling the ball to a wiry young woman on the fringes. Deftly hooking the ball from the air, the receiver turned, flicking her racquet and sailing the ball to yet another. That woman, in turn, pelted toward the blue's goal. Defenders shifted to meet her. Despite her efforts to dodge, one of the defenders hit her full force, tumbling the young woman on the beaten grass.

Another free-for-all scramble for the ball found the blacks outnumbered. A series of rapid passes by the blues sent the ball down the outside, leaving the mass of players in the middle running to catch up.

Which was when Seven Skull Shield noticed Fire Cat. The Red Wing stood with feet braced, muscular arms crossed. His face was a mask of conflicting emotions as he watched the play.

Stepping over, Seven Skull Shield asked, "Think your lady can bring them back from two down?"

"She's done it before." Fire Cat seemed to bite off the words.

"I'm surprised to see her playing today. Heard that she's betrothed to that fancy-dressed foreign lord." He paused a beat. "Or is she not kindly disposed to that idea?"

"She'll do her duty," Fire Cat said. "Not that it's any concern of yours, thief."

At that moment, Seven Skull Shield caught sight of Night Shadow Star as she hammered an elbow into the side of an opponent's head, dropping the woman like a clubbed deer.

"Maybe playing today has certain recuperative aspects. She certainly doesn't look like a swooning dove overcome by impending marriage to the man of her dreams."

Night Shadow Star, teeth bared in a grimace, used a

shoulder to knock an opponent onto her ass as she cleared a
path to the action. A melee had broken out where women
crowded, racquets clattering, as they battled for the ball.

Fire Cat glared sidelong at Seven Skull Shield. "Don't . . .
say . . . another . . . word." The man was vibrating with rage.

Seven Skull Shield raised a soothing hand, sensing that the
Red Wing was teetering on the edge. "For what it's worth,
Fire Cat, I don't like the guy either. He's thick with Blue
Heron's ex-husband, and she trusts him less than last year's
moldy acorns. And remember the Little Sun's missing cloak?"

Barely mollified, Fire Cat asked, "You found it?"

Seven Skull Shield tilted his head toward the Men's
House, where the Natchez were congregated on the veranda
to watch the stickball game. "I found it in a storage box last
night while they were feasting up at the Morning Star's. It's
back at the Keeper's, safe for the moment. But that's between
you and me."

Fire Cat turned his thin-eyed glare on the Men's House.
The Itza lord was seated on a raised stool, his face placid as
the Natchez explained something to Dead Teeth, one of the
Itza's warriors, who in turn translated to the lord. From
the man's slight nod, it was obviously an explanation of the
game.

Seven Skull Shield stifled the urge to take a half step back
lest Fire Cat explode like an overheated water bottle. He had
the notion that if he whispered, "Let's go kill him," in the
Red Wing's ear, it would be like releasing an infuriated wolf
on a pack of clueless dogs.

"You. Skull," an accented voice intruded.

Seven Skull Shield turned to see Newe, Wooden Doll's
barbarian girl servant, arms crossed on her skinny chest,
one leg forward in an irritated stance. Her dark eyes hinted
of disdain. "She thought you be here."

"What's wrong?"

"Nothing. She say little man looking for you. Want talk."

"And where do I find the little man? At your master's?"

"He come Crazy Frog's. After dark. Tonight. You be there."
She turned on her heel, stalking away through the crowd.

Fire Cat, his anger slightly dulled, asked, "The little
man?"

"Flat Stone Pipe. Lady Columella's dwarf. On occasion
we share bits of gossip the other might find rewarding."

"Who is this Crazy Frog?"

"A man who knows more about playing chunkey than
even the Morning Star up there who supposedly invented it.
Crazy Frog lives for the games at River Mounds City."

Fire Cat glanced up at the sky. "You'd best be on your
way, thief. Or, given the way she talked to you, that skimp of
a girl will have your balls for missing that appointment." He
smiled slightly. "On second thought, stay. If she rips your
balls off, I can trade them for a sack of rat shit. Not that
they'd be worth it. Then I could dry them out and throw
them at Clay String when he annoys me."

"I can see you don't know much about women. After she
lifted my shirt, saw what a real man's shaft looks like, curiosity would get the better of her. By the time she'd exhausted herself, she'd have forgotten what she was after in
the first place."

Seven Skull Shield looked back at the stickball game,
where two women were helping a third off the field. She had
her arms over her companions' shoulders, feet stumbling
and dragging. Blood streamed from the dazed woman's
mouth and nose.

Fire Cat had wrinkled his nose in disgust. "You never
cease to amaze me."

"Yeah," Seven Skull Shield agreed, "underestimating my
effect on a woman is never a smart thing to do."

Thirty-three

They'd won by a mere point. Sweat trickled down Night Shadow Star's face as she gasped for breath. Her black-clad teammates leaped for joy, clacking their racquets together on high.

She felt alive.

Whistles and shrieks of delight arose from the sidelines where people were crowding around the stakeholders to collect their winnings. While for the most part entire fortunes weren't bet as they were during the ritual games held on ceremonial days, few missed the opportunity to wager on a practice scrimmage such as this.

She sucked a final deep breath, wincing at the feel of her bruised ribs. Her right breast was sore from a hit, and her elbows would be sporting bruises from the damage she'd inflicted on others. Tomorrow was really going to hurt.

Tucking a racquet under her arm, she wiped the sweat away and walked, loose-limbed, toward where Fire Cat waited on the sideline. His muscular arms were crossed, a ghost of a smile on his lips.

She shot him a sly grin. "Well? Right up to the last heartbeat, Power alone knew how that one was going to end."

"Wasn't even a contest, Lady."

"Really? What did you see from the sidelines that I couldn't on the field?"

"Overall? Better play among the blues, but to make up for it the blacks had you."

"I didn't make a single point, and I barely even got the ball during those last plays."

"No, Lady. But I counted. They dedicated no less than ten women to cover you. They were so concerned with containing the threat you posed, your teammates were consistently left open to score."

A flicker of delight warmed in what had been an angry and depressing day. Not only had she enjoyed almost a hand's time during which her world had become the game, but someone had actually recognized her contribution.

She gave him another smile, saying, "All games should be as—"

"Lady Night Shadow Star?" a voice interrupted.

She turned, seeing the Natchez squadron first, the one called Wet Bobcat. He bowed, touching his fingers to his forehead.

"What is it?"

"I am asked . . ." the man swallowed, obviously nervous. "The Itza lord, he would talk with you."

"Would he? I thought he didn't speak our tongue. I find it even more interesting that you do." She studied him through a slitted eye.

"As a youth I served here. In Cahokia. For my people. I learn to speak, yes?" Wet Bobcat told her. "It was one of the reasons I was chosen to accompany the Little Sun and Itza lord." He smiled weakly. "I am . . . the words sometimes . . . um, come poorly."

"Then perhaps I should speak to the Itza when the words cannot become mangled and a misunderstanding be born."

"Oh, no." Wet Bobcat waved his arms. "He would know about game. Why you, a noble, play? If your life is forfeit if you lose."

She shot a glance at the Itza; their gazes locked. Bracing her racquets over her shoulder, she marched toward him and stepped up on the veranda where he was seated beside the *kukul*. She could feel the thing's Power. The War Serpent watched her with malignant green eyes, its fanged snarl provoking images of Piasa's gaping mouth in the instant before it had crushed her head.

The Itza's warriors stepped back to accommodate her as she strode arrogantly onto the veranda—a brazen act to hide her discomfort at the churning unease the *kukul* had triggered. She pointedly fought to ignore the thing.

Without his makeup and mask, Thirteen Sacred Jaguar looked oddly ordinary. She also realized he was a head shorter than she. And when it came to heads, his was curiously shaped with jutting cheekbones, receding jaw, and a broad, back-slanting forehead that accented his hooked nose. His eyes looked slightly oversized in his wide face, and she realized that his head had been purposely deformed. They'd bound his skull as an infant to flatten the forehead and back—a fact that hadn't been apparent in his ceremonial dress.

The four Itza warriors stood behind him, also looking odd with their deformed heads, but they carried themselves well, as blooded warriors should. Their hard eyes were inspecting her from head to toe, and perhaps lingering a little too long on her breasts.

Thirteen Sacred Jaguar, too, was staring, something distasteful in his eyes as his gaze ran up her long legs, lingered on her hips and flat stomach, and finally fixed on her naked breasts. Only then did a slight smile cross his lips.

"Translate, Natchez," she ordered. "Tell the lord of the Itza that I play for the Powers of the Underworld and the glory of Piasa and Old-Woman-Who-Never-Dies. The rules are to score twenty points. In desperation people have been known to wager their lives when fortune has forsaken them. I play because I'm good at it. And I enjoy myself."

She gave him a threatening smile. "And, as you saw today, my life wasn't forfeit. First, I hadn't bet it, and second, I ensured that my team didn't lose."

She turned, having delivered her message.

Thirteen Sacred Jaguar barked something, and the Natchez cried, "Wait!"

She hesitated at the edge of the veranda, shooting a glance over her shoulder. Fire Cat was half a step behind her, clearly uncomfortable. The Itza warriors were wide-eyed, muttering angrily to each other.

The Natchez spread his arms, chattering to the Itza, his hands flying as he tried to sign the words he didn't know.

One of the warriors, a muscular man with curious snake tattoos running up his arms, stepped up to Night Shadow Star, speaking incomprehensible Itza in a low and hostile voice, obviously angry.

"You might want to take a step back." Fire Cat interposed himself between Night Shadow Star and the angry Itza. The warrior thumped Fire Cat hard on the chest, knocking him back a half step.

"Hold!" Night Shadow Star ordered an instant before Fire Cat launched himself at the man.

"Wait! Wait!" the Natchez was crying as the other Itza started forward to back up their friend. "Stop this!"

Thirteen Sacred Jaguar, still seated, snapped some command, and the Itza warriors backed up, fuming, their smoldering gazes flicking from Fire Cat to her and back.

"Anything else?" she asked, prepared to leave.

"Lady, please," the Natchez pleaded. "It is . . . misunderstanding."

"I warned you that might happen."

"It is way you spoke. Tone of voice. The lord Thirteen Sacred Jaguar's men think you not show . . . um, what is word? Honor? No, is way you say . . ."

"A lack of respect?" Fire Cat tossed out, his sour smile no doubt meant to further incite the Itza.

"Yes! He is lord. Lady need to address him with proper behavior. Show respect."

She pointed, finger like a lance. Thirteen Sacred Jaguar's eyes widened, and his warriors hissed like angry snakes. "As he is a guest in Cahokia, I was kind enough to interrupt my schedule and answer his questions."

"But it is not the way the Itza treat—"

"I don't care how the Itza are treated at home. I may have to marry him, but by spit and fire, I do not have to respect him. Respect is earned, and he has a long way to go to earn mine."

She turned, stalking off the veranda, aware that a sizeable Cahokian crowd had gathered and were watching with amazed delight.

The obnoxious Itza warrior started off the porch in pursuit as the Natchez translated Night Shadow Star's words.

Fire Cat wheeled to meet him, only to have the warrior called back by Thirteen Sacred Jaguar's harsh order.

"Piss and vomit, Fire Cat," she said through gritted teeth, "and I was having such a good day. What came over me?"

"He did, Lady," Fire Cat answered. "The way he was looking at you? I was ready to take him apart myself."

"I have to be smarter than this. More in control."

"Are you sure?"

"What do you mean?"

"Lady, not all battles are won by wits and guile." Fire Cat was tossing a hard look over his shoulder at the Itza warrior. "Sometimes it comes down to blood and fury."

Thirty-four

The warm evening came as a relief after the hot and muggy day. A thousand insects silvered the sunset skies; they hovered on diaphanous wings over the ponds and lakes. Which, of course, presaged a miserable swarm of mosquitoes as the skies darkened. Cahokia was a haven for mosquitoes, with its oxbow lakes, creeks, and marshes. And the summer had been a wet one. Remarkable stands of corn and bountiful gardens, like all things in life, were counterbalanced by the humming misery of endless airborne bloodsuckers.

Grease, puccoon, larkspur, gumweed, and any other combination of insect repellents had been in great demand. Some said that what was asked for in Trade for a good repellent was criminal.

Heeding that, Seven Skull Shield stole a pot of something odd-smelling from a roadside stand, figuring one good crime deserved another.

Now he strode through the thick warren of society houses, warehouses, craft shops, temples, and granaries. His nose wrinkled at the sweet stench of a Panther Clan charnel house when he wound through the densely packed clutter around River Mounds City. He followed a beaten path in the black sandy soil to where Crazy Frog's two-story house rose beside what passed as an avenue.

Fronting the structure was a relatively spacious yard with a large ramada and a round sweat lodge off to the side. A collection of gaudily dressed athletic young men had gathered around the central fire pit. A cadre of equally adorned young women laughed and ate behind them. This was the nightly gathering of victorious chunkey players and their women. To be invited to Crazy Frog's for whatever feast Mother Otter had concocted was considered to be a high honor.

Seven Skull Shield stopped short, batting at a mosquito that hummed in defiance of the greasy mixture he'd slathered over his skin. Crazy Frog had five wives as of the moment, each of them remarkably attractive in her own way. Call them exquisite.

But it was Mother Otter, the oldest, that always left Seven Skull Shield sighing. That she was ten years his senior, had borne twelve children, and for the most part treated him like scum didn't matter. She just had something—a special quality that stated "I am all woman, and more than you can handle." He'd been fascinated for years.

Now he watched her as she moved gracefully around the fire, collecting plates, sharing jokes with the chunkey players, and giving more than one that lift of the eyebrow that so convincingly communicated a dismissive wry amusement.

Seven Skull Shield chuckled at himself and started forward, tired from his hurried journey and wishing he'd stopped to steal more than mosquito repellent. His stomach was empty.

As he walked into the firelight, Mother Otter glanced up, her full-lipped smile tightening into a thin line.

"Greetings, Mother Otter," Seven Skull Shield told her with a lascivious grin. "You ready to toss that withered wreckage you're married to and run off with a man who'd give you what you deserve?"

"Assuming I could ever find such a man, he'd know I deserved better than to be plagued by two-footed vermin and thieves. And that means he'd drive the likes of you away with a club." Her forced smile tightened. "So, you'd better be grateful that I stay with Crazy Frog. Among his few failings, he tolerates you on occasion."

The chunkey players laughed, and Seven Skull Shield's grin widened. "You've always been my favorite, Mother."

Her frozen smile bent into a wince. "And you've always been my worst nightmare, thief." She hooked a thumb. "He wants to see you around back." She hesitated. "Oh, and I know you're driven to steal stuff, but could you leave the contents of the latrine alone this time?"

The chunkey players broke into unrestrained guffaws, and she turned her attention back to the plates.

Shaking his head, Seven Skull Shield made his way around the corner of the house to the rear, where Crazy Frog's storage building was wedged between three structures. The only way in was through the narrow passage. Like usual, a large man armed with a war club stood in the shadows.

"Who comes?"

"Seven Skull Shield. Crazy Frog sent for me."

"You know how it's done?"

"Been here before." Seven Skull Shield walked up to the door, called out his name, and slipped under the heavy cloth hanging, then parted the thick curtains that allowed him into the room. A second man, club in hand, gave him a nod instead of bashing his brains in.

The room was larger than it looked from the outside despite the double-set log walls. Here Crazy Frog kept his wealth. Most of it he'd won betting on chunkey games. The rest came from less savory activities. As a result of his wealth and political acumen, the man had built a network of obligations and alliances throughout the riverfront community. Some agreement had been brokered with High

Chief War Duck, which created a mutually beneficial relationship.

Crazy Frog reclined on a litter chair placed atop two large and ornately carved wooden boxes. He had his elbows braced on the chair arms, feet kicked out before him. The rest of the room was packed with boxes, bales, baskets, and shelving brimming with pots, carvings, statuary, and other prestige goods.

Across from him, atop a thick and folded buffalo robe, sat the dwarf known as Flat Stone Pipe. When standing, the little man's head barely reached the middle of Seven Skull Shield's thigh. But only a fool judged Flat Stone Pipe by his size. He served Matron Columella, the ruler of Evening Star Town and the territory west of the river. Though Columella's younger brother—a man named Burned Bone—had succeeded High Dance as high chief of Evening Star House, she still called the shots.

That she had survived in the first place, let alone emerged supreme after Walking Smoke's treachery and the burning of her palace, was a testament to her political skill. In addition, Flat Stone Pipe's acumen and network of informers had been indispensable. Rumor had it that he was not only Columella's lover, but the father of several of her children.

The little man had his head cocked, inspecting Seven Skull Shield.

Seven Skull Shield gave him a smile. "I hope whatever it is turns out to be worth it. I left a remarkable stickball game to make it here in time."

"I'm delighted that you still have amusements. I hear you've come on hard times," Flat Stone Pipe said thoughtfully. "Old friends would sooner associate with maggot-infested corpses than be seen talking to you."

"They'll come around. Everyone likes a little charm in their lives. And if I'm anything, it's charming."

Crazy Frog chuckled. "You couldn't charm a fly off a

week-old turd." His expression hardened. "Was the Keeper satisfied with the information I provided?"

"She was. Wish you'd had something that would have let us keep the Natchez Little Sun alive. It would have made a lot of things easier."

"How so?" Flat Stone Pipe asked.

"He'd have been the new Great Sun."

Crazy Frog lifted his hands. "What would that have changed? The Natchez would have still brought the Itza here. What's one Great Sun instead of another?"

"Maybe nothing," Seven Skull Shield admitted, then added, "Maybe everything."

"The Itza is really going to marry Night Shadow Star?" Flat Stone Pipe asked.

"It appears so." Seven Skull Shield glanced back and forth between the two. "Why, specifically, did you ask me here?"

Flat Stone Pipe gave him a thoughtful appraisal. "A whispered voice told me that the man called Horn Lance, the one who came in advance of the Itza, paid a visit to High Chief Green Chunkey. Among other things, they talked about the Keeper and her allies. In particular, anyone who might have acted as her agent in stealing that now-infamous feather cloak you were looking for."

Seven Skull Shield kept his face blank. "I see. Anyone found it yet?"

"You might know better than I. Word is that Green Chunkey mentioned a certain thief who is known to work for the Keeper. Horn Lance has begun making inquiries among various parties about how to locate the thief." Flat Stone Pipe paused. "Fortunately, Horn Lance is new to Cahokia and its ways. He hasn't asked the right people."

"Yet," Crazy Frog added. "But he will."

Flat Stone Pipe pasted a humorless smile on his face. "Loyalty is such a fleeting thing, isn't it? Old friends, once boon companions, suddenly find themselves disposed to sell out a comrade for the price of an exotic Natchez pot or re-markable Itza knickknack."

"Why does he want me?" Seven Skull Shield scratched his cheek. "I'm not going to tell him anything, even if I knew it. And taking me isn't going to gain him any leverage with the Keeper. She could give a moldy acorn if I get in trouble or not."

"You took the cloak. An act that both humiliated and threatened Horn Lance and the Natchez." Crazy Frog leaned forward and propped his chin. "You are one of the Keeper's agents. Capturing you, torturing you to death, and dropping your body someplace public sends her a most eloquent message."

"Why warn me? This Horn Lance might have Traded you some extraordinary Itza artifact in return for my hide."

"I might still do it," Crazy Frog mused. "Having you gone would simplify my first wife's life. She wouldn't have to dedicate so much of her day searching for ever-more-derogatory ways to describe you to people who haven't made your charming acquaintance."

Seven Skull Shield glanced at the dwarf and lifted an eyebrow.

Flat Stone Pipe said, "You did me a service once. In re-turn, I can keep you safe. It might mean removing yourself to Evening Star Town until—"

"I appreciate that, but I'll take my chances."

Crazy Frog added, "You won't know who to trust. They'll be hunting you everywhere."

Seven Skull Shield shrugged. "This is my city. Nobody knows it like I do."

"It's your life, no matter how little you value it." Crazy Frog shook his head.

"My offer remains open." Flat Stone Pipe pointed with one of his small fingers. "I pay my debts."

"Anything else?" Seven Skull Shield asked.

"The Itza," Crazy Frog said. "What does his arrival here

mean? Are there going to be more of them coming? Is there going to be Trade?"

Seven Skull Shield laughed bitterly. "There's only going to be trouble. Come on, think! The Itza and Horn Lance arrived among the Natchez, offering the potential for miraculous Trade. The next thing, the old Great Sun and White Woman are dead. A new lineage is in charge, and to keep it that way, they kill Nine Strikes before he even knows he's the new Great Sun."

"Then why even bring the Itza to Cahokia? Why not keep him and his potential Trade in Natchez?" Flat Stone Pipe wondered.

"Because he came all this way to see the Morning Star." Seven Skull Shield shifted on his feet since there wasn't room to pace. "The Natchez don't want to be just another bead on the string, one among a series of Nations between Cahokia and Chichen Itza. They want it all."

Flat Stone Pipe, smart as he was, straightened. "That means the Natchez have to discredit Cahokia and the Morning Star. Make it so the Itza have no reason to seek relations with us."

"How would they do that?" Seven Skull Shield fingered his chin.

Crazy Frog shrugged. "Lots of ways. Incite the Houses to turn on each other. Nothing new there. And Horn Lance has already started laying the groundwork with Green Chunkey. Attempt an assassination of the Itza lord, murder some of his warriors, make him think the Morning Star is a fraud like so many people up and down the river already do. The choices are endless just as long as they end up with the Itza in a canoe headed back to the loving arms of the Natchez."

"Or," Flat Stone Pipe offered, "it could be that even Horn Lance is being played."

"Could be," Crazy Frog agreed. "However it works out, why do I think the Natchez end up as the only winners?"

"Because they are the only ones who know what the real

goal of the game is." Flat Stone Pipe pressed his small hands together. "In the meantime they sow discord. Horn Lance, brewing trouble among the Houses, keeps everyone off balance. The perfect distraction."

"And the Itza?" Seven Skull Shield wondered.

"He's the fool in the center, completely unaware that he's being played by everyone." Flat Stone Pipe gave a shrug of his diminutive shoulders. "That doesn't mean he, too, isn't dangerous in his own way. Even a fool can let loose a maelstrom."

"He'll be lucky to get out of this alive," Seven Skull Shield said thoughtfully.

"No more so than you," Flat Stone Pipe reminded. "The Natchez want you dead. And in light of what we've been talking about, killing you might have just become a really important part of their plan."

Thirty-five

Matron Columella wondered if she shouldn't have made the journey to the Morning Star's palace in central Cahokia so that she might be present at the arrival of the Itza lord. Not going might have been a mistake. But she still had nightmares about the last time she'd been in the Morning Star's presence. Not only had her fate hung by a thread, but so, too, had her children's and her dead brother's children.

Being anywhere close to the Morning Star's physical presence always carried an element of risk. Living gods, she'd discovered, were capricious things.

She ran her gaze around her palace, fully aware of the impression it would make. The walls were freshly plastered, still smelling of damp clay. A sweet smell of fresh-cut grass perfumed the air since the last of the new thatch had only been tied to the center pole six days ago. Looking up, she could see the new peeled-pole rafters, bindings, and honey-colored ridge pole. Smoke and soot had barely fingered them, let alone darkened the wood.

Everything, down to the tamped clay underfoot, was fresh and new, which only partially excused the stark white plaster covering the bare walls that left the room looking huge, cavernous, and unfurnished.

But then all of her old furnishings had been burnt. Right down to the statuary. Victims of Walking Smoke's madness. The ashes of her lineage's trophies, carvings, and mementos were now irrevocably buried beneath her feet, covered by the thick layer of clay that capped her old mound.

She glanced around at her household staff, all busy with their usual duties. Her children, nieces, and nephews were gone. She'd insisted they accompany Burned Bone, acting in his new role as high chief, as he led a pilgrimage to the Sacred Caves two days' travel to the west. Her hope was that getting out, seeing the world, would help settle their souls, heal the scars and soothe the nightmares left by the things they'd witnessed as Walking Smoke conducted his perverted rituals.

"Worried about the children?" Flat Stone Pipe asked from where he sat beside her seat on the dais. He'd always been too good at reading her facial expressions.

"They'll be fine. An entire squadron of Deer Clan warriors is accompanying them. And Burned Bone is fully aware of the importance of caring for them."

Flat Stone Pipe leaned his head back, staring up at the new ceiling. "We were told when Horn Lance's canoe landed. What's taking him so long?"

"Plotting treason should never have been done in haste. Though I find it fascinating that he comes to me immediately after paying his respects to Green Chunkey. Are we really that transparent?"

Flat Stone Pipe glanced sidelong at her. "You have something of a reputation for causing trouble, my love."

The corners of her lips twitched. "By coming straight to me, he might as well wave a burning torch, jump up and down, and shout out to Blue Heron, 'Hey! I'm plotting with your enemies!' Or is the man no smarter than a stone in a creek?"

"Hard to say until I can actually take his measure." He shot her a smile.

Cracking Clamshell, one of her cousins bound in service, hurried in, stating, "His litter is at the foot of the stairs, Lady. Shall I escort him in?"

"Please. Bid our visitor welcome."

"And now we shall see," Flat Stone Pipe whispered.

"The rest of you"—Columella raised her voice—"find something to do outside, if you please. I would speak to the Itza's emissary alone."

As they scurried out, Flat Stone Pipe asked, "Should I be in my hole?"

He referred to the hollow under her dais, a place from which he could hear but not be seen.

"No, stay where you are. I want you to see his expressions, watch the movements of his body. If I desire your counsel, I want it ready at hand."

"Gladly."

Cracking Clamshell appeared at the double doors leading out onto the veranda, announcing, "Lord Horn Lance of Horned Serpent House seeks your counsel, Lady. A man of the Four Winds Clan, now in service to the Itza Lord, he asks that you might receive him."

"Send him in."

She lifted an eyebrow as he strode in. *So this is the banished lord?* The exotic outfit with its crimson feathers, peculiar breastplate, and breechcloth, the interesting arm guards and feathers, gave the man a gaudy and outlandish look. That he hadn't painted his face struck her as alien.

His stride was arrogant as he approached, stopping just before the central hearth, bowing, and touching his forehead.

"Welcome, Horn Lance, of the Horned Serpent House, of the Four Winds Clan." And she pointedly added, "Servant of the Itza."

"Matron," he replied with a smile. "I thank you for receiving me." He glanced around at the huge empty room. "Have I come at a bad time? It seems that no one is here? I would have thought the renowned Evening Star House would be thronging with household servants and supplicants from the Earth Clans you administer."

She smiled. *Arrogant bit of two-legged trouble, aren't you?* "Your timing is perfect, Horn Lance. The high chief is off on a pilgrimage to First Woman's caves. Evening Star Town and the lands it administers is a well-run and efficient concern. The Earth Clan chiefs who serve me know their jobs well. My business with them was concluded in a short session this morning. As for the household staff, I dismissed them in order that we might speak more freely."

She purposefully did not introduce Flat Stone Pipe. If Horn Lance knew who he was, Flat Stone Pipe needed no introduction. If he hadn't a clue, he'd no doubt pass the dwarf off as ornamental. In which case, all the better.

"I see." Horn Lance continued his inspection of her new palace, the action an insolent breach of protocol.

"If you'd like I could summon one of the engineers. We're still completing the construction. He could show you the details." She allowed just the right bite to her words.

"No, but thank you." He turned his attention to her, apparently having achieved exactly the effect he'd wanted. "I would rather discuss the arrival of the Itza, and what it might mean for Evening Star House."

"And what might that be?" She leaned forward, fingers steepled.

Horn Lance, ignoring Flat Stone Pipe, inclined his head in the slightest. "The opening of a whole new world, Lady. With the arrival of the Itza, opportunities present themselves before your very eyes."

"What sort of opportunities?"

He fixed her with his clever dark eyes, a faint smile on his lips. "Why, High Matron, anything you might have imagined—even if it seemed impossible—might suddenly be within your reach." His smile widened. "Assuming you make the proper choices and alliances."

"Anything I might imagine?" She lifted an eyebrow. "That covers a lot of territory."

"Matron, for all intents and purposes, with the arrival of Thirteen Sacred Jaguar in Cahokia, the size of our world just doubled. There's now a great deal more territory, and Trade, and prestige, and those with the means are going to wield their will like mighty fists."

"Presuming those in authority seize the opportunity," she added.

If Horn Lance's grin grew any wider it was going to split his face. "Your reputation is that you are a remarkably clever woman, Matron. I'm delighted to discover that was no exaggeration."

She tapped her fingertips together, giving him a prolonged inspection before asking, "Then perhaps I'm at a loss. My sources have informed me that the Itza lord is marrying into the Morning Star House. It would seem the chance to capitalize on your claimed opportunities has already been offered to others."

He nodded, took a couple of paces to the right, and shot her a sidelong glance. "I should not take this liberty, Matron. And hopefully it will not turn out to be the case, but what would happen if the living god was demonstrated to have some . . . shall we say, questionable attributes?"

He pressed his palms together as he took another step. "What if he were questioned by someone knowledgeable about the Beginning Times, and the Morning Star couldn't answer the questions correctly? If it turned out there was a *different*, more *accurate* chronicle of the Morning Star's activities in the Beginning Times?"

"I don't follow you."

He shrugged. "It probably doesn't matter, Matron. If different stories exist, surely a *living god* will know all of the variations told about him. Even in far-off Nations."

Interest piqued, she shifted. "You suddenly have my full attention. And yes, surely a Spirit Being as Powerful as the

Morning Star would know all the stories, no matter which people told them. But what if he *didn't*? Such a thing could eventually lead to the collapse of his rule."

"Unless an alternative were provided," Horn Lance admitted. "A different miracle. Something the people could marvel over. Perhaps a miracle from the distant and exotic south. An Itza miracle, like a soaring stone pyramid carved into the shape of Hunga Ahuito, or Horned Serpent. Perhaps something built on *this* side of the river, and administered by a different House than the Morning Star's?"

Columella settled back in her seat atop the dais. "A most fascinating concept, Lord Horn Lance. Fascinating indeed."

She glanced down at Flat Stone Pipe, seeing the thousand thoughts that now possessed his souls.

How, she wondered, should a smart woman play this?

And if she bet wrong?

The last time, she'd sidestepped the Morning Star's wrath by the narrowest of margins. The memory of her terror as she knelt before the Morning Star's dais, her fate and her family's hanging by a thread, sent a shiver through her. More than anything, she'd love to turn the tables on Morning Star House, see the living god trembling as disaster, pain, and hideous death seemed inevitable.

"Lord Horn Lance," she said, coming to her decision, "Evening Star House is delighted to offer its support to the Itza high chief. Please do not hesitate to ask if there's any service we might offer."

Horn Lance bowed his head low, touching his forehead.

At her side, Flat Stone Pipe stared up at her in disbelief.

Yes, this would have to be played very, very carefully.

Thirty-six

Blue Heron knew she was dreaming. Dream or not, the sensation of impending doom continued to grow. Her heart now pounded in her chest. A tickle played through her guts.

In the dream the wedding was her sole responsibility, and to her horror, the feast had been presented half raw, half burned. The people lining the room, eating the stuff, were making faces. Then they began to vomit, and worms wriggled in the goo they expelled onto the floor.

Through it all, the Morning Star sat, silent, no expression on his painted face. All he did was watch her, his dark eyes seething with rage.

She kept fidgeting, pulling on her fingers. The bride and groom sat before the fire, looks of disgust on their faces as they watched the guests averting their faces.

In the back, musicians played poorly, hammering on drums, tooting on flutes, and plucking bowstrings. Someone was singing an off-key song about raccoon kits. Raccoon was a harbinger of the dead, so the song reeked of sacrilege and poor taste.

At the other end of the room, the *tonka'tzi* stood, arms crossed, shaking her head as she gave Blue Heron an outraged glare.

Blue Heron wheeled about, appalled to see the Itza dressed in his gaudy regalia. With one hand, he ripped off the colorful loincloth with its feathered and tasseled ends. His penis jutted stiff and proud as he grabbed Night Shadow Star by the hair, pulling her through the plates of half-eaten food spread before them.

With one hand he held her by the throat, his other ripping the black wedding skirt from her hips. As she struggled among the plates, Thirteen Sacred Jaguar screamed to one of his alien gods and used a knee to spread Night Shadow Star's thighs. With a final cry, he dropped onto her struggling body and rammed his shaft into her. . . .

At which moment, Blue Heron blinked wide awake.

For a time, she stared up at her dark ceiling, heart pounding. She couldn't seem to catch her breath.

It had been a long and miserable day spent in planning. They had two days left. The wedding—given the Itza's status and the Morning Star's interest—had to be extravagant and without flaw. A statement of Cahokia's grandeur for their exalted guest.

And, while it wasn't her sole responsibility—that fell to Wind—she'd take part of the blame if anything went wrong.

She filled her lungs, wishing her souls would still and allow her to sleep. Resettling, she lay there, a thousand thoughts vying for attention.

Something clunked in the night.

She froze.

After what seemed like an eternity, she was just drifting off when a sandal scuffed the matting beside her bed.

Images of the assassin who'd tried to slit her throat mere months ago returned, and terror washed through her.

She could see the dark form as it shifted, bending over one of her storage boxes. The lid was back, the stealthy figure reaching inside, fingering her folded skirts and capes within.

Enough is enough!

She angrily threw her blanket back, lurched to her feet, shouting, "Thief! I've had it! If I ever catch you in my—"

The dark shadow moved like a blur, twisting around toward her. Something seemed to leap at her face. Lights blasted behind her eyes, pain, like lightning in her head.

She remembered falling, hitting the side rails on her bed before slamming onto the floor. Dancing dots of light filled her vision, her ears ringing. She tasted blood in her mouth.

Stunned, she was finally able to gasp a breath.

"Keeper?" Smooth Pebble's panicked voice penetrated her dazed pain.

The next thing she knew, the berdache leaned next to her, lifted her, and asked, "Blood and dung, Keeper, are you all right?"

"Did you see . . . ?"

"Just a shadow running across the room and out the door. Did he hurt you? Are you all right?"

She forced herself to wipe the blood from her lips and nose. They were stinging with that numbing pain. Arms, legs, everything still seemed to work. "He just hit me. In the face! The pus-licking maggot hit me in the face!"

Smooth Pebble, her expression hidden in the darkness, was looking around. "Who hit you? What was he after? Was it my imagination, or did I hear you say it was the thief?"

"No. Not Seven Skull Shield." She pushed herself out of Smooth Pebble's lap. "Somebody else."

"Who would dare?"

"Someone with a great deal to lose," she whispered, wishing her nose would stop leaking blood.

Thirty-seven

In the softness of her bed, Night Shadow Star stared up into the darkness. If she had asked the soul flier, Rides-the-Lightning, about the dream she'd just had, he would have told her that it was a longing of the souls, and that if left unfulfilled, it would lead to soul sickness and illness. The old shaman would have told her to fulfill the need, or run the risk of any number of maladies.

What is wrong with me?

The dream had been so real, so perfect. He'd come to her, a smile on his face, warmth in his eyes. Laughing, he'd taken her by the hand, and told her it would be all right as he pulled her into his strong arms.

She'd melted against him, desperate for his strength, frantic for the feel of his body. The first slight tingle had grown to fill her pelvis, her breasts sensitive as they pressed against his chest. His lips had moved on the curve of her neck, nibbling, tickling, sending a thrill through her.

She had tightened her grip on him as though to crush him to her, only to feel herself shift as she was laid on a soft hide. The muscles beneath his warm skin knotted as he lowered himself to cover her. She'd reached down, guiding him into her warmth. No sooner had he filled her than her loins exploded in pulsating ecstasy.

The dream was an old companion that had slipped into her souls after Makes Three left for the north. It had intensified after news of his death.

Now she reached down, pressing gently on her tender ovaries.

Soul sickness. Longing.

In the past, it had always been her husband who had lifted his head to look at her as she gasped with pleasure.

This dream was different, unsettling.

She blinked, wishing there were some way she could forget that the man who'd raised himself to look into her eyes was Fire Cat.

Thirty-eight

Seven Skull Shield was used to being on the run. Normally, however, he had places to hole up. A jealous husband who might be searching for him in River Mounds City meant that Seven Skull Shield might relocate to the Grand Plaza, or up north to Serpent Woman Mounds. Never had anyone placed enough of a price on his head that he couldn't outbid the offended party and buy protection.

The very notion that he was being forced to hide—in *his* city—absolutely infuriated him. And by strangers, no less!

Late as it was, he made his way to Wooden Doll's. By this time, perhaps she'd finished entertaining her last man for the night.

As he slipped through the darkness, he noticed that a litter lay on the ground beside the ramada. Porters were scattered about, wrapped in their cloaks for protection from the mosquitoes.

Seven Skull Shield started past, feeling irritated, then one of the men sat up, scratching at his ear.

"Hey?" Seven Skull Shield called. "How long is your master going to be in there?"

The man squinted in the darkness. "Go away. He Traded

her an exquisite Natchez basket full of yaupon leaves for the entire night."

"He's a Natchez?" A cold fist clenched in his gut.

"Nah. Some Four Winds noble that's been down south. Haven't you heard? He came with an Itza!"

"Yes. I might have heard something about that."

Seven Skull Shield glared at the door, thinking about the man in there. All he had to do was wait until the porter drifted off to sleep. He could quietly unlatch the door. Wooden Doll had that stone hammer. Or there was the bone stiletto she hid by her bed in case a man got too rough. Or, for that matter, Seven Skull Shield could just pick up a length of firewood and beat Horn Lance to death.

He took a step toward the door.

Stopped.

His hands knotted into fists. So many problems would be solved. They'd never dare hunt him after this. He'd be doing the Keeper a huge favor, and maybe Night Shadow Star and the living god, too.

But it wasn't just him. What would Wooden Doll say? How would it change things if he killed a man in her bed? If it were anyone but Wooden Doll . . .

Turning on his heel, he stalked away into the night, a feeling of desolation aching between his souls.

Thirty-nine

The sun had cleared the eastern horizon by a couple of fingers; and the Morning Star's mound-top palace cast a long shadow to the southwest. From the feel of the humid air, it would be another hot and muggy day.

The stone cupped in Fire Cat's hand, he stared down the long chunkey court and tried to shake all the distractions from his souls. Tomorrow, Night Shadow Star would marry the Itza, and the man would move into her palace. His four smug warriors, and who knew how many Natchez, would accompany him.

Everything would be different.

What did that mean for Fire Cat? He was the one who ran the palace, slept outside her door, and kept her safe. He protected her back when she was out among the people. And what happened if the Itza raised a hand to strike her?

"I'll break his pus-rotted arm!"

The man will be her husband. You're nothing but her slave.

He glared all of his hate and anger at the chunkey court. The strip of clay seemed unconcerned.

Souls burning with frustrated rage, he started forward. With a roll of the shoulders, he released the stone. Shifting the lance, he launched it in a graceful arc just before the mark. As he trotted after it, he watched the lance drive itself into the clay a couple of arms' lengths short of the stone.

Muttering to himself, he picked up the lance and stamped the clay flat.

By Piasa's swinging balls, he *had* to do better than this. What was wrong with him? He'd never played this poorly in his life!

An image of the Itza flashed between Fire Cat's souls. The man was grinning, reaching for Night Shadow Star's naked body. Running his hands down her soft skin, cupping her breasts.

Emptiness and despair.

Stop it!

A knot of men stepped off the avenue that ran along the western side of the Morning Star's mound.

The hollow in Fire Cat's gut turned acid as he recognized the Natchez Little Sun. Accompanying Swirling Cloud were the Itza warriors. The one called Dead Teeth had a sneering grin. Split Bone reeked of insolence, while Shaking Earth had that quiet deadly quality about him. And finally there was Red Copal, the snake-tattooed piece of dung he'd wanted to destroy after the stickball game.

"In the name of the Morning Star," the Natchez interpreter, Wet Bobcat called. "Greetings."

"In the name of the Red Wing Clan, greetings yourself," he answered back, noticing that Swirling Cloud carried a stone and lance. "If you want to play, the Morning Star's courts are right over there. As his guests, you are welcome to use them. It is said they are the best in the world."

"Here will be fine," Wet Bobcat replied with a provocative smile. "These are Four Winds courts, yes? And the Morning Star has granted us the Four Winds Men's House. What is Four Winds is ours to use."

"Fine. Have at it." He gestured, stepping back to collect his cape and bag.

"My master, the Little Sun, is a player of some renown in the south." Wet Bobcat waved around. "I see no one here worthy of his challenge. He would show the Itza warriors how chunkey is played."

"He doesn't need a challenger to do that. If you will excuse me."

Dead Teeth muttered something to the Little Sun, the others all smirking and laughing.

Wet Bobcat smiled triumphantly, saying, "They understand why you are leaving. Swirling Cloud's reputation has no doubt traveled even as far as Cahokia. Perhaps there will be a player with the courage to face him somewhere else?"

Swirling Cloud's mocking smile added to the insult's sting. *Don't do this!*

But Fire Cat, livid, heard himself say, "My mistake. I didn't know he wanted to be beaten that badly in front of his guests. Of course I'll play him."

"What will you bet? That stone and lance against Swirling Clouds'?"

"They are not mine to bet."

"Ah, it is true that in extreme cases, a player can bet his life. Would you bet your life against Swirling Cloud's?"

Fire Cat cocked his jaw as he took Swirling Cloud's measure. No doubt he was a good player. It might even be worth finding out just how good. "My life is not mine to wager. Were it, and if the stakes were high enough, I would."

"Of course. You are a slave. I should have remembered. Your clothes, then?" Wet Bobcat asked. "Do you at least own them?"

"Against his stone and lance?"

"Of course." Wet Bobcat's smile was mocking as he turned to Swirling Cloud and rattled on in Natchez, the Itza warriors apparently catching a word or two as they all discussed it.

Red Copal was grinning, and to Fire Cat's surprise the man had little blue stones set into his front teeth. One day, he swore, he would knock those teeth out of the man's head.

Swirling Cloud said something, Wet Bobcat interpreting, "My master says we will play to—"

Fire Cat glared his annoyance at Swirling Cloud. "You speak our tongue fine. Why the charade of a translator?"

"You are a slave," Wet Bobcat told him. "Sun Born do not address other people's slaves."

The word sent a hot rage surging through him.

Swirling Cloud smirked in satisfaction as he shrugged out of his Natchez-cut cape and began to roll his shoulders. With a thin smile, he gestured that Fire Cat should take the first cast.

Stepping into position, Fire Cat took a deep breath. The time had come. All he had to do was concentrate, clear his souls of the distractions, and play. And it wasn't like his life hung in the balance.

He filled his lungs, led with this left foot, and started down the court. Time to win.

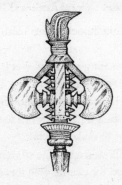

Forty

Seven Skull Shield had been walking since dawn. Down deep in his chest, just below his beating heart, a knot had pulled tight. Seeing Horn Lance's litter in front of Wooden Doll's festered like a cactus thorn.

He shouldn't have cared who she Traded herself to. That was her business. But to lay with a man who had put a price on Seven Skull Shield's head? Take his Trade? Gift him with the arts of her body?

"She couldn't have known," he growled.

But why, of all women, had Horn Lance gone to her?

"Because she's the best, fool."

Which didn't ease the hurt or loosen the constriction under his heart.

Surprised by the depth of her betrayal, he'd considered "borrowing" a canoe and rowing over to Evening Star Town. Maybe even signing on with a Trader and getting shut of Cahokia altogether. It wouldn't have been the first time Wooden Doll had driven him to such an extreme. But in the end, he had decided that even if they were after him, it was early in the game. Word wouldn't have circulated about how much the Itza would Trade in return for his sorry carcass.

And what was he going to do? Just turn tail and run? Go

to ground like a panicked mouse? He was the renowned Seven Skull Shield. Romancer of women, crafty thief, and clever raconteur of song and story.

No, two could play hunter, and he had the advantage. When it came to the back ways, who knew the city better? It would take at least a day for word to travel. And in that time, he had plans to make.

That said he followed a beeline straight down the Avenue of the Sun, headed for central Cahokia. He'd have to warn the Keeper that they were after him. But once that was done, he'd take the war right to the Itza and his sneaky Natchez allies.

"Just who do they think they're dealing with?" he muttered to himself. "Some clanless dolt of a dirt farmer? Some bit of human flotsam that can be discarded like an old pot? This is me! No one kicks me around like some old dog!"

Sometimes, he'd swear, the Spirit World heard him.

A dog's panicked squeal broke the early-morning stillness, and Seven Skull Shield fixed on the man ahead of him. In the center of the rutted boulevard, a wiry fellow in a dirty loincloth was tugging on a rope with one hand, beating a peculiar-looking dog with a length of wood and cursing.

The dog thrashed, trying to jerk free, growling and snapping at the club as the man cursed and swung. With each impact, the dog shrieked, trying to duck away.

Maybe it was because Seven Skull Shield still ached from the injustice of Wooden Doll's betrayal, or that he was feeling persecuted. Maybe it was because it had been a peaceful morning up that point. Or it might have been that nothing the dog might have done in the middle of the road could have merited such a beating.

"Hey! How about a little quiet?"

The man continued to whack the dog; the creature strangling on the tight end of the rope. The dog's eyes were rolling back in its head, the mouth gaping, tongue lolling and bloody. It staggered sideways and collapsed, lungs heaving against the restriction around its neck.

"Mind your own business," the man growled with a side-long glance before whacking the half-conscious dog again. "Stupid beast! Make me late?"

Again he clubbed the trembling dog.

When the skinny man raised the club yet again, Seven Skull Shield grabbed it and wrenched it away.

"What the . . . ? Give me that back!"

"Stop beating the dog."

It was something in the man's eyes: a violent rage that was burning through souls that had somehow grown to be twisted and sick. The dog-beater leaped at Seven Skull Shield. Maybe he was better at beating dogs. Or he'd forgotten the club.

Seven Skull Shield hammered him across the face, breaking his thin nose, peeling skin from the man's cheeks.

In surprise, the man staggered back, eyes unfocused. He stopped short, clawing for balance. Raising a hand to his face, he cried, "You *hit* me!"

"How does it feel?" Seven Skull Shield looked the wiry man up and down, seeing no evidence the dog had bitten him. "What did the dog do? Why were you beating it to death?"

The thin man wiped at the blood leaking from his nose, eyes squinting from the sting. "It ran off. Made me late."

"So beating it was going to make you on time?"

"I was teaching it a lesson! Why did you hit me?"

"Maybe I was teaching you a lesson."

"Just go away! It's my dog. I won it! It's a pack dog. Traded from the far-off Shining Mountains! The people there use them to fight the great silver bears. It's worth a fortune."

"It barely looks like it's more than a puppy!" Seven Skull Shield bent down, yanking the knotted rope loose so the animal could breathe.

As he did, the man pulled his leg back. Tipped off, Seven

Skull Shield ducked the kick, coming up under the man's leg and dumping him flat on his back. Before the fellow could rise, Seven Skull Shield rapped him on the side of the head.

"You don't learn." He glanced at the dog, now panting as its eyes started to clear. "And you're not good enough to deserve a dog. Not even one as ugly as this one is going to be."

With a flick of the wrist, he slipped the rope off the animal's neck. The dog, puppy, or whatever it was, struggled to its feet.

"Hey, you piece of two-footed dung! You just let my—"

Seven Skull Shield caught the man square under the chin, the club making a *smack-click* as it drove his jaws shut. Might have broken some teeth, too. Seven Skull Shield didn't care.

"Come on, dog," he called as he reached in his belt pouch for a length of jerky he'd stolen from a drying rack the night before. "Let's be gone before he comes to and makes me hit him again."

The puppy sniffed the dried meat suspiciously, then wolfed it down in two snaps of its rather impressive jaws.

Seven Skull Shield turned his steps eastward again, aware that people had ducked out of their houses, drawn by the screams and shouting.

He glanced back, seeing the dog, wobbling, but following along. Well, the beast was free. Like Seven Skull Shield, he could go wherever he willed.

Natchez and Itza be cursed for thinking otherwise.

Forty-one

Nothing. Not his ignominious capture at Red Wing Town. Not the deaths of his children. Not hanging, ready to die in the square. Not even his fear that he might break under torture. Nothing had ever unmanned and humiliated Fire Cat like watching the Natchez Little Sun make the final point.

Not *just* the final point.

The final *five* points!

Fire Cat had said nothing as he gritted his teeth, stripped off his breechcloth and sandals, and laid them on the ground before the Natchez.

He avoided the delighted eyes of the Itza and wished he could stuff his ears with mud to shut out their clicking and broken language as they laughed and joked.

Stunned and shamed, he walked on unsteady feet to pick up the beautiful black stone and lance. He would have lost them, had he bet. Thank Piasa's foul breath that they hadn't been his to lose.

Heart hammering, he made himself walk. The steps were instinctive, separate from any conscious thought. One foot ahead of the other. Back straight. Just walk.

His skin might have been on fire with shame.

I failed.

Better to die.

He could take one of the flint knives, or perhaps use the keen copper edge on Night Shadow Star's war club, and slice deeply into a wrist.

I will not have to look her in the eyes. Will not have to explain that I failed her. Failed my ancestors.

His vision blurred. *What would Uncle say?*

Thank the blessed Spirits that the man was dead.

From the time Fire Cat had been a child and Uncle had fitted that very first clay chunkey stone into his pudgy little hand, Uncle had schooled him on the game.

"It's a matter of soul and feeling," Uncle had said. *"You must be smooth. Live the cast the moment before you release the lance. See the arc as it follows the stone."*

And it had all deserted him.

Uncle would have wept.

On leaden feet, he stumbled toward Night Shadow Star's palace. People on the beaten path stopped and stared as he passed, his naked body a symbol of utter defeat. Vaguely he was aware of the dirt farmers, some packing loaded baskets, as they gawked and pointed. One of Night Shadow Star's cousins gaped openly, her servant giggling.

Two Four Winds warriors smirked and elbowed each other, finally having their moment as the once-arrogant Fire Cat avoided their eyes.

But the worst was the gloating Natchez and his pus-licking Itza. They followed along behind, waving Fire Cat's breechcloth like a flag. They kept calling out in their incomprehensible language, as if invoking their rogue gods.

Fire Cat placed his foot on Night Shadow Star's lowest stair, head down. He couldn't meet the guarding warrior's curious gaze. Couldn't stand it.

Taking the first step, his leg almost gave out, his will to climb as numb as his souls.

Power has deserted me. There is nothing left.

But he willed himself, step by step, as if there were nothing left but that last climb to the palace. All he had to do was reach the head of the stairs.

At the top, he hurried, almost in a run as he passed the Piasa and Horned Serpent guardian posts. He barely felt the matting covering the veranda. Then he was inside, blessedly out of sight.

Clay String called something, amazement in his voice.

In one of the dark corners, Fire Cat settled on the floor. He laid the black stone and polished lance to the side.

Only then did the insane laughter burst from his lips. He laughed, and laughed, and continued laughing until his ribs ached, and the world shuddered into silence.

Forty-two

Five Fists stood beside the central hearth in Blue Heron's palace. His muscular arms were crossed on his chest, his lopsided expression grim.

That Five Fists had come personally was proof of how seriously the living god took the incident.

Smooth Pebble dabbed at Blue Heron's sore face with a damp cloth. The rest of her household looked nervous, glancing uneasily at the Morning Star's scarred warrior, or speculatively at the door leading to Blue Heron's personal quarters.

Night Shadow Star paced anxiously before the hearth, her worried gaze taking in the benches and wall hangings. She kept whispering as if arguing with herself.

Or with Piasa.

One never knew with Night Shadow Star.

Only Dancing Sky, the old Red Wing Clan matron, and her daughters, White Rain and Soft Moon, so recently come to the Keeper's household, appeared unshaken. But then, to them, any misfortune that befell the Four Winds Keeper would seem a just retribution.

"Ouch!" Blue Heron cried as Smooth Pebble poked too hard against her swollen nose.

"Oh, stop it," Smooth Pebble chided too quickly, her disquiet barely hidden. "You'd have my hide if I let you outside with bits of dried blood on your face."

"What bothers me," Five Fists declared, "is that the assailant got past the guard and made it all the way to your personal quarters without anyone hearing or seeing him."

Blue Heron told him, "Since Walking Smoke met his end, people have gotten lax. Given how the thief seems to slip in and out of here as if he were a ghost, why should I be surprised? Even after threatening to cut Clay Bell and Fire Temper's balls off, nothing seems to have improved."

The two warriors in charge of her personal security were no doubt wincing where they stood outside her door. She would have to tend to them personally and immediately.

"The thief? You are sure it wasn't him?" Five Fists asked. He'd never liked Seven Skull Shield—had despised him from the moment he'd first seen him. But then, the thief had been dancing around naked, swinging his unnaturally large penis around as if it were a section of overstuffed buffalo gut. Not the finest of first impressions.

"It wasn't the thief." She waved Smooth Pebble back. "In the first place, he doesn't need to steal from me. Our deal is that he can have anything he wants. In the second, he wouldn't have struck me. It just . . ." What? Wasn't right?

She smiled. "I know what you think of him, Five Fists. And yes, he's a clanless, insolent, and no-account bit of human driftwood. But even if you hung him in a square, he'd die before admitting that he lives by an inviolate set of rules. His own rather tortured code of honor."

Five Fists snorted his disbelief. "Then who?"

"The Natchez. If it wasn't Swirling Cloud it was one of his warriors."

"Why? What could possibly tempt them to ruin everything by sneaking into your palace, getting caught, and inciting a potential disaster between our two Nations?"

"The Morning Star's cloak," she told him. "The one gifted

to the Little Sun at the conclusion of the Busk. The one Swirling Cloud stole from him the night the old Little Sun was murdered."

The room went silent, all eyes on the Keeper, but Night Shadow Star's. She appeared oblivious, preoccupied with the voices in her head.

"You found the cloak?" Five Fists asked.

"The thief did. He lifted it out of one of the Natchez's storage boxes the night of Thirteen Sacred Jaguar's welcoming feast."

"Does the Morning Star know this?"

"He does."

"Well . . . where is it?"

"I sent it off with Notched Cane yesterday. Call it a hunch, but it worried me to have it here. I just didn't think they'd come after it in this fashion." She prodded tenderly at her swollen nose.

Five Fists sighed. "Tell me where Notched Cane went. I'll send warriors to retrieve the thing before anything else happens to it."

Blue Heron winced as she stood, feeling the bruises and stiff joints from her fall. She was too old to take this kind of abuse. Nevertheless, she walked up to look Five Fists in the eyes. "You're too late. I had Notched Cane give it to an Anilco Trader the thief recommended. It's going—"

"*You did what*?"

"Old friend, you must trust me with regard to this. It's a deeper game than even the Morning Star thinks. Or, if he's playing this many layers down in the blankets, he'll understand what I've done and why."

Five Fists worked his lips back and forth, frown lines deepening. "Second-guessing the Morning Star can be a most dangerous—"

"I haven't forgotten when you rounded us all up last spring. If you'll remember"—she held up her thumb and forefinger, a tiny gap between them—"I came this close to hanging in a square. And someday, that's where I'll probably end up. But for now, I'm doing what I think best." She paused. "Or, if the Morning Star would prefer, *Tonka'tzi* Wind can name someone else Keeper."

"You take risks."

Still holding his gaze, she laughed bitterly. "Living in the shadow of the Morning Star? By Piasa's swollen balls, we all do."

"The Keeper has my protection," Night Shadow Star stated from the side. "Whatever she's done with the cloak, she has my approval . . . and Piasa's."

Five Fists growled under his breath and scuffed a nervous toe across the new matting. He still hadn't grown used to the notion that Night Shadow Star now wielded such Power and authority in opposition to the living god. Taking a breath, he said, "That still leaves the problem of someone sneaking in and striking the Keeper. This cannot be tolerated. Not after last spring."

Blue Heron made a face as she fingered the scar on her neck. In all of her life—even during the worst of relations with ex-husbands—she'd never been so much as threatened. Now in a matter of moons, she'd been attacked in her sleep by two midnight invaders.

Night Shadow Star said cryptically, "The battle is just being joined."

"What battle?" Five Fists gestured with an open hand. "Who are we fighting? The Natchez? We could sweep them away with three squadrons."

"Which is why the battle is being fought in a more cunning way," Night Shadow Star told him with a smile. "In order to win, they have to weaken us, one by one. Eat away at our strength. Distract us and turn us against each other."

"That's nonsense." Five Fists shot her a distrusting glance. "How can a bunch of foreigners do that?"

At that moment, Clay String uncharacteristically burst through the door, a panicked look on his face. He dropped to his knees, touching his forehead as he glanced anxiously at Blue Heron, then raised pleading hands to Night Shadow Star.

"Lady?" he asked plaintively. "I'm sorry, but . . ."

"Yes?"

"It's Fire Cat, Lady. I've never seen him like this. It was the Natchez. The one they call the Little Sun. He beat Fire Cat at chunkey. Took his clothes. Mocked him all the way to the palace steps." He swallowed hard. "If you don't come I'm afraid Fire Cat's going to kill himself."

For a heartbeat Night Shadow Star didn't seem to understand. Then, spinning on her heel, she started for the door, moving in long strides as she tossed her thick hair behind her.

Blue Heron turned her attention back to Five Fists, asking dryly, "You were saying?"

Forty-three

Now that he had had time to really get a look at the dog, Seven Skull Shield wondered what that fool with the leash had been so proud of. This was a grizzly-bear-hunting pack dog?

The beast was somewhere between a puppy and dog, large-boned, with huge floppy feet, and an oversized bear-like head mostly made up of huge jaws. It stared up at Seven Skull Shield with one brown eye, one blue. The dog's coat was a sort of messy brindle-brown with black speckles.

"Go on. You're free." Seven Skull Shield waved as he hurried down the Avenue. "I don't have time to take care of a dog. People are hunting me. Beat it!"

The dog however, continued to follow as he had for the last finger of time.

Seven Skull Shield stepped out of the way to allow a gang of sweating men to stagger past. Perhaps thirty of them, they bore a long, red-cedar pole on their shoulders as they chanted and bulled their way east under the load. No doubt it would be raised as a new World Tree pole before some temple being constructed up on the bluffs.

He wondered if some hapless young woman was going to be strangled and sacrificially buried at its base as an offering to Old-Woman-Who-Never-Dies. While Seven Skull Shield had always been skeptical about the rituals, priests, and the ceremonies used to coerce people into acting against their own best interest, he had more than enough respect for the doings of Power. He just couldn't convince himself that killing a girl and burying her under a pole was the best possible use a young woman could be put to.

The dog had seated himself, looking up with those peculiar eyes.

Seven Skull Shield bent down, getting on the dog's level as he explained, "I don't have time for a dog. I don't *need* a dog. Dogs are trouble. I'm trouble. That's two troubles in the same place where there should only be one. That means that you and I are not supposed to be together."

The dog licked him in the face.

"Stop that. You're supposed to be listening to me. I'm talking about the precarious world balance of Spirit Power and how you can't be messing it up." He pointed. "So, go away. Make a life. Just don't end up in someone's stew pot."

The dog looked in the direction he pointed, seeming unconcerned that it was only toward a granary and a Deer Clan council house.

Seven Skull Shield stood, wiping the slobber from his nose and cheek, adding, "On the other hand, if you're not smart enough to listen to me, maybe some dirt farmer's stew pot is where you belong."

With that he trotted off in the wake of the log bearers, knowing they'd clear the way for him. The dog gleefully bounded along at his side.

"You really don't listen well."

Saying it brought a smile to Seven Skull Shield's lips. How could he condemn a mere puppy for something he didn't do well himself?

"Actually, dog, I do listen well. And then I go ahead and do whatever I want."

Which, to be fair, was just what the dog had done.

"All the more reason you should go away."

As the sun rose higher and the midsummer heat drew a fine sheen of perspiration from Seven Skull Shield's skin, the dog continued to follow. He might dart off to the side, or stop to sniff at something, but then he was right back, tongue lolling from his oversized mouth, ears flopping.

Seven Skull Shield had just reached the bend in the Avenue of the Sun near Black Tail's tomb. The high ridge mound, charnel houses, and temples to Old-Woman-Who-Never-Dies stood just north of the road. Beyond that was an abandoned mound with the ruins of a burned temple and then the swampy bottoms and Marsh Elder Lake.

From here, the road ran straight past the foot of the Morning Star's mound, up the distant bluffs, and clear to the Moon Mound complex a day's travel to the east.

As Seven Skull Shield rounded the curve he saw Slick Rock coming toward him. Their eyes met. A triumphant smile bent the man's lips as he raised his hand, gesturing three poorly dressed companions forward.

Slick Rock, perhaps thirty summers of age, had been cast out of Snapping Turtle Clan while still in his early teens. The story was that he'd beaten a cousin near to death over a coveted hardwood bow. Something about the man had never struck Seven Skull Shield as being quite right. When asked why he had battered a young woman on another occasion, Slick Rock had just shrugged, saying, "She brought me soup with a dead fly in it."

It was the way he'd said it: emotionless. Cold and uncaring. Nor did it make sense as a reason. Cahokia—with its teeming tens of thousands, its charnel houses and countless open latrines, uncovered cook pots, and piles of garbage—swarmed with flies. The meddlesome beasts got into everything.

Slick Rock bent his lips into a ghastly grin, his eyes going slightly glassy with anticipation. The three scruffy men who accompanied him carried lengths of hardwood—the kind just right for beating someone senseless. And they were no more than a bowshot away.

Hesitation had never been one of Seven Skull Shield's faults. He immediately darted behind a potter's workshop, then dodged left, circling a sweat lodge before ducking behind a women's house. When he would have hidden in the latrine out back, an old woman was already crouched over the pit, her skirt pulled up and bunched in her lap; she glanced up, eyes wide.

"Sorry!" Seven Skull Shield turned, feet hammering the ground as he charged back to the southeast. The trick was to stay among the dwellings, society houses, temples, and workshops where they clustered along the road. Stray too far north and he'd be exposed along the marshy banks of Cahokia Creek or visible in the open area around Black Tail's tomb with its associated temples.

The joke he told was that his body was built for strength, not for speed. And that's when he saw the Bear Clan charnel house atop its low mound. He pounded his way up the slope, around the corner of the plaster wall, and darted in the door, pulling it closed behind him.

The smell hit him first, and then the patter of flies as his passage disturbed them from their feasts.

Taking a moment, he blinked, trying to adjust his eyes to the gloom after the bright sun outside.

Had Slick Rock and his cronies seen him?

As his vision started to adjust, Seven Skull Shield began to make out the corpses laid in rows on plank benches in the center of the room. These were the newly dead. The ones the priests were still preparing. Ornately decorated pots holding the recently removed entrails were resting on the ground beneath the bodies.

As soon as he could see well enough, he wound among the corpses to the rear of the room. Shelves were built into the surrounding walls, and older corpses, either desiccated or stripped down to bare bone, had been placed on them for safe keeping.

More flies buzzed in the darkness, making him wonder why he'd thought of Slick Rock's fly in the soup, only to end up covered with the little beasts.

In the rear he found the priest's sacred box with its carved lid. He didn't need to open it to know that it contained various flint and obsidian knives, chert scrapers, thread and needles, and the other sacred tools. Some were used to remove organs, others to scrape the bones of those whose flesh had softened to the point they could be stripped down.

What mattered was that the box was large enough that he could step on top of it and climb up to the highest shelf. There, an ancient woman's corpse, long dried and partially mummified, lay on its back, arms at its sides.

"Excuse me, Grandmother," Seven Skull Shield apologized. The rickety shelving creaked and swayed as he eased his bulk over the desiccated remains. "Won't be here long, and if I'm the first man ever to lie beside you, your life must have been a tragedy."

He settled behind her, shoving her out toward the edge to get more room. The shelving kept wobbling under his weight. He made a warding sign with his fingers in the hopes it would keep the whole thing from collapsing. The shelves had been built to support dried corpses, not flesh-thick and burly thieves.

He'd no more than taken a breath before a hollow thump was followed by a dog's pained squeal. Then the door was jerked open. Slick Rock stood silhouetted by sunlight as he peered around. His cohorts crowded up behind him.

"He's in there?" one asked.

"That dog of his was sniffing at this door."

Seven Skull Shield strangled a groan deep in his throat. He turned his attention to the gap between the thatch and the wall. Way too thin to allow him to wiggle his bulk through.

"Seven Skull Shield?" Slick Rock called. "We know you're in here. We can do this easy, or we can do it the hard way. We just want to talk."

Seven Skull Shield forced himself to breathe deeply, stilling his desire to do something rash. By blood and spit, there was still a chance they wouldn't see him. Maybe think the dog had just smelled the rotting meat?

"It's the hard way then," Slick Rock said through that flat and emotionless voice of his. "They just want you alive. They didn't say we couldn't mess you up a little in the process." That flicker of empty smile bent his lips. "And I've never liked you. Thought you were a loud-mouthed braggart. You and that oversized rope you call a penis. You're like duck shit in a lake . . . sinking ever lower to the bottom."

Slick Rock had edged in, waving at his companions to spread out as they worked their way carefully through the benches and supine corpses.

"You sure he's here?" asked the young one.

"Oh, he's here."

"I don't like this," another, older and nervous, said. "Only an idiot would anger the souls of the dead. You think he'd take that kind of chance?"

"This is Seven Skull Shield. He'd not only anger the dead, but brag about it later." Slick Rock was squinting, his eyes starting to adjust. Louder he called, "Isn't that right, you bit of worm-infested turd?"

"Hey! Look!" a big man blocking the door called. "The dog's back!"

Seven Skull Shield heard a soft whine, not daring to raise his head.

By Horned Serpent's hairy shaft, why had he ever let that fool dog off its leash?

Skull, this time your idiocy may have finally killed you!

He filled his lungs, trying not to inhale flies, as he sought to quell his rising anger with himself.

The shelving creaked in reply.

"There he is," satisfaction filled Slick Rock's voice. "Up on that high shelf. It's over, thief. Come on down."

Seven Skull Shield clamped his jaws against the curse that bubbled up from his throat. His hands knotted into frustrated fists.

"I'll get him," the closest man said, reaching up to grasp the high shelf and pulling himself up as if he were chinning on the pole rail.

With a crack the whole thing let loose and pulled away from the wall. In a mass, shelving, poles, corpses, and Seven Skull Shield went crashing down onto the benches where fresher bodies lay.

Beneath the mass, the erstwhile climber shrieked and wailed in pain.

Whatever the ghosts of the dead thought, they couldn't have been too angry. Otherwise Seven Skull Shield wouldn't have landed on top of Grandmother, a still-soft and rotting young man, and a plank platform that bowed on impact before giving way. With a loud crack it deposited him and his cushioning corpses gently on the ground.

In an instant, Seven Skull Shield was on his feet. Even as he started for Slick Rock, the anger was burning free.

"Call me duck shit? I'm gonna squeeze your neck until your head pops like a rotten gourd!"

The remaining two of Slick Rock's companions, including the one afraid of the dead, had backed against the shelving on the far side, their eyes wide.

"Take him. Now!" Slick Rock started forward, his club slapping his free hand.

Seven Skull Shield let out a bellow and charged. As Slick Rock swung, Seven Skull Shield ducked. The club swished through his hair. Then he plowed into Slick Rock. The man backpedaled before crashing into another of the corpses atop its table. With a splintering of wood, they hit the floor.

Howling, Seven Skull Shield cried, "Gonna gut you! Gonna *eat your balls!* You *shit-blood maggot sucker!*"

He got one hand on Slick Rock's throat, raging, "Gonna rip your lips off! Gut-eating *pus maggot! Piece of filth!*"

Slick Rock was clawing like a snared raccoon, his legs kicking in the wreckage of shelving and corpses. A mewling sound escaped his mouth as Seven Skull Shield clamped fingers deep. The windpipe and voice box collapsed under his grip.

Which was when a club thumped painfully into his back and his arms went numb. A second blow left him reeling, and a third blasted lights through his vision.

Breath seemed to stick in his lungs, leaving him gasping as he rolled to one side, unable to make his arms work.

"Got him."

Seven Skull Shield barely managed a breath, glancing sidelong in agony at the third man. The big man raised the club again, but at Seven Skull Shield's flinch, lowered it.

"Come on. Let's get him out of here." The big man grinned as he threatened Seven Skull Shield with his club. "See if Slick Rock's going to make it."

The wary older man, his eyes large as he stared in horror at the tangled mass of corpses and broken shelving, was making warding signs with his fingers as if to save himself from all the evil in the world.

The big man grabbed Seven Skull Shield by the hair, jerking his head up. He lifted his club, saying, "Slick Rock just said we had to get him to the Natchez alive."

The blow wasn't full strength or it would have crushed Seven Skull Shield's cheek, broken his jaw, and knocked out half his teeth. It still blasted lights behind his eyes, rocked his head, and hurt like thunder in the morning.

Half dazed, but breathing, Seven Skull Shield watched the man's club rise again for a better blow. Some part of his bruised souls read the glee in the big man's eyes, the parting of his lips in anticipation.

This is gonna hurt.

A flash of brown flickered through Seven Skull Shield's vision and fastened on the man's arm.

It might have been a ghost of the dead given the sound it made: a squealing growl that was half yip.

The man uttered a horrified shriek as he was bowled over backwards. Seven Skull Shield identified the brindle-brown fury, amazed as the dog savaged the big man's arm. The snap of crushed bones could be heard. Shrieking man and growling dog crashed down into the broken shelving and sprawled corpses.

Slick Rock had recovered, coughing, pulling himself upright and reaching for his club.

Seven Skull Shield clumsily laid hands on a large ceramic jar, its side decorated with some incised Bear Clan design. He raised it just as Slick Rock swung. The jar took the impact, shattering to cover them both with foul-smelling wet goo.

Something solid landed in Seven Skull Shield's lap. He reached down; the thing had a texture like a slimy fish. Realizing it was a human heart, and the jar had been full of organs, he threw it at Slick Rock. The heart hit the man full in the face. Gathering up hands full of slithering and ropy intestines, he slopped them onto Slick Rock's head, leaving the man to claw his way through the tangle.

Got to get out of here.

Seven Skull Shield staggered to his feet, hearing the wailing and horror-torn cries of the man beset by the ghost fury dog. He blinked. Realized his vision was doubled.

Slick Rock was coughing through his damaged throat as he struggled through the mass of ropy intestines.

Seven Skull Shield managed to catch the club as Slick Rock gave it a half-hearted swing. Wrenching it from the man's hands, he took his own swing. Off balance as he was, the blow caught Slick Rock on the shoulder, skipped up, and glanced off the side of his head. The man dropped in the draping of guts as if his strings had been cut.

People were standing in the doorway, staring in, expressions aghast.

The last of Slick Rock's men looked paralyzed, the club falling from his hands as he backed away. His terrified eyes flicked from the brown fury still mauling the shrieking man, to the screaming fellow buried in shelving and corpses, then to Slick Rock, now moaning in the tangle of half-rotted humans and the stench of necrotic organs.

Seven Skull Shield bulled his way to the door, wavering on his feet. "Get them!" he told the crowd as he pointed. "I caught them doing witchery on the dead! Tried to stop them, and they attacked me!"

For what seemed an eternity, the crowd just stared at him, eyes wide, mouths agape despite the smell.

Then, with a howl, they charged in, fists knotting, curses on their lips.

Seven Skull Shield gratefully slipped out the door, lost his footing and tumbled down the slight incline of the mound. He scrambled to his wobbly feet on the flat below. He was halfway to the nearest farmstead when a series of shouts caused him to look over his shoulder.

The dog emerged from the charnel house door, sniffed for his scent, and then came like a shot, his oddly colored eyes alight, tongue bloody and lolling out of the side of his mouth.

As Seven Skull Shield rounded the farmstead and out of sight of the charnel house, he paused, propping hands on his knees to pant. Blood was dripping down from his nose and coating his chin and chest. His head ached like a cracked walnut. He smelled worse than buzzard shit mixed with maggot puke.

He grinned despite his double vision.

"What do you think, dog? Was that fun, or what?"

And then Seven Skull Shield's stomach pumped and he threw up.

Forty-four

As Night Shadow Star approached the foot of the staircase leading up the ramp to her palace, it was to find a knot of Itza warriors surrounding the Natchez Little Sun. They stood just out from the bottom stair, beyond reach of the Four Winds warrior who kept people from bothering her.

As she approached, one caught sight of her, nudging his companions and pointing. They laughed, obviously amused. The big Itza warrior, the one with the snake tattoos, was grinning, as if savoring a victory.

The Natchez had Fire Cat's loincloth and cape hung from the end of his chunkey lance. Using it like a banner staff, he waved them back and forth.

She felt her heart harden, Piasa's voice oddly silent as a slow fire began to burn around her heart.

"Greetings, Lady!" the Natchez known as Wet Bobcat called, eyes glittering with mirth. "Good to see you. We came to see where the *ahau* Thirteen Sacred Jaguar would be living two days from now." He glanced up at the palace. "Not as nice as the Morning Star's, but it will probably do for the time being."

"Let me order them removed," Clay String protested where he followed behind.

"You would have warriors beat my future husband's servants?" she asked in a cold voice.

"Why not?" he asked reasonably.

"If I answer that, I might be tempted to follow your suggestion, Clay String."

Instead she walked up to the leering men, a deadly stillness between her souls. "Natchez. Take these vermin and remove yourself from this avenue."

"We are guests of the Morning Star," Swirling Cloud replied, bowing low and touching his forehead in a mockery. He looked up the stairs. "Your simpering slave doesn't appear to be much, does he? Wretched chunkey player." He pointed at the snake-tattooed Itza. "My companion here is named Red Copal, after the Powers of the color and the incense they burn in his homeland. If you ask submissively, perhaps your future husband will assign him to protect and accompany you. Surely it will be an improvement over that naked and trembling worm that used to wear the clothes hanging on my lance."

Swirling Cloud lowered the lance, but when she reached for Fire Cat's clothes, he flipped them up with a twist of his wrist.

A considerable crowd had gathered.

"I might indeed submissively ask my new husband for something," she told him with a smile, and narrowed her eyes to slits. "It is the custom of the Itza to grant sacrifices for special occasions, is it not? Given the stakes behind this marriage, perhaps I should ask for Red Copal's heart to be cut from his chest."

She pointed. "Right up there. At the head of my stairs and within sight of Piasa and Horned Serpent." Fixing her gaze on Swirling Cloud's she added, "You and I could make wagers on whether Red Copal's corpse would tumble all the way down the stairs to the dirt here."

Swirling Cloud's expression thinned, violence behind his

eyes. "You take chances, Lady. As High Pine discovered to her misfortune, one's future can become a fleeting thing if she should make the wrong enemies. Nor are you the only living sister to the Morning Star."

She smiled warily, nodding to herself. "I hear between and beneath your words, Little Sun. Your meaning is clear. But the making of enemies works both ways. Nor would Lord Thirteen Sacred Jaguar find my sister a suitable wife. Her souls are scattered and broken. Her nights and sleep are filled with terrors that leave her weeping. Or perhaps such a woman would be more to his liking than one that comes with Power and anger in her souls?"

"Thirteen Sacred Jaguar could care less about your souls or your sister's." He leaned close, his smile as piercing as a deer-bone stiletto. "His only concern is if that noble sheath of yours will carry his seed to your womb. And should that become a problem, your sister need not have any wits to serve a similar function."

She felt a flicker of fear, like a chilling tendril that slipped up through her gut. "One day I will see you on your knees, Natchez . . . a bloody stump where your neck now supports your head."

"Brave words, Lady." He laughed, flicking his chunkey lance to dash Fire Cat's clothes at her. "As brave as your slave's words before he lost everything that was his to wager."

She caught Fire Cat's clothes with a quick grab, watching as the Natchez led the leering Itza warriors off toward the plaza.

As she started up the stairs, something made her stop, turn. She lifted her eyes and saw a figure high on the palisade wall that surrounded the Morning Star's palace. While she couldn't distinguish features from that distance, sunlight glinted in a polished copper headpiece.

So, Morning Star, the stakes are raised. I know what I am willing to give up in order to prevail. Do you?

Another shiver ran through her as she hurried up the stairs to the sanctuary of her palace—or at least it was a sanctuary for the little time that remained before Thirteen Sacred Jaguar would call it his home.

Forty-five

Seven Skull Shield tried to curl away from the pain in his head, as if by instructing his souls to hunch into a fetal position and drop a little deeper into dreams, the agony would ease. Somewhere down there, Wooden Doll was waiting. He kept catching glimpses of her. If only he could get close enough, reach out and grasp her, she'd turn to him, smiling. Her arms would go around him and the pain would vanish.

From beyond the gray haze a reedy voice intruded as it ordered, "Hey, you. Wake up. Drink this."

Seven Skull Shield winced as the pain speared through his brain with renewed intensity. His skull felt cracked and shattered.

"Go away." It hurt to talk.

Somewhere, back in the dream, Wooden Doll had vanished into the gray.

A litter had been parked out front of her dwelling. That maggot-breathed ex-husband of the Keeper's. A rich man. The one who'd paid to have him hunted down.

He went after her because of me.

At the thought, he blinked awake and groaned as light drove hot stakes through his eyes.

"About time," the reedy voice said. "Now, drink."

A rough ceramic cup was pressed against his lips. Out of instinct he sucked down the warm liquid, taking until the third swallow to realize it tasted vile.

On the verge of spitting it out, the voice snapped, "Drink it all! It's medicine for that headache."

Seven Skull Shield's eyes had cleared enough to focus on the clay cup held to his lips. He chugged down the rest, making a face as the cup was withdrawn.

He lay on a blanket on a packed-clay floor. A soot-coated roof was overhead. Around him, the walls were clay-covered and hung with herbs and dried plants. Mismatched and chipped ceramic pots lined the floor.

"Where am I?" His voice sounded hoarse, the words cracking like rocks as they echoed through his shattered skull.

An old woman, her hair white and thin, leaned into his field of view. She might have been someone's greatest of grandmothers. Her brown and shriveled face consisted of endless patterns of conflicting wrinkles atop long-faded tattoos. She grinned toothlessly at him. Intense brown eyes—laid deep in folds of dry skin—were studying him thoughtfully.

"You're in a shrine. The small one just to the north of Petaga's forbidden mound with Lichen's burned temple. The dog brought you here stinking of death."

"What dog?"

"That one." She pointed, and he followed her knobby and age-bent finger to where the young brindle-brown pup lay inside the door. The beast was watching him with those oddly mismatched eyes.

Memory came flooding back. The dog giving him away, the fight in the Bear Clan charnel house. That last whack of the club. He'd made it out, gotten away. Then he'd thrown up, and everything had gone hazy.

"How could the dog bring me here?"

"He's a Power dog. Says you saved his life, so he saved yours."

"*That* is a Power dog? He told you this, huh?"

Her old eyes seemed to sink deeper in their folds. "Among other things, thief. You're in a great deal of danger. All of you are."

"All of us?"

"You, the Keeper, the Lady Night Shadow Star, Fire Cat, and Cahokia itself."

"Right." He sat up, gasped as a staggering pain left his wits swimming, and eased back down. "Blood and vomit, that hurts."

"Your brain took a quite a wallop. It's mostly water. Sloshes around inside the skull. Takes a while to settle out . . . and for all the ripples to subside."

"How do you know that?"

"I've boiled enough brains over the years. When I was younger, I tried to figure out just what a brain does. Lichen piqued my interest in the beginning. When she was a little girl her father cut a hole in her skull. Allowed her to hear voices most of us can't."

"So . . . what's a brain do?"

"Hearts and lungs are easy to figure out. So are stomachs and intestines and kidneys. But the brain? The eyes and ears and nose are attached to it by fibers, so it has something to do with them. Behavior, too. I studied people with bad head wounds. Sometimes they remained the same; other times they came out acting like different people. I think the souls store memories in the brain. Which is why I tried drying them. Thought I could preserve them. Tried eating them, too. But no matter how many I ate, I never had anyone else's memory pop up among my own."

"What did you give me to drink? Brain juice?"

"A concoction of willow bark, mint, datura, and coneflower." She was looking into his eyes as if studying them closely. "Pupils are the same size. That's good. You'll be fine."

"Did you see my souls in there?"

Her whole body rocked as she nodded. "Seen your souls. Seen a lot about you. More than you can know. No wonder that dog chose you. Both of you, creatures of Power."

"You're not making sense."

"Power rarely makes sense in human terms." She gave him a weak smile that exposed receded pink gums. "I didn't always understand that, but my time is past. The Four Winds Clan changed the world, changed everything when they incarnated the Morning Star in Black Tail's body. Powerful as Lichen was, she didn't fully grasp the change. Neither did Petaga."

"I'm starting to wonder if you weren't hit in the head yourself once upon a time."

"What do you think set me on this course?"

The dog whined, and she turned, head cocked.

"What did he say?" Seven Skull Shield asked unkindly.

"That he hasn't eaten since you gave him a strip of dried meat that you stole."

He shot her a disbelieving sidelong glance. "So, I must have been raving, my souls loose. I found the dog *after* I stole the meat."

Ignoring him, she told the dog, "He doesn't need to understand these things. Power chose him because he has other skills."

The dog made a harrumphing sigh.

"Well, of course," she replied. "And you can help yourself to the last of the stew in that bowl by the fire."

Seven Skull Shield watched the dog rise and walk over to the central hearth. He sniffed at the middle of three bowls, then gratefully began slurping up its watery contents.

"Looks like you and the dog are going to get along fine. I've got to be going." Seven Skull Shield placed a hand to the side of his head. Despite how it felt, no broken shards of bone met his fingers.

Memories of that litter out front of Wooden Doll's, and what it might mean, kept haunting him. He should have figured it out the moment he saw it. He tried to rise, only to sink down again as his head erupted in agony.

The old woman watched him with amused eyes. "You have a couple of fingers of time yet before you'll be ready to go. And even then, you should rest for a day."

"People might need me."

"Of course they will. Why do you think the dog brought you here?"

"Huh?" Maybe she'd eaten too many brains over the years and all the thoughts were starting to confuse her.

She almost glowered at him, as if reading his souls. "The time for you to go isn't right yet. You still have things to learn."

"About what?" He rubbed his face, aware that the dog had finished licking out the bowl. His own stomach was grinding emptily against itself, reminding him that it had been . . . how long since he'd eaten?

She began rocking softly, eyes half-closed and dreamy. "About the Tortoise Bundle."

"What's the Tortoise Bundle?"

"Old Power. Some say it's the heart of Cahokia. And for the moment, I'm its guardian."

Forty-six

Horn Lance batted at flies as the crowd parted and his litter was lowered before the Four Winds Men's House. The hot sun had wicked a sheen of sweat from his skin, and for whatever reason, it drew a swarm of the noxious beasts. Not that Cahokia was particularly hot, though its people complained. That they thought the heat uncomfortable amused him, having lived for as long as he had among the Itza and Yucateca in their sweltering forests and brush lands.

Ignoring the calls from the surrounding crowd, he rose from the litter and walked stiffly to the veranda where Swirling Cloud, a couple of his Natchez, and the four Itza warriors lounged.

"What news?"

Red Copal gave a desultory wave as he disdainfully surveyed the gawking spectators who hovered just beyond the ring of Natchez guards. "How long will this go on?"

"Until you are no longer a novelty," Horn Lance said with a yawn as he reached for a long-necked water bottle and drank. Wiping his lips, he added, "By next week the crowds will have dwindled."

"What took you so long? You were supposed to be here

at first light," Swirling Cloud called from where he rested on a box.

"I was held up. Some melee in a charnel house, of all things. Apparently miscreants got into a fight. Started tossing corpses around. Most disrespectful of the dead. When the local Bear Clan lineage found out, they finished what the fight started. One was dead. Two more were being hung in squares for sacrilege. And two apparently managed to get away."

"What of Horned Serpent House? Will they back you?"

"I had a nice visit with my cousin Green Chunkey and planted the seeds of discontent. From there I traveled to Evening Star Town, where I met with Matron Columella. She barely survived Morning Star House treachery last spring. My visit was pleasant, and I hinted that in the future, Morning Star House might not be as dominant as it is now."

"She will side with us?"

"Perhaps. When the time is right. For the moment she struck me as particularly cautious. Who could blame her? But she's a smart and clever woman nevertheless." He glanced at Swirling Cloud. "Did you get the Morning Star's cloak?"

Swirling Cloud made a face. "The old woman awakened. Called me a thief and started making noise. As hard as I hit her, I hoped it might have broken her neck. Or at least permanently addled her wits."

"You went in there? Yourself? I told you to hire it done. To use a third party."

Swirling Cloud gave him a smug smile. "Why delegate to others what you can do more efficiently yourself? She's an old woman. They frighten easily. The way I hit her? She's shaken. Hasn't been out of her palace. She won't sleep soundly for moons to come."

Horn Lance narrowed his eyes. "You're an idiot. This is Blue Heron we're talking about."

"I thought you were going to see to pulling her teeth."

"I've got half the city searching for the man she hired to steal the cloak from us. Turns out he's really just a common scoundrel. Has quite a reputation as a no-account seducer of women."

Which turned his thoughts back to the night he had just spent with Wooden Doll. The woman had left him with a honeyed glow. Driving himself into a woman was always pleasant, but she'd done things to him that still left him breathless. No wonder the thief favored her. Nor did she have any reticence when it came to discussing the man. Especially after Horn Lance indicated that Seven Skull Shield was such a good a friend of his. Women could be so gullible.

Her detailed knowledge of Cahokia and its workings had surprised him. Wooden Doll, it turned out, had proved to be an unexpected asset. One he would be making further use of.

Swirling Cloud grunted noncommittally. "I know you fear the Keeper, but so far she hasn't impressed me." He yawned. "And in the meantime I have dealt the *ahau*'s betrothed a blow. The slave? He's really not a very good chunkey player. I sent him back to her naked, broken, and humiliated. You should have seen her cheeks, burning with rage and despair. If you ask me, the great Morning Star House is off balance and stumbling."

Horn Lance sighed. "Perhaps." He paused. "What of Thirteen Sacred Jaguar?"

"He's inside. Purifying himself before the *kukul*. He's been burning *pom*, doing that odd drawing with dots and lines on *juna* sheets, and setting it on fire."

"The dots and lines? Those are mathematics. Great Power lives in the numbers and how they add and subtract. Powers your people and these ignorant Cahokians cannot understand. The Maya have made a study of it for generations. Each number has its own name, its own Power. Thirteen Sacred Jaguar is running all the permutations, prophesying the future."

"So you keep saying." Swirling Cloud gave him a sour look. "Isn't it easier to just count on your fingers and toes?"

Horn Lance gave him a placid smile. No sense in arguing. The concept of the calendar, the *baktun*, *katun*, *tun*, *uinal*, and *kin*—the units of time that made the great wheels of time and their calculation—were so far beyond the Little Sun's comprehension as to be meaningless.

Nor did it matter in the end. For the moment, the Natchez were necessary, and as the future played out they'd remain useful and valued middlemen. If Horn Lance could manage it with finesse, the Natchez wouldn't even realize they'd been used as tools in his grand plan.

For the time being, everything hinged on establishing Thirteen Sacred Jaguar's position in Cahokia. Once that was accomplished and the man had begun to lecture on the teachings of the Council Book, the *Popol Vuh*, and the ways in which Cahokia's stories and interpretations of the Beginning Times were in error, it would be like loosening a round stone from the top of a hill. Try as the Four Winds Clan might, they'd never be able to stop, let alone reverse, that stone's growing momentum.

He turned his attention back to the crowed that ebbed and flowed beyond the ring of Natchez warriors. People had flocked from all over Cahokia to see the Itza. Their curiosity continued to rise, and in the end, that was his mightiest weapon. They would want to know all about the great Chichen Itza, and about Mayan mathematics, science, engineers, and religion. Through Horn Lance, Thirteen Sacred Jaguar would tell them. He'd elaborate on the stories of First Mother Maker. His eloquent words would narrate the story of First Father Heart of the Sky's descent to Xibalba. The Cahokians would begin to wonder why the stories were different from their own.

Tomorrow, Night Shadow Star would marry Thirteen Sacred Jaguar. Once that happened, Horn Lance would be unstoppable.

An insidious fungus would have infested the Four Winds Clan, one that would eat at its heart, taint their Morning Star, and eventually expose their living god as the fraud he was.

"In the end, Cahokia will be Chichen Itza's northern vassal." Horn Lance smiled. Revenge was indeed as sweet as forest honey mixed with warm cacao.

Forty-seven

"Leave us," Night Shadow Star ordered as she strode into her palace. Clay String stopped short at the door, waited to ensure the rest of the household servants scurried out, and then he, too, slipped away.

Night Shadow Star crossed to the corner where Fire Cat huddled on the floor, his back braced against a sleeping bench. His knees were drawn up, his head down. The sight of him brought a knot to her throat.

As shivering and vulnerable as he'd been that first moment she'd seen him hanging in the square, he hadn't looked this broken. The depth to which Swirling Cloud had hurt Fire Cat sent currents through the impotent rage within her.

She settled herself beside Fire Cat, her back supported by the bed. She carefully laid his breechcloth and cloak on the matting before his feet. Then she took a deep breath, propping her forearms on her drawn-up knees.

"This, too, shall pass, Fire Cat. Our time will come."

He reached out with a trembling hand, feeling the fabric of his breechcloth. "You got my clothing back?" He swallowed hard. "I am even more ashamed."

"They waited around long enough to taunt me with it."

She ground her teeth as a way of burning off her frustrated rage.

"I have failed you, Lady."

"You haven't. Not yet."

"Had I been able, I would have bet your lance and stone. Even my life. As it was, all I had was my clothing." He took a wavering breath. "I lost by five!"

Doing her best to sound reasonable, she said, "Power has its ways. Are we supposed to learn something from this, maybe take it as a sign?" But of what? Why had Piasa insisted that Fire Cat prepare for a critical game of chunkey?

"Ultimate defeat?" His fists knotted, the muscles in his forearms bulging. "You *marry* him tomorrow!"

"I will do my duty. In the end, I am told, it is the only way to destroy him."

"That . . ." Unable to finish, he shook his head. "I don't understand."

"I don't either. Not completely. Old-Woman-Who-Never-Dies insisted that the Itza has her protection. You and I are not permitted to kill him. Yet Piasa has cleverly hinted that a way exists to get him to destroy himself."

"How?"

She lifted questioning hands. "Do you think I haven't asked? All Piasa will tell me is that I must wait, learn, and that if I am clever enough, the way will become clear." She paused. "That he won't tell me straight must mean that Piasa fears Old-Woman-Who-Never-Dies' wrath should he be found out."

Fire Cat dropped his head again. "I was to play an important part. You warned me. Gave me the chunkey stone. You said our lives might depend upon it." His voice dropped to a miserable whisper. "I didn't want to play him. Not yet. And then, because of my pride, I did. And I failed you."

"This may not have been the game Piasa—"

"I wish to be released from my oath."

Her heart seemed to stop. "Why?"

"If I am not in your service, Old-Woman-Who-Never-Dies cannot hold you responsible for any actions that I might take."

"Do you know what you're saying?"

His head bobbed in a nod. "I thought Power had abandoned me when Spotted Wrist sacked Red Wing Town. And again when I gave you my oath. When I fought the Tula, and saved you in the river, Power flashed in my souls. Bright. Pure. Perhaps in a way I would never have known had I not been taken captive and sworn to you."

"A setback is not the end."

She saw his cheeks line with a bitter smile. "Tomorrow, you will marry the Itza, Lady. The Natchez, the Itza warriors, they will be here, in *this* house. And I . . ."

"Yes?" Her throat had gone dry, her own hands knotted into fists.

"I . . ." He swallowed a groan deep in his throat. "I will have to wait just beyond your door when he takes you to your bed. While the Itza and Natchez watch and grin, I'll have to . . ."

Her souls went mute as she closed her eyes, her own distaste at the coming ordeal surfacing. She'd tried so hard not to think about it.

Instinctively, she placed her hand on his knee, squeezing in reassurance. "It's just a mating, Fire Cat." She smiled wistfully. "If I can endure, so can you."

"Knowing that you don't . . ." He bit off the words, avoiding her eyes.

To spare him, she said, "My souls will be somewhere else, thinking about other things. If I think hard enough, I won't even realize he's done until he rolls off."

He sat silently.

She tightened her grip on his knee. "If you would serve me, you would help make this as easy to endure as you can. I need you strong, proud, and in control. We're not beaten, Fire Cat. We're playing for time. Can you do that for me?

Give me your word?" She took a deep breath, adding, "I have no one else to rely on."

He lifted his head, a glittering pain behind his eyes. "Whatever I have to do, Lady. Whatever it takes."

"Then, for just a moment, let me sit here." She wound her arm into his, leaning her head against his shoulder. "I just want to pretend that life is simple, and that I have at least one friend."

The crazy notion came to her that they were one, she and this man—this supposed enemy who served her. If only she could open his skin, crawl inside him, and escape to where it was warm and dark, and safe. Where his heart beat only for her.

Forty-eight

The majority of the planning for Night Shadow Star's marriage was carried out in the Council House ramada. For the most part *Tonka'tzi* Wind had orchestrated the arrangements. With her usual brilliance for detail and efficiency she delegated the procurement of venison, breads, fowl, fish, stews, and drink to various Earth Clan chiefs. Meanwhile cousins were tasked with putting together a stickball tournament, chunkey, and celebratory Dancers.

Blue Heron chafed as she sat under the ramada, listening as a long line of Earth Clans chiefs and matrons arrived with their final reports and offers of assistance.

Then there was the final curious request.

"The Itza insists on a ritual combat," Blue Heron muttered. "Why can't they be happy with chunkey and stickball like everyone else?"

Tonka'tzi Wind lifted a hand, forestalling Matron Red Temple before she turned her attention to Blue Heron. "They're Itza. Maybe that's explanation enough."

"And what does this 'ritual combat' consist of?" Blue Heron asked as she massaged her hip where it had been bruised in her fall.

"His warriors will fight an equal number of our best

warriors." Wind stated the obvious. "It's something about the way Itza see balance. He wants sacrifices to be made before the wedding. As I understand, the warriors' blood, suffering, and death bring luck and good fortune to the marriage."

"And just where do you expect to find warriors willing to gamble their lives on the odd chance of making a happy marriage?"

Wind threw her head back, laughing. "Are you joking? As soon as word went out, we had a flood of volunteers. From every Men's House in Cahokia. What's a little risk compared to the opportunity to kill an Itza warrior? It's the chance of a lifetime to gain prestige and status. All over the city War Medicine is being conjured. Warriors are fasting and sweating, purging, praying, hoping they will be chosen by their squadron firsts. Names are being submitted from every clan, every lineage. Five Fists will choose the finalists to stand against the Itza warriors."

Blue Heron narrowed her eyes, glancing around at the crowd surrounding Wind's raised dais. She waved off a fly. "I don't like it."

"Who are we to decry any peculiar traditions held by the Itza? Willing men are going to fight each other for bragging rights. The Itza gets his good luck sacrifice; the winners get to preen for the rest of their lives." Wind pointed a finger. "What's different than men betting their lives on a chunkey game? It's up to Power."

"Horn Lance is behind it; that's what's wrong."

"Sister." Wind used her "argument's over" tone. "The finest of our warriors—men blooded in combat—are going to fight these Itza. What do we care if the foreigners are slaughtered on their chief's wedding day?"

"I tell you, it's going to end badly. And I'll remind you that I said so." Yawning, Blue Heron winced. Any movement of her face—from scowl to smile—hurt. And as the day wore on, her bruises bothered her more. It would take days for the effects of the blow to fade.

The knowledge that the Natchez were living in the Four Winds Men's House, just over there, diagonally across the plaza, and she couldn't do a thing about it, irritated her to no end.

Nor did this "ritual combat" the Itza demanded sit well with her.

"Bide your time, woman," she muttered under her breath as *Tonka'tzi* Wind graciously thanked Matron Red Temple of the Fish Clan for coming up with firewood for the cook fires. Revenge would come.

Wind finished, saying, "And give my best to High Chief Two Throws. Tell him my prayer is that Power grants him a speedy recovery."

"He will be honored, *Tonka'tzi*." Red Temple bowed low, touching her forehead. "For myself, I will do everything within my ability to make Lady Night Shadow Star's wedding the most festive of days."

Blue Heron pulled at her sagging chin as she nodded and watched the matron depart. The first humming of mosquitoes could be heard as sunset turned the northwest into a purplish gloom.

"What else?" Blue Heron asked, yawning again.

"You could look at least a little enthusiastic," Wind muttered as she shifted on her litter atop its dais.

"I didn't sleep well last night. Maybe you'll recall the details?" Blue Heron glanced over at Five Fists where the old warrior crouched beside a council ramada support pole. He'd been watching one of the recorders who sat with a deerskin spread before him. The man had painstakingly strung different beads on his string to record what each of the clans was donating for the success of the occasion.

"You should keep strange men out of your bedroom," Wind growled in mock severity as she propped her chin on a fist. "Pus and blood, Sister, have we thought of everything? A moon wouldn't have been long enough to perfectly plan such a marriage."

"It will do," Blue Heron declared. "We'll have enough food, and as for the Itza all that matters is that we awe him with the spectacle. We've got stickball games running from dawn to dusk, chunkey, and half the city is going to be crowding around for as far as the eye can see. No one's ever married an Itza in Cahokia before—let alone a Four Winds noble as exalted as Lady Night Shadow Star. The Traders and hucksters will be as thick as these blood-sucking mosquitoes." She waved at the growing column over her head.

"Not that Night Shadow Star is bouncing with joy." Blue Heron glanced sidelong at Five Fists. Anything she said was going to be passed to the Morning Star the moment the old warrior returned to the high palace.

"She hasn't complained," Wind noted. "Maybe she's ready for a man again?"

"You just hold onto that thought, dear sister. I'll remind you that you said it come equinox, and we'll see how right you are."

Wind, aware of Five Fists, and whom he served, barely narrowed an eye in response.

"Me?" Blue Heron winced as she stood. "I'm going home, standing two guards at my door, and getting some sleep. Tomorrow is going to be a busy day."

"According to my sources, Night Shadow Star hasn't been attending to the rituals. I don't care if she doesn't propitiate Power. That's her business, and maybe Piasa's. But I do care about public perception. She's Morning Star House, a noble woman. People look up to her as a role model for good behavior."

"I'll see what I can do." She eased her way across the beaten courtyard, slapped an incautiously desperate mosquito dead, and walked to the Council Terrace Gate. Below her, the dusk-filled plaza was busier than usual, people already flocking in for the wedding. She took her time, descending step by step in deference to her bruises.

Blood and snot, as bad as the blow to her face had been,

her body bouncing off the bed frame and floor had really hurt her.

On the avenue, Smooth Pebble had Blue Heron's litter ready. Blue Heron's porters lifted her as soon as she was seated, and the guard ran ahead calling, "Make way for the Keeper!" as he parted the crowd.

"Is everything ready?" Smooth Pebble asked from beside the litter as dirt farmers, Traders, and craftsmen gave way to the warriors in Blue Heron's guard. Several teams of men carrying heavy logs slowed, stepping to the side and touching their foreheads as they let her pass.

"As ready as it will ever be. Some of the Earth Clans aren't getting much sleep tonight, raiding their storage, getting water and firewood delivered to the plaza by morning. I doubt half the food will be cooked by the time we're supposed to feast."

"And Night Shadow Star?" Smooth Pebble lowered her voice. "Did you let Wind know what happened with the Red Wing? I tell you, Night Shadow Star was upset when she left. I saw Clay String while you were up at council. He said she confronted the Natchez, got Fire Cat's clothes back, and ordered everyone out of her palace before she went in to see him."

"Huh! Maybe she took the young man by the hand, dragged him back into her quarters, and used him for everything a healthy young man is good for." She tried a crooked smile. "I sure as fire would have."

"That snoop Winter Leaf said that Night Shadow Star and the Red Wing just sat side by side on the floor."

"What's wrong with young people these days?"

"Maybe she's saving herself for marriage?"

Blue Heron shook her head. "The Night Shadow Star I once knew never saved herself for anything. As a girl she was wilder than a weasel. When she married Makes Three, she threw herself into the marriage and worked to learn a matron's skills. She did it with all the passion in her souls.

When Makes Three was killed, she took grieving to new heights. What she is good at is deluding herself over the simplest of things." She paused. "Any word from the thief?"

"Not a squeak, though one of your spies showed up about a hand of time ago." Smooth Pebble looked up at her in the growing gloom. "He reported that Horn Lance spent most of yesterday morning in Green Chunkey's palace. The Horned Serpent House nobles were asked to leave, including our source." She hesitated. "Green Chunkey hasn't had much love for us since you hung his cousin Red Mask in a square last year."

Blue Heron considered that. "Whatever they discussed, it wasn't the good health and well-being of the Morning Star House."

"Probably not. For as soon as Horn Lance concluded his business with Green Chunkey, he was borne posthaste to Evening Star Town."

"Ah, where he began to insinuate himself with Columella!" Blue Heron clapped her hands in understanding. "My ex-husband didn't waste any time picking scabs off old wounds, did he? Good thing we've currently got friendly relations with Serpent Woman Town, or he'd have had to run his porters into the ground to get up north in the attempt to ingratiate himself with High Chief Wolverine."

They were approaching her palace, where a warrior, a war club on his shoulder, dissuaded anyone who might be inclined to climb her stairs.

Blue Heron let the porters carry her up her ramped staircase. She touched her forehead as she passed the eagle guardian posts and sighed as she was set down on her veranda.

It took her three tries to get up. Then she minced her way inside with one hand to her bruised ribs. To her relief Notched Cane was back; a cheery fire crackled and sent its yellow light through the room. Food steamed in pots beside the fire. Notched Cane rose from one, touching a finger to his chin.

"How did it go?" she asked without formality.

"As you ordered, Keeper, I found the Trader the thief suggested. He was actually delighted to assist."

"Good." She gestured at her door. "I'll eat in my room. If anyone shows up looking for me, speak with Smooth Pebble before you decide to disturb me."

"Of course." The man bent down to the steaming pots beside the fire. In the corner Dancing Sky and her two daughters were sewing beads onto one of Blue Heron's skirts.

Blue Heron sighed as she pushed the door hanging aside and plodded into her room.

She started as Seven Skull Shield's weary voice announced, "Before you rip all your clothes off, or jump out of your skin, it's only me."

"Phlegm and vomit! How do you do that?"

In the gloom she could see where he had seated himself on her biggest storage box. He seemed to be leaned forward, looking a little worse for wear, and maybe in pain.

"How do you keep getting in here? Five Fists detailed new guards with the admonition that he'd have their scalps if they failed to keep out intruders."

"What happened to your face?" he asked, apparently having better night vision than she did.

"That Natchez, Swirling Cloud, woke me up last night pawing through that box you're sitting on. When I started to get indignant about somebody uninvited in my quarters, he took offense."

She peered more closely at him. "What happened to you? Some young husband catch you in his wife's bed?"

"This?" He pointed at his bruised face. "Your ex-husband's got the word out to every unsavory scoundrel in the city. He and the Natchez want me. Alive. And they're offering a fortune in exotic Trade to get me. They came close. Caught up with me in a Bear Clan charnel house."

"That was you? Heard it was quite a mess. The lineage that owns that charnel house hung the two who survived in squares. Bear Clan know you were involved?"

"Probably," Seven Skull Shield told her morosely. "If Slick Rock was one of the ones who survived, he'd have screamed out that it was my fault."

That the thief spoke so dispiritedly shook her. Even in the worst of times she was used to a ribald humor lurking just under the surface. "I can deal with Bear Clan for you. You'll have to make your own peace with the ghosts of the dead."

"Keeper, I don't worry about ghosts." He seemed to shift, favoring his back. "And Bear Clan's the least of my problems. I needed to see you, and then I'm going to have get as thin as fog for a while."

"I don't understand."

She caught movement at the corner of her vision an instant before something wet touched her foot. Yipping, she leaped back, only to recognize a dog as it retreated to the safety of Seven Skull Shield's feet.

"Where'd the dog come from?"

"A skinny guy on the avenue. That's another story. I came to tell you that your husband and I—"

"*Ex*-husband."

"Ex-husband," he agreed. "He's gone too far. I can't let him put a price on my head. And I can't run. He was at Wooden Doll's last night. Because of me. If he's hurt her, threatened her? I can't have that. You understand, don't you?"

Wooden Doll. The fancy woman who Traded her bodily skills down at River Mounds City. Her name had cropped up last spring when Blue Heron had been hunting Seven Skull Shield. The inflection in his voice indicated that she was more to Seven Skull Shield than just a mere night's entertainment.

"I do understand." She shied away from the dog, her eyes having adjusted to the dark. Was the beast as homely as it looked, or was it just too dark to make it out clearly? Seating herself on the bed, she asked, "Have you eaten?"

"A bowl of stew this afternoon. I could stand another."

"Notched Cane!" she raised her voice. "Two helpings. Bring one for the thief."

"That's who you've been talking to? How'd he get in there?"

"That does seem to be the eternal question, doesn't it?" she mused dryly.

"Keeper?" Seven Skull Shield asked, "What's the Tortoise Bundle, and why is it so important?"

For a moment, she just stared in disbelief. "Talk about the last thing I'd expect to come out of your mouth. Where did you hear about the Tortoise Bundle?"

"From a woman who calls herself its guardian."

As if she'd swallowed a chunk of ice, a cold chill ran through her stomach.

Forty-nine

The startled look on the Keeper's face told Seven Skull Shield that he'd struck a nerve.

"The Tortoise Bundle . . ." The Keeper's words trailed off as Notched Cane cleared his throat suggestively from outside her doorway. She gave Seven Skull Shield a warning look and raised a hand to still any question before calling, "Come."

Notched Cane entered her gloom-dark room, two bowls in his hands. "It's like midnight in here. Let me get you a lamp, Keeper."

"Thank you, we'd appreciate that. And then we're going to need some privacy."

"Yes, Keeper."

With smooth efficiency, Notched Cane set the plates down. He returned a moment later with a small hickory-oil lamp, its floating wick flickering. He placed it on one of her storage boxes, touched his forehead, and left.

Seven Skull Shield winced as he reached for the bowl, his battered body protesting. Raising it to his lips, he sucked down the flavorful stew. One thing about eating at the Keeper's: the food was always exceptional.

As he drank down the brothy mixture, thick with rabbit,

ground nuts, and mashed black walnut, he kept a wary eye on the Keeper, reading the churning thoughts behind her eyes as she sipped at her bowl. In the light he could see the darkening bruise on her face, the pain she tried to hide.

Finally, she set her bowl down, dragged a forearm across her lips, and pinned him with a sidelong glance. "Where did you hear about the Tortoise Bundle?"

"From an ancient-looking woman who treated me after Slick Rock and his braggarts laid into me with clubs in that charnel house." He gestured to the beast on the floor. Drool was leaking out of the corner of the dog's mouth as it stared fixedly at the bowl. "She says the dog led me to her. For all I know, that was true. I was so skull-knocked I was seeing double and puking my guts out. Then nothing until I came to my wits in her temple."

Blue Heron sighed. "Well, whatever she told you, the bundle's gone. Burned up in a fire when I was a girl. That was in the aftermath of the wars. Petaga and Lichen. Blood and thunder, that was so long ago. We all lived in fear. When warfare flares out of control, it consumes entire peoples."

She paused, eyes gleaming in the lamplight as she watched him. "The great priestess Lichen was Petaga's strength, but the man just didn't have the skills that make a man a great leader. Lichen's Power came from the Tortoise Bundle. It was old, its origins going back . . . huh, perhaps to the Beginning Times. It was old Power, Underworld Power. Of all the great bundles, the Tortoise Bundle was one of the few that somehow survived when Petaga burned Tharon's palace. No one knows how. It should have been consumed along with the rest. And it was said that Nightshade collected—"

"Who?"

"A great and Powerful witch. According to the stories, she called down mad Tharon's destruction when she discovered he'd committed incest. Afterward she collected the bits of bundles that survived and took them off to the Land of the Palace Builders."

Blue Heron paused. "All but the Tortoise Bundle. Along with a little carved stone wolf, it was said to be Lichen's most treasured link to the Spirit World."

"Then why have I never heard of it?"

"Because it's supposed to have been destroyed, thief. After Petaga's army was defeated, the Four Winds Clan sacrificed him and his female relatives and successfully resurrected the Morning Star in Black Tail's body. People had been praying for an end to the wars. The miracle of the Morning Star's resurrection brought all the clans under the Four Winds banner. The Morning Star's decrees, being just, enticed the warring parties to symbolically and ceremonially bury their weapons."

"What about Lichen? The story is that she didn't submit."

"Do you know that old abandoned mound north of Black Tail's tomb? The one with the burned timbers sticking up?"

"I was just there."

"Rather than pay homage to the Morning Star, when warriors were sent to escort her to the living god, she set fire to her temple, and burned alive inside it."

"Along with her Tortoise Bundle?"

"That's what we've always believed. Whoever this old woman is, and if what she says is true, she's kept the secret of the Tortoise Bundle's existence. And done it right under my nose. That takes some skill."

Blue Heron pulled at the wattle under her chin as she studied him. "And now you pop into my room and tell me you've talked to the guardian of the Tortoise Bundle? After all these years?"

"She says the Power's changed. That Lichen didn't understand."

"Power's changed, all right. And her announcing herself to you? That wasn't coincidence." Her gleaming eyes betrayed the thoughts racing between her souls. "Why now? The Tortoise Bundle was said to be Lichen's Spirit Helper, a link to First Woman. Is it because now the Itza comes, threatening to skew the whole world?"

Blue Heron's eyes narrowed further in thought. "Does the guardian of the Tortoise Bundle know that you serve me?"

Seven Skull Shield crossed his arms. "I don't serve you, Lady. We have an arrangement. Though everyone else in this rotted city seems to think I've become your creature. I suppose she does, too."

"Curious," Blue Heron said thoughtfully, "that she'd pick this moment to disclose her existence."

"She didn't tell me so that you'd know, Keeper. She told me—and these are her exact words—'When the time is right, inform Lady Night Shadow Star that the Tortoise Bundle will aid her.'"

Understanding flashed in the Keeper's face. "Of course! It's Night Shadow Star. Underworld Power. A balance to the Morning Star's Sky World Power. What else did she tell you?"

"Her words didn't always make sense."

"That's the problem with priestesses and holy people. They always speak in riddles that no one sane can understand. The more vague the speech, the less likely their prophecy is to be proven wrong."

Seven Skull Shield grinned at the acidic tone in her voice. "One of the things she said that made no sense was that the Red Wing's souls were suffocating both stone and lance. And it was up to me to lead him to the teacher. What could that possibly be about? Fire Cat and me? We despise each other."

Blue Heron was tugging harder at her wattle, a tell that she'd made a connection; her eyes thinned further.

"Want to tell me about it, Keeper?"

"The Natchez, the same one that hit me last night, beat Fire Cat at chunkey, humiliated him, and left him to walk home naked and broken."

Seven Skull Shield caught himself pulling at his own chin as he considered. "Disgraced at chunkey? And she's marrying the Itza lord tomorrow? As stiff-necked as he is, I could see him cutting his throat."

"Stone and lance? His chunkey game has been the topic of some conversation."

"Why would the guardian of the Tortoise Bundle care if Night Shadow Star's bound servant is losing at chunkey?"

"Even more to the point, who's this teacher you're supposed to lead him to?"

"No idea."

She shook her head slowly as she considered. "Is this old woman someone I should be wary of?"

"Keeper, my impression? That old woman has stared into the eye of the abyss; and when she saw what was staring back, she didn't so much as blink."

Keeper Blue Heron nodded to herself, lips pursed. "Then things are more convoluted and dangerous than we thought."

"How's that?"

"When even ancient enemies offer an alliance against a new threat, a wise man should tremble in his moccasins."

Fifty

On bare feet Night Shadow Star eased her door hanging to the side and crept out into her palace great room. At his place beside her door, Fire Cat finally slept. She'd listened to him toss and turn until his breathing had finally deepened.

She'd relished the time she'd had to just sit beside him, the voices in her head stilled for the moment. To feel another human being's presence, that warmth against her arm, the security of her head on his shoulder, had flooded her with a seldom-known contentment.

When she'd finally pulled away, he'd said, "You don't have to do this. We could leave, Lady. There is a whole world out there. A couple of necklaces, a piece of copper, would be more than enough Trade for a light-hulled canoe. There are other places. Split Sky City. Cofitachequi. The Ockmulgee. The Caddo. Pick a direction. I can serve you in a foreign land as well as I can in Cahokia."

His words had drawn tendrils of desire from her souls, stirred a longing she hadn't known existed within her.

"No!" Piasa's voice, absent since she'd hurried from Blue Heron's, sent a sibilant shiver through her.

Now she walked through her palace, aware that this was the last night that it would be inviolately hers. She might still own it, but tomorrow a strange man, his servants, and warriors would invade her haven. His presence would insinuate itself, filtering into the very walls and benches. Here, where she and Makes Three had laughed and loved, the memories would be tainted, corrupted.

She tilted her head back, drawing in the scent of smoke, thatch, floor matting, and the lingering sweetness of the corn stew Winter Leaf had cooked. The odor of her people, their clothing and robes, would be contaminated by the strange sweat and oils of invaders.

"Did you delude yourself with the belief that the world stopped with Makes Three's death?" Piasa's whisper just behind her right ear made her glance his way. Only dark shadows met her gaze.

"Delude myself? No. It was a hope, master. Only a desperate, fading hope."

Fifty-one

Horn Lance yawned and rubbed the back of his neck as he stepped out the Men's House door. The faintest hint of dawn grayed the eastern horizon. A ring of Natchez warriors, their weapons at hand, slept in a semicircle between the structure and the open plaza. Bitter Wood, the squadron second, hunched in the misty morning, back braced against the Men's House wall as he kept watch.

"Good morning, Lord," the war second greeted.

"You have seen the *ahau*?"

"He's around back. Had his medicine kit."

Horn Lance nodded his thanks and walked quietly around the building. The Men's House was built upon a low mound, barely enough to lift it above plaza height. On the apron of dirt in the rear, Thirteen Sacred Jaguar was removing the last of his clothes. Beside him stood Burning Ant, his hands clenched on the *kukul*'s staff. The carved image of Waxaklahun Kan snarled at the reddening horizon, the War Serpent's fangs gleaming as if bloody in the light.

Thirteen Sacred Jaguar neatly folded his breechcloth and laid it aside. He spread a red, yellow, black, and white blanket on the beaten grass. A small ceramic pot, its sides painted in the *k'ak b'utz* hieroglyphs for fire and smoke, rested beside his blood-letting kit. Glowing embers were visible within the small pot. A small ball of *pom* incense burned before him, its aromatic smoke rising in a blue plume.

"Greetings, *Ahau*. Are you prepared for the day?"

Thirteen Sacred Jaguar shot him a brief glance, then knelt naked on his blanket. "Offerings must be made. Last night I held vigil for the Nine Lords of Death. This morning I send offerings to the Thirteen Lords of the heavens. If I am to succeed here in this nest of ignorant monkeys, the Powers of both Kan and Xibalba as well as the will of the gods must be with me."

"My travels have laid the groundwork for several valuable allies, *Ahau*. As in all things, there must be a beginning. A seed planted. At both Horned Serpent House and Evening Star House I have made the fertile suggestions that opportunity exists for the other Houses. I will follow up with them again after a *uinal* has passed."

A *uinal* marked twenty days, a basic unit in the Mayan calendar.

Thirteen Sacred Jaguar nodded, his eyes on the brightening horizon as he removed a sheet of *juna* from his sacred snake-skin bag.

Horn Lance could see the prayer, its hieroglyphs carefully drawn. The different colors of ink added their Power to the words themselves.

"Fertility?"

"I am hoping that this very night I will do some planting of my own. The prayer asks that the Zero-One Portal where the Canoe of Life opens in the northern sky will produce a new soul. That it will join with my semen as I take this ugly woman."

The lord referred to the northern terminus of the great white band of stars in the night sky. It was believed that there, in the constellation the Itza and Yucatec knew as the Cracked Turtle Shell, souls reentered the world from the realm of the Dead.

"May it be so, *Ahau*."

He watched respectfully as Thirteen Sacred Jaguar spread his knees, placing the *juna* with its prayer hieroglyphics on the blanket so that he straddled it. Then he laid his sacred stingray spine beside his right knee.

Humming a prayer, Thirteen Sacred Jaguar raised his hands and eyes to the eastern horizon.

The first spectators, having risen early, caught sight of the Itza where he continued to pray, hands raised. They were pointing, calling to each other. Others appeared, rounding the society houses and temples that packed the space around the Men's House.

Walking to the Men's House front, Horn Lance called, "Second, if you could rouse a couple of the men, Thirteen Sacred Jaguar is in prayer. People have started to approach. If we don't keep them back the *ahau* will be mobbed."

"Yes, Lord." The Natchez yawned and began kicking his warriors awake.

Horn Lance returned to the rear, relieved when the first of the Natchez warriors created a protective ring around the Itza as he earnestly prayed to the rising sun.

More people arrived, a crowd building.

Thirteen Sacred Jaguar's voice continued to rise and fall; as he prayed, his naked body reflected the morning's orange glow. Cupping the *pom* smoke in his hands, he bathed his body with it.

The first bright spear of orange sunlight cleared the eastern bluffs. Thirteen Sacred Jaguar shouted in triumph. As the light spilled yellow onto the back of the Men's House, he reached for the stingray spine.

Horn Lance shot a curious glance at the now-silent crowd.

Thirteen Sacred Jaguar grasped his dangling penis in his left hand, pulling the foreskin out above the glans. He lifted his voice in prayer as he used the sharp point to pierce the foreskin.

An audible gasp rose from the crowd as Thirteen Sacred Jaguar directed his penis over the *juna*. Blood, the highest form of *ch'ulel*-laden *itz,* dripped onto the paper in scarlet starbursts.

Letting his penis bleed, Thirteen Sacred Jaguar lifted the paper, offering it to the sun, to the four directions. With his left hand he reached for the *k'ak b'utz* pot and poured hot embers onto the paper. Holding it just so, he blew. The embers reddened before the *juna* burst into flames.

"Rise, sacred smoke!" Thirteen Sacred Jaguar cried in Itza. "Take my prayer and my offering to the thirteen heavens. Tonight, as I join my wife, let a soul come to our union! With the sacrifice of my blood, born of my pain, hear me!"

Within moments, flames consumed the parchment, and a spiral of gray smoke rose toward the morning. Several tendrils Danced along the *kukul*'s fanged face before weaving their way through the gaping jaws and vanishing as if inhaled by the war god's *ch'ulel.*

The crowd seemed stunned, having never seen the like of it. Yes, let the word travel. Let the Morning Star wonder. Horn Lance could not care less if the Zero-One Portal spit out a soul to join Thirteen Sacred Jaguar's semen. An heir would eventually come. If not tonight, then sometime in the coming year.

It was the crowd he wanted. And the story they would tell about the remarkable offering the Itza had made on the day of his wedding. Yes, let that go from lip to lip. The most Powerful of weapons were not always *yaotlatquitl* in the hands of dedicated warriors, but the questions in the common man's mind.

Fifty-two

Fire Cat moved as if his souls were made of wood. Carved like the images of Hunga Ahuito on the temple roofs, and just as unfeeling. Some remote part of him ensured that breakfast was made, that it was taken to Night Shadow Star before the Keeper came to collect her for her ceremonial preparation. Marriage—like everything in life—required the proper ritual.

When he dared to glance in, Night Shadow Star was busily going through her boxes and storage baskets, sorting garments.

"Lady? Can I be of assistance?"

"There are things I don't want others going through." She hesitated, fingers running over the fine fabric of a shirt he recognized as once having belonged to Makes Three. "When I'm finished could you carry these things to my storage room? Perhaps rearrange the boxes so they are on the bottom?"

And away from casual rummaging by Itza or Natchez fingers.

"Of course, Lady."

Her voice was small when she said, "Thank you."

Fire Cat glanced at the rest of the household staff, reading their worry.

"It will be all right," he told them, trying to force a smile.

"Will it?" Clay String asked while the others raised questioning eyebrows.

"She knows what she's doing," he insisted without belief.

It was Winter Leaf who said, "You brought her back to life . . . for a while at least."

"Thought you all didn't like me." He bent over the breakfast pots, scraping what was left into a single jar.

"We don't," Clay String told him with an absent smile. "But we're expecting to like the Itza even less."

He paused, looking at the man. "She is going to need us more than ever. All of us."

"And how do you, Red Wing, think you're going to be able to find the strength to just smile and take it? Yesterday you were on the verge of weeping over the loss of a chunkey game."

Fire Cat took a deep breath. "I'll find it. Somehow."

Clay String spread his hands wide. "You're the great war chief who destroyed entire Cahokian armies. If you can't save us, who can?"

He stared down, flexing the muscles in his right arm, watching them bulge under his sun-browned skin. Something had gone wrong. As if a shadow of witchery had tainted his very flesh. Like a deep-rooted fungus that sucked at the marrow of his bones and muscles when it came to chunkey.

The solution lay just beyond the fringes of his consciousness. Elusive. If he could just reach out, grasp that fleeting understanding . . .

Clay String's desperate voice intruded: "Whatever you have to do, Red Wing, we're all depending on you."

"Whatever?" A swelling emptiness sucked at his heart.

Fifty-three

What do you think, dog?" Seven Skull Shield asked his new companion as they walked through the crowd gathering around the plaza. People were coming from all directions, Cahokia's great avenues thronging like rivers of human beings that flowed toward central Cahokia. A festive feeling seemed to carry on the very air.

The locals—anyone with a cooking pot, dried meat or fish, corn or nut breads—were looking for a good day's Trade. Others were already hawking beaded jewelry; some dangled crude statues of the Itza, hastily carved and painted. To Seven Skull Shield's way of thinking, the images didn't look anything like the Itza. The green dye, made from hastily rubbed grass blades, wasn't going to last out the week, but the hawkers were still asking a string of shell beads in Trade.

And often getting it.

On the southern end of the plaza, the first of the stickball teams had assembled. Wearing bright yellow girdles with trailing bustles, the young men were loosening up, passing deerhide balls back and forth. The old referees with their colored sticks were chasing up and down the sides, motioning people back in an attempt to keep the field clear.

The dog ambled happily at Seven Skull Shield's side, tongue already hanging from the side of his bear-like jaws. The beast's tail cut lazy arcs in the air, his oversized paws padding on the packed ground. Each time Seven Skull Shield addressed him, he looked up with his oddly colored eyes sparkling in wordless response.

"Quite the crowd," Seven Skull Shield noted, thrusting his thumbs into the rope that belted his ratty-looking hunting shirt at his waist.

To his relief, Keeper Blue Heron had offered him one of the beds outside her door. Partly he supposed his presence added to her sense of security; partly it was no doubt that she was so exhausted she wasn't thinking straight. But he hadn't had to sleep on someone's ramada mat and face discovery in the middle of the night, or the endless clouds of mosquitoes.

The early-rising Smooth Pebble had seen to it that he got a good breakfast, and the berdache had disdainfully tossed a loaf of stale acorn bread to the dog. Fortunately she'd been looking the other way when the brindle beast squatted in puppy fashion and peed on the new matting.

When Blue Heron had appeared in her doorway, he'd used the distraction to cover the wet spot with a handy seed jar. Maybe in the predawn rush no one would move the pot until after it dried.

"Dog?"

The beast looked up, tail swiping a bigger arc.

"You're either going to figure out where and when you can pee, or I'm not going to be able to save you from the stew pot."

On the eastern side of the plaza he slowed as he approached the Four Winds Men's House. A seething mass of people surrounded it, the strongest shouldering in to get a peek, and then shouldering back out to tell companions what they'd seen.

"You wouldn't believe it!" a Hawk Clan man told his

friend. "The Itza was there at dawn. Praying. As the sun crested the horizon, he slit open his shaft! A fountain of blood shot out. And he burned it in offering!"

"He burned his penis?"

"No. He burned the blood!"

"How's Lady Night Shadow Star going to like that? Her husband comes to her marriage bed with a bleeding rod? Any pleasure she's going to get tonight will be stoked by her own fingers."

"What kind of fool slices his penis on his wedding day?" another wondered.

"Maybe Itza can magically heal themselves?" The Hawk Clan man shrugged. "Who knows what foreign and exotic Power he controls? Undoubtedly it's a great magic, given that he comes from the other side of the world."

"Next thing, you'll tell me he has a second shaft? Like those stories they tell out west about Coyote?"

Seven Skull Shield stopped the man. "Did you see this? He truly cut his shaft and burned the blood?"

"Indeed! Think of the Power! Penis blood, carrying the essence of a man's prayer. He sent it to the Sky World the way we do tobacco smoke. I tell you, he has Powerful gods."

Seven Skull Shield raised an eyebrow. "That . . . or very dangerous witchery."

"Huh?"

He pointed to his own crotch, saying loudly, "Think about it. If you split your penis on your wedding day, how long do you think it would take you to recover . . . if ever? And what kind of evil Power would it take to mend a man's shaft back whole again?"

He left them staring suspiciously at each other, the others who'd overheard muttering under their breaths.

It was a small barb in the body of retribution, but who knew where the battle might end up, or what slight margin the Keeper might need to garner a victory?

He passed a knot of dirt farmers, their hair coiffed in an

odd fashion, their language unintelligible. Given the delight in their eyes, the coming of the Itza might have been like a second resurrection. One man pointed at his crotch before gesturing with animation and fluttering his fingers toward the sky.

The story about the Itza's morning ritual was spreading like a wildfire.

Seven Skull Shield glanced down at the dog. "You know what I think? Maybe the Itza believes this nonsense. Or maybe it was a trick. But whatever it was, the people are eating it up like honeysuckle nectar on blueberries."

The dog's ears pricked as if fascinated by every word.

"Yeah, I'm glad that you agree. But I think it's going to be trouble in the end."

As he said it, he heard someone say, "There you are."

He turned to see Slick Rock, his face battered and bruised. A war club—pogamoggan style, the kind with the rounded wooden ball on the end—hung from his scabbed-over hand.

"How'd you get away from the Bear Clan?" Seven Skull Shield asked reasonably.

"You're going to pay." Slick Rock swung his club.

Instinctively Seven Skull Shield grabbed the dirt farmer who'd been marveling at the Itza's split penis and yanked him sideways into the blow. At the smacking thump, the dirt farmer shrieked in surprise and pain.

Before Seven Skull Shield whirled to run, he glimpsed the consternation on the faces of the farmer's friends. For a heartbeat they stood frozen in disbelief; then with a chorus of howls, they leaped. As Slick Rock disappeared under the avalanche of bodies, Seven Skull Shield was slipping artfully into the press, the brindle dog bounding gleefully behind.

Fifty-four

Blue Heron sipped her cup of rosehip tea, the red liquid sweet on her tongue. The midmorning sun had just cleared the Women's House roof, and the day was already too warm. She lowered the cup as Night Shadow Star emerged from the sweat lodge: a low dome-shaped structure sealed with an earthen roof. A gush of escaping steam swirled around her naked body as though in a caress, then rose toward the light blue morning sky.

Blue Heron had been attending her niece since she'd collected her just before dawn. As Night Shadow Star's closest female relative, it was traditional. *Tonka'tzi* Wind should have shared the duties, but had her hands full with the last of the wedding preparations. Not that Blue Heron was doing such a good job with her niece.

Certain behaviors were expected of a woman before her marriage.

Night Shadow Star had summarily refused to participate in most of them.

The common belief was that to omit such important personal and spiritual preparations brought bad luck to a marriage.

Hence Blue Heron's insistence that Night Shadow Star at least accompany her to the Four Winds Clan Women's House to ritually bathe, cleanse, and purify her body before the late afternoon ceremony.

Night Shadow Star straightened to her full height and tossed damp black hair over her shoulders. She tilted her head back in what must have felt like delightfully cool air after the steam's sweltering and hot sting.

Blue Heron smiled at the sight. Night Shadow Star gleamed, her skin luminous as perspiration pooled in the hollows created by her collarbones and broad shoulders. The light seemed to mold itself to the woman's muscular arms and runner's thighs. Her high breasts—brown nipples hard—arched as she filled her lungs. The action emphasized her narrow waist and the swell of her hips. She had a flat belly and muscular abdomen that culminated in the water-beaded mat of pubic hair.

First Woman must have looked like this in the Beginning Times, Blue Heron thought. If ever there were a perfect image of a female in her prime, it was her niece, here, at this moment.

"Come. Let me rinse you off." Blue Heron reached for the heavy pot of water, climbed up on a stump, and carefully sluiced the contents over Night Shadow Star's head and hair. Measuring her pour, she let the cool water run in sheets down Night Shadow Star's smooth skin.

"Feel better?" Blue Heron asked as she climbed down and placed the empty pot on the ground.

Scrubbing water from her eyes with both knuckles, Night Shadow Star blinked. "Well, that sets the blood running."

"The sweat lodge cleanses the body as well as the souls. You don't do it enough. Honestly, niece, you worry me."

Night Shadow Star shot her a mocking dark-eyed glance. The tiny beads of water on her lashes resembled little sparkles. "Be glad you don't share the terrors swirling around my souls. You'd be as tempted as I am to sink myself in the river and let Piasa devour my drowned and lifeless corpse."

Blue Heron said nothing, reading the truth of it in Night Shadow Star's eyes.

"Then perhaps a stricter adherence to the rituals might lessen the effects of—"

"Spirit possession comes with a price, Aunt." Night Shadow Star fixed her gaze on the empty water pot. "Holy men spend their lives seeking the ways of Power, crying out to be filled with it. When I first came back from the Underworld after being consumed by Piasa, Rides-the-Lightning placed a Piasa cloak over my shoulders and invoked the water panther's essence inside me." She smiled wistfully. "If I could shift Piasa's presence, like that cloak, to another's shoulders, I would do so in an instant."

"And then what?"

"I would laugh, Aunt. I would Dance, and run, and fling my arms about. I would be light, and free, and bursting with joy. Happy tears would slip from my eyes, and my souls would float like cattail down on a warm summer day. Beyond that, honestly, nothing would matter but freedom from the whispers, fears, and terrors in the night. I just want to be left alone to live without the hissing voices in my head. As it is, each breath I draw is taken in fear." She swallowed hard, adding, "And it's never going to end."

"Is that why you're sabotaging your marriage? Failing to observe the rituals? We do these things to ensure fertility, happiness, and ask Old-Woman-Who-Never-Dies and the Powers of the Earth to bless a union. Good marriages strengthen the clan. They provide us with a foundation from which—"

"*You*, Aunt? Of all people? With your string of discarded men behind you? Lecture *me* on good marriages?" Her laughter dripped with ridicule. "I *had* the perfect marriage. I *loved* my husband so much that I wrapped him in my souls. Even after what the Morning Star and my brother did to me, I healed, surrendered myself to one remarkable man." She knotted her fists, face strained. "And then Power took him away from me."

"Niece, it's not like—"

"Oh, yes it is, Aunt. Those parts of me that didn't die with Makes Three were crushed between Piasa's jaws, pierced by his sharp teeth. They were chewed, and swallowed, and digested. What he vomited back into the world was reborn as Piasa's creature. Piasa's *thing*. I do his bidding, exist in his shadow."

Blue Heron shivered despite the rising heat. "Why, then, are you marrying this Itza? You could have refused. Was it Piasa's order? Some game that Power is playing between our peoples?"

"The Itza brings the first roots of a new Power to Cahokia. It comes hidden beneath the wonders and potentials for stupendous Trade and exotic goods. But in the end, unchecked, it will change who we are and how we serve Power."

"Hunga Ahuito and Old-Woman-Who-Never-Dies will allow this?"

"The Itza has Old-Woman-Who-Never-Dies' protection. She has ordered me not to kill him."

"Let me get this straight: you want to kill him, but you can't. So . . . you're going to marry him?"

The smile that bent Night Shadow Star's lips hinted of madness. "It's the only way to destroy him."

"That makes no sense, girl."

"It makes all the sense in the world."

"Dense wood that I am, could you explain?"

"If I can't kill him, I have to convince him to destroy himself. Break him in a way that convinces him he's lost. Failed. Somehow I have to shatter his faith in his personal Power. Send him fleeing in defeat."

Blue Heron gestured toward the sweat lodge. "While you were in there, Smooth Pebble sent a runner. The story is that the Itza split his penis down the middle at sunrise. Then he burned the blood that jetted from the wound." She shook her head. "I have no idea what madness would possess him to mutilate himself so, but apparently you won't revel in the joys of his shaft this night." She winced. "Or perhaps any other."

Night Shadow Star's expression hardened. "Stories, like penises, grow on their own, Aunt. No doubt by sunset it will be told that he castrated himself. The Itza might have drawn a blood offering for the Powers of the Sky, but I suspect that he will be functional tonight. If anything, he will be hoping that his wound opens during our joining . . . a blood offering to mix with and empower his semen."

Blue Heron read the disdain and resolve behind her niece's expression. "Any chance it will take root?"

"From the feeling in my loins, my heat has passed for this moon." She smiled warily. "Assuming, despite his offering and prayer, that his Power to impregnate is no more potent than mine to remain barren. And if I'm lucky, by the time my cycle is full again, he'll be dead."

Blue Heron shook her head. "You're taking a man into your bed to destroy him? It's an odd way to fight for Cahokia's future."

Night Shadow Star's eyes were fixed on a distance only she could see. "I thought Fire Cat could save me. Why do women do that? Look to others? Now I fear this is the only chance we have left." She shot Blue Heron a fragile look. "If I fail, Thirteen Sacred Jaguar and his rogue god win."

Fifty-five

When Horn Lance found Thirteen Sacred Jaguar the *ahau* was in the process of Spiritually caring for the *kukul* atop its pole. Standing behind his right shoulder stood Burning Ant, his head raised, hands up in the supplicant's position.

The carved effigy of the War Serpent always sent a shiver down Horn Lance's spine. He had been there the day Waxaklahun Kan's *ch'ulel* had been ritually invoked and had taken possession of the standard.

Horn Lance himself had led the war party that had captured more than a hundred human beings from the city-state of Mayapan. On the day of the ritual, he had offered his own blood and pain. But it had been nothing compared to Thirteen Sacred Jaguar's offering as he first pierced his hands, thighs, and tongue, then pulled a knotted cord through the wounds. As tears had leaked from the man's tightly clamped eyes, his blood was collected by the priests, spattered on *juna*, and burned in a sacred offering plate.

At the same time the priests continued to torture the naked, blue-painted captives from Mayapan, beating them, breaking their jaws, wrenching their joints out of socket. Only when Thirteen Sacred Jaguar fell into a drug-induced trance, his voice plaintively calling past his swollen tongue to

Waxaklahun Kan, did the priests order the warriors, Red Copal and Shaking Earth, to drag the captives one by one to the altar.

Atop the stone bench carved in the shape of a supplicant warrior, the blue-painted captives were sliced open, their beating hearts cut loose from the arteries and veins, and pulled from inside spastically quivering rib cages.

Blood. So much blood. An impossibly crimson and vibrant offering of *itz*: the Power and essence of life. He'd never forget the smell of it as it mixed with the heady clouds of burning *pom*. The slick and clotting pools through which the warriors and priests waded.

Images clung to his souls, flickers of memory as limp bodies, blue-painted and gore-splotched, tumbled lifelessly down the blood-bright stone stairs to the plaza below. Had he actually seen the hideous Lords of Death rise from the soil to feast on the rubbery corpses? Or was that just a figment of his imagination, a vision made whole in dreams?

As Horn Lance had stood by Thirteen Sacred Jaguar's side that day—his own souls swaying in the Power Dance of balche, morning glory, and powdered mushrooms—he'd felt it: blood, death, and pain amplifying Thirteen Sacred Jaguar's rasping pleas. They had attracted Waxaklahun Kan's *ch'ulel*. Following the blood, the War Serpent had been drawn inexorably to the carved image of itself. As the priests slathered the *kukul*'s open mouth, opening a link between the Spirit World and this, the god's essence had taken possession of the standard.

Horn Lance had felt it happen. From that moment on, every time he was in the *kukul*'s presence, it served as a reminder of the incredible Spirit Power and magic the Itza controlled.

Poor Cahokia. In comparison with the Itza, let alone the Yucatec, Puuc, and their neighbors, how could the Cahokians ever hope to evoke the same *ch'ulel* from the Lords of the Sky, Earth, and Underworld?

In Cahokia, a hundred people might be sacrificed once a generation in the dangerous ritual to reincarnate the Morning Star's soul into a living man's body. But the Itza routinely cut the living hearts out of a thousand human beings in a day just to manipulate the divine scales. Only through an orgy of suffering, torture, blood, and death would the gods be forced to respond by bringing rain, health, prosperity, and good luck.

Cahokians were ignorant of the underlying truth: The whole of Creation teetered, eternally struggling for balance between pleasure, health, comfort, prosperity, joy, and success on one hand, disease, pain, suffering, war, death, and misery on the other.

The beautiful terror.

"Are you ready, *Ahau*? The time has come to prepare yourself. I have water for your bath. Your clothing is laid out, and your mask and cloak are being made ready."

Thirteen Sacred Jaguar turned, an expression of peace on his face. It slowly shifted to one of distaste as he focused his attention from the *kukul*'s Power to the duties of the day. "What of the sacrificial combat? Is that prepared? Have the Cahokians swallowed the bait?"

"They have, *Ahau*. Warriors have petitioned from all over Cahokia. Five have been chosen to face our warriors. They are the best of the best, Lord. Men who have killed at least ten opponents in man-to-man combat."

Thirteen Sacred Jaguar smiled thinly. "And they have no concept of the *macuahuitl*?"

"None. They've spent their lives with either the bow, war club, or war ax. As you like to say, they are like monkeys. And this afternoon they are about to face men for the first time." Horn Lance inclined his head slightly.

"I still dislike the notion that we cannot call it what it is. They are *ch'ab*, a sacrifice. A gift to the Lords of Death."

"And the Lords of Death shall partake of their blood, *Ahau*. They understand that things cannot yet be done as they are in the civilized world we come from. That we can offer the Lords of Death the lives of these warriors in celebration of your marriage is miracle enough for the time being. As we change these people, bring them to an understanding of the true nature of Creation, the Lords of Life as well as the Lords of Death will finally receive their just due."

At that moment, Red Copal leaned in to say, "War Leader? The woman you summoned has arrived. She awaits outside on a litter."

"Have her seated on the veranda. And ask Dead Teeth to see to her needs. Tell her I'll join her as soon as I can."

"What woman?" Thirteen Sacred Jaguar asked.

"Her name is Wooden Doll. A well-respected paid woman of remarkable talents . . . especially in this backwater. But more to the point, one who has a deep and sophisticated understanding of the intricacies of Cahokian politics. I've asked her to accompany me today."

"As you will." Thirteen Sacred Jaguar glanced reverently at his precious *kukul* and then at Horn Lance. "I should not question you as I do. Since arriving in this land of wild and ignorant monkey people, it has been just as you said. Back home, you served my father and the *multepal* before you came to serve me. Now, it seems, to obtain our goals, I must accede and serve you."

"*Ahau!*" Horn Lance protested, his hands out as a measure of his shock. "I *never*—"

"No, you've never exceeded your status or position." Thirteen Sacred Jaguar stepped forward and reached out to push Horn Lance's hands down. "But let us recognize this reality as it is: Here, for the time being, I follow your lead, take your advice."

Again he waved down Horn Lance's protest. "I understand that you are working to your own ends, my friend. As I look around this savage monkey world, I see little enough worth saving. So, tear it down in any way you wish. Inflict all the suffering you can upon those who once caused you harm. In the end, the darker their misery and defeat, the brighter our success and triumph. Each victory, beginning with this day's marriage to that hideous woman, brings us closer to the day when the first fleet of Itzan canoes lands here with priests, scribes, and warriors to begin the true transformation of these savages."

Horn Lance nodded, his thoughts racing. "We'll know in ten days, *Ahau*. If, in that time, we have established ourselves in Night Shadow Star's palace, if the other Four Winds Houses have begun sending emissaries, and if the people have begun to spread word of your Power, we can chance dispatching Split Bone and Dead Teeth back to Chichen Itza with a request for a major expedition."

Thirteen Sacred Jaguar studied him. "A mere ten days? Isn't that a bit presumptuous? We won't even know if the new Natchez White Woman and Great Sun have secured their hold on political authority, let alone on the river Nations. Nor can we be sure if our standing here—"

"Think, my Lord." Horn Lance pressed his hands together in a display of humility. "Given the distances involved, the risks and perils of the journey, the soonest we can expect our people to arrive is a full year away. And that's if everything goes according to plan."

Thirteen Sacred Jaguar stared thoughtfully at the *kukul*, as though reassured by its immense Power.

Horn Lance added, "Time, *Ahau*, is at once on our side, and our greatest enemy. On one hand, we need not succeed immediately."

"And what if we fail before they can arrive?"

"The gaming pieces will have been cast, Lord. The fate of these 'monkey people,' as you call them, will be sealed. Your commission from your father and the *multepal* was to determine if my stories and the rumors were true. You're here. In Cahokia. You've been face to face with the man pretending to be Hun Ahau. You have seen the sacrilege committed here, and how the Cahokians have perverted the sacred stories and gods. All Split Bone and Dead Teeth have to do is reach Chichen Itza and whisper what they've seen here. From that moment on, the *multepal* will move the god Witz and his mountain to reach Cahokia and cleanse its pollution from the world."

Thirteen Sacred Jaguar's young face lined in worry. "So much could still go wrong."

Horn Lance dropped to his knees before the lord, bowing his head. "As long as you manage to get a message to Chichen Itza, *Ahau,* even if your soul has been devoured by the White Bone Snake and is being tortured in Xibalba . . ."

Thirteen Sacred Jaguar's face brightened. "Like Hun Ahau, the sacred One Lord who reincarnated his dead father in the Underworld, I shall have won."

"And Cahokia, like the Lords of Xibalba in the Third Creation, will be doomed."

"Fetch me my box, good friend," Thirteen Sacred Jaguar said with a relieved grin. "For this day I shall partake of the mushrooms, a pinch of powdered toad, and ground mescaline. Make me a tea. I want to watch this world through a haze of *ch'ulel.* It will make my victory that much sweeter."

Fifty-six

"Pssst! Keeper!" came the whisper from outside Night Shadow Star's door.

Blue Heron turned, seeing Seven Skull Shield's bruised face as he peered around the door frame. And, being Seven Skull Shield, he took more than a moment to ogle Night Shadow Star's shapely body as she lifted a lean leg and stepped into her skirt.

"What do you want, thief? And keep a civil eye in your head. She's about to be married."

"You're starting to sound like Fire Cat," the thief replied, using her response as permission to step fully into the room. The ungainly bear-headed dog followed, its nose wiggling as it scented the air and looked around with those mismatched eyes.

"I asked what you wanted."

Seven Skull Shield made a face and gave her a shrug. "It's been a difficult morning. First I barely avoided having my brains knocked out by Slick Rock, and not a hand of time later, as I was enjoying a most succulent roasted rabbit, Mad Leg and some of his relatives appeared out of the crowd and grabbed me. I barely got away with my life."

Night Shadow Star inspected him as she tied a beaded

belt around her narrow waist to secure the midnight-black skirt. The garment didn't exactly communicate the usual gaiety of a wedding skirt, looking more like something worn for a state visit or other somber occasion.

Blue Heron arched an eyebrow. "So what do you expect me to do about it? And stop staring at Night Shadow Star's breasts like you're a starving infant."

Night Shadow Star's smile was fleeting. "At least the thief's lust is stoked by honest appreciation for a woman. I'll remember that when this day concludes." She pointed at her bed, now perfectly made, the opulent blankets and hides seamless on the frame. "Given that I'll end up there as nothing more than a prize to be bred."

Blue Heron's souls cringed at the bitterness in Night Shadow Star's voice. "With an attitude like that, you're certainly—"

"There are other, better fates, Lady. I can have you out of the city and gone," Seven Skull Shield told her bluntly. "No doubt I'll regret it, but you can take the Red Wing, too."

"Thief"—Blue Heron ground her few remaining teeth— "you go too far! If Night Shadow Star doesn't order you hung in a square, so help me—"

"It's all right, Aunt." Night Shadow Star shot the thief a half-felt smile. "Thank you. Now I can at least tell myself that it's my decision to stay and fight."

Seven Skull Shield's lips twitched; then he uncharacteristically bowed his head and touched his forehead. "Whatever you need, Lady. Just ask. And I do mean *anything.*"

Night Shadow Star's expression tightened, her eyes slightly losing focus. She seemed to be listening to something, then nodded. To the thief she said, "Fire Cat lost at chunkey. Piasa says he needs your help. Can you do that for me? Help him?"

"Help Fire Cat? Pus and blood, Lady, I was hoping you'd ask me to break someone's knees, or drown somebody in the swamp. The Red Wing and I? That's like mixing his swamp mud and my fine hickory oil." His expression soured under Night Shadow Star's slightly arched eyebrow. "I'll, uh, do what I can."

Blue Heron shook her head. "Why are you even here? We're almost out of time, and you're wasting more of it."

Seven Skull Shield hunched his big shoulders. "Keeper, half the city is hunting me. Um, you wouldn't mind if I sort of followed along behind, would you? Sort of out of the way until nightfall when I can really start to take things in hand?"

"Are you out of your mind? This is a Four Winds Clan wedding! You? You're a clanless, footloose, womanizing—"

"Look through the clothing stored in the great room," Night Shadow Star interrupted. "And have Clay String paint your face to hide that bruise. Tell him I want you to look like a noble."

"Niece!" Blue Heron thundered. "You can't—"

"If inviting the thief to join us brings me joy on this terrible day, who are you, or the clan for that matter, to deny me?" With a flourish, she whipped a stygian-black raven-feather cloak over her shoulders. "Even Piasa finds a perverted relief in the notion."

"It's your wedding," Blue Heron agreed.

"Which is why I'm dressed for a funeral, Aunt. Black skirt, black cloak, blackest of days."

Fifty-seven

Nothing in Seven Skull Shield's life had prepared him to be a noble. Even if he could have seen himself, he wouldn't have recognized the man who looked back. Clay String had painted his face white, then laid a thick black line from ear to ear over his eyes and the bridge of his nose. A red circle ran across his lips and under his jaw.

Seven Skull Shield worried that it made a perfect target for anyone who wanted to smack him on the chin.

His hair was greased, pulled into a bun so tight that it made his scalp hurt, and a wooden bundle box containing two scalp locks had been affixed to its front. The scalp locks, Clay String had told him reverently, had been taken by Night Shadow Star's dead husband in mortal combat. She had asked Clay String specifically to honor Seven Skull Shield with their Spirit Power.

No one, ever, had bestowed such an honor upon him, let alone such a high-status individual as Night Shadow Star. He wasn't sure how he felt about it. Uneasy, nervous, totally unworthy, and ready to reach down the Itza's throat, grab a handful of lungs, and rip them out by the roots if the gaudy foreign fool so much as gave Night Shadow Star a disdainful sidelong look.

Nor did the transformation stop there. A fine cardinal-feather cloak lay over his shoulders, and a white hemp-fiber apron hung from a tightly folded cloth breechcloth. Its front had been embroidered with two turkeys facing each other on either side of a spiral-decorated World Tree pole.

White leather wrist guards and feathered ankle bands finished the ensemble.

"I wouldn't believe it possible," Blue Heron muttered as they climbed the broad stairway from the packed Grand Plaza. She kept looking back at him, only to shake her head and climb the next couple of steps toward the Council Terrace Gate.

Ahead of them, Night Shadow Star rode in her litter, its sides decorated with strings of sunflowers, lilies, honeysuckle, and morning glory. Her porters advanced in measured step, as though in a slow, orchestrated climb.

Behind her litter, Fire Cat, dressed in full battle armor, followed in his usual position. Seven Skull Shield hadn't had time to so much as share a word with the Red Wing. But if the man's expression were any indication of how he felt, he needed only an excuse to let loose with the copper-bitted war ax he carried.

The procession ascended another slow step.

Pus and blood, boys, get it over with. She's dying inside, and all you're doing is dragging it out.

He glanced down at the dog. The beast seemed totally unconcerned, looking this way and that, sniffing a slight westerly breeze that carried the musky odor of tens of thousands of human beings.

Atop her litter, however, Night Shadow Star looked as if she were carved of ancient wood. She sat unflinching, eyes forward, knees together, arms braced on the litter sides.

As the procession finally reached the top, the crowd below let out another thunderous roar.

The warriors standing guard at the top of the stairs

dropped to one knee, bowing deeply and touching their foreheads in a sign of utmost respect.

Seven Skull Shield, tight on the Keeper's heels, followed the party inside as if he'd been a noble all of his life. The dog didn't know he was now on sacred ground.

"Keep your pus-rotted mouth shut," the Keeper had warned him, shaking a finger under his nose in emphasis. *"Remember that you're there on Night Shadow Star's sufferance.* Don't you dare *embarrass me or the lady. Or, gods rot you, I'll have your carcass hanging in a square so fast your blood will boil."*

Inside the gate every high chief, matron, and noble from the Four Winds Houses and the Earth Clans crowded the enclosure. Dressed in splendid finery and feathers, their faces painted to reflect their clans, most had chosen brightly colored clothing consisting of red for fertility, white for peace and contentment, and yellow as the symbol of new beginnings. Every form of hairdo could be seen, some elaborate, others subdued.

The ruling lords of Cahokia bowed their heads as Night Shadow Star's litter was carried past. Their fingers rose respectfully to their foreheads. Only as they looked up did expressions of surprise fill their eyes. Night Shadow Star's dark garb made an unmistakable statement. So did her tightly coiled hair pinned with copper arrows, and her face, painted light gray with the black tri-forked design of the Underworld surrounding her eyes. She looked less a bride and more an avenging Spirit from the darkest Underworld.

The sight created such a stir that only a few paid any heed to Seven Skull Shield as he walked along behind the Keeper. He kept his expression blank as puzzlement filled the eyes of the few who tried to place him. Then they gave the ugly beast at his heels another look before shaking their heads.

He waited while Night Shadow Star's litter was placed under the ramada on the central dais usually occupied by

Tonka'tzi Wind. Night Shadow Star remained still as a statue while chiefs and matrons crowded around, offering their congratulations. Her murmured acknowledgments were graciously polite, though remote.

Spit and fire, couldn't the callous fools see she was dreading the whole affair?

Fire Cat had taken his position to the rear, his posture rigid, his face a mask of conflicting anger and distaste.

Seven Skull Shield surprised himself by actually feeling sorry for the man. Fire Cat's arrogance had always been his worst feature. He constantly projected a self-important, over-inflated superiority. The last of the Red Wing Clan, he liked to think of himself as honor incarnate, having vowed to serve his enemy. No doubt the fool had never allowed himself to consider that he might actually be in love with the woman.

Then he'd been skinned by that cocky Natchez Little Sun? Knowing full well the man had murdered his predecessor? That he was in bone-deep with the Itza who was marrying the woman he secretly longed for?

That had to sting like cactus thorns pulled sideways through the man's souls.

Since Blue Heron was surrounded by Earth Clan nobles come to offer their well-wishes, Seven Skull Shield drifted back to the Council Terrace Gate and glanced out.

The Itza's procession, led by its Natchez guard, was parting the huge crowd on the Avenue of the Sun as it rounded the Great Plaza's northeast corner. The sight reminded Seven Skull Shield of a stick being pushed through debris-choked water as the crowd parted around the Itza party and flowed along beside it, only to remerge behind to trail in its wake.

Warriors in the plaza kept the multitudes from trampling the Morning Star's sacred chunkey courts. Beyond the high World Tree pole in the plaza's center, a massive stickball game was in progress. The way the teams moved hearkened back to schools of minnows, as players—one side in red, the other black—surged toward the eastern goal.

The society houses, temples, clan houses, and charnel mounds surrounding the Great Plaza seemed to float in a roiling sea of humanity. Seven Skull Shield could feel the Power of them: tens of thousands of human beings come to celebrate Lady Night Shadow Star's wedding.

People would be talking about this day for the rest of their lives.

The Itza's party was now climbing the stairs. First came the *kukul* standard, held high by an Itza warrior decked out in bright red, yellow, green, and blue. The snake totem with its gaping and fanged mouth glared out at the world though baleful green eyes of polished stone.

Atop his litter, and next in line, Thirteen Sacred Jaguar looked like a god himself; his dazzling and oversized head-dress, topped with its iridescent feather plume, gave him an otherworldly appearance. His sloped face, protruding lips, and slanting forehead had been painted with a black spot on either cheek. Depending on how the light hit his quetzal-feather cloak, it shone in any combination of green, blue, silver, or purple. The remarkable colors of his apron and the feathered arm guards and exotic necklaces of blue and green stone beads had never been equaled in Cahokia.

Behind came Horn Lance wearing his red-macaw-feathered helmet and his Itza warrior's armor. An exotically dressed woman climbed at his side, her face painted white with red sunbursts.

Then came the Natchez Little Sun, wearing the feathered finery of his people; the man climbed thoughtfully. And well he might. Nothing he'd ever seen among the Natchez or the southern Nations would have prepared him for the sea of humanity that washed up around the great mound.

Seven Skull Shield narrowed his eyes to slits as he studied the Little Sun. The man had dared to invade the Keeper's personal quarters, and, by Piasa's balls, he'd hit her hard enough to really hurt her. Nor was there any doubt that the sneaking little intestinal worm had murdered his predecessor.

Nothing about this entire situation smacked of any good.

At the foot of the stairs, the Itza warriors, led by the one called Red Copal, had stopped in a knot surrounded by the Natchez guard. They'd dressed in armor, carrying shields with curiously designed face decorations. Some kind of cased long weapons were carefully rested on their shoulders.

Word was that they would fight Cahokia's finest warriors atop the *tonka'tzi*'s newly recapped mound. Combat to the death? To celebrate a wedding? Unheard-of. And Hunga Ahuito help the luckless Itza who had to face the deadliest of Cahokia's skilled killers.

The people, however, had gone giddy in anticipation. Food, dancing, games, and celebration were one thing. Blood sport? That was the sweet nectar atop the corn cakes!

Seven Skull Shield stepped back as the *kukul* bearer marched the standard through the gate. Then the porters had to duck slightly lest the high plume atop the Itza's intricately ornate headdress rake the lintel.

Murmuring ran through Cahokia's nobility as they made way for the procession.

Seven Skull Shield couldn't help but grin to himself. It wasn't just every day that Cahokia's mightiest were awed by pageantry. It was a good lesson for the overstuffed—

He stopped short, heart skipping as he recognized the woman accompanying Horn Lance: Wooden Doll! Dressed like he'd never seen her before. Her face was perfectly painted, the wealth of her raven hair in a forward bun held in place by a stunning white-swan-feather splay. Her languid walk, hips undulating with each long-legged step, drew the eye of every man and half of the women; they whispered to each other, wondering at her identity.

To her credit, Wooden Doll acted oblivious, leaning toward Horn Lance to subtly indicate certain high chiefs like old one-eyed War Duck and Matron Round Pot from River Mounds House, Kills Four of the Snapping Turtle Clan, and Matron Red Temple of the Fish Clan. As she did she'd whisper additional information to Horn Lance.

"You know that woman?" Blue Heron asked, appearing at his shoulder.

"Wooden Doll," he almost whispered. "But . . . *with him*?"

"Ah, your paid woman. But I'm left to wonder: Why would he bring her here? What's his game?"

Seven Skull Shield reached up to rub his jaw, realized his face was painted, and barely avoided smearing his red circle. "She's acting as his guide to the high and mighty, pointing out the chiefs. Explaining to him who they are and why they are important."

"Surely they don't *all* patronize her."

"You'd be surprised, Keeper, but no, they *all* don't. Some, however, do. So do those who serve them, and those who deal with them. And Keeper, just because Wooden Doll is a paid woman, only a fool would underestimate her wits, or what she commits to memory."

"She's a most attractive woman," Blue Heron noted. "She's almost as much a sensation as the Itza. When you get the chance, thief, I'd like to make her acquaintance."

And with that she fixed her eyes on where the Itza's litter was being placed on the dais beside Night Shadow Star's. Neither of them appeared to be happy. Both kept their stares fixed forward, faces like graven stone, though the Itza's eyes seemed unfocused and dreamy.

"Oh, happy day," Seven Skull Shield muttered, seeing the corpulent Green Chunkey nodding as Horn Lance bowed respectfully before his clan chief. The two had walked off, leaving Wooden Doll standing chastely, her hands interlaced before her.

Taking the opportunity, Seven Skull Shield stepped up beside Wooden Doll, his heart in his throat as he said, "Every woman here is diminished by your presence."

He surreptitiously kicked the dog back when the mongrel extended its blocky nose to sniff at Wooden Doll's leg.

Startled, she turned, eyes flashing wide with recognition. "Skull? What are you doing here?" She glanced around in sudden panic. "Pus and blood, whatever you're planning to steal, it's not worth it! These people know each other. Dressed like a noble or not, someone's going to ask, 'Who's he?' and you're going to—"

"Shhh." He fought the urge to raise a finger to her reddened lips. "I'm not here to steal anything. Lady Night Shadow Star herself had me decked out like this. But your concern touches me."

Her dismay quickly shifted, a rapid calculation now reflected in her dark gaze. "So . . . you're a step deeper into Morning Star House's deadly swamp?" A pause. "You worry me."

"And you worry me." He inclined his head to where Horn Lance was being introduced to High Chief Thin Otter of the Raccoon Clan. "Serving him? He's the enemy."

"He's the Itza's second . . . and he pays well."

"Listen to me, he's in deep. You remember that cloak? The murder of the Natchez Little Sun? That was just the beginning. There's a catastrophe brewing here, and Horn Lance is the one throwing oil onto the fire. He's going to lose."

Her lips had tightened in that old familiar way. "Don't bet on that, Skull. You should hear the stories he tells. Our world is about to change forever. This marriage today? It's the first step in building a relationship with the Itza. Horn Lance sees it as a way of binding the world together. In his words, 'extending a mighty net of Trade and alliance from Cahokia to Chichen Itza and pulling them tight.'" She paused, a slight frown on her face. "But . . . I thought you were his friend. He's asked me a great deal about you."

"He's using you."

"And the Keeper's using you. Makes us even in a curious sort of way."

"Please, don't do this. He's danger—"

"Ah, Wooden Doll," Horn Lance asked as he appeared at Seven Skull Shield's side, "which young lord is this?"

Before she could respond, Seven Skull Shield told him, "Seriously, you'd ask? Figured you'd know, given what you're paying to have me captured, beaten, and tortured. I'm Seven Skull Shield, high chief of thieves and scoundrels, you sack of bleeding pus."

Wooden Doll's expression had frozen, her back stiffening.

"Ah." Horn Lance smiled grimly. "Should I simply bide my time, or call out that a common thief has slipped past the guards and watch you thrown down the steps?"

"Call out," Blue Heron interjected as she stepped between Seven Skull Shield and Horn Lance. "Please do. Since Seven Skull Shield is my niece's guest, the insult might be just enough to stop this farcical marriage. At the very least, it will provide the most sensational fodder for future conversations, don't you think?"

For long moments the two stared their hatred at each other. Seven Skull Shield shot Wooden Doll a sidelong glance of warning.

Apparently she was way ahead of him, her expression blank, head slightly turned as if unaware of the drama.

"Our time will come, my old love," Horn Lance whispered softly.

"Until then, perhaps you and Seven Skull Shield should get to know each other. You might withdraw your reward to have him captured as a way to get at me. It might do you good to meet a man with actual integrity."

She placed a hand on Wooden Doll's arm. "And while these men get acquainted, let's wander off for a talk. I've heard a great deal about you, and to be honest, I'm curious to know what kind of woman Seven Skull Shield thinks so highly of."

To the average eye, Wooden Doll's expression might have appeared composed. Only through his years of intimate association did Seven Skull Shield know how terrified she was as she inclined her head, saying, "You do me great honor, Keeper."

Seven Skull Shield kept his eyes locked on Horn Lance's as Blue Heron led Wooden Doll away. "If you harm that woman in any way, by Piasa's blood and fury, I'm going to—"

"The threats of a two-footed piece of trash like you are meaningless." Horn Lance smiled. "Enjoy your afternoon of playing high lord, you clanless fool. I've taken everything you thought you had: your woman, your freedom, your friends, and next I'll destroy your beloved Morning Star House. You're a bunch of pathetic fools, all of you. You've already lost, and you don't even know it."

Seven Skull Shield heard the low growl, and looked down to see the dog, hackles raised as he lifted his lip in Horn Lance's direction.

"Don't waste the effort to bite him, dog. He's just rotten meat." To Horn Lance, he added, "Keep right on thinking you've won, piss head. It'll make it hurt all the worse when I finally break you down and snap you in two."

Throwing his head back, Horn Lance broke into mocking laughter. He muttered "Pathetic idiot" as he walked away.

Fifty-eight

Columella smiled to herself as she watched the interplay between Horn Lance and the Keeper. Definitely no love lost there, nor had she been close enough to overhear the conversation between Seven Skull Shield and Horn Lance. It had taken her some time to recognize the thief, out of place and dressed as he was.

That the Keeper had dragged the exotic paid woman to the side just added to the fascinating social dynamics playing out before her. Flat Stone Pipe's spies had already informed her about the price Horn Lance had placed on the thief's head. Seven Skull Shield was a paradox. Columella had made a considerable number of inquiries about him in the days since Walking Smoke had come so close to snuffing her lineage in blood and fire: who he was, why the Keeper had drawn such a man into her service.

Knowing as much as she did about him, she was startled to see him here, let alone dressed like a noble in his finery. That didn't smack of Blue Heron's doing. Night Shadow Star, however, wouldn't have cared about appearance, let alone propriety. Was that the explanation? And if so, what did it imply about the thief's influence?

That Seven Skull Shield stood face to face with the man

who'd put a price on his head without reaching out, grabbing Horn Lance by the throat, and howling like a maniac as he beat him to death indicated that he fully understood the crosscurrents in the deep waters of intrigue.

As Horn Lance walked away from the thief, his lips twisted in wry amusement, Columella sauntered over to intercept him. She arched an eyebrow, cocking her head as he met her eyes.

"Greetings, Matron," he said neutrally. "You honor us with your presence here today. Myself, I am delighted to see you. You have met the *ahau* Oxlajun Chul Balam?"

"Not yet." She directed her gaze to where the Itza sat on his litter beside Night Shadow Star, a line of chiefs and matrons paying their respects, though the opulently dressed Itza seemed to be staring into space with glassy eyes. "Perhaps you will make the introduction?"

"Of course, Matron."

"A moment first, if you would, Lord Horn Lance," she added as he started toward the seated Itza.

Curiosity rapidly replaced irritation as he followed her off to one side and out of earshot of the others.

She glanced around to be sure, then began, "I've been keeping track of your activities over the last couple of days. My congratulations. You're the talk of the city."

The satisfaction of a satiated cougar lay behind his dark eyes. "These are exciting times, Matron. The Itza's presence here is forever changing our world. The people realize and understand the momentous events unfolding around them."

She glanced up at the palace. Its presence dominated the proceedings, a looming reminder of where the ultimate authority over Cahokia resided. "And how is your campaign to undermine credibility in the Morning Star progressing?"

"Matron! Surely you don't mean to imply—"

"Neither of us is a fool, Horn Lance. You wouldn't have come to pay your respects to Evening Star House hot on the heels of the visit to your cousin Green Chunkey if you hadn't understood Cahokia's underlying political structure. So let us talk bluntly. You've begun the process of undermining the Morning Star. The Itza provides a surrogate for the people, a new exotic with potentially more Powerful gods, assuming you can continue to awe the dirt farmers and Earth Clans. You've stabilized the south by assassinating the Natchez chiefs and installing new ones. Your arrival in Cahokia was magically orchestrated to dazzle us with wonder. The Morning Star has been lulled and distracted by remarkable gifts. Now the Itza marries Night Shadow Star. That roots his presence and acceptance as firmly as hard-packed ground around a World Tree pole. Now you're whittling away at those who could sabotage your plans."

"I think you're seeing more than is really the case, Matron."

"Oh?" She tilted her head toward where Seven Skull Shield stood, arms crossed, his hooded gaze on Blue Heron as she talked to the paid woman. "You've quite a price on the thief's head. If one of your ruffians can finally waylay him without wrecking another charnel house, what are you going to do with him?"

"Who said I'd placed a—"

"Like I said, neither of us are fools." Her gaze burned into his. "Did you come seeking Evening Star House's help or not?"

"What does that have to do with the thief?"

"There's no love lost between Blue Heron and myself. Your instincts were correct. For reasons that defy logic, she actually cares for that foul bit of human trash. Where were you thinking of holding him, or were you just going to sink his corpse in the river some night?"

Horn Lance pursed his lips, thoughtful eyes darting to the thief. Then he said, "We owe him one."

She gave him a cold smile. "Dead he's of no more use to you. Alive you can use him to torture the Keeper. Providing you can stash him somewhere where the Keeper can't find him. Someplace where he can linger for a long time and add to Blue Heron's dismay."

"And why would you take a risk like that?"

"Like I said, the Keeper and I have never liked each other." She paused. "Paying old debts is such a perilous business, wouldn't you say?"

Fifty-nine

The only way Fire Cat could stand it was by turning his heart and souls into stone: cold, unfeeling, and impervious. He forced himself to shut off his thoughts and just stand, back straight, war club in his hands. He convinced himself he *was* stone. Granite. Heavy. Hard.

The moments passed in a drawn-out blur. His gaze focused on the back of Night Shadow Star's head, as though he could see through her carefully combed hair where it was pulled up and pinned in place by the polished copper arrows. Past her scalp and skull and into her frantic thoughts.

How does she do it?

Quiet. Stone doesn't think. It doesn't question.

She hates this! She hasn't even glanced at him.

Night Shadow Star and the Itza might have been carved of rock themselves; neither seemed to take the slightest joy as they sat on their litters, looking for all the world like they were victims of malicious fate.

As if a counterpart, the standard bearer stood behind Thirteen Sacred Jaguar, his face stoic as he propped the snarling snake effigy, like a guardian, behind the Itza's litter.

At most Night Shadow Star or the Itza might incline his or her head slightly when a well-wisher offered congratulations.

The Itza, of course, had no idea what was being said to him, nor could he move his misshapen head much given the size of his soaring headpiece.

From where Fire Cat stood, it would be so easy. All he had to do was step to his right, raise his copper-bitted war club, and hammer it into the back of Thirteen Sacred Jaguar's neck before the standard bearer could shout out a warning.

One. Two. Three.

It would all be over. Night Shadow Star would be free.

And I would have broken my vow to her.

Not for the first time did he wish he hadn't been born a Red Wing. To have been anyone else would have released him from the inviolate code imposed by his ancestors. He could kill the Itza, the Cahokians would kill him, and the balance would be restored.

Be like a stone.

Don't think.

There was a moment of confusion when the Morning Star appeared at the top of the steps and started down from his palace.

A stillness fell over the crowd as the so-called living god descended, step by step. Chunkey Boy had overdressed the part of the Morning Star, complete with copper head-dress, white apron, the usual face paint, and shell-mask ear coverings.

That familiar deep-seated revulsion grew in Fire Cat's heart as people knelt. How could the fools debase themselves before a living lie?

How could Night Shadow Star acquiesce to her perverted brother's will and marry this foreigner?

Then, lost in the maze of disbelief, and the howling of his souls, Fire Cat realized the Morning Star was standing before Night Shadow Star and the Itza. For the first time, they both rose, stepping forward as Horn Lance moved up behind Thirteen Sacred Jaguar. The *kukul* bearer crowded in close, as if the gaudy snake totem were a party to the proceedings. Was that a gleam in the eerie green eyes, or did the light just reflect from the polished stone?

The familiar words, once said during Fire Cat's own marriages to Fall New Moon and False Dawn, repeated in his head as they came droning out of the Morning Star's mouth.

At the Itza's side, Horn Lance continued to translate for Thirteen Sacred Jaguar. At the appropriate time, he even took the Itza's hand, extending it to grasp Night Shadow Star's.

Both seemed to recoil from the other's touch.

Fire Cat might loathe the imposter who played the Morning Star, but some voice down between his souls reminded, *"He's her brother, Chunkey Boy. Which makes the marriage valid."*

And then, as the final words were spoken, Horn Lance coached Thirteen Sacred Jaguar through the Cahokian pronunciation. The highly decorated ceremonial blanket was brought forth. As it was draped over their shoulders, man and woman were married.

In that instant, Fire Cat struggled for air, as though a chokehold had been placed on his throat. A tingle of fear tickled his insides, and a desperate sensation ran electric and crackling, like rubbed fox fur, through his bones.

She's no longer . . . mine. As if she ever was.

People were whistling, clapping, and shouting. High chiefs and elegant matrons, their faces glowed with delight. When had the world gone so blurry, his vision wavering?

"Here," a soft voice intruded into Fire Cat's freefall of loss. He jerked in surprise as a hand was laid gently on his shoulder.

Somehow he turned, shocked to recognize Seven Skull Shield behind the ridiculous face paint and hairdo. Clay String had outdone himself.

"Look at me," Seven Skull Shield ordered. "Walk over here. That's it."

"What . . . What are you doing?" Fire Cat's voice sounded hoarse and strained. He fought for balance as the thief literally dragged him. "Get your hands off me!"

Seven Skull Shield tightened his grip, scarred hands on Fire Cat's shoulders. "Hold still, Red Wing. Let me help you."

"Help? I've got to get back to my lady."

"Wait." The thief reached up, wiping a cloth over Fire Cat's wet cheeks. Wet? How had that happened? When?

Even more unsettling was the concern in Seven Skull Shield's expression. "An interesting choice was mentioned to me earlier: biding one's time, or creating a scene. For the moment we're biding our time. Can you do that?"

"This happened because of me."

"You lost a chunkey game."

"Power deserted me."

"Your game was off. You made mistakes. They can be fixed."

"How?" Fire Cat glanced down at his trembling hands where they clutched the war ax.

Night Shadow Star and Thirteen Sacred Jaguar were surrounded by well-wishers. A deep, keening howl sounded in the depths of his souls.

"Of course. That's who the old priestess meant." Seven Skull Shield glanced at the knot of people swarming the newlyweds. "I know someone who knows more about chunkey than anyone alive. But the only people he can help are those willing to listen and learn. I don't know if you've got the sense or guts to do either."

"She thinks she has to destroy him on her own." His voice sounded faint, as if spoken from someone else's mouth.

"She might," Seven Skull Shield agreed, wiping Fire Cat's latest tears away. No one had wiped his face like that since he was a child. "But here's the thing: Are you tired of hurting like this? Do you want to be the man she needs, instead of this sniveling piece of shit? If so, you come see me."

"I don't understand."

"I'm just beginning to, Red Wing. Now, reach down into those priggish souls of yours and grab onto some of that arrogant pride you're so fond of strutting out for the world to see. I've got the beginnings of a plan."

"What sort of plan?"

"The kind you're not going to like for a whole lot of reasons. Mostly because you'll find it to be demeaning." The thief shot a hard look at where the Natchez Little Sun was grinning, talking to Horn Lance and the Itza lord. "But those pus-licking curs are hurting too many women we care about. And they've sent both of us scurrying like frightened mice in the process. Me, I've about had it."

"So . . . what do I have to do?" The ache in Fire Cat's heart eased slightly. Was this actually a chance?

"Tomorrow, early. You and me need to go to River Mounds City, and with no one the wiser."

"And *leave* her unprotected? With *him*?"

"The man's her *husband*. He's not going to hurt her on his wedding night. Usually it takes a few days before even the slimiest man sinks that far." The thief grinned, distorting his facial paint. "Trust me, I know."

Fire Cat gave him a sidelong look.

"Tomorrow, Red Wing. Before dawn. Bring your chunkey gear."

"I have duties."

"You swore." The thief's smirk vanished, and he glanced speculatively down at the ugly dog that had been following him around. "Fire Cat, something tells me that by tomorrow morning, you're going to be desperate for a reason to be out of that palace."

Sixty

So, it's done," Blue Heron said as the Morning Star wrapped the ceremonial marriage blanket around Night Shadow Star and Thirteen Sacred Jaguar's shoulders. The *kukul* standard seemed to be leering in triumph as it swayed above the Itza's head.

Her niece's expression, behind her black-and-gray facial paint, showed not a flicker of emotion.

Blue Heron stood by Wooden Doll's side, having been interrupted by the arrival of the Morning Star and the performance of the ceremony.

As people flocked forward to congratulate the new couple, Blue Heron blocked Wooden Doll's line of flight, studying the woman carefully. To her credit, the paid woman gazed back through wary but unflinching eyes.

"You swim in dangerous waters," Blue Heron began. "Aligning yourself with my ex-husband against Morning Star House either takes exceptional courage and political agility, or a death wish."

"I am a paid woman, Keeper. My 'alignment,' as you put it, is nothing more than a business arrangement."

Blue Heron glanced sidelong to where Horn Lance was

translating congratulations from the crowd of chiefs and nobles. "That might not be enough to keep you alive."

"I'm not a fool, Keeper."

"Coming from where you do, a woman doesn't gain your stature and prestige by being stupid. I'm catching a glimmer of what the thief sees in you." She paused. "Tell me. What happens to you on the day when Horn Lance waves his hand dismissively and says, 'Begone.'"

"That depends on how this all plays out." With a graceful gesture she indicated the crowd around the newlyweds. "If this is truly the first of a long series of contacts with the Itza, a smart woman might profit in the most incredible ways."

"And if it isn't?"

Wooden Doll's eyebrow barely arched in reply. "That same smart woman needs to get what she can, while she can, and remain agile enough on her feet that she makes no enemies in the process."

"Even if that means sacrificing Seven Skull Shield in the process?"

The woman frowned, her hardening gaze fixing on Horn Lance where he interpreted for the Itza. "He told me that Skull had sent him. I had no reason to doubt it. Men often send friends to my door." As quickly she countered, "Though I find it odd that the Four Winds Clan Keeper would care what happened to a clanless man like Skull? What is he to you?"

Blue Heron bristled at the woman's tone. Then a deadly smile bent her lips. "You do live dangerously. What's he told you about me?"

"Straight out? Nothing of consequence, except that he trusts you. But knowing Skull like I do, you're like sweet nectar on bread, and he just can't get enough. Working for you the way he does, he gets to feed that sick craving he has for excitement and challenge. And my guess is that you'll play him like a hollow-reed flute, right up until the moment you don't need him anymore." Her dark gaze hardened. "And it will break his heart, because fool that he is with his insane sense of honor, he thinks you're really his friend."

Blue Heron's lips quivered as a spear of truth made her heart skip. "I'm not the one who sold myself to the man who's offered a chief's Trade to anyone that will club Seven Skull Shield in the head and drag him in to be tortured."

"Until Skull told me today, I wasn't aware that Horn Lance had placed a price on his head. So for the moment I don't know who I trust less when it comes to his safety. You, or Horn Lance."

"I don't owe you any explanations, woman. But then, I'm not the one warming Horn Lance's bed. Tried it once. Didn't like it. You, however, are—"

"Earning a small fortune, Keeper." She glanced at where Seven Skull Shield had pulled Fire Cat to the side. "Men come and go. So, I'll get what I can, while I can. And if I were ever fool enough to try to save Skull, change his life? Settle him down? Pus and blood, Keeper, in the end he'd break my heart."

"So it's all about who pays the most?"

"Always, Keeper. Always."

Sixty-one

Had Piasa himself arisen from the Underworld and asked Fire Cat to plan a more disagreeable afternoon, he would have been hard pressed to do so. Nevertheless the thief's insistence that he reach down and cling to that pride that simmered at his core kept him, barely, from breaking down or striking out violently.

It was bad enough that he had to maintain his discipline as he followed Night Shadow Star and her new husband, pacing beside the hated *kukul* borne by the Itza warrior named Burning Ant.

Somehow he had to keep the pain out of his eyes when he met Night Shadow Star's stoic gaze. He had to stand firm when he only wished to scream and unleash fury with his war ax. But along with his pride, he fundamentally understood that if he failed her again, Night Shadow Star would collapse in despair—that for whatever reason, she clung to his projected strength, lie that it was.

Steadfast, he endured the reception, heedless of the empty wishes proffered to Night Shadow Star by the high chiefs of various Houses, matrons, and Earth Clan chiefs. Then came the feast, and finally the long descent to the Avenue of the Sun, where the huge crowd was held back by

what looked like half the Four Winds Clan squadrons—
the warriors in long formations that kept the way open as the
newlyweds were carried atop their litters to the large white-
clay-capped mound where the *tonka'tzi*'s palace was in the
process of being rebuilt.

After *Tonka'tzi* Red Warrior was murdered last spring,
his palace had been burned. Since then a new layer of white
clay had been added, raising and enlarging the mound. The
first posts had been erected to create *Tonka'tzi* Wind's new
palace, but the flat at the top created the perfect elevated stage.

Thirteen Sacred Jaguar had requested the location for the
ritual combat as a fitting honor to his new wife's clan.
Tonka'tzi Wind had initially objected, given that the mound
had just been reconsecrated after her brother's murder. She
supposedly had relented when reminded that it would be symbolic of Four Winds authority and Power when the foolish
Itza went down in defeat. After all, what chance did the
southern foreigners have against the very best in Cahokia?
Which, essentially, meant the best in the world?

Fire Cat himself had no doubts about the outcome as he
followed the litters up the newly laid squared-log steps that
led to the mound top. Thirteen Sacred Jaguar and Night
Shadow Star would be seated upon a raised platform hastily
constructed for the affair. The actual combat was to take
place at the head of the stairs so that the huge crowd could
observe the action.

Those who spilled their blood, Horn Lance had noted,
would be sanctifying the newly capped mound, covered as
it was with white clay.

Fire Cat didn't know any of the Cahokian warriors, but
just from the look of them, each was battle-hardened, scarred,
and fit. They stood in a small knot, mature men in their early
thirties. Wooden and leather helmets covered their heads;
arm guards, chest protectors, and shin guards filled out their
body armor. Each carried a shield and a beloved war club,
those being the terms of the fight.

As the Itza warriors climbed the stairs, they made a most unusual spectacle with their plumed helmets, folding shields with abstract facial designs, feathered arm and leg guards, and curious carapace armor. Their war clubs looked long and slender, the business ends cased in what looked like decorated bark scabbards.

"How do they expect to win with such skinny and delicate-looking clubs?" someone asked. "A good war club has weight at the end. Those things look so light they'll barely give an enemy's skull a knock."

As Horn Lance was handed one of the clubs by Swirling Cloud, the first stirrings of premonition sent uneasy fingers through Fire Cat's gut. Not a year ago, he'd derided the notion that Cahokia could ever take Red Wing Town. A quarter-moon ago he'd have scoffed at the notion his lady would be married to a strange foreigner in fewer days than he had fingers. A mere two days ago, he'd have laughed at the notion that a Natchez could beat him at chunkey.

Now, watching the Itza as they prepared, his sense of alarm built.

"Lady," he said, leaning close to Night Shadow Star's litter, "you must stop this."

She actually turned, the first break in her graven expression all day. "What's wrong, Fire Cat?"

"Something. I don't know. But if there is a way, stop this now."

"Dressed as the Itza are, with all those feathers? And though their clubs are still cased, they don't seem the slightest bit dangerous. With one good counter-blow they look like they'll shatter."

"Then why have they not been uncased? Lady, the Itza are too sure of themselves. Figure a way; stop this now."

Horn Lance, where he stood beside Thirteen Sacred Jaguar, couldn't have heard their whispered words, but apparently he read Fire Cat's expression.

In a loud voice, he shouted an order in the clucking Itza

language, and his warriors, led by the snake-tattooed Red Copal, leaped into formation. Horn Lance stepped into position in the middle, Dead Teeth and Red Copal to his left, Split Bone and Shaking Earth to his right.

He barked another order. With a single swing of their clubs, they sent the bark scabbards flying.

"Wait!" Night Shadow Star cried as she raised her hand.

So unexpected was her protest that Thirteen Sacred Jaguar jerked his head around, almost dislodging his soaring headgear.

Night Shadow Star, rose, calling, "If the joining of our peoples—"

"*Attack!*" Horn Lance called in Cahokian so that there was no misunderstanding.

A roar went up from the crowd below, and the Cahokian warriors, taken somewhat by surprise, dropped instinctively into a defensive formation, shields up.

Fire Cat had his first glimpse of the Itza's weapons. Long-handled, with a slim flat blade, they were nearly as tall as the warriors wielding them. Something glittered along the thin edges, catching the light in a vitreous shine.

As the Itza warriors carefully approached the defending Cahokians they began chanting.

At the same time, Thirteen Sacred Jaguar rose from his litter, barking something to Burning Ant, who started forward with the *kukul*. At the sight of the standard, the Itza warriors called out in joy, singing, half dancing as they closed on the Cahokians.

"*Squadron!* Rush!" the Cahokian squadron first called.

In perfect precision, his five warriors charged forward, shields aligned. The tactic was sound. Break the Itzan advance, hammer their light shields aside, and crack a few bones as their opponents broke and retreated. By keeping tight, wheeling, advancing, and maintaining integrity and formation, Cahokians had crushed all comers for generations.

As if choreographed, the Itza warriors split. Horn Lance, in the center, backed slowly, his wary eyes on the advancing line of shields. The remaining Itza, in teams of two, circled eagerly to either side. The flanking warriors skipped lightly around the Cahokians, their long thin weapons feinting at the shields, then flicking low before they leaped back.

As they did, the squadron first called, "Left! Attack!" sensing that Red Copal and Dead Teeth, menacing the Cahokian's left, were slower. The instinctive call was correct, but the two warriors guarding either Cahokian flank were already limping, blood welling on their bare thighs. At each touch, the Itzan weapons had laid open long gaping wounds.

The Cahokian on the right stumbled and went down.

A cry of dismay rose from the spectators.

Instinctively the squadron first ordered a move to cover the man. The Itza had already circled like eager coyotes, leaping in, slashing, dancing away. As before they struck for the bare thigh, just above the knee.

For the most part the Cahokian warriors managed to block the blows, but working in unison, the Itza reached past the guarding shields. In the wake of each stroke, a bleeding gash was left behind.

Fire Cat stared in a sort of paralyzed horror as the Cahokians were lamed, bleeding and hobbling as they tried to keep formation.

The first warrior who'd fallen was struggling to put pressure on his wound. Red Copal leaped close, swung his thin blade, and neatly cut the downed warrior's throat before skipping away.

"Stop this!" Night Shadow Star barked. "You've proven your point!"

"My lady," Swirling Cloud said, bowing his head and touching his forehead respectfully. "They fight in honor of your marriage. There is no point, as you call it, to be made. This is a blessing for you and the *ahau*."

"I said, stop!" She rose from her litter, fists balled.

Thirteen Sacred Jaguar barked something, his questioning look going first from Night Shadow Star to Horn Lance.

Not that it mattered. The final Cahokian standing was the squadron first, and blood was streaming down both of his legs. As he turned to block an attack from his right, Red Copal flicked his long thin weapon in from the left, neatly slicing the squadron first's throat open.

The last Cahokian raised his shield where he lay in a spreading pool of blood. Four of the Itza Danced in, striking, one severing the warrior's hand from his forearm with a swinging blow, another flicking his blade across the man's throat.

At the same time Burning Ant was singing, raising the *kukul* high as if to allow the fanged snake to better observe the bleeding corpses.

Thirteen Sacred Jaguar now rose from his litter, stepping over to kneel above the squadron first's corpse. He reached his hands into the gaping throat wound. Then, his fingers covered with blood, he stood. Burning Ant lowered the *kukul*, and Thirteen Sacred Jaguar wiped his bloody fingers across the snake's mouth, as if feeding it. The colorful snake's jade-green eyes seemed to glow from an inner fire.

Frozen in stunned fury, Fire Cat heard Thirteen Sacred Jaguar praying joyously, repeating the words *Waxaklahun Kan, itz,* and *ch'ulel* over and over.

All thought gone, Fire Cat started forward, driven by insane rage. All he could see was that slope-headed face peering from the elaborate mask, eyes dancing in rapture. He would drive his copper-bitted ax right between those eyes, knock that gaudy, high-plumed mask off the Itza's head before he split the man's skull. . . .

"Fire Cat?" a firm hand grasped his arm.

He had half raised his war club to strike down whoever dared to restrain him, startled to find himself staring into

Night Shadow Star's desperate eyes. He froze, heart thundering in his chest.

"I can't lose you, too. That would kill me."

Her words hit him like a stone from above.

The Itza warriors, sensing threat, had placed themselves around the *ahau*, their long-handled wooden swords at the ready.

Fire Cat blinked, seeing the weapons up close, realizing those deceptively thin edges were inset with deadly obsidian blades. So that was the secret.

"Stand down, Fire Cat," Night Shadow Star pleaded. "Please."

The desperation in her voice penetrated his fog of pain and defeat.

"Yes, Lady." But all he wanted to do was charge the Itza, bellow his rage, and show them the true meaning of courage even as they cut him apart.

Sixty-two

Ritual combat?

That might have been the name the Itza gave it. But to Blue Heron the memory of what she'd seen would linger for the rest of her life. She sat beside *Tonka'tzi* Wind at the final feast. It had been laid out in the Council Terrace compound while everyone had been watching first the "ritual combat" and then accompanying the wedding party as they oversaw the final stickball game and chunkey tournament.

Instead of a joyous occasion, a pall had been cast over the proceedings by the one-sided slaughter of five of Cahokia's finest warriors. The blow had gone straight to the city's heart.

The question possessed every soul in the city: Who were these Itza? How could they be invincible? Did they bring a new Power, or did they just serve more potent gods?

Where Night Shadow Star and Thirteen Sacred Jaguar sat under the ramada, they might have been exiled and estranged gods. Blue Heron knew that expression on Night Shadow Star's face. The woman was desperate.

Thirteen Sacred Jaguar, however, had an unfocused look and a beatific expression, his wide lips in a slight smile. He had ordered the War Serpent standard to be placed before him that he might stare up at it with his rapt eyes.

"He looks as if he's dancing with Sister Datura," *Tonka'tzi* Wind declared.

Horn Lance overheard, saying, "The Itza, and the Maya scholars before them, have discovered that this world is an illusion. We see only a shadow of the reality lived by the gods. The *ahau's* standard? It holds Waxaklahun Kan's *ch'ulel*. Linking it between this illusory existence and the real existence of the gods. Today *Ahau* Thirteen Sacred Jaguar sees this world through the eyes of reality, looking into this world from what you would call the Spirit realm."

Beside him, Wooden Doll gave him a measuring, side-long look as she picked at a piece of roasted duck breast. The woman had been glancing periodically at the outlying ranks of Natchez where Seven Skull Shield sat.

Funny that the thief would pick their association. But then Seven Skull Shield wouldn't be welcome sitting among the nobles. Nor had he apparently disclosed his identity to the Natchez warriors, who mistook him for a Cahokian lord.

"Hmmph!" Wind snorted, lifting a horn spoon of steaming buffalo broth spiced with wild onions.

"I understand your reluctance, *Tonka'tzi*." Horn Lance leaned his head back slightly, head cocked. "I, too, shared your skepticism when I first heard of their great cities and the Power they controlled. So I went. Walked their elevated stone causeways, marveled at their mighty stuccoed buildings painted every color under the sun. These things I saw with my own eyes. The sacrifice of your warriors earlier today just reflects how what you call Power, and we call *ch'ulel,* are projected from the reality of the gods into our world of illusion."

Blue Heron pointed to where the Morning Star sat atop his litter at the foot of the stairs leading up to his palace. The living god was smiling, talking with two young women, one or both of whom no doubt would accompany him up to his private chambers for the night.

"There's a living contradiction." *Tonka'tzi* Wind pointed. "The reincarnated Morning Star, a Spirit from the Sky World, returned to earth to take possession of a human form. If anyone would know if the Itza were right, it would be him. Yet he tells us that our stories about the Beginning Times are true."

"No doubt he does," Horn Lance agreed amiably. "I expect that in the end, it will be a matter for the priests to work out as they peer through the sacred books where the words of the First Mother and First Father, One-and-Seven Lord, and the . . . Oh, wait. That's right. You have no books. Just the beaded record mats, and those only detail which leaders have done what."

"What's a book?" Wooden Doll asked the question that Blue Heron wouldn't permit herself.

Condescending, Horn Lance turned to the paid woman. "It is an ancient art going back a thousand years among the earliest of the Maya. They record the actual words, drawing them on *juna*, then binding them together and passing them down, generation after generation. The word for such a book is *jun*. But then, you would not understand, having only the stories told by your grandfathers as they heard them. That and a few beaded mats." He smiled. "Pity."

Blue Heron caught the dark flash of Wooden Doll's eyes, though her smile remained in place.

Turning back to Blue Heron and Wind, Horn Lance added, "I think great changes are coming to Cahokia. You saw the expressions on the faces of the common people as we returned here from where your warriors were sacrificed. This day they witness a rebirth for Cahokia." He pointed to where Thirteen Sacred Jaguar reached for his bowl of succulent bison meat, chewing thoughtfully as he stared up at the *kukul*. "And today a new lord has aligned himself with the Four Winds Clan and demonstrated the Power of his gods and beliefs."

He narrowed his eyes. "From here on out, nothing will ever be the same."

Sixty-three

By torchlight, Night Shadow Star and Thirteen Sacred Jaguar were borne down the Avenue of the Sun to her palace. Around them, in the darkness, crowds of well-wishers shouted their salutations. But the calls were tempered, carrying a note of worry, as the people warily studied the Itza and wondered what new marvelous and dangerous Power was rising in their midst.

The Itza had prevailed at each turn until she herself wondered if Thirteen Sacred Jaguar, Horn Lance, and their Natchez weren't invincible.

Now I must take him into my bed.

Distasteful as that was, her thoughts kept flashing longingly to Fire Cat. He'd been a pillar of strength. Every time her spirit was at the breaking point, all she needed to do was glance back. Just the sight of him—tall, strong, standing at attention with the deadly ax in his hand—had stiffened her resolve.

After the Morning Star had placed the ceremonial blanket over her shoulders, binding her to the Itza, she'd caught a glimpse of Seven Skull Shield wiping what had to be tears from Fire Cat's eyes.

Stricken, she'd been on the verge of weeping herself. Just

as she'd felt the sting behind her eyes, she'd glanced back again, only to see Fire Cat once more in position, jaw clenched, a fire burning in his pain-bright eyes.

If he could bear it, so could she.

He'd been right at the beginning of the combat. She should have stopped it before it started. That Horn Lance had realized what she was about, and initiated the slaughter, only made her hate him that much more.

Then when Thirteen Sacred Jaguar had run his bloody fingers over the hated *kukul*'s mouth, she'd never craved a human being's death with such longing. Stopping Fire Cat at the last moment before he attacked the Itza had been one of the hardest things she'd ever done.

But for the alert warriors with their bloody *macuahuitl*— and the certainty of Fire Cat's death—she might have let him try. Had she her own weapons, throwing Old-Woman-Who-Never-Dies' warning to the winds, she'd have joined him.

Patience, fool!

Piasa's voice startled her, as if the Spirit beast loomed behind her.

"Yes, I know," she whispered miserably as she was carried up her long steps. Bathed in the flickering light of torches, Horned Serpent and Piasa's guardian posts seemed alive, their eyes gleaming, snarling faces enraged.

She ground her teeth, jaws clamped as her litter led the way to the veranda. Behind her, jubilant and jovial, trooped the hated Itza warriors and their Natchez allies.

Her stomach twisted as the *kukul* was carried between the guardian posts. At that instant, the air felt electric, as if lightning could strike from the partly cloudy night.

She fought off a shiver and stood, barely glancing at Clay String and the rest of her household where they waited in traditional respect beside her door. Fire Cat behind her, she refused to look back, walking head held high through her door and into the great room.

A fire snapped and crackled, illuminating the benches, wall hangings, and opulent surroundings. She walked woodenly across the newly laid cane matting, past the fire, and turned at the door to her personal quarters. Her heart like a stone, she watched the Itza and his warriors pour through the door, their eyes taking in the grandeur of her palace.

Thirteen Sacred Jaguar stared around with his Spirit-drugged eyes. Burning Ant stopped beside him, smiling as he held the *kukul*. Horn Lance grinned, tucking fingers in his belt as he took in the wealth of copper, fine ceramics, and sculpted wood. The rest of the Itza were nodding in satisfaction, while the Natchez gaped like fools.

"Clay String," she said through a tight throat, "make my husband's retainers comfortable. They can see to their own cooking and cleaning. They are also capable of supplying their own needs. If anything isn't clear about that, they can come to me for an explanation."

"Yes, Lady."

To Fire Cat she said, "Should my husband decide to join me, we are not to be disturbed."

Fire Cat swallowed hard, lips quivering. Hoarsely he said, "As you order, Lady."

She hesitated, willing her souls into her gaze. "If you are not here in the morning, I will understand."

"My Lady?"

"Take whatever steps you must, Fire Cat. I trust you."

As he took his position before her door, she stepped into her quarters. Two hickory-oil lamps burned, the flame on their floating wicks casting a soft yellow light through the room. To the side her altar stood. She ignored it as she walked to her bed and seated herself, arms crossed.

Feeling numb, her heart pounding, she waited. A tickle of anxiety unsettled her gut; nervous energy played along her bones.

Beyond the door, she could hear the Itza discussing something in their clacking and rattling tongue. Then someone laughed. The Natchez were joking among themselves in a way that sounded ribald.

"Come on. Just get it over with."

Her throat had gone dry, every instinct urging her to escape. If only she and Fire Cat were on the river, headed anywhere but—

She glanced up as Thirteen Sacred Jaguar entered, having removed his ponderous mask and cloak. He glanced around the room, gaze stopping at her altar with its well pot.

Then he fixed on her. Only an idiot would misread the distaste in her eyes as she met his. Smiling, he said something in Itza and stopped before her. Reaching out, he fingered her hair, talking to her in soft tones. With the tips of his fingers, he traced out the three-forked design around her left eye. At the same time his voice rose, questioning.

She tried not to flinch at his touch.

A ghost of a smile crossed his lips as he lifted the raven-feather cloak from her shoulders and let it fall. His hands cupped her breasts, fingers—just short of painful—digging into her as he massaged them.

Staring into her eyes, he asked something she couldn't understand. As if amused at himself, he smiled and shook his head.

"Let's just get it over with, shall we?" She finally broke her silence and unhooked her skirt, letting it fall. As it did, she slid onto the bed, positioning herself on her back. Pulling her knees up and spreading wide, she choked a swallow down her dry throat.

He took his time undressing, never meeting her eyes, his attention focused solely on her body. To her surprise, his penis hung limply.

Whispering something under his breath he climbed onto the bed and knelt between her legs. She forced herself to breathe normally as he stared at her through those oddly protruding eyes. He fixed his gaze between her legs, reached down and grasped himself. Fingers working, he kneaded himself until his shaft hardened.

"Wait." She raised a hand as he started forward.

Shifting, she dipped her fingers into the edge of the hickory-oil lamp before reaching down to grasp his erection and slather it with oil.

As he lowered himself onto her, she turned her head to the side, closing her eyes. From beyond her door came the sounds of rude male laughter and foreign song.

This isn't anything women haven't endured since the be-ginning of time, and far from the worst you've ever known.

Sixty-four

Burning Ant had taken a position opposite Fire Cat and stood with the hated serpent standard atop its pole, as if guarding the doorway. The hideous snake's gaping mouth reminded him of a leering and lecherous grin, given what Night Shadow Star was enduring.

Fire Cat fought to ignore what was happening in her once-private quarters. Instead he stared his hatred at the *kukul*.

Can you sense my rage, snake god? Can you feel my souls burning as they imagine what it would be like to smash you into kindling and urinate on your splintered remains? One day I will burn you for the rogue god I know you to be.

The *kukul*'s eyes gleamed in the firelight, as if mocking him in return.

He turned his attention to the Itza warriors and Horn Lance where they crowded around the fire. He let the hatred burn like a wildfire through his chest. One by one, he focused on their faces, wishing their destruction: Dead Teeth, Split Bone, Shaking Earth, Red Copal, and finally Horn Lance.

He could hear Thirteen Sacred Jaguar talking softly in

the room behind him, though no answer came from Night Shadow Star.

At some joke by Horn Lance, the Itza burst into laughter. Even Burning Ant chuckled. Then the standard bearer cast a wry glance at the door behind him.

I'll kill them all.

The thought kept replaying in Fire Cat's souls. To destroy them and free Night Shadow Star, he'd gratefully sacrifice all that he was, and die hideously in the process.

She serves you with all of her soul. How could you let this happen, Piasa?

The Spirit Beast, no matter how vocal with Night Shadow Star, didn't grant him even the faintest of whispers.

He flinched when he heard Night Shadow Star's statement of "Wait."

And then silence.

Fire Cat ground his teeth, grip tightening on the wood of the war ax, every muscle in his body knotted in the effort to remain at his station.

Horn Lance huddled with the Itza at the fire, his animated face accented by the gestures of his hands as he talked.

By the great room door, Seven Skull Shield, still dressed as a noble, had sneaked in and was chatting amiably with the Natchez called Wet Bobcat. What idiotic game was the thief playing, anyway? If Horn Lance turned and saw him . . .

Even as he thought it, the thief was leading Wet Bobcat out into the night, a bottle of something apparently being the lure.

Fire Cat's thoughts fragmented as he heard a distinctively male groaning followed by a gasping intake of breath from the room behind him.

Burning Ant's lips curled in satisfaction.

I can't stand this!

But he had to. She'd asked. Pleaded.

The single hot tear tracking down his cheek barely registered.

Sixty-five

Seven Skull Shield blinked awake, his left side aching
where he slept on the cane-mat floor. Something heavy lay
on his leg. The sound of snoring men was accompanied by
the faint creaking of the beds that supported them.

Shifting, Seven Skull Shield winced and flipped the blanket off. The dog—who'd been sleeping with his head on
Seven Skull Shield's leg—yawned, then sat up to scratch behind his ear.

Pulling himself into a sitting position, Seven Skull Shield
rubbed his eyes. Night Shadow Star's palace was dark. From
long habit, he'd awakened a couple of fingers of time before
dawn.

At the pattering sound of water, he winced, took a swipe at
the dog, but the beast was peeing on the floor just beyond
his reach.

"If you don't learn, you're going to be stew meat by the
end of the week, beast. And I might be the one to smack you
in the head and throw you in the pot."

Rising, he folded the blanket, careful to avoid the wet
spot. Slurping sounds indicated the dog had found one of
the stew pots.

It had been a most interesting evening. Dressed as Seven

Skull Shield was, the Natchez had had no idea he was the same infamous thief for whom Horn Lance had offered a fortune. Nor had they cared that he tagged along at the rear of the wedding party. He'd enticed Wet Bobcat out onto the veranda and out of sight with a bottle of blackberry juice.

"Well, there it is," Seven Skull Shield had told Wet Bobcat as they seated themselves on the step. "Itza and Cahokia, joined shaft and sheath. Wouldn't it have been better if the White Woman had married the Itza? As it is, you're sort of a small stone caught between two big rocks."

The Natchez, delighted to have a Cahokian "lord" hanging on his every word, had talked the night away. And what a wealth of information the Natchez squadron first had been.

In the morning stillness, Seven Skull Shield veered wide of where Horn Lance slept. Fire Cat huddled before Night Shadow Star's door. Still dressed in his armor, head bowed under the weight of the helmet, the copper-bitted ax laxly gripped, the Red Wing looked about as comfortable as a catfish crammed into a clam shell.

Seven Skull Shield squinted in the dim light, located the black chunkey stone and lance, and used the lance tip to prod Fire Cat awake.

The Red Wing started, muttered, and almost toppled as his blood-starved and cramped limbs betrayed him.

"Shhh." Seven Skull Shield placed a finger to his lips. "If you can get up without collapsing in a heap, we have work to do. Let's go."

"Thief?" Fire Cat whispered questioningly.

Seven Skull Shield grinned to himself and started tiptoeing toward the door.

Glancing back, Fire Cat was following on wobbly, blood-drained legs and making faces as his circulation was restored.

Outside, Seven Skull Shield paused between the guardian posts at the head of the landing, breathing deeply of the smoky and damp air. The familiar smells of the city carried on the muggy dawn.

"What are you doing?" Fire Cat asked, glancing up at the guardian posts as he rubbed the back of his neck with one hand, the other cradling the war ax.

"Now that you've had your fill of the Itza, it's time you set about beating them."

"You still talking that foolishness about going to River Mounds City?"

"I had a long conversation with the Natchez last night." He lifted the chunkey lance and stone. "Swirling Cloud isn't just a good chunkey player. He's the best anywhere on the southern river. Maybe good enough to beat the Morning Star himself. The miracle is that he only beat you by five that day."

"How do you know all this? Why are you still dressed like a noble? Why are you even here? If Horn Lance had seen—"

"I know why you got beat at chunkey. I know how to fix it. But you've got to come with me."

"I can't leave her! Not now!"

"Did nothing I told you yesterday sink into that bone-thick head of yours? You want to stand around like a miserable grieving log with tears running down your face? That's Red Wing honor? Fine, I'll tell her you refused. No, *you* tell her you refuse. I want to see the look on her face when you do."

"She's surrounded by enemies."

"And you're the only man who can defeat Swirling Cloud. But you've got to do it my way. Right now. Make your decision, Red Wing."

Fire Cat shifted his uncomfortable armor, glanced worriedly back at the palace, and said, "I can't just leave her."

"Your choice. Can't say I didn't try."

Seven Skull Shield set the chunkey lance and stone on the top step and started down toward the avenue below. Behind him, the dog's oversized paws thumped on the wood as he bounded in pursuit.

With each step he shook his head, muttering, "All right,

Piasa, it's all up to you now. Night Shadow Star better be smarter, trickier, and tougher than we all think she is."

Grinding his teeth, he turned west down the Avenue of the Sun, glancing north toward the Keeper's, wondering if he should drop in on her, fill her in on everything the Natchez had spilled.

Or did he dare venture to Wooden Doll's? She hadn't accompanied Horn Lance to Night Shadow Star's, no doubt having been dismissed as an unnecessary complication for the evening.

But who knew what sort of valuable information she might possess? Horn Lance didn't strike Seven Skull Shield as the kind of man who'd consider Wooden Doll more than a convenient and temporarily useful tool. Men were continually underestimating Wooden Doll—a trait she'd learned to exploit for her own benefit.

Decision made, he hastened his steps to the west, figuring he could be at her house just before mid-sun. Still dressed as a noble—though his face paint was smeared—not even Slick Rock would give him a second look.

The chatty Natchez, flush with the heady feeling of success, had talked way too freely. Now, if Seven Skull Shield could just learn where Horn Lance's vulnerabilities were, he could bring him down, too.

And then there was the Tortoise Bundle's keeper to consider. The old woman had claimed that she'd appear with the bundle when the time was right.

"And we're to believe that?" Seven Skull Shield wondered as he glanced at the ungainly dog trotting beside him. "Right. And you're a Spirit dog, too, huh?"

The beast, its tongue already lolling, wagged its thick, whip-like tail.

The pounding of feet on the packed clay avenue caused him to turn: Fire Cat emerged from the pre-morning gloom. The chunkey lance and stone were in the Red Wing's hand, the ax hanging at his belt.

"You can really tell me how the Natchez beat me? You know how I can win?"

Seven Skull Shield chuckled under his breath. "Me, no. But I know the man who can."

"A priest? Some sorcerer who can fill me with Power?"

"Never trust a priest or sorcerer to do what a scoundrel can do better. And when it comes to scoundrels, Crazy Frog is the best. But if you can be fixed, he'll know how." He paused. "Got to make a quick stop at the Keeper's for a bit of Trade. Then we'll be on our way."

For the first time, Seven Skull Shield felt a glimmer of hope. He looked down at the dog, the beast having fixed its curious blue and brown eyes on his. "You know, dog, if this works, we might just have a chance."

Sixty-six

Horn Lance yawned, stretched, and sat up in the dim light of dawn. He looked around Thirteen Sacred Jaguar's new palace and grinned appreciatively. The location couldn't have been better. He and the *ahau* were now literally perched at the Morning Star's right hand.

He drew his blanket back and lowered his feet to the floor. A faint blue haze of smoke rose from the central hearth. He glanced at the door to the *ahau*'s private quarters, noticing that the Red Wing was gone, though the *kukul* stood in its holder beside the doorway. Burning Ant snored on the sleeping bench to the right.

Horn Lance pulled a ceramic jar from beneath the bed and relieved himself. As his urine splashed into the vessel, he noticed it was a Four Winds Clan design for the storage of ritual foods, not a chamber pot. That amused him.

Walking down the benches he kicked Clay String awake, and as the man cried out and sat up, he shoved the pot into his hands, saying, "Empty that. And then the *ahau* and my men need to be fed. We want a worthy breakfast, not just reheated slop from last night."

Clay String, still blinking, glanced down at the pot, his

nose wrinkling at the odor of urine. "This is a ceremonial pot! And you peed in it?"

Horn Lance backed the blow with his entire body; the force of the slap knocked Clay String's head sideways, a spray of urine sloshing out of the bowl to spatter both man and bedding.

"You serve the *ahau*. Now move."

Clay String, gasping, one hand to his cheek, said, "My lady gave me precise instructions that I was not to—"

Horn Lance's second slap caught the other cheek, the smack of it loud in the room. "Are you a fool, or do you want me to beat you to death? In the name of your *ahau* I gave you an order. Now get that pot emptied and get the rest of this lazy household to work making us breakfast."

"Fire Cat is going to . . ." Clay String didn't finish, his tearing gaze going to the vacant place beside the door.

"Fire Cat is going to what?" Horn Lance asked mildly. "If he has the sense of a stone, he'll be on a Trader's canoe headed south by sunset. But you, you surly little maggot, will have my men fed within a hand's time, or your severed head will hit the avenue long before the rest of your body tumbles down the palace steps."

Horn Lance pulled his hand back to deliver another blow, but Clay String scurried away, dripping urine as he headed for the door.

The commotion had brought the rest of the room awake, Itza warriors and Natchez, grinning and yawning. The rest of Night Shadow Star's servants, wide-eyed, expressions shocked, were tumbling out of their beds. Even as they did, they shot anxious glances at the back room, no doubt desperate for Night Shadow Star to emerge and rescue them.

Horn Lance swaggered to the door, leaning in as he called, "*Ahau?* Do you or the lady need anything?"

"What time is it?"

"Dawn, my Lord."

He heard a hearty yawn, and moments later, Thirteen Sacred Jaguar appeared, a kilt hung on his hips. "Where is the woman?"

"She's not with you?" Horn Lance asked.

"Her bed is empty."

"I did not see her leave, *Ahau*. But I doubt she will be difficult to find. She took her slave with her."

"Let her do with her days as she will. My only concern is with her nights." He shared a secret smile with Horn Lance. "I have discovered that as long as I only concentrate on her naked body, I can forget I'm not copulating with a true noble woman."

"Perhaps when this is all over, *Ahau*, a marriage worthy of your rank and status can be brokered with the *multepal*. A suitable lady, or several for that matter, could be sent north."

"Let us hope."

Thirteen Sacred Jaguar stepped out and raised his hands to the *kukul*, praying, "Grant me strength, terrible lord. Settle my seed in the woman. Help me to bring your truth to these vile monkey people."

When he straightened, smiling, he fixed Horn Lance with knowing dark eyes. "With the marriage complete, the time has come to take the next step. The monkey people have seen their most prized young lady bedded, their finest warriors cut down like hollow-stemmed grass, and their false god humbled by my magnificence. All that remains is to sow the seeds of the Morning Star's destruction."

"With me as an interpreter, we only need to begin reciting the true story of the gods and the origin of the world. Start the controversy among the people, *Ahau*, and everything else will fall into place."

Sixty-seven

Night Shadow Star climbed the steps to the Earth Clans' temple as the first rays of sunlight speared over the eastern bluffs. A bitter smile bent her lips as she heard the melodic voices of the priests. Lined along the mound's eastern side, they sang the traditional greeting to the sun.

She stopped at the top of the stairs, looking back at the misty plaza that was now dotted by a handful of early risers. A few were laying offerings at the foot of the World Tree pole, and beyond them, on the other side of the chunkey courts, the Morning Star's mighty pyramid rose, topped with the living god's palace.

Piasa's sibilant whisper was barely audible, as if he but mumbled under his breath. She shook off the feeling of anxiety, almost irritated that her master wouldn't speak clearly.

She touched her forehead as she passed the lightning-scarred red cedar pole before the temple, then waited as the morning ritual on the eastern side of the temple was completed and Rides-the-Lightning led the small procession of his acolytes around the corner of the building.

Two young men walked in advance of the old soul flier, both acknowledging her with a respectful nod as they passed.

Rides-the-Lightning smiled, his white-blind eyes seeking her out, as if he saw with a different vision than ordinary men.

"Elder," she greeted.

"Night Shadow Star. Why am I not surprised to find you waiting at my door?"

"I need to speak with you."

"You? Or your frightening lord?" Before she could answer, he added, "You, I would guess. The Water Panther casts but a dim filament of shadow upon you this morning."

"You see a great deal for a man who is blind."

"It was only after my eyesight faded that I began to see anything, my lady." He smiled, the action exposing his toothless gums, the wrinkles on his ancient face rearranging around his flat mushroom-shaped nose. "Come. Share a cup of tea with me, and tell me how I can be of service."

She followed him into the dark interior of the great temple, taking a seat on one of the blankets by the fire as he lowered himself beside her.

One of the priests dropped to his knees to dip tea from the ceramic pot that rested beside the coals. He handed a cup first to Rides-the-Lightning and then one to Night Shadow Star before rising and walking off to join the others who occupied themselves at the benches in the back.

Rides-the-Lighting sniffed at the steam rising from his cup and nodded. "Mint and phlox tea with rosehips. Most refreshing in the morning when shared with a good friend."

Night Shadow Star smiled at that and sipped her tea before saying, "Thank you."

Rides-the-Lightning studied her across the rim of his cup, his opaque white eyes seeming to burn right through her. "I cannot help you to deal with the terrible Spirit that inhabits the Itza's war standard. That is beyond me. Nor do I see any foreign enchantments or magics cast upon you in the form of witchery."

"Piasa would have warned me." She smiled wearily. "My needs lie more along the lines of Spirit plants like squaw root, wild celery, juniper root, mistletoe, and anything else you might suggest."

"I see." He nodded, his ancient fingers caressing his cup with its extended handle. "Such medicines would be available in the Four Winds Clan Women's House. Why would you come to me instead?"

"Gossip would blow like a relentless wind from within the Women's House to cover the entire city. Some aspects of my relationship with my new husband, I would prefer to remain private."

Rides-the-Lightning grinned. "The arrival of the Itza has given the people enough to talk about as it is. What need do they have of even more distraction, eh?"

He turned, calling, "Would one of you be so kind as to bring the lady that black-and-white bag from inside the frog jar beneath Blue Serpent's bed?"

She watched one of the priests walk to a bed in the rear and bend down to rummage among the storage beneath.

Rides-the-Lightning lowered his voice. "We teeter on the edge, Lady. These are very dangerous times, and none of my auguries are reassuring. With the arrival of the Itza, Power could shift as violently as it did when Black Tail resurrected the Morning Star. As radically as Cahokia changed then, it could just as easily swing toward the Itza."

"He has Old-Woman-Who-Never-Dies' protection. I can't kill him. Nor can I allow him to win."

"The ways of the Itza are not evil, Lady. Just different. As different as the Four Winds' ways were from Petaga's. As though we are seeing another face of Power, but one with completely different features. If you win, we stay the same. If he wins, we become a different people. Either way, we nevertheless remain a people. Or so Power sees it."

She nodded, a sense of futility filling her.

"Tell me of yourself, Night Shadow Star. Not of gods, Spirits, and Power, but of the worried young woman living inside your skin."

"Fire Cat was gone this morning." She stared down into her tea. "I think . . . I hope he went with the thief. As soon as the Itza slept, I removed myself from the bed. Huddled on the floor with a blanket over my shoulders. Spirit voices filled the darkness. I could hear them whispering, making curious buzzing noises. They told me terrible things. That because I married the Itza, Blue Heron was plotting against me. That Fire Cat hated me."

She shook her head. "Can these things be true?"

Rides-the-Lightning placed an age-withered hand on hers. "Lady, you must listen to me and hear my words. Make them part of your souls. The Itza comes with foreign and mysterious Spirit Power that he uses in ways we do not understand. A terrible Power inhabits that serpent standard that accompanies him wherever he goes. The whispers you hear which are not Piasa? They are lies to weaken you, separate you from your friends."

"They seem so real."

"Would they be persuasive if they didn't? Ignore them, Night Shadow Star. They seek to mislead you and divide you from the people who love you. If they succeed in distracting you, you will be destroyed along with all that you hold dear."

She nodded, taking a deep breath.

The priest walked forward, extending the frog-shaped jar.

Rides-the-Lightning received it, caressing it with his age-callused fingers.

She said, "I find it interesting that you would put the Spirit plants I seek in a jar crafted to look like a frog."

"You understand the nature of the Spirit plants you've requested?"

She nodded. "They will keep his seed from taking root in my womb. Their Power and my will to remain barren against his Power and will to impregnate me."

"Use them with discretion, Night Shadow Star. No more than one cup of tea a day. And do not be surprised if your moon passes without bleeding." He reached into a pouch by his side, removing an intricately tied knot the size of a green walnut. "Take this. The dark stain you see around the cord is menstrual blood. Soak it with your own when your moon comes. Hide the knot beneath your bedding when he lays with you. The knot will draw the Spirit of his seed, confuse it, and bind it within the knot. Keep it from finding its way."

She took a deep breath, a faint sense of relief flickering within her for first time. "Thank you, old friend."

"Be very careful, Night Shadow Star. Do not underestimate the lengths he will go to, or the Power that resides in that snake standard of his."

"Yes, Soul Flier."

Taking the knot, she clutched it to her breast and rose. "And the voices . . . I will remember that they are lies."

"If they should persuade you otherwise . . ."

She nodded. "Then I am lost."

Sixty-eight

Anyone who spent any length of time in Cahokia had heard of the chunkey games at River Mounds City. While the Morning Star kept his chunkey courts immaculately groomed for his sacred ceremonial games, High Chief War Duck of River House had a far more pragmatic attitude about his chunkey grounds.

Located in the elongated plaza, overseen by his mound-top palace, the River City chunkey courts were talked of up and down the river. Just up from the canoe landing, they drew every Trader, embassy, and visiting lord, noble, or war chief. From the swampy gulf coast in the south to the cold forests in the north, good players dreamed of visiting River Mounds City and testing themselves against the best in the world.

So keen was the competition that some of the best players had come to River City—and never left. Those rare individuals lived and breathed for the game, many having amassed significant wealth and standing in the community. With names like Wins-His-Cast, Long Throw, and Hits-His-Stone, they had adopted gaudy costumes and accumulated followings who flocked to watch them play.

And in the process, War Duck had figured out how to skim a percentage of the professional players' winnings.

Among those who followed chunkey with a near-religious fervor was Crazy Frog. Fire Cat had heard rumors of the man and was familiar with the role he'd played in bringing an end to Walking Smoke's reign of terror.

As they approached River Mounds City with its high temples and palaces, travel on the crowded Avenue of the Sun slowed as people packed the narrow thoroughfare.

"This way," Seven Skull Shield called, ducking off between a pigment dealer's hut and a weaver's. The pack he'd picked up at Clan Keeper Blue Heron's bobbed on his wide back.

Fire Cat had no idea what the sack contained, Seven Skull Shield having left him on the veranda while he stepped inside. He had heard some tense-sounding conversation between the thief and Smooth Pebble, though the words had been incomprehensible.

Traveling with the thief had been both entertaining and harrowing. First off, Fire Cat still wasn't sure he'd made the right decision about leaving Night Shadow Star in the clutches of her new husband. Second, he'd never condoned thievery. The act was unthinkable. Therefore he'd bitten his tongue to keep from protesting when Seven Skull Shield deftly stole a roasted duck from where it cooled at a meat-seller's stall.

At first he'd refused so much as a single bite, empty though his belly was.

"Don't know why you'd make such a fuss about it," Seven Skull Shield had muttered as he stripped meat from one of the legs. "The duck's not going back to its previous owner any time soon. It's going to be digested whether it's just me and this dog eating it, or you helping. It's the same outcome for the duck either way."

Irrefutable logic. Seven Skull Shield was full of it.

And the duck had been decidedly tasty, cooked with a sage and beeweed rub for added flavor.

Now he shook his head as he followed the thief and his

ugly dog through a maze of buildings, walls, granaries, sweat lodges, and storage houses.

"How do you find your way?" he cried.

"Like the lines on your grandmother's face," Seven Skull Shield called over his shoulder. "Once you've seen them, you never forget."

"It's a stinking maze in here. And I do mean stinking," he growled distastefully as he stepped over piles of human crap and wrinkled his nose at the smell of urine.

"People have to go somewhere." Seven Skull Shield threw him a look over his shoulder. "Ah, I understand. You're noble-born. You've never had to see how my kind of people make do. Well, Red Wing, welcome to my world."

They had to retreat and wedge themselves out of the way as an old man, back bent under a remarkable load of thatching, took up the narrow passage.

In the wake of the old man's passing, Fire Cat heard a shout go up as he resumed his pursuit of Seven Skull Shield. "What's that?"

"That, Red Wing, is what we've come for."

Moments later, he and Fire Cat emerged from between a moon temple and a Panther Clan charnel house into a crowded plaza.

Fire Cat immediately placed himself. The high palace at the end of the narrow plaza was High Chief War Duck's. The building-studded mounds along the elongated plaza housed a Four Winds Clan House and charnel mound along with a Men's House, Women's House, and temples dedicated to Old-Woman-Who-Never-Dies, Morning Star, Hunga Ahuito, the sun and moon, and various Spirit Beings. Then came the inevitable Earth Clan palaces, their council and charnel houses, and the various society houses.

The usual hawkers crowded the peripheries offering food, drink, ceramics, chipped and ground stone tools, fabrics, carvings, jewelry, and anything else imaginable.

But most of the people were crowded along the edges of the chunkey courts. Through the press, Fire Cat caught a glimpse of sprinting players. An instant later their lances glimmered in the sunlight as they arced through the sky in pursuit of a fast-rolling stone.

Shouts of delight and dismay rose as the lances disappeared behind the mass of bodies, indicating that the play had been decided.

Seven Skull Shield slipped through the crowd with a remarkable ease given his bulk. Fire Cat, with his long lance, was pressed to keep up.

At the foot of a raised wooden platform, Seven Skull Shield stopped and shaded his eyes as he looked up.

Sitting atop the platform was an average-looking man wearing a fine fabric tunic, his head shaded by a flat-topped sun hat.

"Crazy Frog!" Seven Skull Shield called. "Do you have a moment?"

Fire Cat squinted up as he studied the notorious "lord of chunkey." For such a renowned figure, he looked absolutely unremarkable with his bland, round face, nondescript clothing, and ordinary wooden-beaded necklace.

The man looked down, recognized Seven Skull Shield, and sighed. "What kind of trouble are you in now?"

"Trouble? None." The thief made a face. "Well, that is but for a disruptive Itza, a bunch of despicable Natchez, and a recently returned Four Winds noble that I've got to put in his place."

"Ah, the one who is bedding Wooden Doll and has put a price on your head?"

"You've heard?"

"Given how much he's offering for you, I find it curious you'd be here, announcing yourself. Even if you are dressed like a noble. I could make a fortune."

Seven Skull Shield jerked a thumb at Fire Cat. "I brought

protection. My very own warrior. And yes, you could make a fortune. But you can make a bigger one with considerably less risk by helping me."

"What do you want? And why should I waste my time on it?"

Seven Skull Shield unslung the sack on his shoulder, reached in, and tossed up a polished copper bracelet.

Crazy Frog caught it with a snap of his hand, studied the gleaming metal, and a lopsided smile curled his mouth. "Suddenly and remarkably, you have my attention."

Again Seven Skull Shield hooked a thumb in Fire Cat's direction. "This one would like your opinion on his chunkey game. Consider him a pilgrim from a far-off land. A babe cast loose in the cold and brutal world of real chunkey players. A lost soul who desperately needs your expertise on how to improve his game and is willing to listen and learn."

Fire Cat ground his teeth as a flush of embarrassed heat warmed his ears and cheeks. "I don't need any riverside scoundrel to—"

"Ah! You must be Fire Cat," Crazy Frog said with dawning recognition. "Word is that you had to send your lady to get your clothes back from the Natchez."

"I don't need this," Fire Cat muttered through gritted teeth, turning to leave.

A hard hand slapped down on his shoulder; Seven Skull Shield whirled him back around. Face jutting into Fire Cat's he said, "You *do* need this. You want to save your lady? You'll stay, you'll show Crazy Frog what you've got, and you'll listen and learn."

"But he's—"

"The best in the world when it comes to evaluating players. And he'll see what's wrong with you in a single match."

"A single match?"

Seven Skull Shield looked up at Crazy Frog. "How soon can he play?"

Crazy Frog studied Fire Cat through half-lidded eyes, as

though taking his worth. After a long hesitation, he turned, bellowing, "Hey! Four Fingers! Got a substitution for the next match. Take Lightning Lance out. Someone else is playing Skull Pinner."

"Who?" a voice called from the other side.

"I wouldn't use his name," Seven Skull Shield suggested with emphasis.

Crazy Frog glanced down at the ugly dog that was sniffing the support pole of his platform; then he glanced back. "It's a new player. A man called Wounded Dog!"

"He's up next!" the voice called back.

As Fire Cat's ears continued to burn, Crazy Frog studied him with a cocked head, then said, "I'd shed that armor, helmet, and ax. They just get in the way. You're up next, so if I were you, I'd be quick about it before someone changes his mind and decides this is all folly."

Sixty-nine

Seven Skull Shield perched beside Crazy Frog atop the rickety scaffold. From the elevated platform, he could see everything. Crowds were always bigger in the afterglow of holidays, and Night Shadow Star's wedding to the Itza had been that. In addition was the uncertainty cast over Cahokia by the inconceivable slaughter of the Cahokian warriors. The people sensed a change, as if the world were no longer the same familiar place. When the people felt that way, they were more interested in congregating and listening to gossip and rumors than in working.

At the head of the court, Fire Cat warmed up. Stripped of his armor, he wore only a simple light tan hunting shirt, sweat-stained and wrinkled. He had pulled his long hair behind his head and bound it with a string.

Beside him, the player known as Skull Pinner soaked up the sun's rays wearing his gorgeous black-and-yellow outfit with its splays of brilliantly dyed feathers and polished leather. A copper headpiece rested on his immaculately coifed locks. His face was painted black, his eyes, nose, and mouth in bright yellow to mimic that of a grimacing human skull. A yellow-and-black striped breechcloth was tied at his waist. He'd oiled his muscular arms and legs so that they glistened in the sunlight.

The crowd was mumbling, many shaking their heads as the odds makers worked the fringes asking for bets.

Crazy Frog grinned and gestured futility as he placed colored beads on the scoreboard he kept in front of him. "Your man can't even get odds that he'll be beaten by fifteen out of the twenty possible points."

Seven Skull Shield fingered what was left of the paint on his chin, hoping he still looked enough like a noble that no one would recognize him. Or that if they did, being on Crazy Frog's platform would be protection enough to keep him from being grabbed.

"I don't care what he loses by. I just need to know how to fix his game."

"He was said to have been pretty good when he was the war chief of Red Wing Town."

"Piasa told Lady Night Shadow Star that he had to win at chunkey and combat."

"You really believe she's possessed by the underwater panther?"

"Old friend, you haven't seen the things I have."

"I thought you were a skeptic."

"I am. About priests and temples and ceremonies. About Power? That's another thing."

A whining came up from below, and Seven Skull Shield craned his neck to stare down at the dog. The beast paced around the pile of Fire Cat's armor where it lay under the guarding eyes of Crazy Frog's men.

So . . . was the mongrel really a Spirit dog like the keeper of the Tortoise Bundle insisted? He really doubted it.

Applause went up from the crowd as Skull Pinner and Fire Cat took their places. As the favorite, Skull Pinner had the first roll and cradled his stone in his right hand.

At his side, Fire Cat crouched, his lance in his right hand, eyes fixed on the court.

Skull Pinner launched himself, muscles flexing as he sprinted forward. Four paces later, his arm went back and whipped forward to release the stone. It shot down the smooth clay.

Skull Pinner shifted his lance, arm going back. Just before the penalty line he and Fire Cat both released, the lances catching the sunlight as they curved upward. In a gentle arc, they sailed down toward the slowing stone.

Meanwhile Fire Cat and Skull Pinner raced in pursuit, their cries echoing with the crowd's as the lances impacted point-first and fell shivering to the earth.

"Skull Pinner by a couple of hand lengths." Crazy Frog moved one of his beads into a hole on his scoreboard as the players retrieved their lances and headed back to the start.

"What about Fire Cat?"

"Not bad. But it's only one throw. I need to watch him for a while. Learn his habits and faults."

Crazy Frog watched intently as Fire Cat positioned himself, leaning forward, eyes on the court. Beside him, Skull Pinner was grinning, hefting his lance as if testing its balance.

Fire Cat launched, powering forward, Skull Pinner matching pace for pace.

Whipping his arm back, Fire Cat bowled the black stone. It hit the ground with a bounce and jetted forward. Fire Cat never broke stride as he shifted his lance. Three steps later he cast, sending it flying after the stone. Slightly behind now, Skull Pinner made his cast a half a heartbeat later.

"Skull Pinner wins," Crazy Frog declared.

"How do you know?" Seven Skull Shield asked, watching as the two players chased their flying lances, clapping hands, calling as if their desperate shouts could influence the lances in flight.

"Fire Cat isn't smooth. He's bowling the stone too hard, too high on the release. He's thinking where he wants the stone to be when he casts his lance. Not watching it, reading its path."

"I thought that's how the best players won. By knowing

where the stone was going to be and hitting that spot with their lances."

Crazy Frog nodded as Skull Pinner won by an arm's length. "That's how they do it." He paused for effect. "But it means the player must actually control the stone well enough to roll to that particular spot. And do it consistently."

"And Fire Cat can't?"

"We'll see, won't we?" He shot Seven Skull Shield a side-long look. "The question is, will he be smart enough to take the criticism, or will he stalk away in a huff?"

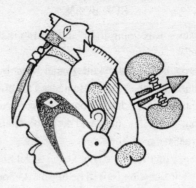

Seventy

One of her spies sent a runner, which gave Clan Keeper Blue Heron just enough warning that she could throw a shawl over her head—no doubt a feeble quest for anonymity—and wander down to stand at the edge of the crowd that had assembled itself around the bottom of Night Shadow Star's mound.

On the fourth stair up, no more than a pebble's toss from the Avenue of the Sun, Thirteen Sacred Jaguar stood in his quetzal-feathered finery, his great mask perched atop his head. Its vivid yellows, blues, greens, and black shone vividly in the midday sun.

Two steps down stood Horn Lance, resplendent in his Itza war finery. And before him Burning Ant held the Waxaklahun Kan standard high. War Serpent's hot green eyes glared menacingly at the crowd, the fangs mottled and stained.

The way it seemed to glare at her, she could well believe the carving was possessed. Whenever those malignant green eyes met hers, a shiver ran down her spine.

Thirteen Sacred Jaguar gestured emphatically as he spoke, his Itzan language unintelligible to the growing crowd of Cahokians drawn from the avenue. Barring the foot of the

Morning Star's stairs, no other place in Cahokia was better suited to draw a crowd.

As Thirteen Sacred Jaguar lectured, Horn Lance translated, saying, "In the Beginning, at the Creation, Heart of Sky, the Maker and Modeler, went to Lord Plumed Serpent and the Begetters in the dark and formless waters. Using a cord, they surveyed out the sides, corners, and ends of Creation, marking them with stakes. Next, by halving the cord and making angles, they began to demark and measure the space contained within Creation.

"Together the three uttered the name of the earth, and it rose from the dark and formless water. The male sky force was concentrated into the First Father's being, the female force in First Mother Maker, born of water. Having Created earth, they brought forth upon it the sacred tree called Yax Cheel Kab, what you call the World Tree. From its branches came the plants and flowers. Then First Father and First Mother fashioned the birds, fish, reptiles, and all the animals. But these creatures couldn't speak the Creators' names, nor could they worship their Creators. The Father-Mother banished them to the wild places and told them their purpose would be as food to the beings who came later.

"In the second Creation, the Father/Mother created people from mud, hoping these beings would worship them and pronounce the names of their Creators. But the mud people were too soft and melted in the rain.

"In the third Creation they crafted people of wood only to discover that they were too hard and stiff and couldn't remember the names of their Creators. Nor did these wooden humans have any concerns for their fellows, the animals, or their gods. Those who survived the devastating flood sent by the Mother-Father survive as monkeys today."

At the whispering among the crowd, Horn Lance stopped, smiling graciously. "Monkeys, my friends, are hideous little caricatures of people and are found in the high trees in the lands of the Itza."

Blue Heron pulled at her wattle, eyes half-squinted as she took in the awe-filled crowd around her. The gullible fools were hanging on every word.

Thirteen Sacred Jaguar spread his arms wide, his clicking voice filling the air.

"While Creating the third world, First Woman gave birth to the magical One-and-Seven Lord, who was both one individual and two. A being with reflecting and linked souls in both the spirit and created world. They in turn sired the Hero Twins, who, in our language are called Hun Ahau and Yax Balam, or One Lord and First Jaguar.

"No sooner were the Hero Twins born, than One-and-Seven Hun Ahau created the ball game. This he played in the sacred court, but the bouncing of the ball awakened and disturbed the Lords of Death in Xibalba, what you call the Underworld. Irritated, the Lords of Death invited One-and-Seven Lord into the frightening depths to play ball against them. One-and-Seven Lord naively traveled to the Underworld. Full of pride as he was, the Lords of Death tricked him, tortured him, and finally beat One-and-Seven Lord at ball playing. They cut off his head and placed it upon a pole, then buried his body beneath the ball court."

Blue Heron squinted skeptically as she watched the crowd. Some were nodding, other faces reflected confusion, while a few appeared to share her skepticism.

Horn Lance raised his hands, smiling. "The story sounds similar, doesn't it? You might think of First Man, the Morning Star and Thrown-Away Boy's father, playing chunkey with the giants. But consider this: perhaps one of the stories is but a reflection of an older one. And who is to say which story came first? Perhaps the answer to that lies in which tellers of the tale are endowed with superior Spiritual Power by the gods. That superiority would be measured by their grandeur, their dress, the potency of their rituals, and perhaps their military prowess."

This the audience could definitely agree with. Horn
Lance got nods in return.

Clever, you piece of dung. Not even the simplest of the
dolts could help but draw comparisons to Thirteen Sacred
Jaguar appearing in his colorful panoply, being feted and
received by the Morning Star, marrying Night Shadow
Star, and then the stunning ease with which Cahokia's finest had been laid low in ritual combat. By evening the story
would be all over Cahokia, the people wondering whose
Power was greater: the Morning Star's, backed by the Four
Winds Clan, or the newly arrived and exciting Itza's, with
all the exotic allure it represented.

"Gods," she whispered as the brilliance of Thirteen Sacred Jaguar's plan became apparent. "We've been played like
fools the entire time."

She glanced up at the Morning Star's high palace, seeing
a single individual perched atop one of the bastions and
looking down. She didn't need to see the gleam of his copper headpiece to know it was the Morning Star.

*Living god or not, if this pack of lies takes root, he's going
to bring you down. And the rest of us with you.*

Seventy-one

How are you doing?" Seven Skull Shield asked.

It was a fair question, and it caught Fire Cat off guard as he spooned baked squash from a gourd container. He was just finishing it after having demolished a freshwater clam stew made on a goosefoot-seed stock, spiced with wild onions, greens, and hominy. That had been preceded by fire-roasted fingers of swan breast wrapped in steamed grape leaves.

"I couldn't eat another bite. The food is magnificent." He looked around Crazy Frog's yard and at the other chunkey players who sat in ranks around the great fire where Mother Otter handed out bowls of the most savory treats. The yard fronted an imposing two-story house more suited to a lord than a common gambler. Two wooden mortars stood to the side, and a spacious ramada filled the spot where normal people would have had their garden.

Fire Cat had been introduced to Crazy Frog's five wives, and to his flock of children aged eleven on down. The extent of Crazy Frog's wealth was just sinking in. *Five* wives? The resources necessary to support them and their children? Not to mention that all of the furnishings, ceramics, the clothes Crazy Frog's family wore, the jewelry, and imposing house would have challenged a chief's resources. Yet Crazy Frog was nothing more than a footloose ruffian akin to the thief and his ilk?

"You come here often to eat?"

Seven Skull Shield's sigh was the sort he'd waste on an idiot. "I *never* eat here. We're here because I paid for us to be. That sack I picked up at the Keeper's? It bought you an afternoon of playing chunkey. The fact that we're invited to eat? That's because Crazy Frog is no one's fool. He knows that you're close to the heart of Morning Star House politics, tied to Lady Night Shadow Star. The story of her cutting you down from the square at Piasa's insistence, the fact that you saved her life? That she went out of her way to retrieve your clothes?"

Fire Cat felt his ears burn as he watched two of Crazy Frog's younger wives picking up wooden bowls from the fancy-dressed chunkey players. He hadn't caught their names, just Mother Otter's. Nor was he surprised that the other players, including Skull Pinner and Lightning Lance, both of whom he'd played that afternoon, barely wasted a glance in his direction. Not only was he dressed like a common man, but he'd lost every match he'd played.

If anything, they were no doubt wondering what had possessed Crazy Frog to stoop to inviting "Wounded Dog" to join the winners at his evening gathering.

As Seven Skull Shield rubbed his ugly dog's ears, Mother Otter stopped before them. She crossed her arms under her full breasts and glared down at the thief with obvious distaste. That earned her special points in Fire Cat's opinion.

Then she turned her attention to him, saying, "Wounded Dog? My husband would like to see you. Thief? If you value your sweat-stinking hide, you'll stay right where you are."

"But Mother Otter"—Seven Skull Shield spread his arms wide—"I've never been a nuisance, let alone been allowed to wander around to admire all of your wonderful things."

"Which is why all of our possessions are still ours. When

you're around, not even a red-hot hearth stone is safe from your fast fingers."

"You just can't resist my charm, can you? That's why you say these things. As if you're trying to talk yourself out of feelings you can't deny."

"A steaming pile of fresh feces behind a charnel house has more charm than you do, thief. Now stay put. And keep that dog out of trouble." She made a disgusted humph. "Figures. He's the only man alive could find a dog uglier and more unsavory than he is."

Fire Cat climbed warily to his feet as Mother Otter studied him suspiciously.

"You're a friend of his?" She hooked a thumb at the grinning thief.

"Usually, when I think about Seven Skull Shield, I'm imagining how it would feel to split his head with an ax."

Her faint smile didn't extend to her eyes. "You, I might like."

She led him toward the house, arriving at the door just as Crazy Frog emerged surrounded by five children. They were laughing, pulling at his apron, and hanging onto his legs.

"Go on!" He waved them off, shaking a particularly persistent five-year-old from his right leg. "I've got business with Wounded Dog."

He grinned as the children ran giggling and shrieking toward the fire. Then he turned his attention to Fire Cat. "You got enough to eat?"

Fire Cat shot a glance at Mother Otter, who'd again crossed her arms, concerned dark eyes taking his measure. "The meal was the match to the finest I've ever eaten." He touched his forehead as he bowed to Mother Otter. "Superb."

For the first time her expression thawed.

"Come." Crazy Frog led him around the seated chunkey players. They called greetings and praises to which Crazy Frog replied with a good-natured banter. Stepping under the ramada he gestured to the blankets and seated himself.

Fire Cat dropped, propping his arms on his knees, unsure of what was coming next.

"I live for chunkey," Crazy Frog told him with a smile. "Most of this"—he gestured around at his grounds—"comes from my winnings. I have other interests, of course, but the game is my passion. Perhaps because myself, I have no talent for it. I can't roll a stone in a straight line or throw a lance well enough to keep it in the court. Couldn't do it if it meant saving the lives of my children. But I've spent my life watching, learning how to evaluate a player and what his chances of winning are."

He gave Fire Cat a distasteful wince. "The smart ones now wait to see who my agents bet on before placing their own bets. I have ways of dealing with that. Playing them against themselves. Otherwise they ruin the odds."

"The thief says you can help me."

"That's up to you."

"What's wrong with my game? Have I been witched? Perhaps by the Natchez? Or by foreign Itza magic? I used to play better than this."

Crazy Frog steepled his fingers and studied Fire Cat in the dying afternoon light. Squeals from the playing children mixed with laughter as the chunkey players shared a joke. Hopefully it wasn't at his expense.

"When it comes to chunkey, Power gifts some men over others." Crazy Frog hesitated, and Fire Cat's breath caught. It was insane. What did a commoner, a gambler who didn't even play the game, know?

Crazy Frog then added, "You are such a gifted man."

"But I keep—"

"Losing. Yes. I've heard Seven Skull Shield's version of the story. About Piasa and the lady you serve. Now you tell me. And if you expect me to help you, you must open your very souls. So, just what exactly is at stake?"

"Everything," Fire Cat whispered.

Nevertheless, he hesitated. How did he tell this stranger,

this parasite on the underbelly of Cahokia, how much hung in the balance? Open his heart? To Crazy Frog?

"I am the last of the Red Wing," he began, figuring to skirt the sensitive parts, but once the words started, they just seemed to keep coming, flowing out of his soul as he tried to explain his worry, his failure, and ultimate humiliation.

"I can't see how beating the Natchez that day would have made a difference," Fire Cat finally admitted. "How winning his lance and stone would have stopped the marriage and defeated the Itza. But I lost. Saving our world now falls on Night Shadow Star's shoulders. She married a man who will destroy her and Cahokia. And I am here, wondering at the depths of my own desperation."

Crazy Frog nodded, as if some critical bit of information had fallen into place.

"The problem isn't magic or foreign Power. It's you, Red Wing. Down deep in your souls."

"What?"

Crazy Frog smiled grimly. "Confront your greatest fear."

"That the Itza will win?"

"You delude yourself. The thing that terrifies you is that you will not live up to the expectations of others. I don't know the ways of Power, but I do know chunkey and chunkey players." He waved at the players seated in a ring around the fire. "Why do you think I spend so much time with them? I want to know them, what they think, how their souls work. Why one wins and another loses. Perhaps you had to lose to the Natchez. Perhaps you had to be forced into what you call the depths of your own desperation as a means of bringing you here. I'll leave that up to the priests."

"You think I can beat the Natchez?"

"First, you have to beat yourself."

"Beat myself? That doesn't make sense."

"Of course it does. Tomorrow morning. At false dawn. Meet me at the courts. We'll start with the basics. How you hold the stone. Timing your release. Shifting the lance."

"But I know all those things."

"No, you don't. Otherwise you would have won today's matches."

"And if you can fix my game, what do you get out of it?"

Crazy Frog smiled, eyes narrowing. "If you can reach the potential I think you have, I'll make a small fortune betting against the Natchez. If you don't measure up to what I know is within you, I won't even bother to wager against you."

Seventy-two

"Show me how you grip the stone." Crazy Frog stood with a foot out, arms crossed as Fire Cat took his position.

Seven Skull Shield yawned, scratching the back of his head. The first light of dawn had turned the River Mounds chunkey grounds misty pink and violet. He glanced down at the dog, who yawned and laid down at his feet.

"Really ought to find a name for you."

The dog thumped its thick-rooted tail, the action eliciting an irregular fart.

They'd been allowed to spend the night beneath Crazy Frog's ramada. A small blessing. But apparently not enough to have merited a hot-cooked meal out of Mother Otter's kitchen.

Instead, Crazy Frog had appeared in the faintest of dawn light, kicking Fire Cat awake and saying, "Let's go."

Seven Skull Shield had followed along as Crazy Frog led them to the River Mounds chunkey courts. He scratched at a mosquito bite as Fire Cat offered his hand where it gripped the black stone.

"That's good. The best players use their fingers to drive the stone forward and into a spin. The more a stone slides when it first hits the dirt, the more chance for a wobble. The finest of players actually give the stone a flip with the fingers at the last instant of release."

Fire Cat studied the way his fingers cupped the smooth black stone. "How do you know all this?"

Crazy Frog gave him the sort of stare he'd give an imbecile before continuing. "Even more to the point, finger pressure can make the stone curve in one direction or the other. Just as the angle that you release it does. If it's not straight up and down, it will go in whichever direction it's leaned."

"I knew that."

Seven Skull Shield looked down at the dog. "Sounds like they've got it all sorted out here."

"Then thief, you know less about chunkey than I thought you did." Crazy Frog gave him a sidelong glance.

"Which is why you're working with good old Wounded Dog here, and I'm off to find something to fill my gut."

"Watch yourself," Fire Cat added as he took his mark at the start, Crazy Frog watching the placement of his feet. "There's still a price on your head. You may be dressed like a lord, but your fellow thieves and ruffians will look twice. You should wait until I can go along."

"Hey, Red Wing, this is me we're talking about." He jammed a hard thumb into his breastbone to emphasize the point and gave the warrior a lascivious grin.

He left Crazy Frog making suggestions about Fire Cat's feet, and with the dog following, he slipped between the engineers' society house and a moon society temple. From there, taking the dawn-shadowed back ways, he arrived at Wooden Doll's in short order.

To his relief, no litter was sitting in her yard, nor were men sleeping before her door.

He took his time, ensuring that no one watched the place, before easing along the wall to the wooden plank door. With a knuckle, he tapped lightly.

Moments later the slave girl lifted the door open a crack, staring out into the gray morning. She started to smile, then got a closer look and recognized him. "Oh, it's you. Wait."

Seven Skull Shield looked down at the dog. "Don't pee on the floor. We've got enough against us as it is."

The dog stretched his front end out and down, back and tail raised high in reply, which stimulated another odiferous release of gas. Seven Skull Shield made a face and tried to wave the noxious smell away.

When the door finally opened, Wooden Doll, her hair sleep-mussed, leaned against the frame. She crossed her arms, a shapely brow lifted. "Still dressed as a lord?" She shook her head. "Skull, you never know when to quit, do you?"

"We need to talk."

She sighed. "And let me guess. You haven't eaten yet, either."

"Well . . . things have been busy this morning."

She glanced down. "And that mongrel that's been following you around has an empty belly, too, right?"

"Can I come in? I scouted around before I knocked. No one's watching your house yet, but that doesn't mean Slick Rock or Fish Grease, or one of the more ambitious latrine stranglers looking for me won't think to check here in hopes of picking up Horn Lance's reward."

"Why do I even try?" She clamped her eyes shut and shook her head. "Come in." She winced. "And that beast, too. I suppose I owe you that much."

He gave Newe a wide smile as he entered, one that she didn't reciprocate.

"Newe, find us something to eat," Wooden Doll said.

As the servant girl ducked out the door, Wooden Doll turned her attention back to Seven Skull Shield. "What are you doing here, Skull? I thought you'd be sticking to the Keeper like horn glue in hopes she could keep you safe."

"There's no such thing while the Itza, your *friend* Horn Lance, and his Natchez maggots are in the city. I had a long talk with the stupid Natchez night before last night. They expect to create a whole new order of political influence up and down the river, clear to the Itza lands across the gulf."

"That's ambitious. Even Cahokia has avoided messing with the Nations on the lower river."

He shook his head, as if baffled. "Had you asked me a half-moon past, I'd have said anyone who proposed such a thing was head-struck. After the things I've seen, and what the weasel-brained Natchez say, they might just be able to pull it off. With Cahokia as an anchor in the north and the Itza using the Natchez lands as a base for Trade, preaching their religion, and military expansion, they can control the entire river."

"And is that a bad thing?" She shrugged, settling next to him on the bed poles. "You should see the piece of fabric Horn Lance Traded for my services. That one square of cloth is worth everything you see here, including the house and grounds. Morning Star himself hasn't the like."

She lifted an eyebrow. "And there's more where that came from. A whole world of wealth just beyond the horizon across the gulf. Horn Lance told me about people called the Yucatec and their great ocean-going canoes. About how they can bring riches beyond compare."

"At what cost to us?" He searched her clever eyes. "They started with murder on our most holy day. They've ingratiated themselves like a slow poison with their wealth, their grandeur, and exotic gifts. The Itza has married Night Shadow Star, inserted himself into the Morning Star House. They've threatened the Keeper. Put a price on my head. How long before the Morning Star himself is poisoned?"

He paused. "You saw how easily they mowed down our best warriors. What happens when an army of Itza warriors paddle up the Father Water in these big canoes? Who stops them then?"

Her eyes slitted. "Not my problem, Skull. From where I sit, the kind of Trade the Itza and their supporters will give for my services beats anything a Cahokian or any river Trader can offer."

"So that's your ultimate concern?" He paused. "Whatever makes you the most? Even if it means selling out Cahokia and its people?" He swallowed hard. "Selling out me?"

Her lips thinned. "Horn Lance told me that you sent him here. That he was your friend. That he . . ."

She chuckled, amused at herself. "Maybe I'm not the woman you think I am, Skull. Maybe I'm irritated because if I'd known he wanted you dead, that he was playing me, I'd have figured a way to skin him out of *two* of those Itza fabric pieces."

He studied her for long moments, arms crossed. She met his glare, eyes sultry and dark with challenge.

"That's really how you feel?"

"You made your choice. And you chose the Keeper. Sold yourself to that old woman. Do you really think, no matter what she says, that she cares any more for you than Horn Lance cares for me?"

"She's my friend."

Wooden Doll burst out in hard laughter. "Sure she is! Who do you think you're fooling? Dressed up, playing a noble? No matter how many flowers you rub on a skunk's ass, you can't change his stink. You're a tool to them. And as soon as they wear you out, they're going to rid themselves of your odor." She shrugged. "Them, or Horn Lance. If you're going to wind up dead anyway, I might as well profit from it."

He stood, walking to the door, the dog rising to his feet and following. "Maybe I'm not hungry after all."

"Just as well. I've got to get ready. A litter is supposed to pick me up before midmorning. I've got an appointment. Someone important who lives near the Grand Plaza wants to talk business. Being seen at the wedding is already paying off." She blew him a kiss, adding, "Oh, and Skull, watch your back out there, huh?"

He lifted the door to the side and stalked out into the morning, the dog following along behind.

Of course Wooden Doll would be looking to her own interests, but didn't she see the bigger issue? The Itza would bring a new ruling class, one that dominated the Four Winds Clan, who dominated the Earth Clans, who dominated everyone else. A new religion meant the Morning Star had to be replaced. Eliminated. And somewhere in the mix would come rebellion against the new masters. When that happened, Cahokia would explode in chaos, mayhem, and murder, with tens of thousands of human beings turning on each other.

He shook his head as he took the familiar path between a council house and basket weaver's.

"She doesn't realize how fragile Cahokia is," he muttered under his breath as he passed a latrine screen behind a potter's. "Just like with Walking Smoke, all it takes is the wrong spark and the whole thing goes up in—"

He had the barest impression of movement. Of someone leaping out from behind the latrine's woven cattail screen.

A blur of something dark and heavy.

The blow to his head shot lightning behind his eyes, the impact like thunder through his skull and senses.

He didn't feel his body hit the ground.

A dog shrieked and squealed in pain, as if someone were beating it to death.

The last image he had was of Slick Rock, club in hand.

And then the world went away . . . .

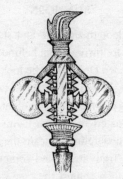

Seventy-three

Piasa whispered disjointedly into Night Shadow Star's ear as she climbed past the Natchez guards to her palace. Lovingly she ran her fingers across the polished wood of the Horned Serpent guardian post, recalling the Spirit Beast's gleaming crystalline eyes. How they'd glowed with an internal light as the creature peeled away layers of her memories.

At the time—her souls lost in the Underworld—she'd faced only death and eternal nothingness. Not the yawning sense of desperation and distaste at what she now was about to endure.

She'd returned at dusk the night before, only to have Clay String, Green Stick, and the rest of her household servants throw themselves at her feet, pleading that she put Horn Lance in his place.

When she'd faced the man, he'd smiled wickedly, crossed his arms, and told her: "Your people serve *Ahau* Oxlajun Chul B'alam. As do you. He would like to find you in his bed tomorrow morning instead of waking to empty blankets."

"Who my people serve, and where my body is in the morning, are my concern. My people—"

His hand flashed in a blur, slapping her hard across the cheek. Staggered by the force of it, she'd barely avoided a fall.

"Your husband would like you to share his supper before retiring to his bed. He believes a woman with a full stomach is better disposed to accept his seed."

Cheek still burning she'd glanced desperately around the room, seeing the Natchez. They'd all witnessed her humiliation and were grinning that she'd been put in her place. Especially Swirling Cloud.

Where's Fire Cat?

His place by the door remained vacant, Horn Lance having removed his bedding and replaced it with his own.

In her ear, Piasa had whispered, *You are abandoned by everyone. You have no one left, Night Shadow Star.*

She'd awakened that morning before dawn, her skin crawling, hearing voices whispering from the dark corners of her room.

Soundlessly, she'd slipped from her husband's side, grabbed her clothing, and tiptoed past the sleeping form of Horn Lance where he lay in Fire Cat's place.

That entire day, she'd wandered around the Great Plaza, listened to the people as they talked about the Itza, about what his stories meant, and if the Morning Star was the same as the Hun Ahau the Itza told of.

Abandoned! Piasa's disembodied voice seemed to hiss from the air.

She shot a glance at the guardian post carved in his image and walked hesitantly toward her palace where Natchez warriors sat in a row on her veranda.

She ignored them as she entered, walking slowly toward the fire. Again her desperate eyes searched for Fire Cat, finding only the Itza warriors, Horn Lance, and her husband in some sort of conference. They stopped, all turning to watch her with speculative eyes as she approached the fire.

There she lowered herself, extending hands to the heat,

wondering how long she could stand the pain were she to thrust her hands into the bed of coals.

Though she concentrated, she could see nothing in the glimmering embers. No pattern, no clue as to the future.

She was only vaguely aware of Horn Lance squatting beside her, offering a plate.

"I'm sorry about yesterday, Lady. I should not have struck you. Here. Freshly cooked. The spice comes from the *ahau*'s home country. It's called achiote. The meat is bison. I'm told it's from a young cow. Tender and sweet."

She took the plate, refusing to meet his eyes, and tried the succulent meat. The achiote filled her mouth with a unique and tangy flavor. She'd originally thought to try it and then pitch the rest into the fire—a statement of what she thought of his apology. The unique flavor, however, led her to a second piece, and then a third.

"I thought you'd like it," Horn Lance replied as he stood and walked back to the other men.

Finishing the plate, she found her cup and filled it with tea, washing down the last of the meat.

Taking a deep breath, she laid the plate to the side, continuing to stare at the fire.

I should have left with Fire Cat. He offered, suggested taking a canoe, heading south.

She glanced again at where his bed had been, seeing Horn Lance and the rest of them. They waited by the door to her personal quarters like vultures, silent, each one studying her, as if waiting.

For what?

On the far side of the room, her household staff huddled, talking softly among themselves, anxious eyes on her. She sniffed disdainfully. As if she could do anything to help herself, let alone them.

I could leave. Tomorrow. Sneak away. Go in search of Fire Cat and . . .

A curious hazy feeling swam up from her gut. She blinked,

a warm wave rolling around her insides. Her vision seemed to smear, colors brightening. Heat, like an infusion, ran down her bones, pulsed with her blood, and conjured a prickling sensation in her hands and feet.

She shook her head, trying to shake off the odd euphoria.

Horn Lance was smiling as he rose, crossing the room with Red Copal in tow to lower himself beside her.

"Feeling better, Lady?"

"What is this?"

"A mixture, Lady. Scrapings from mushrooms that grow in the forests of the Yucatan added to *bache*, an herbal that opens the doors to the Spirit World."

She took a deep breath, seeking to stabilize the room.

"Let me go."

Horn Lance had taken one arm, Red Copal the other.

"I don't want to go there."

But they were walking her inexorably toward her bedroom.

This time when she looked up at the *kukul* the terrible alien war god was glaring back. The green eyes gleamed, alive with a victorious essence. She could feel its Power, throbbing, hot, and angry. Its predatory gaze followed her as she was led past it and into her room.

Guiding her inside, Horn Lance led her to the bed. She pawed awkwardly in a feeble attempt to stop him as he yanked her skirt down over her hips.

He and Red Copal tossed her onto the bed, backing away as Thirteen Sacred Jaguar stepped between them. He studied her with his oddly bugged-out eyes, a resigned set to his lips.

He was pulling off his clothes when Horn Lance said, "Lady, you'll find yourself much more responsive to your husband's caress. You might not even need the hickory oil."

The room had become unreal and liquid. It seemed to swirl, shifting sideways. Some distant part of her knew she should care. That this was wrong and she should fight it.

Then she saw Piasa, like a soot-soft darkness in the corner; his three-forked eyes burned yellow and gleaming.

She was still staring into the Spirit Beast's glistening eyes when her husband's body settled onto hers. She stifled a cry as he drove himself into her.

Abandoned . . .

The word seemed to echo around her empty skull.

Seventy-four

Slick Rock squatted on his heels, his arms braced on his knees, a smug satisfaction almost radiating. It could be seen in his eyes, in the set of his mouth and the lift of his eyebrows. The slight smile distorted his facial tattoos. Bruises were fading on his hide, white edges having formed on some of the older scabs. He'd pulled his thick black hair into a bun and pinned it with turkey-bone skewers.

His only movement was the slow flexing of his hands, fingers extending, then tightening, rearranging the pattern of old scars on his knuckles as the tendons rose.

Seven Skull Shield would have conjured his best murderous glare, but the brutal pain in his head sapped him of the will, let alone the energy.

He'd awakened on the dirt floor of a Panther Clan council house. Or so he assumed given the building's round shape, the low benches around the periphery, and the cat images drawn on the poorly plastered walls. A cold fire pit filled with gray ash lay between him and Slick Rock. Three scruffy and scrawny-looking men dressed in worn breechcloths hunkered to the side, watching him with bored stares. A hot shaft of white midday sunlight poured through the oversized smoke hole, its brilliance doing nothing good for the searing pain in Seven Skull Shield's broken head.

He'd already tried the ropes that bound him up like a trussed bear. All he'd managed to accomplish in the struggle was to pull hide from his wrists and ankles. Each time he strained against the bindings, it augmented the agony in his head by a factor of ten.

"You really are going to regret this." He studied Slick Rock through slitted eyes. "Every time you've taken me on, you've come out second best."

"So I've noticed." Slick Rock's fingers spread and closed again, as if squeezing the air into a tiny ball. "Which is why you're lying on the floor, a lump the size of a goose's egg on the back of your head. Given your expression, it hurts just to breathe. Which is just an itty bitty hint of the pain, horror, and misery waiting for you when I finally get you to Horn Lance."

"Where am I?"

"River Mounds City." Slick Rock rubbed his palms together, the callused skin making a rasping noise. "Waiting for dark."

"Why?"

"'Cause I'm not an idiot. The Keeper's got spies all over. I've gotta get you to Horn Lance without anyone the wiser."

"And how you gonna do that?"

"By learning from you, you big maggot. Got ten Panther Clan men gonna bring a canoe up just after dark. We're gonna whack you in the head again to remind you to be quiet. Then we're gonna toss your meat into the canoe and carry it to Horn Lance's." His smile widened. "Clever, huh? Just like you did with that foreign warrior last spring. The one you smuggled to the Keeper's."

Slick Rock tilted his head in enjoyment. "The idea of doing to you just like you did to others brings a unique pleasure to my heart, you loud-mouthed piece of maggot crap."

Seven Skull Shield worked his tongue around his mouth. "You got any water?"

Slick Rock looked at a leather bag off to one side. "I do. But not for you. It's probably the only favor I'm doing for you. Letting you thirst and starve."

"How's that a favor?"

"Do you think that even as much as I hate and despise you, that I'd let Horn Lance torture you to death without giving you a chance to work up to what's coming? Just let you start suffering without any preparation whatsoever? What kind of a man do you think I am, anyway?"

"You've kicked over a pile of manure before?" Seven Skull Shield asked.

"Of course."

"Then you've seen the little white worms? The ones that tunnel through the shit and end up down at the bottom pile, where it's wet and moldy? That's the kind of man you are."

Slick Rock's smile only grew wider while the man's eyes narrowed to menacing slits.

Seven Skull Shield asked, "How much did you give Wooden Doll for giving me up?"

"That part was too easy. I just had to crawl between her legs. At the feel of a real man she melted. Offered me everything she had if I'd just stay with her forever. Instead I pulled out and told her I'd never slip it back in again if she didn't send me word the minute you showed up." He glanced absently off to the side, as if considering. "I imagine she's panting right now. Wondering what's keeping me."

"You're a lying pile of fly-infested vomit. What did you Trade her for me?"

Slick Rock shrugged. "Two shell necklaces."

Something deep inside Seven Skull Shield went hollow.

Reading his expression, Slick Rock added, "You really are something. You *actually* thought you *meant* something to her?" Then he chuckled. "You self-deluded fool. I can't wait to tell this story to the others. We'll be laughing our guts out for the rest of our lives."

Seven Skull Shield gritted his teeth, wincing at the pain it triggered.

"I never thought victory could taste like this—a delight to be tucked into the heart for eternal joy."

"Oh, it can indeed," a voice called from the door. A big man with Fish Clan tattoos on his face ducked into the room. He carried a war club, his hair done up in a bun. A beaded forelock, denoting a blooded warrior, hung down over his nose.

Four more warriors followed, crowding in around Seven Skull Shield. One of them leveled a war club at Slick Rock's henchmen, ordering, "Get out. And if we see you again, you'll wish we hadn't."

"Who are you?" Slick Rock demanded, rising warily to his feet, his right hand dropping to a deer-bone stiletto at his belt.

"Admirers of yours." The Fish Clan warrior smacked the stone head of his war club against the hardened palm of his left hand. "You've sent a runner to Horn Lance? Told him you've caught the thief?"

Slick Rock nodded, eyes flicking back and forth in his uncertainty. "You are in his service?"

"After a fashion."

"I don't know what that means. Why are you here?"

The Fish Clan warrior spread his arms wide in mockery. "Like I said, we're admirers of yours. We're here in admiration of the tricky way you caught the thief. We just wanted to thank you, tell you how much we appreciate it, and how impressed we are."

Slick Rock's wariness mixed with confusion. "I don't understand. If you're not Horn Lance's . . . then whose men are you?"

The big warrior shrugged. "You didn't really think that you'd be the only one with an interest in the thief, did you?

Now, we've told you how much we appreciate you grabbing him for us—which, given the circumstances, is more than we needed to do. So if you'll just disappear we'll consider it a token of the high regard we hold you in and call it even."

"I'm not giving up the thief! I've got Trade coming!"

A grin split the Fish Clan man's broad face and exposed peg-like teeth, some of them broken. "I just explained that part. You get to live. That is, you do if you trot those feet of yours out the door, out of River Mounds City, and we don't see you again. If we do, our first thought is that you didn't appreciate our kind gesture. We'd take that as an insult. Something happens when we're insulted. We just lose all sense of restraint."

Even as he said it the other warriors began to nod in agreement and growl under their breaths. War clubs made a hollow popping as they were slapped suggestively into cupped hands.

Seven Skull Shield, his heart hammering, drove a swallow down his dry throat. At the same time, Slick Rock looked like a man in agony as he shot glances at Seven Skull Shield and then back at the Fish Clan warrior.

"I guess you didn't appreciate the depth and sincerity of our offer, which means you think we're shit," the Fish Clan man said with a deep and supposedly heartfelt sigh. He turned to the man behind him, asking, "I think we're insulted. What should we do?"

"Can't let that go, Squadron First. Gotta kill him." The man took a step forward, dropping into a crouch, his war club at the ready.

"Wait!" Slick Rock raised his hands, edging away. "It's all right! I'm going. He's all yours."

With that, he scuttled around the curved wall and ducked out through the door.

The big Fish Clan warrior stared thoughtfully at the door; the hanging swung in Slick Rock's wake. "Guess he appreciated us after all."

"Good to see you," Seven Skull Shield told the man amiably. "The sooner you cut me loose, the quicker you can take your pick of the Keeper's finest Trade. She's a most generous woman."

"I'm sure she is," a familiar voice called from the doorway. "But I'm afraid there's a complication."

Seven Skull Shield twisted his head to stare over his shoulder. A renewed blast of pain brought tears to his eyes, but through the shimmer he could see Flat Stone Pipe.

"What's the complication?"

Flat Stone Pipe sighed, extending his small hands. "I'm sorry, old friend. It's just that in politics, the structure of influence and authority continually changes. When that happens, prudence dictates new alliances. Horn Lance and the Itza have offered Evening Star House certain concessions in return for our support. Disagreeable as it may seem, that includes you."

"I *saved* Columella's children that day! But for me and the Keeper, they'd have burned! I was going back for Chief High Dance when the roof collapsed!"

"We are more than aware." Flat Stone Pipe actually looked torn. "Which is one of the reasons political reality has such an ugly aspect. Unfortunately, it is just the way things are."

He pointed at the Fish Clan warrior. "Squadron First, I assume you can secret the thief across the river to the location I have specified?"

"I can, Lord."

"Oh," Flat Stone Pipe added, "and could you send a runner to inform the good Horn Lance that despite what he may have heard from less-reliable sources, Seven Skull Shield is safely under our control?"

"Yes, Lord."

Head reeling, Seven Skull Shield felt himself lifted. A thick mat was rolled out beneath him. They let him drop, the impact blasting his head apart with pain.

Within a heartbeat they had him rolled up in the mat,

lifted, and he felt himself being borne from the council house.

"I saved her children!" he bellowed in disbelief.

A war club thumped hard against his ribs, the matting barely dulling the blow.

"Quiet! The next time I have to whack you, I'm breaking bones. And thief, hanging from a square when your bones are broken is even more excruciating. The sharp ends stick out through the skin. I hear it really hurts."

Seventy-five

Oxlajun Chul B'alam!" the crowd chanted as they packed the avenue between Night Shadow Star's mound and the sloping sides of the Morning Star's great earthen pyramid. Worse, the swelling mob blocked the Avenue of the Sun as those on the outside pressed forward in an attempt to hear Thirteen Sacred Jaguar's morning sermon, translated by Horn Lance, from the heights of Night Shadow Star's stairway.

Blue Heron scowled distastefully from her litter as the warriors in her guard cried with near-futility, "Make way! Make way for Clan Keeper Blue Heron."

"Why should we?" a soot-stained man hollered back. "She serves a false god! All the Four Winds do!"

With a flick of his wrist, Big Right, the squadron first in charge of her security, cracked the miscreant on the side of the head, sending him staggering.

A shout went up from the press, expressions hardening, some raising fists.

"Make way!" Big Right bellowed. "Or we'll break a lot more of your idiot heads!"

A ripple went through the crowd, like a wave. Blue Heron's fists tightened. People's attention turned from where

Horn Lance lectured on the step below the gaudy Itza and his *kukul,* to where her guard surged forward, war clubs waving menacingly.

Blue Heron's anxiety turned to fear—a cold certainty rising within her as she read the massed faces before her. Their excitement turned to irritation, and then to anger as whispers ran from mouth to ear.

"She serves a false god!" someone cried.

"Her guard just killed a man!" another shouted in disbelief.

"Who are the Four Winds to order us around?"

That question was followed by grunts of agreement, eyes hardening as they fixed on hers. She knew it the moment they turned against her.

She had ten warriors in the guard, most of them crowding forward.

"Squadron First!" she barked. "Back away. We'll go the other way."

He shot her the briefest of questioning glances before ordering, "Back away."

Blue Heron's litter bearers deftly reversed course, the guards shifting to cover her retreat.

Moments later, they'd broken free, pursued only by shouts and insults as her porters trotted back toward the relative safety of the busy avenue. East-bound traffic had piled up, blocked by the crowd. At least here, people made way as her warriors cut south, skirting the western side of the *tonka'tzi*'s great white mound, then past the Moon Society house, and across the Great Plaza.

As her heart rate dropped, she took a deep breath. "Piss and snot! This has got to stop."

"Yes, Keeper," Big Right called up, a grim expression on his face. "I've never seen the like. They were within a hare's whisker of turning on us. Here! In the shadow of the Morning Star's palace!"

Her litter was lowered before the great staircase, and Big

Right offered her a hand as she got to her feet, asking, "Do you want me to call out a squadron and disperse that bunch, Keeper? Shut this Itza nonsense down once and for all?"

She glanced back at the crowd swelling around the mound base. Hawkers were working the fringes, offering trinkets carved to resemble the Itza, the *kukul*, and miniature replicas of *macuahuitls* that were little more than flattened sticks with tiny stone flakes stuck in the edges. The attention of the crowd had now gone back to Horn Lance, individuals on the outskirts straining once again to hear over the press.

"For the moment, leave them be. But prepare your men. After I speak with the *tonka'tzi* and the Morning Star, I might have orders for you."

"Yes, Keeper." Big Right touched his forehead reverently. The rest of the warriors traded wary glances.

She started up the stairs, futility hanging on her bones like a too-heavy blanket. Wind would back her. And surely the Morning Star would finally have come to the conclusion that Thirteen Sacred Jaguar and his preaching were like cactus juice poured on copper, eating away at the city's peace of mind.

"Nip it in the bud now," she said between breaths as she cleared the top of the stairs and passed through the gate and into the Council House yard. Like an unstoppable force she bulled her way through the cluster of officials and dignitaries awaiting their audience with the *tonka'tzi*.

Wind was seated on her litter atop its dais beneath the Council House ramada. She glanced up from a discussion with what appeared to be representatives of some colony, given the record mats and deerhide maps spread before her.

Blue Heron picked out Dead Bird from the officials behind the dais, pointing at him and snapping her fingers in a beckoning gesture. She said, "*Tonka'tzi*, excuse me. We need to talk."

Like a flock of grouse, people fled, and within moments, she, Dead Bird, and Wind were alone.

"What's happened?" Wind demanded, her expression pinching.

Blue Heron stepped up to Dead Bird. "We need to see the Morning Star. Now. Tell him we're on our way up."

Dead Bird read the smoldering worry and anger, and nodded; the young man turned on his heel and bounded for the stairs.

"Since the wedding, Thirteen Sacred Jaguar has been preaching from Night Shadow Star's steps. That's five days now. Each day the crowd grows larger. Today the mob blocked my way, called the Morning Star a false god, and would have attacked me. It's got to stop."

Wind pursed her lips, the expression wrinkling her face. "I know they're blocking the avenue, but only for a couple of fingers time. It's just a novelty that will wear off. And there are always a handful of malcontents who—"

"You weren't there. It's not just novelty. Nor is it just a handful of malcontents. Horn Lance is fanning embers that almost caught fire this morning. If it had come to a fight between my guard and the crowd? My warriors killing a couple of dozen people? Or worse, me being pulled down from my litter? Beaten? Perhaps worse? Spit and vomit, sister, think it through!"

"What's he saying? You're the one with the spies, the one who's been listening."

"He started with the Itza story of Creation, telling their myths about the Hero Twins. How they—similar to what's told in our story about the Morning Star and the giants—played ball with the Lords of Death. And won. And resurrected their father. But the preaching has changed as the crowd has grown. Now he's asking questions, like how could the Morning Star not understand Itza? Why the Morning Star couldn't answer simple questions Thirteen Sacred Jaguar asked him. How if the Beginning Times were really the Beginning Times, then Morning Star would also be the Hun Ahau of the Itza legends, so why does the Morning

Star only play chunkey? Thirteen Sacred Jaguar gave him a ball, so why doesn't he practice with it like in the stories? The implication is that if the Morning Star were really the hero from the Beginning Times, he'd explain why the Itza stories are so different from ours, and which one is right. That's what's so dangerous. The people are starting to question. And so far we've done nothing to discourage it. Meanwhile Horn Lance and the Itza have been triumphant at every turn from the murder of Nine Strikes, to the opulence of Thirteen Sacred Jaguar's reception, to the wedding, to the murder of our warriors."

Wind's nostrils thinned as she inhaled. "Very well. Let's go."

She climbed to her feet, leading the way to the stairs.

"What do you suggest we do about this?" Wind asked as she started up the steps. "Have a couple of squadrons move in? Disperse the crowd?"

"That could be just as provocative in the end. Play into the Itza's hand. I can hear Horn Lance now, 'What does the Morning Star fear? Would a true living god have to rely on warriors to enforce my silence? Or is he using them to protect a lie? Were he really the hero incarnate, he would descend from his palace and face Thirteen Sacred Jaguar, answer his questions about the Beginning Times, and prove his identity.' "

Blue Heron's lungs started to labor. "The other alternative is to plant our own people in the crowd. Order the Earth Clans to have their people mass at the bottom of the steps to shout their opposition. Make fun of every statement the Itza makes. Ridicule is a Powerful weapon when used with discretion."

Winded, Blue Heron passed the high gate, acknowledging the guards as they touched their foreheads respectfully.

She led the way, brushing her fingers on the lightning-scarred World Tree in the center of the courtyard.

After the bright sunlight, the dim interior of the great room left her blinking.

"He'll see you in his personal quarters," Dead Bird said, emerging from the doorway in the back.

Blue Heron shot a questioning glance at her sister, but Wind just shrugged and plodded forward across the matting, past the fire, and to the rear behind the high dais.

The Morning Star's door hung to the side on leather hinges, the room even darker. Blue Heron stopped, letting her eyes adjust. "Morning Star?"

"Here, Keeper," he replied.

She turned her attention to the left and made out the Morning Star as he draped a pale cloak over a young woman's shoulders. He placed his hand to her abdomen, saying, "I pray your wishes come true."

"I am honored, Lord," the woman whispered shyly, shot a doe-like glance at Blue Heron and Wind, and scuttled out the door like a panicked puppy.

Morning Star, a wrap around his loins, stepped back and settled himself on the corner of his opulent bed. He studied Blue Heron through half-lidded eyes, then asked, "Yes, Keeper?"

She took a deep breath, recounting her near disaster with the crowd, and began to elaborate on the contents of Itza's speeches, only to have the Morning Star lift a hand.

"You need not be concerned, Keeper."

"Lord? Don't you understand? He's poisoning the people against you. Lying to them. Questioning your very—"

"Of course he is. It is the only thing he knows."

"What do you mean?"

"I mean it's the only truth he possesses. In his way he is as blind as you are in yours."

"Blind, Lord? I don't understand."

"Thirteen Sacred Jaguar and Horn Lance are more capable than I thought. I shouldn't have underestimated them so. I do hope Lady Night Shadow Star hasn't made the same mistake that I have."

Blue Heron shot a confused look at Wind, who gave a

suggestive lift of her hands to communicate her own dismay.

"Lord, let me try again. The Itza and Horn Lance are working against you. They are succeeding. All of Cahokia is talking about them, speculating if the Itza are more Powerful than Cahokia. Now, based on the foul lies spewing from Night Shadow Star's steps, they are beginning to wonder if you are an imposter!"

Morning Star smiled wearily. "While I appreciate your concern, it will not matter in the end."

"We have to *do something*!" she cried.

"What?"

"Fight them! Counter their arguments. Listen, I don't understand how this works between you and Night Shadow Star. She thinks she had to marry the Itza to destroy him. Which makes no sense whatsoever. You don't seem to care if he wins or loses, even if losing means your own destruction and the city tearing itself apart in the process. We've got to take matters into—"

"Where is the Red Wing?"

Blue Heron stopped short, fist half-raised in a gesture of defiance. "Haven't seen him since the wedding."

"And your thief?"

"Haven't seen him, either." She gestured futility. "Maybe they both showed more sense than the rest of us and left. Nor do I blame them. If I'm any judge, Night Shadow Star taking the Itza into her bed tore Fire Cat's heart out. And as for the thief? Horn Lance put a price on his head. For all I know they've got him tied in a square somewhere while they cut strips from his hide as a way of punishing me."

"And Night Shadow Star?"

"Haven't seen her, either. Word is that she's keeping to her palace. I'm told she's dedicating herself to her new husband."

"Which we don't believe for a minute," Wind said with a snort.

Morning Star sighed then, averting his eyes for the first time. "Then perhaps she, and Piasa, made the same mistake I did."

"What was that? Letting that Itza scorpion set foot in Cahokia in the first place?"

"Underestimating his ability," he replied, before lifting a hand to dismiss them.

As Blue Heron turned to go, he added, sadly, "Do nothing to hinder Thirteen Sacred Jaguar, Keeper. You are not to interfere. Do you understand?"

"Yes, Lord."

Seventy-six

True to form, the old woman awakened in darkness. As the decades had passed, so had the need for deep and dreamless sleep.

She shifted on her aching bones, the action causing her to cough up a gob of phlegm that had caught below her voice box.

She sat up and spit into the pot she kept beside her bed, then swung her feet out, wincing at the pain in her hips, back, and ankles.

A soft whine was barely muffled by her door hanging.

Grunting with the effort, she rose and hobbled to the door, slipping it to the side.

The dog let out a low whine, struggling to stand, managing to find a purchase with two legs. A third was cocked, the fourth, a right front, it held high in pain.

"Ah, it's you. Come to trouble, have you?"

The beast looked up at her through a half-swollen blue eye, patches of fur missing from its scabbed head.

"Well, I can't pick you up. You'll have to make it inside on your own."

The dog hobbled forward, that high-pitched whine of pain deep in its throat each time the wounded back leg took weight.

Inside it collapsed in the darkness next to her hearth.

"Let's see what we've got, shall we?" She knelt by the fire, teased a glowing ember free of the ash with a stick, and used the ember to ignite a handful of shredded bark to which she fed kindling.

Once the fingers of flame Danced light around the room, she cocked her head, squinting her old eyes as she felt along the dog's body with practiced fingers. As light as her touch was, it still brought pitiful cries from the dog.

"Mostly they are bruises. The big bones seem all right. Red willow bark will help, along with coneflower. It'll take me a moment to mix it up in something you'll eat."

The dog watched her, uttering a guttural rejoinder.

"How long ago did this happen?"

A soft growl came from deep in the dog's throat.

"Five days? If you were going to die, you'd have done it by now."

The dog made a muumphing sound.

"Hurt that bad, did it? Took you that long to get here?"

A sighing whine was the answer.

She propped herself against her bed, closing her eyes and breathing deeply. "It's time, then. Can't say I'm sorry the day's come. I just hope we're not too late."

Seventy-seven

Notched Cane had the fire going outside; a pot filled with ground goosefoot seed, sunflower seeds, and little barley bubbled on the flames. Being too hot to cook inside, he had chosen to cook the meal in the protection of the ramada.

A soft night breeze carried cool air, though it smelled of smoke and city. Between the smoky fire and the concoction of crushed fir needles, gumweed, and puccoon he had rubbed on his skin, the mosquitoes weren't much of a bother.

He had the stock boiled down to just the right consistency and fished out the two shredded lengths of sassafras root, having boiled them long enough to impart just the right flavor. From within a wrapping of grape leaves, he took long strips of white sturgeon meat and tossed them into the pot. After they'd cooked he would add fresh chokecherries and wild plums.

Somewhere in the distance, a dog began barking, only to be answered by several others. But beyond that, the night was quiet.

He glanced again toward the east, not even seeing the first hint of false dawn. He had plenty of time. Everything would be cooked to perfection by the time the Keeper rose to greet the day.

He scratched at his jaw before slipping another stick of firewood under the pot. The Keeper was worried. He'd seen it in her before and knew the extent to which she was punishing herself. This time it wasn't just the political situation, or the fact she'd almost been mobbed on the avenue. The problem of the Itza was bad enough, but he and Smooth Pebble knew it was the thief who'd really gotten to her.

Seven Skull Shield had been gone too long without word. Nor had any of her spies been able to locate him.

"So . . . did he walk off and leave her? Or did someone collect Horn Lance's reward?"

Notched Cane made a face. The Keeper would see the first as a betrayal, the second as her fault. Either way she'd suffer for it.

He used a horn spoon to stir his stew and straightened. Bats fluttered just over his head, their clicking peeps fading into the night.

Making sure that everything was under control and the fire just right, he took the opportunity to retrieve his old brownware chamber pot from inside the door, and walked around the side of the Keeper's palace. Dropping his breechcloth, he squatted, thankful for the night. During the day, the avenue below would have been thronging with people.

Straightening, he pulled up his breechcloth and stepped around the front of the palace. A dark shadow moved behind the ramada.

"Who's there?" he called.

The shadow seemed to flatten itself as the fire flared up.

Running forward, Notched Cane peered into the darkness, seeing and hearing nothing.

So, had that been a person? Or just the afterimage of the fire?

Walking to the stairway, he called down, "Did you see anyone pass?"

"No. All's quiet here. We've got guards on all four corners."

"Awful dark out there," Notched Cane insisted.

"Guard check!" the warrior called out.

"Here." "Here." "Here." "Here." The warriors chimed in from all directions.

"You can inform the Keeper that you not only checked, but we were all awake," the commander called up jocularly.

"She'll be delighted to know that."

"Go back to your cooking, Notched Cane, and know that you're torturing us. It smells wonderful."

He chuckled to himself and walked back to the pot. Reaching for the spoon, he was going to stir the stock again, when he noticed what looked like a chip of wood floating on the surface.

Frowning, he used the spoon to lift it out, then glanced up at the roof, wondering if it had fallen from the thatch.

Sniffing, he caught a curious odor, lifted the spoon to his mouth, and tasted. The stew had a pungent tang, a sort of musty fullness that coated the tongue. Not unpleasant, but surely nothing that would have come tumbling down from the ramada roof. Taking the chip he held it up in the firelight. It looked like it had been cut out of something, perhaps a piece of root.

Shrugging, he touched it to his tongue, then nibbled at it, determining it was the source of the pungent taste.

But where had it come from?

He glanced up again, slowly shaking his head.

Seating himself with his back to one of the ramada posts, he glanced again at the eastern horizon. Dawn would be coming soon.

When he decided that the stew needed stirring a finger of time later, he was surprised to discover that his legs had gone numb. Nor would his fingers work.

"Help!" His voice came out as little more than a croak, his body suddenly as distant as the faint pale glow in the eastern sky.

Seventy-eight

Fire Cat cleared his souls of all but the moment, calming himself, setting the stone into the cup of his hand, his index and little fingers pressing in from the sides where his two middle fingers conformed to the stone's rounded rim.

Feet placed as Crazy Frog insisted, he bent forward, his concentration on the court. This was the game point. He and Lightning Thrower were tied. Nineteen to nineteen.

Silence filled the crowd lining either side of the court. Only the occasional whisper broke the tense anticipation.

A small fortune was bet on this game. That fact brought a smile to Fire Cat's lips as he loosened his shoulders and took a final breath.

"Wave it all farewell, Wounded Dog." Lightning Thrower rapped his lance with hard knuckles in an effort to distract him.

Fire Cat charged forward, driving with each step. Timing. Everything was timing. Crazy Frog had started him at a walk. Built to a run, watching Fire Cat the entire time. Correcting his balance, explaining how to hone his movements. Everything hinged on the release.

Now the court was forgotten, Fire Cat's attention on the

distance. On a peaked roof that rose dead center in line with the middle of the court: his target.

This, too, was new. Uncle had taught him to look at the court, to pick a place on the flat clay where his lance and stone would meet. Crazy Frog had insisted that the very best players looked beyond to a post, or something on the skyline, and aimed for that.

Fire Cat's arm went back in balance with his stride, a slight bend at the waist. Whipping his arm forward, he felt that faint contact with the clay; then his fingers were imparting a final spin as he released.

Straightening, he concentrated on a smooth stride, shifting the lance between breaths like Crazy Frog had instructed. He didn't even look at the penalty line. Crazy Frog had taught him to know his pace. Twisting his entire body, he put all of his strength into the throw, fingers imparting a spin to the javelin. Dead on, he watched it sail up into the air, directly in line with the distant rooftop.

Beside him, Lightning Thrower shouted in delight as he launched his spear.

Side by side they ran in pursuit of the flying lances and rolling stone.

Fire Cat hadn't heard the crowd, not until this moment. Some realization in the back of his head knew they'd been screaming, whistling, and stamping from the moment he'd launched.

"Fly!" he bellowed at his lance, willing it to hold course, knowing that in the end, it was now a matter of luck.

Even as he watched, Makes Three's beautiful black stone slowed and veered to the right before toppling on its side. An instant later both his and Lightning Thrower's lances thudded into the clay, not a finger's width between them.

Pounding his way down the court he stared in disbelief. Both lances were an arm's length shy of the stone, each impact dimpling the clay. But which was closer?

The old referee toddled forward with his measuring cord;

the crowd on the sidelines raised a deafening roar of anticipation.

Fire Cat's heart hammered at his chest, driven by more than his exertion as the cord was laid out. The measuring knots marked the distance from the edge of the stone to each lance.

Crouching there with Lightning Thrower, he saw with his own eyes, a sick feeling welling within him.

"Lightning Thrower by a half a knot!" the old man cried.

A great shout rose from the audience; clapping hands and piercing whistles mixed with cries of exultation and bellows of disbelief.

Fire Cat took a deep breath, retrieving his stone and lance.

He glanced sideways, seeing Crazy Frog on his platform, a curious smile on the man's normally expressionless face.

"I wouldn't have believed it," Lightning Thrower told him.

"What? That I lost?"

"No, that you'd ever be this good. Not after what I saw that first day you were here. No wonder Crazy Frog invited you to his house that night." Lightning Thrower paused. "It almost worked, you know. Coming in, acting like a mediocre player to mask your skills. Clever."

Fire Cat stared at him in disbelief. "You think I threw those first games?"

"If you made any mistake it was seeming to get better by the day before this match. If I hadn't taken you seriously, you might have won, and I'd be a much poorer man."

Fire Cat, frustration like a festering stone in his breast, walked on wooden legs through the crowd, barely aware of the nods and smiles men gave him as he passed. He stopped below Crazy Frog's elevated stand, calling up, "I hope I didn't lose you much."

Crazy Frog, his face bland, stared down. "Actually, I bet on Lightning Thrower. By three. You just rolled a very good game, Wounded Dog. A couple of bobbles, but no more than Lighting Thrower made."

"Then why didn't I win?"

"Had the stone veered left there at the end, you would have." He smiled wistfully. "Fire Cat, once you roll the stone and cast the lance, the rest is out of your hands. That's the moment that Power takes over and has its will."

"Can I beat the Natchez?"

Crazy Frog shrugged. "I've never seen him play."

It was only when Fire Cat turned away that he saw the dog. It had to be Seven Skull Shield's. No other dog alive was that ugly. The beast was limping around the edge of the crowd, left front foot held up. Obviously its wounds had been tended to, but as Fire Cat looked around, he could see no sign of Seven Skull Shield.

The dog, however, fixed on Fire Cat, one eye almost swollen shut as it stared at him. As Fire Cat stepped closer, the beast turned, hobbling away, only to look back as if irritated that Fire Cat had stopped short.

"Where's Seven Skull Shield? What happened to you?"

If the dog looked this bad, did it mean the thief had come to grief as well?

"Was it Horn Lance? Some of his people?"

The dog whined, lungs heaving with emphasis.

"If he's in trouble, I don't have time to go looking for him. I've got to practice my game."

The dog barked, tone full of impatience.

"I don't care. I don't even like the thief. I think he's a crude—"

The dog barked again, aggressively this time.

"Go on." Fire Cat waved at the dog. "I'm not going with you. I have more to do here. I've got to practice."

He heard the dog's whine over the roar of the crowd as two more players took their positions on the court.

Fire Cat turned his back on the beast, muttering, "It's not

my fault if the thief's in trouble. If he's gone and gotten himself killed, it's good riddance."

He couldn't leave. Not yet. He couldn't face the Natchez until he was winning again. But how long would that take, if ever?

As he looked back, the dog's eyes seemed to be filled with disgust. It turned away—barely avoiding a kick from a dirt farmer—and hobbled off looking forlorn.

Seventy-nine

If it hadn't been for a spider falling from the roof, we'd have never known," Blue Heron told Rides-the-Lightning as he leaned over Notched Cane's corpse. "It landed splat on White Rain's right eyelid and skittered across her face. Startled her so bad she had to get up and away from her bed. Needing to catch her breath, she stepped outside just as Notched Cane cried out."

They stood in the charnel house where it perched on the elevated platform between the two Earth Clans mounds. A shaft of sunlight illuminated Notched Cane's corpse, his eyes wide, mouth gaping.

Rides-the-Lightning turned his white-blind eyes on her. "She would have been the Red Wing matron after Dancing Sky, wouldn't she? A person you were supposed to torture to death. Fire Cat's sister."

"Yes?" Blue Heron countered uneasily.

"Most convenient, wouldn't you say? Had not Piasa demanded the Red Wing be saved, she would not have been sleeping in your palace. Were she not, the spider would have dropped on the floor and scuttled away."

Blue Heron filled her lungs and shrugged, heedless that he couldn't see her.

Around her, most of the benches, including the wall shelves, were empty—the dead they had once held having been interred or cremated during the Busk celebration.

"What do you see?" Rides-the-Lightning asked two of his assistants.

"His eyes are clear, Elder." One of the young men leaned over Notched Cane's face. "I see no foam on his tongue. Nothing to indicate a struggle." He ran his hands down Notched Cane's right thigh and calf. "The muscles are oddly knotted, the limbs stiff as if he'd been dead for hours. Nor do I see signs that he went into convulsions."

"He did not," Blue Heron interjected. "White Rain says that he whispered the words, " 'Poison,' 'The chip,' and 'Can't feel my body.' Then she said that he just stopped breathing as if his muscles had quit."

"Poison?" Rides-the-Lightning wondered, leaning down and sniffing at Notched Cane's mouth. "There is an odor. Something musty and pungent, but unlike any of the poisons I'm familiar with. This is something different . . . new."

She removed the cup from her pack and tipped it so the little wedge of root tumbled onto the bench beside Notched Cane's arm. "White Rain told us that when he said the word poison, his eyes flicked down at this. She picked it up from the ground. Said it was wet as if it had been in his mouth. A horn spoon was beside it with some spilled stew."

"I see." Rides-the-Lightning's opaque white eyes were fixed on the shaft of light coming through the gap between roof and wall. "Fine Mist, find something to pick it up. Don't touch it yourself. Let me smell it."

"Yes, Elder." The assistant used two copper needles from one of the defleshing kits to lift the little wedge of what looked like a woody root. He held it just under the soul flier's nose.

Rides-the-Lightning inhaled, his nostrils quivering like a dog's. He held his breath for a moment, then shook his head.

"I don't know it. But the odor is the same musty smell as that in Notched Cane's mouth."

"Definitely poison?" she asked.

"I do hope you safely disposed of that stew Notched Cane was cooking. And Three Fox, please run to the Keeper's and ensure that White Rain's fingers are thoroughly and safely washed."

The second acolyte turned on his heel and dashed from the charnel house, feet flying.

The old soul flier turned white eyes in Blue Heron's direction. "You're sure this bit of root is nothing from your household?"

"I'm sure. Any time Notched Cane wanted to cook something new, he'd try it himself first. He was making stew for the whole house." She paused. "The guards said that he thought he saw something, someone. That he called out and they reassured him that all was well."

As the implications sank in, Blue Heron took a deep breath, backed up, and sat on one of the benches. Images of Notched Cane slipped up from her memory, along with the hollow awareness of loss. Over the years he'd always been there, his very competence practically ensuring that she never gave him any thought. Meals were cooked, the water jugs full, the fires hot and crackling, the chamber pots never dirty or foul, the house in order.

With a sense of shock she realized she'd never really known him: What he wanted. What he thought. Who he was as a person.

"Who'd want to poison him?" she wondered.

"Him?" Rides-the-Lightning asked. "You said the poison was found next to a spoon and spilled stew? My guess is that your entire household was the target. You especially, Keeper."

"Foreign poison," she whispered. "Something so different not even you are familiar with it. A poison no one has seen before. One that no one will recognize."

"So it would seem, Keeper," Rides-the-Lightning agreed. "Where do you suppose such a novel means of inflicting death might have come from? And more to the point, who do you think might have delivered it to your stew pot?"

"Horn Lance," she rasped through gritted teeth.

"Then it would seem, Keeper, that he has pulled so much of Cahokia's Power into his grasp that he no longer fears retribution after his actions."

"And if he can act so freely against me?"

"The Morning Star, of course, will be next."

Eighty

The effort to get out of bed exhausted Night Shadow Star. The notion of getting dressed, just walking out into the great room, seemed insurmountable. Merely sitting up, swinging her feet to the floor, and squatting over the ceramic bowl left her completely fatigued and desperate to clamber back into bed and fall asleep.

He's won, Piasa's disembodied voice told her.

She blinked in the dim light of her room, fingers kneading the soft buffalo-wool blanket. So soft. The weavers had separated the downy undercoat curried from a winter hide to weave into such a prized possession.

"Lady?" a roughly accented voice called moments before one of the Natchez entered bearing a bowl.

She stumbled through her memory. Little Sun . . . Swirling Cloud. The one with the hair twisted to look like blunt horns on his head. Yes, that's who this was.

Where do I know him from?

Something tried to form down between her souls, only to drift away like goose down on the wind.

"Time for you to eat. It is the *ahau*'s order. He wants you strong. Better to catch his seed, yes?"

Numbly she took the bowl, blinking, her souls oddly

empty of thought. The world had grown fuzzy, as if all of its edges were gone. Everything soft and oddly warm.

The Natchez lowered himself to the side of her bed, his gaze running down her body. "Eat, Lady."

She lifted the stew to her lips, drinking slowly, stopping only to chew the chunks of meat and hazelnuts. When she'd drained the bowl, she set it down to one side.

Her stomach expanded the way it would if something peculiar were warming it from the inside. Each meal had this effect. First the warm feeling in the stomach. Then it would spread, running out around her ribs, up around her heart, and down into her pelvis to create a tingle in her loins before it crept down her thighs to her feet.

The Natchez shot a wary glance at the door before leaning close to whisper, "I know he thinks you're ugly." He reached out, his fingers stroking down her right shoulder, across her chest, around the swell of her breast to settle on her nipple. As he massaged it between his fingers, she sucked a breath. His touch might have ignited a sparkling fire that burned through her chest into her core.

"I, however, think you are the most beautiful woman alive," he added, grinning as she started to squirm and awkwardly pushed his hand away. Instead of retreating, he let his fingers trace down the curve of her hip and along the sides of her thighs.

"Are you tired of him, Lady? Would you like to share yourself with a man who actually wants you? One who would rather hear you sigh as he coaxed cries of delight from your body?"

Was that what she wanted? His words seemed like flitting birds, going this way and that and making little sense. Confusing words. She tried to find her own, saying, "I just can't . . . it's the warmth . . . don't know . . ." The rest of the thought flew away with the flitting birds and she gasped, suddenly aware that his hand had slipped between her legs.

With his other hand he pushed her onto her back.

"That's it." He was staring down at her, the smile widening as she tried to push his hand away. She clamped her thighs tight around his fingers as they probed and stirred embers of pleasure.

"Fire Cat?" she asked in confusion.

"Sure. I'm Fire Cat if that makes you happy."

The voice was wrong. Her vision shimmered, Fire Cat's face seeming to blend itself into Swirling Cloud's.

He's using you! Piasa's sibilant voice speared through her.

"Get out," she gritted through clamped jaws. *"Get out!"*

The hand was suddenly gone, Swirling Cloud standing beside her bed, a triumphant leer on his face as he loudly stated, "Lady, I don't care. My orders are to make you eat."

Then he leaned close, whispering, "It's just a matter of time until we'll be alone together." He shot her a wink and left.

"What is wrong with me?" She clamped her eyes shut, curling into a fetal ball. Could she summon enough strength to deny the Natchez the next time? Did she have the will? Or would she just surrender? Was it easier to retreat into the fuzzy haze and let him fill her sheath while she pretended he was someone else?

The answer frightened her.

You are losing. Losing yourself. Losing Cahokia.

Piasa's disembodied laughter filled the room.

How does it feel . . . Lady?

Eighty-one

The dog had led him halfway back to the Great Plaza as it limped painfully along the Avenue of the Sun. Again Fire Cat wondered what had possessed him to grab up the sack that held his armor and ax, shoulder his chunkey lance, and follow the beast.

Is it because you're tired of losing?

Was that it? He was running away? Fleeing from the lessons and Crazy Frog's ever-critical eye?

Surely it couldn't be any hidden vestige of concern about Seven Skull Shield. The man was a disgrace. An irritant. A worthless parasite sucking precious blood from the body of decent society.

The dog had led him through River Mounds City's maze of buildings to the Avenue of the Sun where it ran east-northeast toward Black Tail's tomb. The mangy cur stayed just far enough ahead to remain in sight among the endless stream of people, those packing burdens, and travelers. Periodically the dog would stop, glance back to make sure he was following, then limp anxiously forward again.

Once again he was on the verge of giving up when three dirt farmers coming in the opposite direction saw the dog. One pointed and cackled something to the others in their incomprehensible language. A third pulled a folded net from his shoulders and shook it out.

It was common enough: a beat-up and wounded dog, obviously belonging to no one. The mutt was fair game. And Seven Skull Shield's mongrel was big, young, and undoubtedly tender. Just perfect for the stew pot.

The dog, of course, had stopped, and was looking back at Fire Cat, now perhaps twenty paces behind.

"Hey! Look out!"

But at his voice, the dog actually turned to face him, cocking his head as if trying to figure out just what Fire Cat was worried about.

Even as Fire Cat shouted and started forward, the three spread the net, rushing.

The dog let out a frightened yipe, cowering as the net dropped over its head.

Deftly one of the dirt farmers yanked on the net's draw cord. The thing drew tight, trapping their prey. Another had extracted a stone-headed hammer from the pack on his back and was raising it high. In an instant he'd smash it down on the dog's head.

Too far away!

Fire Cat's move was instinctive. In one fluid motion his arm went back. Whipping his body forward, his chunkey lance arced toward the man and thudded into the packed sand that paved the avenue.

The hammer man froze, staring at the shivering wooden shaft embedded in the ground between his feet.

"Let the dog go!" Fire Cat bellowed.

The fellow, his stone-headed maul still raised overhead, gaped in disbelief at Fire Cat. Shock gave way to anger, and he roared something of his own, starting forward. To Fire Cat's ear, the man's mouth might have been full of rocks the way his native language sounded. The stone-headed maul bobbed in menace as the man's face twisted, his eyes burning. He closed the distance in mighty strides.

Run or duck?

In the few remaining heartbeats before the big dirt farmer could strike, Fire Cat's arm whipped back. With an underhand pitch he released the chunkey stone. A black blur, it caught the man just below the sternum.

With a sound resembling a crack, the stone drove deep; a ripple shot through muscle and skin. The man's face rounded in surprise, eyes popped wide, mouth forming a hollow *O* as his cheeks puffed out.

The hammer dropped from nerveless fingers and thumped him on the back of the neck. Carried by momentum, he missed a step, slamming facefirst into the trampled sand at Fire Cat's feet.

There he gasped and rolled onto his side. Mouth agape, eyes staring, a racking gurgle came from his throat as he clutched his gut and gulped frantically for air.

His two stunned companions stood frozen, one having pulled the net up so the dog hung struggling just above the ground.

"Let the dog go!" Fire Cat ordered as he pointed.

The one with the net muttered something to his companion, who hurriedly began shaking out the net.

Seven Skull Shield's dog landed in a pile, whining, trying to protect its hurt leg. Fishing his copper-bitted ax from his bag, Fire Cat started forward.

The two blinked, shot each other a knowing look, and both wheeled and fled headlong into the crowd.

People had stopped to watch. Fire Cat dropped on his knee by the dog, one hand on his chunkey lance, the other patting the dog's scabbed head. The odd blue and brown eyes looked up in apparent relief.

"I'd say life's hard on dogs in Cahokia," Fire Cat admitted. "You going to be all right?"

The dog whined.

A couple of people had bent over the remaining dirt farmer. He'd recovered enough breath to sit up. One hand pressed his stomach, the other the back of his neck where the hammer had whacked him.

Unsure if the dirt farmers were local and might return with reinforcements, Fire Cat retrieved his chunkey stone and lance and followed the dog as it limped off the road, curving around Black Tail's tomb.

Originally a complex of three mounds that had included a platform temple, an elevated charnel house, and a conical burial mound that had held Petaga's grave, it had been turned into a single high ridge mound upon Black Tail's death. Oriented east-west, it lay in perfect alignment, directly on line-of-sight with the Morning Star's high palace. On the equinox dawn, the living god's hatchet-like palace roof marked the point where the morning sun first appeared over the eastern bluffs.

The dog hobbled past the shrines and temples to a small hut on a bare hump of a mound.

There an old woman sat, her face a mass of wrinkles, her eyes like hard obsidian pebbles sunk deeply into her skull. She tilted her ancient head, straggles of wispy white hair floating around it like a halo. Her gnarled right hand rested on a desiccated leather Bundle, its exterior scarred and worn, faint images hinting of long-faded paint.

"So you're the Red Wing," she said softly as the dog dropped wearily at her feet. "I remember the day your grandfather left Cahokia. Circles within circles. The Spiral come alive."

"Who are you?"

"Your oldest ally in Cahokia. But come, we've not much time. And I don't walk so well or so far anymore."

"Not much time for what?"

"Living . . . and dying."

Eighty-two

Blue Heron panted after the long climb to the Morning Star's high palace. The midsummer sun and hot humid air had cooked all the energy from her body. Sweat beaded on her skin, the tickle of thirst clutching the base of her tongue.

She nodded as the two guards at the palace gate touched their foreheads. Despite their athletic youth, they, too, looked wilted and ready to melt.

Inside she found Five Fists leaning against the palisade, his shoulders stooped and arms crossed as he took advantage of the little bit of shade cast by the clay-covered wall.

"Keeper? This is unexpected," he greeted, not bothering to move. "We heard Notched Cane was ill. Hopefully it was nothing serious."

"Ill?" she asked incredulously. Then, thinking it through, had to admit that she'd ordered him carried straight to the Earth Clans' soul flier's temple. Who knew what sort of stories were flying about?

"He's dead, Squadron First. Poisoned. Nor was he the target. The deadly potion was meant for me."

Five Fists pushed himself away from the wall, a tightening behind the eyes. "And you know this how?"

"The soul flier confirms it. Claims the poison is exotic,

something he's unfamiliar with, but very deadly. Had Notched Cane not managed to alert us to the bit of herb, we'd have had no clue. He'd just be dead, his body showing none of the usual signs like foaming, thrashing and convulsions, or seizures."

"Who did this?" Five Fists asked dully. "Do you have any idea?"

"My suspicion is Horn Lance, of course. And we know he and the Itza possess boxes of potions and hallucinogens that we've no experience with. Nor do I think this is the first time they've been employed."

"Oh? I don't recall any suspicious deaths."

"I'm referring to the dead Natchez."

"He was lanced, gutted."

"I meant his brother and aunt. The old White Woman and Great Sun. According to the stories we've heard, they just up and died. And in a manner that didn't raise suspicions. Had White Rain not stepped outside when she did, we'd have found Notched Cane propped against a ramada post. Nothing would have indicated anything except that his souls had slipped peacefully out of his body as often happens."

Five Fists pursed his lips around his misshapen jaw and stared angrily at the trampled grass by his feet.

"What is it?" Blue Heron asked, reading the old warrior's frustrated worry.

"The Morning Star is up there." He pointed to the high bastion that dominated the western courtyard wall.

Following his callused finger, she saw the Morning Star, uncharacteristically dressed in a breechcloth, only his face painted and his hair wrapped around a simple bun pinned with polished copper.

"He hasn't been going to his usual chunkey game in the mornings. He's been up there since dawn." He paused before adding, "Three times now, an eagle has come to land upon the wall beside him. They seem to converse for a while; then the bird takes flight and vanishes."

Messengers from the Sky World?

A shiver, despite the draining heat, whispered along her bones.

She sighed, bent to rub her aching thighs, and gestured that Five Fists stay. "I'll go tell him."

"Be careful, Keeper. I've never seen him like this. Not even when Walking Smoke was threatening us all."

She strode wearily to the ladder that led up to the high platform. As she placed a hand on the polished wooden rung, she glanced around. The palace staff was engaged in cooking under the small ramada shade, and the high World Tree pole cast a slanting shadow, its position marking the date and time of year.

Resigned, she climbed, calling out, "It's me. I need to speak with you."

"Come, Keeper," came the reply through the square hole in the bastion floor. "I've been expecting you."

"Someone tried to poison me last night. Killed Notched Cane. Rides-the-Lightning thinks you're next." She climbed through the hole, scrambled to her feet, and tried to place herself as far from him as possible in the cramped area.

"The soul flier is a wise man." The Morning Star's somber gaze hadn't shifted, his attention on the west, where humid air burned oddly silver as it wavered over the city. Smoky haze softened the faraway river and Evening Star Town's distant bluff.

"Lord? I don't hear the outrage I expected. The Itza is moving against us." She swallowed hard, raising her hands defensively. "I understand that he comes offering Trade, and that Cahokia could gain immensely through establishing relations with the other side of the world. The Itza no doubt have astonishing things to teach us. We've been played like dolls on strings. They arrived with a plan to destroy you. I know that it seemed like a reasonable request to marry Night Shadow Star to the—"

"It wasn't my choice."

"Excuse me?"

He turned to face her for the first time, a vulnerability in those eyes that she hadn't seen since before the living god had been resurrected in Chunkey Boy's body. The smile playing along his lips had a bitter twist.

"I don't care, Keeper. Not in this contest between Cahokia and Chichen Itza. The Powers of Sky and Underworld take no sides. The world was Created as it was Created. Since the first humans, the stories have been told. Like individuals, stories have lives, are born, grow, change, and adapt. Sometimes they split, become different. And stories eventually die; others expand to take their place. The gods and heroes have different names. But beneath it all lies the One. The thunderous silence. The brilliant and blinding darkness. Beginning and end. Everything and nothing. The Spiral."

She tried to swallow against her building unease. "I don't understand."

"Neither does the Itza. He thinks I failed his test."

"What test?"

"When he asked in his language if I was the Hun Ahau. The One Lord. Their name for the Morning Star."

"And are you?"

Morning Star smiled sadly. "I am so much more. And so much less."

He slapped a palm to the worn clay plaster atop the wall. "The extent to which Horn Lance and Thirteen Sacred Jaguar have made inroads into the people's beliefs is surprising. Horn Lance's manipulation of the Itza's arrival, the wedding, and the lord's preaching has been masterful."

"You *admire* him?" She made a face. "He's trying to *destroy* you!"

"He can't."

"If he can get a bowl of poison broth into your—"

He raised a hand to stop her. "Keeper, if he kills this body, that part of it which is the Morning Star will thankfully return to the Sky World where it belongs. Chunkey

Boy's body will molder in its fine new tomb, and most likely Thirteen Sacred Jaguar will convince enough people not to call the living god into another person's body, preferring that they worship him."

"Worship him?" she almost sputtered.

"And he in turn will serve the Lords of the Sky, One Lord, and the First Father–First Mother by spilling the blood of thousands to release the life essence. Use it as a means of drawing the gods from their Spirit World to this. Eventually his story, too, will fade or change into something else. Only the One remains, uncaring, existing for the Dreamers to find and Dance in."

"What about us? What about the Four Winds Clan? The Earth Clans? All the people who have come from great distances to be near you? Do you just desert them? Surrender them to the Itza?"

"I need not surrender anyone, Keeper. They will surrender themselves. More to the point, they will do it in joyous abandon, with a smile on their faces and a song in their hearts. It's just what people do."

"What about those of us who've served you?"

"The Four Winds Clan?"

She pursed her lips, eyebrow arched in a question.

He studied her with veiled eyes, then asked softly, "Do you think living here among you is easy? Putting up with your petty little intrigues? The endless fawning sycophants and flatterers seeking personal gain? The endless supplicants? Everyone wants something from me. And it never stops."

"I . . ."

"Go, Keeper. Leave me. Piasa and I have made our wager. The future of Cahokia is up to you."

Eighty-three

The moon cast an iridescent silver rime around the clouds, accenting their black bodies as they rode in clotted masses across the night sky. Only the brightest of the stars sprinkled in the open patches. For the moment, Horn Lance's way was moonlit as his porters followed two guides carrying lit torches.

He'd been on the road since midday, his porters trotting west along the Avenue of the Sun behind a Natchez escort. Cutting through River Mounds City, he'd arrived at the canoe landing just after sunset. There one of the Trade canoes was hauled down to the water, and he and his party were paddled across the churning, rippling Father Water to the western bank.

The guides had been waiting to lead the way as his litter was unloaded. Borne up the bluff trail, Horn Lance had been led past the guardian posts to the Evening Star Town plaza, across its corner, and past a conical charnel mound, a cluster of society houses, and to this narrow avenue.

The torch bearers slowed before a large trench-wall structure with a low, split-cane roof, one calling, "Master?"

"Here," a voice returned, and Flat Stone Pipe stepped out

from the shadowed entrance of what looked like a ware-house.

"Set me down," Horn Lance ordered.

He stretched and rose as the litter touched the ground. At that moment the moon's ghostly white face vanished behind a raft of inky clouds.

"How was your journey, Lord?" Flat Stone Pipe asked.

"Hot and sweaty for the first part, hot and muggy for the second. By crossing the river after dark, we should have left any spies behind. No one knows I'm here. Is everything in order?"

"It is, Lord Horn Lance. The Lady Columella sends you her greetings and salutations."

"I rather thought she might meet me in person."

"She considered it more prudent to welcome the high chief and her children, nieces, and nephews on their home-coming from a pilgrimage to the Underworld caves. Fewer questions that way."

"Well, let's get this over with."

"This way, Lord Horn Lance." The little man was barely visible in the low flicker of the torches; the pitch was nearly consumed.

Horn Lance waited while the two guides lifted a plank door to one side, and as the torches guttered, he was led inside.

A small fire snapped and crackled in a puddled-clay hearth. Its illumination cast the room in flickering yellow, but the place was sweltering. Around him were bales, sacks, boxes, and ceramic jars. Some were filled with corn, dried roots, coils of fiber, and the other basics of Trade. Others were sealed, their contents unknown.

In the center of the room, behind the fire, stood a wooden frame consisting of two upright posts sunk into the floor, a top crosspiece, and a second crosspiece lashed across the bottom to make a large wooden square. Inside it hung a brawny naked man, wrists bound to the upper corners, feet lashed on either side at the bottom.

Horn Lance smiled in anticipation as he walked forward. Reaching out with a hand, he wrapped it in loose hair and lifted the hanging head.

The man's face was thickly caked with dried blood, the nose swollen and plugged with black clots. The cheeks were puffed out, as if swollen. Then the eyes blinked, swimming into focus as they stared into Horn Lance's.

"Hello, Seven Skull Shield."

The hanging man showed no reaction.

"What? No witty reply? No threats?"

Silence.

"You know, you never really had a chance."

"What are you going to do to me?" the thief finally asked through stained and dry lips.

"Me? Nothing. I couldn't care less. I just needed you out of the way. Another preoccupation adding to Blue Heron's worries." He shook his head in amazement. "It still amazes me. I'd have never believed she was capable of friendship of any kind, let alone caring for a worthless bit of two-footed flotsam like you."

He glanced down at the thief's unusual endowment. "Or perhaps I do understand. She was always a hot-blooded thing under the covers. She'd have ached to ride a lance like that. I even heard that she called you 'Tow Rope' out of admiration."

He paused before adding, "Such a pity. My suspicion is that Columella, or the dwarf here, will be burning that remarkable shaft of yours into ash over the next couple of days."

"Why are you here?" the thief rasped.

"Actually this is just a quick side trip. A chance to gloat. I'm on the way to visit an old friend of yours—the lovely Wooden Doll." He gestured at Seven Skull Shield's hanging pride. "Another woman who will never sigh as you slip your rod inside. I suppose she'll ask about you, but I can tell her honestly that neither I, nor my people, have you."

"Leave her alone," the thief said through a dry swallow. "You're just using her."

"Of course I am." He leaned close, placing his lips next to the thief's ear. "I'll have plenty of witnesses to verify that I spent a pleasant night sliding my shaft in and out of her delicious sheath."

"You seem to have an unhealthy preoccupation with that subject."

"It's not about coupling," Horn Lance whispered so that only the thief could hear. "I needed to be somewhere else while Swirling Cloud slipped poison into the Keeper's stew. It's a bit of root from deep in the Itza forests. People just die. Best of all, your Rides-the-Lightning won't have a clue."

The thief puckered and spat, more a statement than an act since his dry mouth evidently couldn't conjure the spit.

Horn Lance chuckled in amusement. "You've lost, thief. Night Shadow Star's floating in a mist spun by mushrooms. The Itza is preaching to rapt crowds. The *kukul*'s Power is filtering like a haze through Cahokia's warrens. Your Morning Star is about to be exposed for the fraud he is, and replaced by a god king backed by Itza wealth. Blue Heron gone today. *Tonka'tzi* Wind a couple days after that? It's just like the Natchez all over again."

"There's something else," Seven Skull Shield whispered.

"What's that?" Horn Lance leaned his head close to hear.

The thief bucked with unanticipated vigor, slinging his head sideways. The man's skull hit Horn Lance's with enough energy to drive lights through his vision. He staggered in pain and surprise. Barely caught his balance before tumbling backward into the fire.

In anger, he backed a step. Bracing himself, he swung his right leg and kicked the thief in the crotch with everything he had.

Seven Skull Shield bucked and strained against the

bindings. The wooden frame creaked. A rattling came from the thief's lungs as he sucked for air. For a moment it seemed the square would crack and collapse.

Horn Lance turned. To Flat Stone Pipe he said, "I don't care what you do to him—just make it last for as long as you can."

"Of course, Lord Horn Lance. My matron would expect nothing else."

Eighty-four

I can't live like this.

It came to her in the middle of the night. Night Shadow Star's thoughts were clearer then. And by the time Thirteen Sacred Jaguar had awakened, crawled out of bed, washed and dressed, her thoughts were as focused as they would be for the day.

She watched her husband leave the room, his voice calling a greeting to Red Copal and the rest of the warriors. Behind them she could hear the distinctive sound of ceramic clicking against ceramic, the popping of the breakfast fire, and liquid being poured.

This is my moment. The food will be here within a finger's time. After that there will only be haze.

She didn't know when Swirling Cloud would come. He'd bragged the night before that he was playing chunkey this morning, wagering a fortune against Black Toe, one of Night Shadow Star's cousins. But he would come. When he did he would climb onto her and groan as his hot seed shot into her.

Nor would Thirteen Sacred Jaguar know. He and his Itza were touring the Rattlesnake Mound complex south of the Great Plaza on the Avenue of the Moon. The excursion was the latest move in Horn Lance's campaign to topple the Morning Star.

And something was supposed to happen to the Keeper. But she'd lost that in the haze.

She frowned as her thoughts returned to Swirling Cloud. That she had to endure her husband and his nightly ritual of self-stimulation before he could stand to insert himself was bad enough. The idea that she'd have to service Swirling Cloud? And how many furtive men afterward would take the risk? It sent a wave of revulsion washing through her.

Yes! Open the passage, Night Shadow Star. Step through. You know the joy, the peace and tranquility. You didn't want to come back the last time. It's your only way out.

She knotted all of her muscles, wishing she could reclaim that clarity of soul that had always been hers. Even if just for a finger of time.

The haze of gray seemed to cloak her thoughts, muddying even the simplest of notions.

With a deep breath, she threw off the covers and climbed out of bed. She braced herself, one hand on the bed frame. Her balance kept playing tricks on her.

The whisperings of Spirit voices, murmurings that lay just below the level of comprehension, kept trying to distract her.

"Should I do this?" she asked herself softly as she knelt before one of her ornate storage boxes. The lid was carved in the image of Cosmic Spider with its soul bundle tied to its back.

They are all gone. The Keeper is dead. Morning Star will flee back to the Sky World. Fire Cat has left you. If you stay, your only purpose will be to service men as they climb between your legs.

Was that Piasa? Or her own thoughts? She couldn't tell the difference anymore.

Opening the box, she reached in and found the familiar small clay jar.

Walking over to her altar, she knelt, staring into the well pot that sat atop the clay column. Some of the water had evaporated, but she could still see her reflection in the pot's depths.

With trembling fingers she reached into the little clay jar and dipped out two fingers of the greasy substance. Taking a deep breath, she closed her eyes and began rubbing the salve into her temples. Even as she did, she could feel the crushed seeds that permeated the paste.

Sister Datura's gentle touch caressed the edges of her souls.

Breathing in an easy cadence, she leaned forward, staring down into her reflection in the well pot. As Sister Datura tightened her grip and began the Dance, the portal would open.

This time Night Shadow Star would not return from the Underworld.

"I'm sorry, Fire Cat. So very, very sorry."

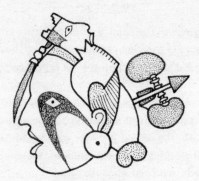

Eighty-five

The midday heat might have bothered the Cahokians, but for Swirling Cloud, coming as he did from the Father Water's lower valley, the warm muggy air almost seemed a relief. It reminded him of home, of desperate chunkey matches, of sparring with his cousins on the bright red-orange courts. He had honed his skills there, playing in heat like this. Not just honed, but prevailed.

He had been trained by the best, and he'd practiced in hopes that one day he would stand here, on Cahokia's most famous court: the Morning Star's. Around him a huge crowd had gathered, come that morning to see the Morning Star play, only to be disappointed when the living god hadn't appeared as was his wont for the daily game.

Nor had there been any reason given for his absence.

All the better for Swirling Cloud. He had not only defeated every player to challenge him, but Wet Bobcat and several of his warriors now stood guard over a huge pile of winnings.

The first game had been close; the Four Winds lord known as Black Toe had been no mean player. Word was he had once come within a whisker of beating the Morning Star, scoring seventeen out of the twenty necessary to win.

Three points.

A lot could happen when a match was that close.

Unless one actually hit the stone, which immediately won the game.

According to the common wisdom, Black Toe had been the local favorite by huge odds. The Natchez foreigner was known only for beating a slave by five and taking his clothes.

Swirling Cloud had stripped half of the furnishings from Night Shadow Star's palace and had them carried down as his bet. The gullible Cahokians had taken the bait, wagering a staggering amount of wealth against the newcomer.

And lost.

Thereafter, challenger after challenger had stepped up in the desperate hopes of beating the Natchez and claiming the vast spoils.

Now Swirling Cloud was ahead nineteen to Marble Mace's seventeen. This final match had proven the toughest of the day. But here it would be decided. Swirling Cloud could feel the Power running through him. This was *his* day. The Hero Twins, playing against the giants of the Beginning Times, might have felt the Spirit within them as he now did.

In the tradition of those mythic heroes, this was an epic chunkey match. The stuff of legends for which he had prepared his entire life.

The Morning Star might not have appeared that day.

But Swirling Cloud had.

He was about to take down the last of Cahokia's fabled Four Winds Clan players. And he was doing it on their court. In the heart of their Power.

He cupped the stone, taking deep breaths, a rising confidence filling him the way a full draught of black drink might. The sunlight, the roar of the crowd, the narrow clay track before him—everything was right.

Marble Mace, standing beside him, might have been but a shadow of reality. A nonentity.

Picking his target point, Swirling Cloud launched, each foot driving him forward. On the fourth pace, his arm dropped, body twisting from instinct. The release felt perfect. Two strides. Shift the lance.

The stone was running straight and true, and from the speed, he picked the spot on the clay where it would stop.

Penalty line coming up.

Arm back, balance, whip it forward.

The lance left his fingers, sunlight gleaming on the polished wood. He thundered across the penalty line, shouting in exultant joy as the lance slipped through the air. Beside it, Marble Mace's lance followed its own gentle arc.

"Home!" Swirling Cloud bellowed. "Ancestors, Sacred Sun, guide my lance! Seal this city's fate!"

As he'd anticipated, his lance thudded into the court no more than a forearm's length short of the stone when it toppled onto its side.

An instant later, Marble Mace's lance nosed into the clay a hand's length behind his own. No cord would be necessary. The results could be seen from the sidelines.

A huge groan seemed to swell, uttered by a thousand throats, as Marble Mace stumbled to a stop to stare stupidly at his lance. So close. But still farther away from Swirling Cloud's distinctive Natchez-style stone with its hole through the middle.

"No," he whispered.

"You read the stone's track perfectly," Swirling Cloud told him. "The cast was just short. You could not have won. Not today. I am blessed by the *kukul*'s Power."

He turned, raising his voice and bellowing, "It's over! A new Power has come to Cahokia. The one *true* Power! The Morning Star knows it. That's why he didn't appear today. Didn't dare to challenge Swirling Cloud and wager his life!"

A gasp rose from the crowd, people shooting speculative glances up at the high palace. The staircase was vacant.

"I serve *Ahau* Oxlajun Chul B'alam. Lord Thirteen Sa-

cred Jaguar. He serves the *kukul*! The Power of the great
War Serpent flows through him. Through me! And with it, we
are going to return Cahokia to the true ways, make right
the corrupt interpretation of Beginning Times, and reveal
the truth of the Creation."

He lifted his arms, aware that he had the crowd's full attention. He could feel their skepticism wavering, could read
it in their faces, see the growing disappointment as they
looked up at the Morning Star's high palace. The fools were
expecting the living god to appear decked out in his finest,
face painted, his copper lance gleaming in the sunlight as
he trotted down the stairs to answer this outlandish, hereti-
cal challenge.

For what seemed a breathless eternity, the entire world
seemed to hang in the balance, and then it passed. Swirling
Cloud could feel the crowd's resolve crumbling.

"Is there no one to challenge me?"

Arms lifted high, he faced the grand stairway. At the top,
on either side of the Council Terrace Gate, the two guards
seemed oddly incongruous, symbolic only of impotence instead of might.

"The living god doesn't answer," he shouted, feeling the
crowd's spirit finally break. This was the critical moment.

"I am Thirteen Sacred Jaguar's champion. Cahokia's best
are vanquished! Look at the sideline. The wealth of the Four
Winds Clan lies there, guarded by Thirteen Sacred Jaguar's
Natchez guard. But no one steps forward. With the *kukul*'s
Power flowing through me, I am invincible! No one can beat
me at the Morning Star's sacred game!"

He clenched his fists, shaking them up at his sacred sun,
founder of his family, his people, and his Nation. The exultation of victory exploded within him.

He'd won the crowd. Convinced them.

As he watched their expressions, read their reluctant acceptance, an image of Night Shadow Star's remarkable body
formed between his souls.

With Thirteen Sacred Jaguar gone for the day, what better way to savor his triumph over the Morning Star and the Four Winds than by enjoying their highest-born—

"I can beat you!"

The voice shattered his reverie.

A whisper, like a wave, ran through the crowd. Mutterings and gasps of disbelief rose as people craned their necks.

The figure that stepped out at the head of the court was dressed only in a hemp-fiber shirt. His hair hung down his back unrestrained like a girl's. At his side stood a battered-looking dog, and an absolutely ancient woman with a pack on her shoulder.

It took him a moment to recognize Fire Cat. When he did, he threw his head back and laughed, great peals of it, silencing the crowd.

"You, slave? What have you to bet? You're my master's property. Leave."

"I am bound to Lady Night Shadow Star. You are a liar and the murderer of your predecessor, Nine Strikes. You are a cheat and a weasel, serving some rogue god whose name you can't even pronounce. And if my words aren't true, Hunga Ahuito can be the judge. Here. On this court. Before all the world."

Wet Bobcat appeared at Swirling Cloud's elbow. "Little Sun, would you like me to deal with him? We could just surround him, take him away. He can't fight us all."

"Do it. Get rid of him. No sense in . . . Wait." He smiled. "He's the key to this. Destroying him here, in front of all these people, after he's bragged about serving Night Shadow Star? The loud-mouthed fool has just handed us Cahokia."

Fire Cat stood with his lance at the ready, a pack of what had to be his armor on the ground at his feet. His copper ax was thrust in his rope belt. The breeze teased his long hair, and his face remained impassive.

The crowd waited. In the thousands, some climbed up

atop vendors' booths to see; others were lifted by their friends as they called down descriptions.

"You have nothing to wager, Red Wing!" Swirling Cloud gleefully announced. "I took everything you owned last time." He pointed at the daunting pile of spoils. "What have you got that will equal the value before us?"

"My life, and all that I own, against your life and all that you own."

The crowd gasped as hundreds drew breath.

"Come on, you Natchez maggot! You just told the whole world that the Itza's *kukul* makes you invincible? I wager my life, the Power of Hunga Ahuito, Piasa, and Horned Serpent against you and your foreign god."

Under his breath, Swirling Cloud whispered, "I could kiss you, you stupid clod of dirt."

Then he shouted, "What is this? Cahokia's champion comes in the form of a *slave*! Is that what this city has left? Very well, it will have its proof! Me and the Red Wing! I only beat him by *five* last time. How many points will I take him by this time? And then, how shall I dispose of him? Make him my slave? Or hang him in a square for all to see?"

Eighty-six

"Cut him down."

The three words barely penetrated the haze of pain and misery in Seven Skull Shield's muzzy head. From some angry knot tied deep between his souls, he pulled up the energy to blink his eyelids open and lift his head.

He couldn't feel his arms or legs. Nothing but the pain that screamed through his shoulders, ribs, hips, and neck. He swallowed hard, thankful that they'd at least given him all the water he could drink. That had been after Horn Lance left.

As he fought to focus, he realized that a woman stood beside the diminutive Flat Stone Pipe. Behind her were the Fish Clan warriors who'd taken him from Slick Rock. Nothing else about the warehouse had changed except that bright sunlight filtered through the gap under the eaves. Looked like late morning if he was any judge.

Flies were buzzing around his blood-caked face.

Which was another peculiarity. The Fish Clan warriors had painted it on, then pressed strips of cloth into his mouth and told him to stuff them into his cheeks. If that was their version of torture, he could live with it. Just hanging in the square overnight had been bad enough.

The woman stepped forward, a pinched expression on her face. "Be very careful as you take him down. He's going to be as limp as river moss."

"Yes, Matron," the Fish Clan warrior replied as he and his men started working on the ropes binding Seven Skull Shield's wrists and ankles.

"Matron Columella," Seven Skull Shield said with a grin. "I'm more than a little disappointed in you. But if the Keeper's been poisoned, there's not many who can stand in your way now."

"She's alive." Columella's smile thinned. "Notched Cane, however, wasn't so lucky. I don't have many of the details yet. Blue Heron's never really confided in me. It will take Flat Stone Pipe's spies a day or so to ferret out the whole story."

"Then she's going to be most interested when she figures out that you've made a deal with the Itza."

Seven Skull Shield gasped as the last of the bindings was sawed in two and his weight sagged into the arms of the warriors. True to the Evening Star matron's orders, they were unusually solicitous as they lowered him to a soft buffalo-wool blanket.

From the back of the room a Healer stepped forward and bent down, running his hands over Seven Skull Shield's body and then massaging his right arm.

"This is going to hurt," Columella told him as she pulled up a wooden storage box and seated herself. "For that you have my apology. There just wasn't any other way."

"Other way than what?" Seven Skull Shield asked as the first tingling began in his clay-like limbs.

"Hanging you in a square," Flat Stone Pipe told him as he squatted down with a wet rag and began washing the dried blood from Seven Skull Shield's face. When the little man grinned, it almost split his face. "The rumor was that you were headed for a square sooner or later. I made the bet it would be sooner. Oh, and you can spit out those cloth strips. We had to make you look rather the worse for wear."

Seven Skull Shield groaned as the prickling turned into an angry stabbing in both arms.

"It was the only way we could be sure," Columella added, a hard set to her lips. "Horn Lance had to know you were no longer a concern. So I ordered you to be hung in the square and made up to look like you'd taken a real beating. It was my decision not to tell you. I couldn't take the chance that Horn Lance might suspect you were playacting. Nor could we take you down after he left until we were certain he wouldn't come back. That's the good news."

"And the bad?"

"Unfortunately, with the exception of Slick Rock, half of Cahokia is still combing the city looking for you. Either Horn Lance has forgotten that he's put a price on your head, or he doesn't care if people occupy themselves so. But it's more likely that it is meant to keep his enemies confused about your fate."

"I don't understand," Seven Skull Shield asked through a wince as his body ached and throbbed. "Matron, why snatch me from Slick Rock in the first place? What's your game with Horn Lance?"

Columella's grim smile tightened. "I don't forget my debts, let alone what Evening Star House owes you. As far as my game with Horn Lance, that remains to be played out. It's no secret that I have no love for the Morning Star, but I don't trust Horn Lance or his magical Itza, either. Too many grand promises."

She slapped her thighs in emphasis. "So, what's a matron to do but play a little bit of everyone's game, hoping she's quick enough on her feet so that whichever side wins, she and her House can profit?"

"And I'm part of the game," he told her as the pieces fell into place. "What if Horn Lance wins? Seems to me it would embarrass you if I suddenly turned up. He might think you couldn't be trusted."

Her eyes narrowed. "You begin to see my problem. How

do I balance my sense of honor against the pragmatic needs of my clan and House?"

Flat Stone Pipe noted, "You could simply take the next Trade canoe headed for the lower river or the Tenasee. Along with your word that you'd never come back as long as Horn Lance was alive."

"That's a problem," Seven Skull Shield told him. "I was sold out by someone I trusted. I can't just let that go."

"I really wish you'd chosen the Tenasee," Columella told him coldly. "No matter what I owe you, my House comes first."

In the background, the Fish Clan warriors had straightened, their war clubs appearing like magic in their hands.

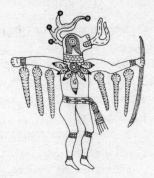

Eighty-seven

The shout from the chunkey grounds barely registered as Blue Heron sat on a stool in the shade of her veranda. Later she would remember that something about it was unusual, but for the moment she was much more interested in the report Splinter Branch, one of her spies in Bear Clan, was giving her.

Blue Heron was fanning herself in the heat, which despite the shade had coaxed a thick sheen of perspiration from her aging skin.

Smooth Pebble hovered in the doorway, a pitcher of water at the ready should Blue Heron's cup run empty. Two older, gnarly-looking warriors stood to either side, their wary eyes on the individuals she waved forward to give their reports.

Everyone seemed to be nervous, as if feeling the fraying threads that had once made up Cahokia. And indeed, the city was starting to fall apart.

She should have been half-frantic, her keen souls plotting which steps to take, how to counter the seeping poison Horn Lance had let flow into the blood and bone of Cahokia's complex hierarchy.

Instead, her thoughts and worries kept turning to Seven

Skull Shield. She refused to believe the thief had abandoned her like the rumors—circulated by Horn Lance, no doubt—implied.

Seven Skull Shield? Cut and run? That wasn't the man she'd seen battling Tula warriors, saving her skinny neck, and risking his life to pull children from a burning temple. Nor was that the man who'd dared to risk her ire, seating himself brazenly beside her, demanding a puff from her pipe. She missed the twinkle in his eye, his irreverent quips, and complete disregard for her status and rank. It was bad enough that he might be dead, but the notion that Horn Lance might even now be torturing him in some dark hole left her feeling distraught.

". . . are worried. High Chief Eight Scars continues to counsel patience, but some of the local chiefs have been extending invitations to the Itza to come and tell people about his new gods," Splinter Branch droned on, as if the world teetered on his report. "In short, Keeper, if he and Matron Red Temple do not receive some sort of guidance from the Morning Star, High Chief Eight Scars fears Bear Clan will split right down the middle over which gods should be worshipped."

She took another sip of her water. "You say the lesser chiefs are sending invitations to the Itza?"

"He has married Lady Night Shadow Star. He lives in the second-largest palace in Cahokia. That implies that either the Itza has the Morning Star's blessing, or the living god is helpless to stop it."

Splinter Branch glanced around uneasily. "And, Lady, the Morning Star hasn't been seen at the chunkey courts. If people are starting to believe in this Waxaklahun Kan, and we hear nothing to dissuade us, what can we expect but that the Morning Star and Four Winds also agree with this teaching?"

"And what are the ordinary people saying?"

"Some are committing themselves to the Itza; others are adamant that the Morning Star is still the resurrected Spirit

Being. Others are confused, waiting for the Morning Star to explain things."

She rubbed her brow, remembering the Morning Star's lack of concern. *Pus and blood! Why? Surely he knows Cahokia is about to shatter like a dropped pot?*

A headache was coming on.

"Give me your personal thoughts on this, Splinter Branch. Where is the city, given what you've seen and heard?"

He pressed his palms together like a supplicant. "Keeper, if you ask me, given everything that has transpired, it wouldn't take much to convince the majority that a new god, more Powerful than the Morning Star, has come to Cahokia for good."

He paused, meeting her eyes. "After all, the *kukul,* the Itza, and his followers seem invincible."

She sighed, nodding. "So it seems. Thank you my friend. Now, go. Keep your ear to the ground. Anything that seems—"

"Keeper!" one of her informants, a bald-headed fellow named Knotweed, came pounding up her steps. He ducked and slapped a hand to his forehead as he passed the Eagle guardian posts, slid to a stop, and dropped to his knees. So quickly did he prostrate himself, he nearly bashed his head into the ground. "Forgive me, Keeper, but you said to inform you! It's the Red Wing! He's playing the Natchez at chunkey. And he's wagered his life on the match!"

She heard another shout carry from the direction of the Grand Plaza, and couldn't miss the gasps uttered by Dancing Sky, White Rain, and Soft Moon as they worked at repairing a section of netting on the other end of the veranda.

"Fire Cat? Is Night Shadow Star with him? Did she put him up to this?"

"No, Lady. I mean, she's not with him. Just some old woman I've never seen before." Knotweed looked up with wide eyes. "When he took the Red Wing's challenge, the

Natchez Little Sun said they were playing for the future of Cahokia. Lady"—he swallowed hard—"from the mood of the crowd today, I believe it!"

Blue Heron rose wearily to her feet, eyes drawn to where Dancing Sky and her daughters sat bolt upright and anxious.

"Oh, blood and piss, he's your son, and I'm a fool. But whatever happens, wait for my orders before you do or say anything I might regret."

The three women scrambled for her door.

"Guards! Get my porters. Best that you be armed and prepared for anything. We might be breaking heads to get away from a mob when this is all over."

"Will it be that bad?" Smooth Pebble asked from the door.

"Might be the end of our world," Blue Heron replied as the implications sank in. "I need you to get a message to my sister. Tell her that we're all teetering on the brink."

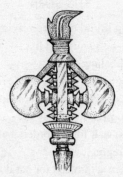

Eighty-eight

Sweat beaded and trickled down the side of Fire Cat's head. The heat, the burning midday sun, the cloying smell of thousands of unwashed, sweat-damp bodies in the humid air—it all closed in on him. Oppressive, heavy, like a weight that crushed the soul and body.

The black stone in his hand almost scorched the skin, cooked as it was by the relentless sun. Fire Cat blinked his sweat away, panting from exertion and heat. The far end of the packed clay court shimmered in waves; the distant Earth Clans mounds wavered and danced in the silvered and runny light.

The screams and shouts from the crowd battered at him as though the sound had presence and form. Again he blinked to clear his vision.

This was his throw. He'd won the last one, his lance closer to the Natchez' stone by a finger length, earning him the right.

Nothing in this match had gone the way it should. In the beginning, for every point he won he'd lost two. The enormity of what he was attempting had struck home, crashing down on him with the weight of the world.

He was playing for his life, for Night Shadow Star's future, for the whole of Cahokia. Even for the so-called Morning Star, the man he despised.

And he was losing. Losing it all.

Think. Concentrate.

Desperately he tried to call back all of Crazy Frog's subtle advice and pointers. But like goose down on a hot wind, they scattered the moment they entered his head. He kept falling back into old habits, forgetting to pick his target, watching the penalty line instead of trusting his pace.

He filled his lungs with the hot air, forcing himself to relax. He wiped his sweat-slick fingers on his shirt to dry them before fitting the stone into his hand as Crazy Frog had shown him.

"Can you feel it?" Swirling Cloud asked as he waited beside him. "Is that why you hesitate? Because you know that with each throw, the end is inevitable? I see it in your face, fool. The despair grows with each cast, each point you lose."

"It's not over."

"In another ten casts, it will be."

Fire Cat knew it the moment he launched. He'd played right into the Natchez' hands, rushing his movements. The release wasn't smooth, nor was his transfer of the lance or the cast that followed.

To his surprise, he won the point. By sheer luck. His uncontrolled stone veered in the same direction as his poorly thrown lance.

I'm playing for Power, for Piasa and the beliefs of my ancestors! Where is the Power? Why won't it fill me?

He turned after retrieving his lance, seeing Swirling Cloud's mocking smile.

Hatred as hot as the day burned within him.

"Clever new plan, eh?" Swirling Cloud taunted as they trotted back to the start. "You were almost out of bounds. So easy to lose a point that way."

"It's not over."

"Keep saying that, Red Wing. But it will be."

Unless he could pull off a miracle and actually hit the stone. But the way Swirling Cloud had been playing, chances were greater that he might achieve the near-miraculous feat first.

As Fire Cat took his position for the next point, he glanced at the crowd, reading the faces, greedy, betting against him. Waiting for him to fail.

And there was the Keeper, Blue Heron. Beside her—to his dismay—stood his mother, a pained worry in her dark eyes. She kept patting at her gray hair, as if it were blown astray. Clutching her arm, as if to reassure her, Fire Cat's sisters seemed to prop her up. From their expressions, they might have been watching slow torture instead of a chunkey match.

I am going to lose.

"Red Wing?" the old priestess called from where she stood beside the court. "Come here."

"Go," Swirling Cloud said with a dismissive whisking of his fingers. "Every delay builds the anticipation. Makes my victory that much more complete."

Fire Cat couldn't meet his opponent's eyes. Instead he walked over to the old woman. The dog was standing by her feet, its tail wagging anxiously.

"What is it?"

For the first time, she reached into her sack, removing an object the size of a cow buffalo's heart. The leather covering looked old, cracked, its surface scuffed and blackened in places as if it had barely survived a fire. The barest impressions of what looked like painted designs had faded into near nothingness.

"Touch it," the old woman whispered through her toothless jaws. "Go ahead."

"What is it?"

"Old. It will help."

"Its Power will make me win?"

"It will only give you the ability to use what you have within you. Nothing more."

Warily Fire Cat reached out with a sweat-damp hand, barely laying it on the firm leather cover. To his surprise the thing felt cool, comforting. A sensation like a spring breeze ran up his arm, settling in his chest. He thought he could smell blossoming forest in the suddenly sweet air. A thousand voices were Singing. He cocked his head, trying to listen over the catcalls of the angry crowd as they verbally berated him for taking too long. But the voices didn't come from the air or the mysterious bundle. They seemed to be inside him, the cadence rising and falling.

"The rest is up to you," she told him as she pulled the bundle back, lowering it carefully into the sack.

A sudden shiver ran through Fire Cat as he turned back to Swirling Cloud. The Natchez leaned on his propped chunkey lance, a smirk curling his lips. "Hope it helped. You can think about it as you hang in a square."

Fire Cat smiled weakly, a calm acceptance having replaced his brooding anxiety. He trailed by three. If Swirling Cloud won the next ten points, everything would be lost.

As he took a deep breath and took his position, the day didn't seem quite as hot, the crowd not as loud. He had lived a good life. Fought proudly for his people. If he lost, Cahokia would fall; nothing would happen that his ancestors hadn't prayed for.

Some second sense made him shoot one final glance over his shoulder.

There, up at the Council Terrace Gate, a single figure stood between the guards. A young man, his hair loose, wearing a red hunting shirt. Chunkey Boy, without his finery.

Come to watch the end of his world. The death of illusion.

Fire Cat placed his feet, picking his target: the guardian

post at the base of the conical Earth Clans burial mound. Crazy Frog's instructions echoed from his memory as he launched, the stone firmly cradled in his hand.

I wonder if the Morning Star will die as well as I will?

Eighty-nine

Waving away a particularly pesky fly, Horn Lance stretched and sighed. He lay with one leg up, his head and back cushioned by textile-covered pillows. His skin felt delightfully cool as the sheen of perspiration dried on his stomach, crotch, and thighs.

He watched Wooden Doll as she stood and flipped her long hair back. A slight smile, as if reflecting a profound satisfaction, lay on her soft lips. His gaze traced the now-familiar lines of her face, her long neck, the angles of her broad shoulders. He relished the curves of her high breasts and jutting nipples, the smooth and muscular stomach. Her hips cradled that lush triangle of thick black hair before surrendering into long thighs. Had he ever known such a magnificent woman?

Even if he had, he'd never experienced a woman who could use her body with such art and imagination. The afterglow of every coupling left him warmly exhausted, a honeyed satisfaction burning from his loins to his core. Despite the vivid memory engraved in soul and flesh, could it have been real? Had he really experienced those sensations? Had she actually unleashed such passions from his aging body?

Or was it illusion, some fantasy spun of magic and Power

that beguiled the soul, since such joys couldn't actually be real?

"You look pleasantly exhausted." She studied him through dark and thoughtful eyes. "Sometimes a nap can make the entire world right again. Most men seem to prefer a short respite. You will awaken refreshed, I assure you."

He lightly fingered the bruise the thief had given him the night before. He had half a mind to go back and spend a finger or two of time adding to the fool's misery.

"I have to go. You've kept me much longer than I planned as it is. I was supposed to be back in—"

She reached down and placed soft fingers against his lips. "Lie back, relax. If you simply must go, at least do so with a full stomach. I shall have a selection of meats, fish, greens, and stews available within a finger's time."

"Pus and blood, woman, I'd almost think you were thinking up ways of detaining me."

"Why wouldn't I?" she asked with a throaty laugh. "Do you think you were the only one to enjoy such an exceptional coupling? I don't frivolously turn loose of a man who can do to me what you just did."

"I pay you. Perhaps too well. No other woman in Cahokia has cacao to drink. And there's not much of it left."

"And you wonder why I don't just toss you your clothes and throw you out?" She settled on the bed beside him. "You are no one's fool, my lover. Nor am I. Here are the facts." She ticked them off on her long fingers. "One. You and the Itza are the new force in Cahokia. Two. Be that as it may, you *don't* know the intricacies of governing its Houses and clans. Three. Yes, you can rely on Green Chunkey, Columella, and some of the others. Four. They will do their best to manipulate you for their own advantage. Five. You do not know the personalities of the players, what their weaknesses and vulnerabilities are. Six. You will need someone you can trust to advise you. And, finally, I intend on being that person."

Ah, yes, there was her angle. "You would be my wife?"

She made a face. "Don't be absurd. And never underestimate me like that again. You need to marry women with a strategic and practical value. So does the *ahau*. I can help you with that. You need to found a ruling lineage, and the truth is you don't have that many years left to do it."

"Then what do you see as your role?"

Her level gaze held his as she said, "The Keeper's position exists for a reason. If you've poisoned Blue Heron like you think you have, you're going to need someone to serve the same function. Or did you think Swirling Cloud—ignorant and untrusted Natchez that he is—would step into that position?"

"Don't underestimate me, either," he shot back. "I've heard that Columella's dwarf has connections." Anticipating the exasperated lift of an eyebrow, implying he didn't understand, he stated, "You're going to tell me he serves her interests first. I know that. But . . . tell me about Columella. She's married. Where's her husband?"

"Gone as often as he can manage it, which suits them both." Now the tilt of her eyebrow communicated agreement. "She'd be a splendid first match, though a bit old for more children. Don't think you'd ever be able to win the dwarf's loyalty. And do expect that he'll be sharing her bed anytime you're not in it."

"Call him a *small* annoyance." He delighted in his wit.

She was watching him the way an osprey did a small fish. "A smart man would give very careful consideration to my offer."

He nodded slowly, eyes locked with hers. "You've already done me a great favor. But if you're smart, you'll get rid of the slave girl. She's engaged in her own game. Just thought you'd like to know."

A slight pinching of her expression was the only reaction. "I see."

"And now, I've got to start back. It will already be dark by the time I reach the Grand Plaza."

She watched him dress, her arms crossed, expression thoughtful.

When he walked out into the hot afternoon, he almost sighed at the sight of his litter. By the White Boned Snake, she'd drained him dry. Thankfully he'd be able to sleep all the way back. He didn't dare let Red Copal and the rest know she'd worn him out; they'd tease him beyond toleration. Instead he flopped wearily onto the litter, already planning how to poison the *tonka'tzi* before the next quarter-moon.

He didn't look back. Didn't see when Wooden Doll opened her door just far enough to signal with a red cloth. Nor did he see the young man in a breechcloth rise from where he'd crouched in the shade of an overhanging roof. Even before the youth passed between the buildings, he'd broken into a hard run, headed east.

Ninety

*L*ocked in Sister Datura's deadly arms, Night Shadow Star's body floated down to settle on the soft mud. Around her a twisting warren of dark caverns converged in the grotto where she stood. Roots clung to the limestone overhead; green fingers of moss streamed out in the slow-moving current.

She knew this place with all of its terrors and promise. Was it a measure of her desperation that it now felt like a refuge?

"A refuge? Do you think you can escape here, Lady of Cahokia?"

She turned. The giant snapping turtle lifted itself from the bottom; sand and streamers of moss traced patterns as they flowed down the horny plates of shell. Immense, huge, the great reptile extended a boulder-sized head, worked its jaws, and stared at her with a round and alien eye. The bluntly pointed nose ended with two nostrils that extended her way as the creature took in her scent.

She froze, having forgotten how terrifying the Spirit Beast was, or the horror of being eaten alive by the dark denizens of the Underworld.

"Do you think we care how many males mount you, or

whose semen settles in your loins? We couldn't care less who you are, who you love, or what you hope. Your existence is fleeting, woman. Meaningless to the process of life unless your womb produces another life, which in turn produces another in the endless propagation of life itself. Think of yourself as a two-legged womb . . . the males as nothing more than mobile penises. In the grand scheme of things neither you, nor they, have any other purpose than breeding. Once you accept that, your sordid and inconsequential existence will be much easier to bear."

"What if I refuse?"

"Refuse all you like. Protest it to all of Creation." Snapping Turtle studied her with a cold eye, then cocked its head. *"I listen, and hear nothing but silence from the universe. Not so much as a ripple of sympathy emanates from the timeless harmony of the Spiral. There is your illumination. Your answer. You have discovered your true place and where you fit into your world. Now leave. Begone. And stop disturbing my realm."*

Night Shadow Star stiffened, back arching, muscles knotted as she shook her head. *"I refuse."*

Snapping Turtle shifted and dislodged swirls of mud. Now both eyes fixed on her, cold, predatory, the pupils like black dots of frigid emptiness. The great head pulled back, jaws gaping as a snapping turtle's was wont to do before striking. *"You refuse? A fleeting and insignificant bit of blood, meat, and bone denies me?"*

"I deserve more."

Snapping Turtle snapped at her, its jaws shearing empty space within a finger length of her nose.

Night Shadow Star's terror left her trembling. She forced herself to glare into the angry Spirit Beast's baleful black eyes.

"Go ahead." Her voice broke. *"Strike. But I will not back down. I will be more than a meaningless breeder in an endless line of breeders. I will be more."*

"She certainly isn't a coward," a soft contralto said from behind.

Night Shadow Star turned, startled to see a slender black-haired woman, perhaps twenty, with large dark eyes. The woman seemed to hover above the soft mud, her dress an ethereal fabric, her hair undulating with the current.

Even as Night Shadow Star watched, the woman's form seemed to flow, appearing slightly older, a tinge of gray in her hair, faint lines in her age-hardening face.

Or was that a trick of the light? Didn't she appear younger now, flushed with the energy of youth?

"I would have expected Horned Serpent," Night Shadow Star whispered to herself.

"He rises each night in the southern sky, guarding the entrance to the Road of Souls." Snapping Turtle sounded sullen, and the great beast shifted, silt billowing as it settled deeper in the mud. To the woman he asked, "Why are you here?"

When Night Shadow Star turned her attention back to the woman, it was with shock that she found a little girl, perhaps three or four summers old. Surely that couldn't be the same . . .

"We are one and many," the little girl's voice piped. "Since you balanced the Power and saved the boundaries between worlds, we have wondered about you."

"Who is we?"

"She knows nothing." Snapping Turtle sounded brittle. "Why Piasa wastes time with her is beyond understanding."

Night Shadow Star wasn't sure that she actually saw the little girl's image waver, but an old woman—jaw undershot, face a mass of wrinkles, her hair but thin white wisps—was studying her through those same large dark eyes. Yes, the eyes, the only constant as the woman's image kept shifting, aging, growing younger, never seeming to fix.

"She may be the one," the woman said, her body momentarily that of a matron.

"She may indeed," Piasa announced, *his form blurring into existence as if materializing from one of the tunnels. "But she is already mine. Why should I share her?"*

The woman, now barely a teen, with budding breasts, smiled beguilingly. *"Nothing is forever, Lord. Not even Spirit Beasts, as someday you shall learn. Bundles know these things. Our Power rises when humans care for and nurture us—and declines subject to their neglect. Given the time we have remaining, we would see the Itza Dream fail. As you would."*

Piasa spread his barred and spotted wings, yellow eyes thinning to slits, the whiskers bristling around its pink nose. *"Nothing given comes without a price."*

"She says she would be something besides a meaningless breeder." Snapping Turtle sounded surly as he bit off the words.

The old woman stepped forward, extending an age-gnarled hand. *"So far the Itza has taken everything from you. The man you love, your possessions, your body, your home, and he's on the verge of taking your people. The choice is yours: Do you want to fight him? Even if it comes at the cost of one of your Dreams?"*

Night Shadow Star glanced warily at the hand, and then at Piasa. The underwater panther was panting softly, long white fangs exposed as the pink tongue curled with each hot breath. The beast's yellow glare burned into her very souls.

"Lord?" she asked.

"The battle is joined, woman. The War Serpent's Power, what they call ch'ulel, has taken us by surprise. We have a chance, but only if you take the Bundle's hand. If you do, it will come at a cost."

Snapping Turtle hissed in disgust. *"Are you a fool? She will choose to remain here, with us, in the safety of our protective tunnels. Here she will no longer feel, no longer ache, suffer, hunger, or hurt. She's not stupid, only ignorant and weak."*

Night Shadow Star shot a sideling glance at Snapping Turtle, then reached out and took the old woman's hand, but in grasping it, realized it now belonged to a young girl.

In that instant, she saw the chunkey courts, the crowds, and Swirling Cloud with his lance. Fire Cat had that pinched look he got at moments of great stress; he grasped Makes Three's old lance and positioned himself. Swirling Cat was on the verge of bowling his stone.

"What do I have to do?"

"It comes down to a single throw of a chunkey lance. We will get one chance, and after that, Waxaklahun Kan will turn his full wrath upon us. To save the people, you will have to condemn the man you love. Are you willing to make that sacrifice?"

Ninety-one

Eighteen even.

Two casts to win.

Fire Cat took a proffered water bottle handed out by a young man in the crowd, lifted the bottle, and chugged the tepid liquid, letting it run down his chin and chest before handing the bottle back to the wide-eyed young man.

"Bless you, Red Wing!" the Deer Clan youth cried before a warrior forced him back from the edge. Warriors lined both sides of the court now; nor did they hold back, whacking people indiscriminately when the huge crowd threatened to spill onto the court. The surging press of humanity was driven by its weight and mass.

Heat rolled off those tightly packed bodies and washed across the court in a permeable thickness heavy with the stench of sweat and breath. Nor had Fire Cat ever heard such a sound; ten thousand voices creating a roar more like a pounding waterfall than anything uttered from human throats.

Throughout the long match, the people had come, word spreading like a wave rolling out from the center. "The Red Wing is playing the Natchez for his life!" "Cahokia's Power against the Itza's!"

Drawn by the sensation, throngs had assembled in a chaos of betting, shoving, shouting, and bobbing.

Down by one, Swirling Cloud had taken the last point to pull even at eighteen apiece. He took his position, his Natchez stone with its central hole clutched tightly in his sweaty right hand. Tendons stood from his darkly tanned skin, the fingernails white from the force of his grip.

Gone were the taunts and threats. Somewhere in the last hand of time—as Fire Cat's game had steadied and Swirling Cloud's lead dwindled and then vanished—the man had begun to panic. The tells were there. His jaw muscles knotted and twitched. A glitter now lay behind his eyes, his gaze half frantic. Two casts back he'd lost the point through a bad release that sent his stone careening out of bounds and into the crowd.

Somehow he'd recovered after that, but tension lay in the angle of his shoulders, the jerky quickness of his step.

Fire Cat took a deep breath—little relief though it gave in the dripping heat and stench of packed humanity.

Swirling Cloud swallowed so hard Fire Cat heard his gulp over the roar of the crowd. Life and death now teetered on each release of the stone, each cast. Sweat slicked their fingers and stung as it dripped into their eyes. Fatigue played its perilous tricks on thew and sinew.

The slightest mistake now would cost the match.

Cost a life.

"Make way! Make way for the *Ahau* Oxlajun Chul Balam!"

Swirling Cloud stopped short at the verge of launching.

Fire Cat turned to see a tumult in the press as Red Copal and the Itza warriors drove a wedge through the crowd. The gaudy Thirteen Sacred Jaguar, his head bare, sun beating on his sloping forehead, rode atop his litter in the wake of the colorful *kukul*. He looked imperious, decked out in his iridescent quetzal feathers and fine fabrics.

Swirling Cloud almost sobbed with joy, rushing to meet

the warriors as they elbowed a space behind the head of the court. Doing so drew jeers and curses from the displaced Cahokian nobles who'd already displaced their lesser predecessors.

It was now Fire Cat's turn to lean on his lance while Swirling Cloud and Red Copal conversed.

He glanced at the old woman. She kept wavering on her feet, eyes closed, looking as if she were about to collapse. The thief's dog kept looking anxiously up at her, head cocked, ears straining.

On the verge of stepping over and asking if she needed help, Fire Cat stopped as Swirling Cloud gave a cry and dropped to his knees. Burning Ant lowered the *kukul* over Swirling Cloud's head.

The Natchez raised his arms in supplication. The snarling serpent's green eyes glistened as if in anticipation. A beatific expression filled Swirling Cloud's face as if he were drenched in cool water. Then he filled his lungs and began singing in Natchez.

Still singing, he picked up his lance and stone. Expression rapturous, he returned to the court and shot Fire Cat a triumphant and joyous look. Taking his place, fingers working on the stone, his feet set, he studied the court before him.

Fire Cat balanced his lance, launching an instant after Swirling Cloud. Matching his opponent pace for pace, he watched the Natchez bowl the stone, studied its path until the last moment. Estimating its track, he cast a heartbeat before the penalty line. He raced after his lance, saw it catch the sunlight.

Shouting his encouragement, he watched in dismay as Swirling Cloud's stone hooked at the last instant and toppled. The Natchez' lance impacted a hand's length from the milky stone. Fire Cat's lance speared the clay two hands beyond.

Point to Swirling Cloud. The next cast would be for the game unless Fire Cat tied again. His heart hammered in his chest. Blood surged in his veins. An odd sensation slipped around his stomach, like a wounded snake twisting and writhing.

"Last Point, Red Wing," Swirling Cloud told him through a rictus-like grin. "The *kukul* has blessed me. It won't let me lose." He started to take his position.

The thief's dog began to bark, insistent, half-panicked. Fire Cat turned—anything to keep from that last awful cast he felt certain he would lose.

The old woman was down, people bending to stare. The dog was leaping, barking, desperate eyes fixed on Fire Cat.

"Hold!" he called, trotting over and pushing people out of the way. "Get her water!"

The old woman's face was slack, her breath coming in odd, labored gasps. Fire Cat pulled her upright, her head lolling. As her eyelids fluttered, she mouthed the words, "Breathe in the Power, Red Wing. Touch the Tortoise Bundle. Your ancestors . . ."

She seemed to fade.

"Red Wing!" Swirling Cloud bellowed over the roar of the crowd. "Are you going to play? Or do you forfeit?"

The dog stared at him through those odd blue and brown eyes, whining.

Fire Cat looked up at the staring faces. "Care for her! Or I'll have your hides." Then he threaded her pack off her shoulder and reached in. Feeling a tingle in his fingers he removed the Bundle, felt its curious warmth. Lifting it to his nose, he sniffed, inhaling the smell of old leather. Like a cool and pine-scented breeze, its aroma curled down through his lungs and into his heart and blood.

Go. Play.

He felt rather than heard the words.

Rising, he shot a look at where the Itza remained high above the crowd, his litter still propped on his porters' shoulders. The man's protruding and wide-set eyes had an arrogant and disdainful look. Before him the *kukul* glared balefully with its polished green eyes.

Fire Cat could feel the thing, its presence like that of a coiled water moccasin lurking in a dark hole.

Above and beyond, at the Council Terrace Gate, the Morning Star might have been a carven image, only his hair flipping in the southwestern breeze. Fire Cat felt his presence, eyes locking across the distance.

He heard the Bundle's voice inside his head: *Do you know why owls die with their wings outspread?*

As the words echoed between Fire Cat's souls, the distant Morning Star extended his hands, as if asking for the answer.

"Because taking wing is their only hope for survival," Fire Cat parroted the words that formed inside him.

Will you give up, Red Wing? Or will you fly for your people?

"I'll fly," Fire Cat growled, his souls seeming to swell with renewed energy.

His gaze took in the hemming crowd, a seething ocean of humanity. He lifted his lance, shouting, "I'll fly for all of you! I'll fly for Cahokia! This game is for our ancestors, for the Morning Star. This final cast is for Old-Woman-Who-Never-Dies! I play this point for Piasa and Horned Serpent. For Hunga Ahuito and the Thunderbirds! I play this for our world!"

The answering roar from the crowd was deafening as Fire Cat took his place beside the smirking Swirling Cloud.

"Your throw." Fire Cat's voice was drowned by the crowd.

Swirling Cloud gave him a last triumphant glance, breathed on his stone, and took his position. He immediately launched, driving forward.

Fire Cat felt the Bundle's Power: cool, possessed. It filled him; voices of ancestral song, soothing and encouraging, echoed in his souls. His fear and desperation vanished as his renewed muscles and bones drove him in pursuit.

The Natchez barely ducked as his right arm curled down. The spinning disc shot forward, straight and true.

Fire Cat had that instant to read its track, could sense its ultimate line. Picking his target he cast with all his might at the same time as Swirling Cloud.

The lances shot through the air like falcons, rising side by side, each spinning, noses seeking the sun. At mid-flight they curved, still tracking the same course. As twins they nosed over, arcing in descent.

Time slowed to a crawl as Fire Cat raced in the wake of the lances. He didn't shout his encouragement, didn't pray as he ran.

Instead, he willed the Power of the Bundle, as if it could flow through his vision and into the slim white-ash lance.

He might have been but a spectator, watching through another's eyes as the lances dropped toward the slowing stone.

As if possessed, Swirling Cloud's lance accelerated, speeding ahead. Fire Cat's lance seemed to slow, waffle slightly in its progress the way it might if it had lost its way or been touched by a mysterious wind.

A worried moan rose from the crowd.

As Swirling Cloud's stone toppled onto its side, his lance thudded into the clay but a hand's length beyond.

The Natchez was already howling his victory, leaping high, swinging a fist in exultation.

It seemed to take forever, Fire Cat's lance arcing down. In the desperate silence between his souls, he could hear the lance point hiss as it cut the air.

Fire Cat was frozen in midstride. He watched in disbelief as the point of his lance speared the hole in Swirling Cloud's stone, wedging tight.

Stopped short in the small hole, the weight of the lance flipped over, lofting the stone. With a high bounce, it slammed down. At the impact, Swirling Cloud's stone cracked into two pieces. They flopped, broken, on either side of Fire Cat's still-shivering lance.

The crowd exploded as if struck by lightning. The very air shivered under the thunderous roar.

Fire Cat paced to a stop, eyes on the impossibility of the broken stone.

Swirling Cloud stared in disbelief, paralyzed. Then, realization sinking in, his expression changed, color draining.

With a shaking arm, he picked up his lance. Unable to even touch his broken stone, he almost staggered back to the head of the court.

Fire Cat picked up his lance and walked back to the start, ignoring the straining warriors who struggled to hold back a crowd gone insane.

The Keeper, his mother, and sisters were bent over the old woman. Smooth Pebble was giving her water. The dog, however, studied him with those odd colored eyes, tail wagging in an "I told you so" manner.

"You lost," Fire Cat told Swirling Cloud as he reached for his sack and dropped his stone inside.

"For today," Swirling Cloud told him, expression glazed. "Tomorrow. I'll beat you tomorrow."

"My life against yours. Everything I own, against everything that is yours."

The smile that tried to form on Swirling Cloud's lips flickered and died. Then, mouth working, he turned to Red Copal, speaking in what seemed even to Fire Cat's ears to be broken Itza.

The warriors stepped forward, surrounding the Natchez.

The wary smile was back on Swirling Cloud's lips. "I don't think so. Not today. You won't interfere. Not when it would turn to bloodshed."

The high chiefs and matrons who'd been watching stood stunned. They began to mutter. Cries of "Coward!" gained in volume. A swell of discord ran through the crowd like a bitter winter wind.

The Itza, atop his litter, straightened. Foreigner he might have been, but a child could have read the crowd's disgust and growing anger.

Thirteen Sacred Jaguar barked an order.

With a hardening of expression, Red Copal and his warriors stepped back in unison. Those in the rear propelled Swirling Cloud forward and beyond their protection.

Fire Cat slipped his hand inside his sack, a cold certainty filling his souls. Images played in his memory: the dead Nine Strikes; Swirling Cloud's suffocating arrogance and his delight at Fire Cat's humiliation at being made to walk home naked; how the Natchez had bragged of what he'd do to Night Shadow Star . . .

Fire Cat found what he was looking for.

"No!" Swirling Cloud screamed as he turned and raised imploring hands to Thirteen Sacred Jaguar. He dropped to his knees, arms lifted. Imploring, he shouted, "You can't let this happen! You *need* me! I *am* the Natchez!"

In the crowd, the Natchez warriors were shuffling uncertainly. Wet Bobcat kept gesturing patience to his warriors as he glanced uneasily between Thirteen Sacred Jaguar and Swirling Cloud.

Fire Cat stepped forward, letting the sack drop free.

As Swirling Cloud read Thirteen Sacred Jaguar's answer in the Itza's implacable eyes and hard mouth, he cried, *"Waxaklahun Kan! Help me!"*

Fire Cat swung with all his might, his copper-bitted war ax driving into the back of Swirling Cloud's neck.

Swirling Cloud's corpse spasmed and flopped. For whatever reason, Fire Cat glanced up. As the Natchez's brilliant red blood spilled over the clay, the Morning Star turned and vanished into the Council Terrace Gate.

Ninety-two

The Fish Clan warriors were good at their job. Too good. A fact that irritated Seven Skull Shield to no end. Columella's parting words were "No matter what he looks like, he's not to be underestimated. The man wouldn't be one of the Keeper's most trusted people if he wasn't among the best. He's known for trickery and sleight, so you don't want to let him draw you into a conversation. Nor do you want to let him get too close. Take whatever steps you must to ensure he stays here."

"Yes, Matron," the big Fish Clan warrior had told her as he bowed his head and touched his forehead.

So Seven Skull Shield sat, massaging his aches, fingering his bruises, and prodding at tender places. They had brought him food: a filling fish-and-turtle stew. He had plenty of water to drink. Through the gap under the eaves he could see the angle of the sun change. But beyond that, the warehouse had more than lost any allure it might have ever had. Which, when he got right down to it, wasn't much since it had a big nasty wooden square standing in the middle of the floor.

"Never been in one of these before." Seven Skull Shield eased his way over and inspected the wood. White ash. Tough stuff. A grim smile played on his lips as he imagined the wood, this very wood, burning in the middle of a large fire.

He slapped it in promise and asked the big warrior, "Do you have a name?"

The man stared at him, face impassive.

"Oh, come on. She didn't want me drawing you into long conversations where I'd subtly suggest that you let me go, and you, having been seduced by my charm and wit, would bow and open the door. We all know that won't happen. A name doesn't hurt anything. And you do have one, don't you?"

The Fish Clan warrior lifted an eyebrow high enough to wrinkle his brow, glanced at the other three, and gave a faint shake of the head.

Seven Skull Shield sighed and worked his arms, wincing as he tried to loosen the strained muscles. The night had been agonizing. How did people stand it for days? And worse, his four-warrior guard could beat him into a pulp and hang him right back up there, on the matron's order.

Keeper. I'm coming. That is, if I can ever get free of these people.

He made a face as he paced slowly among the pots, jars, and stacked boxes topped with storage baskets. Habit made him take inventory. A man never knew what he might need to acquire should the opportunity arise. Mostly the place was filled with sacks of fibers, a pile of planks in the rear, baskets of tool stone, and so forth. Nothing that immediately sprang to mind for a weapon or means of escape.

He lifted a box lid painted with the Four Winds Clan spirals and found it filled with spindle whorls. Where had they come from? Why just put them in a box? Why did humans do anything outside of eating, drinking, sleeping, driving pegs into sheaths, and eliminating wastes? Why fight over someone's idea of Power, Spirit, or totem? Why not just send word to Matron Columella that he'd take that canoe ride south?

He'd done that once, just after Wooden Doll turned him down the first time. Not yet twenty, he'd joined a Tenasee Trader and tried to work himself to death paddling the heavy Trade canoe up the Mother Water, up the Tenasee, beyond the portages, and clear to the river's great bend.

Maybe if his traveling companions had been different, if he'd liked them, fit in better, the life might have stuck. But he'd missed Cahokia. Missed friends. So he'd come back, working like a dog at the paddle. And he'd come back a different man, strapping with muscle and possessed of a finer appreciation of the city and its opportunities.

And there's the Keeper.

So, someone had tried to poison her and killed Notched Cane? That would wound her deep down. And while Notched Cane had always disapproved of and barely tolerated Seven Skull Shield, he'd never done anything outright offensive.

He closed the box, knowing what he had to do. Amazing what a person could learn from spindle whorls.

But first, there were Wooden Doll and Slick Rock to deal with.

If only he could . . .

The door was lifted up and out of the way, late-afternoon light spilling in.

Ah, there were another two warriors outside the door. Columella really wasn't taking chances with him, was she?

The diminutive form of Flat Stone Pipe entered in his rolling short-legged stride. As quickly the door was closed.

"I see you've managed to keep him," the dwarf noted dryly.

"Yes, Lord." The Fish Clan squadron first really seemed to have no sense of humor.

"If what's building up in the west is any indication, there is going to be one nasty storm tonight."

Seven Skull Shield jerked a thumb at the square. "I'm not going back on that thing. Just whack me in the head instead."

"Which would accomplish what?" Flat Stone Pipe cocked his head, the question lying behind his dark eyes. "My informants tell me that you've nothing inside that skull of yours but stone. That you don't have a heart, that your liver is black, and your blood is as cold a turtle's. They tell me the only way to kill you is to starve you to death, that outside of bedding women, your only passion is filling your stomach."

Seven Skull Shield sighed as he spread his arms wide. "I am so misunderstood."

"Then enlighten me." Flat Stone Pipe walked over and seated himself on the square's lower crosspiece, picking at the wood with a thumbnail. "If you could walk out of here, what would you do?"

Seven Skull Shield sensed the little man's uncertainty. Something had changed. But, which way should he bet?

"That would depend. If the Keeper's dead, and that overdressed-and-feathered foreigner has managed to gain the support of the people, Horn Lance is going to ensure my existence is short and not in any manner sweet. A fact that reminds me that I've always wanted to see distant Cofitachequi."

"And if the Keeper's alive? If Night Shadow Star is drugged and captive? If something might have shaken Horn Lance's plans?"

Seven Skull Shield crossed his arms, flexing the muscles to sharpen the pain in his shoulders. "Then that depends. Your matron and I, I think we both see the world the same way. Her concern is the survival of Evening Star House. Mine is the survival of me. So we each do what we have to, make the deals we have to. Given that she plucked me away from Slick Rock? I think I like her."

"And when it comes to my matron and the Keeper?"

"While I like your matron, the Keeper is my friend. As I've found out recently, I don't have many friends."

Flat Stone Pipe kept picking at the wood as he considered his next words. "Relationships between Evening Star House and the Morning Star . . . Well, let's say my matron doesn't trust him."

"Little man, your matron isn't alone. Listen, here's where I think you're going: Evening Star House has its needs and goals, and so does the Keeper and her House. Maybe our job—yours and mine—is to figure out ways so that neither House gets crossways with the other. Even if we have to slap a little pine pitch over the cracks every now and then to cover up the unsightly gaps between them."

"While we did hang you in a square for a night, it was for a good reason."

"What you're saying is that unlike if you'd left me with Slick Rock, I survived it and I'll heal."

Flat Stone Pipe seemed to come to a decision. "You know I have my sources?"

"I do."

"A fast runner arrived moments before I came to see you. The Red Wing just beat Swirling Cloud at chunkey. Bet his life against the Natchez. Won a huge fortune, and cut off the Little Sun's head. As news spreads, the city's going crazy."

"He *did* it!" Seven Skull Shield whispered.

"Can you manage to avoid Horn Lance's agents? Many people still think you're on the loose and worth a fortune."

"I can." He paused. "Especially if there's a storm. But there's a stop I have to make first. Call it a special payback."

"About the woman who betrayed you. It might be a little more complicated than you think. But there's more than one storm brewing outside. I've got a few more things to tell you; then, just after dark, I'll let you go." He paused, "Assuming you can do me a couple of favors in the process."

Ninety-three

A hard rain was falling out of the lightning-riven night as Horn Lance's porters slopped up to Thirteen Sacred Jaguar's palace steps. The clouds had come spilling in from the south at sunset, their black interiors rent by tortured white veins of lightning. As Cahokia fell under the mantle of darkness and storm, a thousand searing bolts flashed, and thunder banged and crashed through the falling deluge.

What had begun as a respite from the day's oppressive heat had rapidly become a misery to be endured. While Horn Lance's porters carried an extended sun shade, the thin fabric rapidly succumbed to the pounding streamers of rain.

Horn Lance had considered taking shelter and waiting for it to pass, but he'd already been soaked to the skin. Nor had it let up, seeming only to intensify in fury as wind, lightning, and deafening peals of thunder hammered out of the night. If there was any good news it was that the constant searing bolts of lightning illuminated the water-silvered Avenue of the Sun as though it were midday.

As his litter was laid on the soaked earth before the palace stairs, another gust of wind drove rain in slashing patterns that almost blinded him.

His arthritic arm raised as an ineffectual shield, he

climbed to his feet, shivering, and made his way up the slippery stairs as the first hailstones clacked and snapped on the wood.

Ducking and wincing as thumbnail-sized balls of ice smacked his head and shoulders, he reached the head of the stairs. Lightning in a strobe-white flash illuminated Piasa and Horned Serpent. Alive, trailing streamers of water, their colors vivid, he saw them leap, the snarling mouths wide.

Howling in fear, he dropped flat. Quivering with each impact of a hailstone, he thought it a flesh-rending fang or claw. Only after heartbeats of time had passed did he realize he was still alive. He summoned his courage and glanced up. A more distant lightning flash portrayed the guardian posts as they'd always been, but sleek with a sheen of water.

Laughing at himself, he rolled on his butt, one hand to his still-pounding heart.

What possessed me? Am I that much of a silly fool?

Disgusted and sheepish, he climbed to his feet and hurried between the guardians into the shelter of the veranda.

"Lord?" one of the Natchez warriors asked tentatively from the darkness.

"It's me. What a storm. Something sure has riled the Nine Lords of the Sky and enraged Tlaloc. You'd think it was the end of the world out there."

"You'd best see for yourself, Lord." The dark shape guarding the door shifted warily. "They need you in there."

Maybe he wasn't the only one spooked by the sound and fury.

Squishing through the door, he stepped into the dimly lit great room. The first thing that struck him was the bare walls. Most of the copper plate, the fine fabrics, the intricately decorated shields, the exquisite ceramics, blankets, and robes—anything of real value—were missing.

Night Shadow Star's household servants all huddled in a protective ball in the dark corner to his left. From the expressions, they, too, were a breath away from panic.

The Natchez warriors were all clustered in the great room's rear, their attention on Wet Bobcat and his war second. At the sight of Horn Lance, the Natchez squadron first seemed to sag with relief. The other warriors glanced Horn Lance's way, hard and worried gazes giving way to a flicker of hope.

"What's happened?" Horn Lance demanded as he began pulling his sodden clothing from his shivering skin. The White Bone Snake might have been shaking his spectral vertebrae the way his teeth were chattering.

Not waiting for an answer, he hunched over the central fire, letting the warmth and smoke trace up his goosefleshed skin. Rubbing his pruned hands, he extended them to the flames and sighed.

"The Little Sun is dead," Wet Bobcat declared. "And so is the Cahokian bitch. The *ahau* is in with her now. He placed the *kukul* at the side of her bed and is praying."

"Swirling Cloud . . . ?" Horn Lance couldn't quite get his cold-muddled thoughts around it.

"Do not use his name!" Wet Bobcat rose from the back bench, picking his way through the warriors. They were all throwing dark glances his way. "The slave. The one they call the Red Wing, cut his head off."

"And you *let* him?" Horn Lance thundered in disbelief.

"It was *just*!" Wet Bobcat bellowed back as he stopped beside Horn Lance, fists knotted, veins swelling in his neck. "The Little Sun *disgraced* us as it is. He tried to hide behind Red Copal and his warriors when he lost!"

"Lost? Lost what?"

"Chunkey, Lord. Look around you. All the furnishings? He wagered them, and won. And won. And won again. He'd taken the day. Defeated the Four Winds Clan. And then this *slave* challenged him. Bet his life against the Little Sun's."

". . . And Fire Cat won." He fought a bone-rending shiver, wondering if he'd ever feel warm again. "You're telling me that a mere slave did what Cahokia's mighty nobles could not? Defeated the finest chunkey player on the southern river?"

"The Little Sun invoked the Power of the *kukul*. He called upon it. We all saw. The Red Wing only had an old woman and some worn-looking Bundle on his side. But on the last cast, he hit and split the Little Sun's stone. We've never seen such a thing. It was a miracle."

Wet Bobcat glanced nervously at his companions. "We want to go home."

"You'll do no such thing. You'll stay, and you'll follow my orders. Now, what's this about the *ahau*'s wife being dead?"

"Go look," Wet Bobcat said sullenly.

Still shivering, Horn Lance rounded the fire. He had no trouble picking his way through the Natchez warriors as they scuttled out of his way.

Entering the back room, he found it lit by hickory-oil lamps. The *kukul* dominated the room; he felt the War Serpent's *ch'ulel* as the hard green eyes and snarling face met his gaze. The Itza warriors crowded the rear of the room, Red Copal with his arms crossed. Dead Teeth had a worried look.

Thirteen Sacred Jaguar sat on the side of the bed and took in Horn Lance's wet and naked body. Something implacable and hard lay behind his wide-set and bulging eyes. His mouth was pressed in a flat and tense line.

On the bed, Night Shadow Star lay on her back, a blanket covering her from the chin down. Her eyes were barely visible behind slitted lids, her face slack, lips parted and dry.

"What happened to her?"

"She was on the floor, there, by that altar of hers. We found her when we returned from the ball game. Your man Swirling Cloud lost his head. Waxaklahun Kan found him unworthy. Refused his pleas and abandoned him. We didn't understand at first . . . when he asked Red Copal to protect him. We didn't know that he'd bet his life, just like in the sacred ball game. When I realized the truth, we gave the Natchez lord to the woman's slave. The slave pulled an ax from his bag and cut off the coward's head. His souls are disgraced. The Lords of Death will turn their backs on him."

Thirteen Sacred Jaguar sighed, rubbed his weary eyes, and winced. "And then we return here, barely escaping that mad crowd, and I find my wife lying dead on the floor. We picked her up. Put her here. I have asked Waxaklahun Kan to try to recall her souls to her body. She remains cold. She does not breathe. There is no response."

"Let me see." Horn Lance, still rubbing his shivering arms, stepped close and bent down.

He lifted an eyelid, studied the rolled-back pupil, and then touched her eyeball. She blinked in response.

"She's not dead, *Ahau*. Not quite. Not yet. But it could come at any time." He leaned close, squinting in the dim lamplight. Running his fingers along her temple, he felt the grease, lifted it, and sniffed. "Sacred Datura. She's in a trance. Her souls are in the Spirit World, seeking the Vision Serpent."

Thirteen Sacred Jaguar glanced up at the *kukul* and took a deep breath. "What if she finds Och Kan there and he inserts his tongue into her mouth? What if he finds her souls unworthy the way the *kukul* did the Natchez? If he devours her, digests her souls, and passes them with his lifeless excrement, her body will die." He lifted his hand in inquiry. "What then, my *cha'k payal*?"

"There are other women to marry." Columella immediately came to mind. Older, yes. But a potent and capable ally. If she, Green Chunkey, and War Duck could be induced into an alliance against the wounded Morning Star House . . .

"My warriors think the Natchez want to leave this place," Thirteen Sacred Jaguar told him. "Would that be a prudent choice for all of us? Especially if the woman should die?

Will her relatives understand that I am not responsible? Or will these monkey people react like the uncultured beasts they are?"

"There is no need to abandon Cahokia. This is just a setback." A deafening crack of thunder shook the palace, causing the others to flinch and look up with frightened eyes. "And it's the darkest of the storm. We're tired, unsettled."

He straightened. "And the Keeper? How did the people take news of her death? Do they suspect us?"

Thirteen Sacred Jaguar's protruding round eyes never wavered as he said, "She lives. If what Wet Bobcat heard is correct, only her slave, the one called Notched Cane, is dead. She even attended the chunkey match. Watched as Swirling Cloud's head was cut off."

"But he did it, right? Sneaked in and placed the poison root in the food?"

"Wet Bobcat says he did." Thirteen Sacred Jaguar's gaze seemed to bore into Horn Lance. "Had he followed instructions, the entire household should have been killed. Just as it was with the old Great Sun and the White Woman in Natchez. I can only assume that, as in chunkey, he failed."

He should have been here, not dallying in Wooden Doll's bed. Had he been, none of this would have happened. Horn Lance felt the energy drain from his legs. He sank to the bed, disbelieving stare going to the comatose Night Shadow Star. "Must I do everything myself?"

"Perhaps, *ch'ak payal*. But for myself, I am wondering if we are not playing ourselves for fools. This Cahokia, I'm beginning to think, may not be worth our effort."

Horn Lance raised a hand. "Fools, *Ahau*? Or like Hun Ahau and Yax Balam in Xibalba we are being tested." He looked up at the *kukul* with its snarling mouth and glaring green eyes. "Power doesn't just grant success. It has to be paid for. We are waging a war. The Spirit World rewards those who offer it *itz* and *ch'ulel*, blood and soul."

Thirteen Sacred Jaguar's face tightened. "How much

more can it demand of us? We set out with ten large ocean-going canoes. After the storms, only seven of us landed at the mouth of the Father Water. *Seven!* In only one canoe. But for the Natchez Traders at the mouth of the river, we, too, would have perished."

"But we didn't, *Ahau*." He stroked his chin. "Perhaps I've been fighting incorrectly."

"How so?"

"Perhaps it is time I went after the Keeper and the *tonka'tzi* myself. Perhaps Waxaklahun Kan would grant us greater favor if we laid their severed heads as an offering on the floor before him."

Ninety-four

Everything was in chaos. Blue Heron rubbed the back of her neck as lightning cracked, boomed, and rumbled across the night. Periodic actinic flashes stabbed through the doorway, filling the room with eerie white and overpowering the central fire and hickory-oil lamps. The aftereffects left her half-blind and with ghostly images fading from her vision.

She watched the rain-soaked messenger as he hesitantly left her veranda and hurried out into the storm, his figure alternately illuminated by flashes of lightning as it passed between the eagle guardian posts.

Should have let him stay on the veranda. Too late now. But at least she knew Horn Lance was on the move.

Smooth Pebble gave Blue Heron a nod. The berdache, overwhelmed by the day's events, hadn't thought to tackle the onerous task of organizing supper. That had been Notched Cane's responsibility. But to Blue Heron's surprise, Dancing Sky had stepped up, ordering her daughters to stoke the fire and set the pots to boiling. Then she had rummaged through the burnished brownware storage jars for whatever could be tossed into make-it-up-as-you-go stew.

"I appreciate your help, old enemy," Blue Heron told the woman.

Dancing Sky interrupted her task to grant Blue Heron a sidelong glance. Then she turned her attention to where Fire Cat ministered to the old woman; she'd been laid on one of the benches by the door. The thief's dog was busily scratching at its bear-like left ear.

"Keeper, you didn't have to let us accompany you today. To have seen my son's victory? Epic. You have no idea what it means to my daughters and me." She shook her head. "Who would have believed that was my son, the heretic, saving Cahokia of all places?"

"I thought Night Shadow Star was head-struck and addled when she had Fire Cat and you taken down from the squares." Blue Heron narrowed an eye. "And you, old rival. In my house? I had my reservations when Fire Cat forced me into it. But I'm curious. Why haven't you been trouble for me?"

Dancing Sky double-checked where Soft Moon stirred one of the bubbling pots of acorn, goosefoot, and maygrass before she said, "You've treated us fairly. Better than I would have treated you had our positions been reversed. Am I bitter about the destruction of Red Wing Town? Of course. But we were at war, and Power chose. You can't make a shattered pot hold water. So the girls and I will stumble along, and do the best we can in these new circumstances."

A sly smile curled Dancing Sky's old lips. "And as Power demonstrated today, one never knows what the future may require."

"You wouldn't be the first former adversary to find a place here. Smooth Pebble did. And Notched Cane."

"Who is she?" Dancing Sky indicated the old woman Fire Cat ladled water to.

"I have no idea." Blue Heron lowered her voice. "I do, however, intend to find out. Call when supper is ready."

Blue Heron almost jumped out of her skin as a white strobe of lightning accompanied a mighty clap of thunder that shook her palace. Before she could catch her breath, the violent pounding of rain on the thatch combined with the musical pattering of runoff from the eaves.

She worked her fingers and took a deep breath to settle her anxiety. Glancing out the door, she saw a drowning world in the lightning's flicker. Fire Cat's wealth—or Night Shadow Star's to be more precise—was now stacked on her porch where she'd ordered warriors to carry it.

Fire Cat looked up and nodded as she seated herself on the bench beside the old woman. "How is she?"

"Better," the old woman replied through a reedy voice. Her gaze flicked up to Blue Heron's. "I still have a blinding headache. Got too hot out there. Can't take it like I could when I was young."

"Do you have a name?"

"I've had many names, Keeper." The woman's dark eyes seemed to deepen like a bottomless pool. "Names, however, are meaningless. Patterns of exhaled vibration uttered by the throat and modified by the mouth. Mere tags to keep track of things or people. All you really need to know is that I'm the current keeper of the Tortoise Bundle." Her gnarled fingers patted the worn fabric pack beside her.

Fire Cat reverently said, "It sang to me."

"They sang to you," she corrected. "The essences of all those who breathed Power into the Tortoise Bundle over the long generations."

"It looked more like a heart than a tortoise," Blue Heron murmured, the fine hairs on her arms and neck rising. It came to her that of all the persons to cross her threshold—including assassins and even Walking Smoke himself—this shriveled and desiccated old woman might be the most dangerous.

"You are wise to fear me, Keeper," the old woman told her, eyes now glowing like molten obsidian. "And in ways you can barely conceive."

"Do you hear my thoughts?"

"I can see the Dance taking place between your souls. I

know the pathways of your heart. I can see the Spirit within you, hold it, or snuff it out." Her gaze turned deadly. "Like this."

A fist seemed to tighten around Blue Heron's throat. She tried to swallow. Couldn't. Fought for a breath that wouldn't come. And a feral panic spiked in her chest; a spear of pain lanced through her heart.

Lasting but an instant, it let go, leaving her gasping for breath, a hand to her throat. Pus and blood, why was it always her throat?

"You and I need not be adversaries," the woman rasped. "I have no interest in your petty intrigues."

"Why are you here?" Fingers of fear continued to flutter along her shaken nerves. She pointed at the blue-and-brown-eyed dog. "Where's Seven Skull Shield?"

"Your friend is facing his own challenges. As to me, I'm tired, Keeper. I've waited a long time."

"Waited? For what?"

"For someone to take the Tortoise Bundle. Provided, that is, she survives to see tomorrow's sunset."

"Who?"

The old lips curled. "Didn't see her taking matters into her own hands . . . that she'd choose Sister Datura as a way out. What life is still clinging to her body is slowly draining away. When that gleaming flicker inside her finally snuffs to darkness, she'll—"

"Spit and vomit!" Fire Cat cried, leaping to his feet. "Keeper, send a runner for Rides-the-Lightning! I've got to get to her. Make sure she—"

"Sit. *Down*!" The old woman's voice was barely more than a whisper, but it hit Blue Heron with the impact of a thrown rock. From Fire Cat's reaction, it had had the same effect on him.

The Red Wing swallowed hard, eyes big, as he dropped back to a crouch. "Elder, you don't understand. Last time she Danced with Sister Datura, she almost didn't come back. Every moment I waste here just lets her slip that much deeper into—"

"The final decision is hers, Red Wing. She has her choices . . . and you have yours."

Fire Cat's forehead lined with concern. "I don't understand."

"We rarely do, warrior." Her face saddened. "Not even the greatest of Dreamers. They can become so lost in Power and Dreaming the One they never realize the world around them has changed." She reached up, fingering a small bundle that hung from a cord about her neck. Her eyes had gone distant.

"What do you want from us?" Blue Heron asked cautiously.

The old woman fixed soul-sucking eyes on Blue Heron's. "First Woman doesn't care if the Itza brings a new Dream to Cahokia, but she is not of this world. A long time ago, like First Woman, I was so lost in the Spiral that human squabbles were not my concern. So what if Petaga initiated another bloody vendetta? Black Tail's vision of requickening Bird Man's soul in a human body seemed insignificant. The Tortoise Bundle barely called me back in time to save it from Black Tail's wrath: I had to walk through fire to carry it to safety. Took years before I could build a small temple beside Petaga's old mound to house it. You see, if one has forgotten how to listen, then having a second hole in the head is for naught."

"Second hole? I don't understand."

"No, I suppose you wouldn't." A ghost of a smile bent the withered old lips. "What matters—and the Itza knows this—is that this world and the Spirit World are inseparably linked. I know where he would take Cahokia. How he would change it. It is my decision that his vision, and Horn Lance's, must be destroyed."

"How?" Blue Heron growled.

"I could walk in and brain him," Fire Cat growled.

The old woman closed her eyes, her visage immediately changing from menacing to frail, exhausted, and ancient. She whispered, "First Woman cannot be disobeyed. The Itza has to do it himself."

"What?" Blue Heron cried.

"That's crazy. As long as he's got that *kukul* to stare at, he's . . ." Fire Cat's eyes lost focus, as if he had reached some terrible understanding.

"Yes, you see, don't you? The Bundle and I will do everything in our Power to aid you. But in the end, victory will come at a price," the old woman murmured wearily, and within heartbeats, she'd drifted off to sleep.

"What price?" Blue Heron asked. "What's she raving about?"

"My life, Keeper. It's the only way to beat him and save Night Shadow Star." Fire Cat's expression had gone white. "That is, if I'm good enough."

Ninety-five

Aching, shivering, wet to the core, Seven Skull Shield slopped his way down the route that led to Crazy Frog's. Lightning crisscrossed the sky, weaving irregular patterns through the clouds and turning the torrential rain silver as it illuminated cascades of water streaming from thatch and split-cane roofs.

In their rage, the Thunderbirds blasted the world as they pursued their war against the Tie Snakes and the Underworld. At the same time Seven Skull Shield could believe they were trying to either drown the world, or confuse the water serpents into thinking they could swim up into the very air—and right into the blasting thunderbolts.

If so, even the Spirit World was made up of trickery and subterfuge.

Thankfully, the raging ache in his head had ebbed to a slight annoyance, irritated only by the incessant battering of raindrops on his skull.

Making a face, he sloshed through a low area between warehouses, knowing full well that every latrine in the city was flooded and overflowing into the pathways. Come morning the flies and stench would be nose-clogging.

A ragged pattern of lightning Danced in different parts

of the sky and cast the house, ramada, and yard in strobes of blue-white. The central fire pit looked like a gleaming black eye that wept streaks of floating charcoal and ash. Rivulets of water shot from the edges of the thatch to spatter in pools of runoff that sheeted across the yard. The roar of the pounding rain and the booming crash of thunder devoured any other sound.

Seven Skull Shield trudged around the corner of the house, slipped between closely spaced walls, and slammed the flat of his wet hand against the dark plank door.

"It's Seven Skull Shield!"

Moments later, a shadowy figure lifted the door to one side, saying, "We wondered if you'd been washed away."

"It's raining so hard I watched a school of fish swim up out of the river. They almost made it to Black Martin's cord-making workshop before a bolt of lightning cooked them through and through. I'd have brought you one, but a baby Thunderbird snapped them up before I could grab one."

"Inside. He's waiting for you."

Seven Skull Shield slipped past the hangings and into the lamplit interior. Crazy Frog was perched atop a thickly folded buffalo robe, a beaded record mat in his hands. He looked up from where he peered closely at the patterns and colors of beads. "Won this in a match today. I wonder what it says. Now I'm going to have to Trade something to a recorder to tell me. Probably cost me a Split Sky City pot just to find out how many jars of corn some colony raised seven seasons ago."

"Or it might be a secret treaty between the Oneota and the Caddo declaring war on the Morning Star and announcing their armies will arrive here in ten days—a fact that will make you so rich you can buy High Chief War Duck and rule River Mounds City from the background."

Crazy Frog's expression didn't change when he said, "What makes you think I don't already?"

"Me? Think? That's not my reputation, so don't start

spreading it around. It would be too much effort to live up to."

"The Red Wing beat the Natchez."

"So I've heard."

"I missed it. Didn't so much as have a clue it was coming. When you see your friend, tell him I'm displeased. *Very* displeased. He owes me. Since you brought him here, you owe me. I've heard that it was the most remarkable match ever played. Tied. Right up until the last cast, when the Red Wing not only hit the Natchez' stone but broke it. Then while the Natchez was pleading to the Itza god to save him, Fire Cat struck his head off with one blow. Can you imagine?"

"I, uh—"

"The greatest chunkey match in years, and I missed it. This disturbs me, thief. Really, deeply, burns me right down to the hollow between my souls. You understand, don't you?"

Seven Skull Shield crossed his shivering and wet arms, head cocked. "And how would you have bet at the start? For or against the Red Wing?"

Crazy Frog's irritated expression leavened slightly. "All right. Against. Your Red Wing was making progress. He was listening, improving. Another week and I would have figured he *might* have a chance against the Natchez."

"So you'd have bet wrong."

"I *could have covered* if I'd been there!" He jabbed a hard finger at Seven Skull Shield. "You and the Red Wing owe me."

"You were paid to instruct him. And handsomely. Just because—"

"You really are a stone-headed lump of shit, aren't you?" Crazy Frog shook his head, eyes raised as if imploring the Sky World for understanding. "It's not the *winnings*, you idiot. It's that I didn't *get to see it*!"

Seven Skull Shield wondered if Crazy Frog was on the

verge of tears. "You have my word. When I see the Red Wing, I'll make rotted sure he understands your disappointment."

A sly smile hid behind Crazy Frog's normally uninspiring lips. "But everyone does know that I trained him. There's no little satisfaction in that."

"Since your man was expecting me, that means Flat Stone Pipe's runner was here?"

"He was." Crazy Frog laid the beaded mat to one side and pointed. "Over there, next to that big wooden box. Lift up the blanket."

Seven Skull Shield crossed the room, wincing at the muddy tracks he left. He reached down to lift the split-feather blanket.

"Been thinking about you," he told the huddled figure, then glanced back at Crazy Frog. "I know Flat Stone Pipe already gave you something in Trade. I'll add my own appreciation as soon as I can."

Then Seven Skull Shield bent down, grunting with the pain as he picked up Slick Rock's tightly bound body. Every muscle screaming, each joint and sinew aching, he tossed the wiggling man over his shoulder and turned.

"One down, two left to go." As he headed for the hanging, he said, "Give my love to your first wife."

Slick Rock was screaming into the cloth gag tied over his face as Seven Skull Shield stepped out into the rain and storm.

The Spirit Beasts understood retribution.

And so would Slick Rock.

Ninety-six

The dream was so vivid: Horn Lance was in the Temple of the Warriors in Chichen Itza. The bright red-and-black feathered-serpent columns cast bars of shadow as the late-afternoon sunlight slanted onto the polished stone floor. His leather helmet with its red macaw-feather crest felt almost too snug around his head. His skin had been painted black, and white armbands circled his biceps.

He grasped a naked man's ankles, could feel the man's warm bones and his racing pulse through the thin veil of skin. The victim was bent painfully backward over the low stone altar, his chest exposed, the skin stretched tightly across his ribs and stomach. The pelvis jutted up as if to make a mockery of his dangling penis and tight scrotum.

Horn Lance bore down, all of his weight keeping the man's feet pressed to the bloodstained limestone. The awkward and painful position deprived a sacrifice of leverage should he resist at the last instant. The tightly stretched torso would gape wide as the keen blade severed skin, muscle, and sinew.

To the victim's left, the black-painted priest raised a beautiful obsidian knife to the dying sun. Its rays shot through the dark volcanic glass: sparkles that danced and leaped with the slightest movement. Then, with a call to the Lords of Death, the priest turned in a Dance-like flourish of feathers. With practiced efficiency he drew the keen blade across the straining chest just below the ribs.

A terrified scream broke from the victim's throat, only to fall silent as his muscles and diaphragm were severed and his rib cage spread wide.

Horn Lance looked up, seeing the multicolored serpent as it gathered itself and rose from the blood-caked stone. Green-blue quetzal feathers bobbed above the creature's scaled head; the mouth gaped, and the tongue flickered between needle-sharp fangs.

Green eyes locked on Horn Lance's; the brilliantly colored serpent's head slipped sideways and down, the neck and body serpentine in movement. As the priest lifted the victim's sacrificial heart the snake's nostrils flared, and it inhaled the fresh scent of *itz*. The priest squeezed; blood spurted from the heart's severed arteries and veins to run down over the priest's fingers and trace patterns down his sinew-thick forearm.

"Dead Teeth!"

The call from another world pierced Horn Lance's dream. Afterimages spilled through his souls. He straightened from the sacrificial victim's ankles, looking down at the man's surprised face . . . and saw Thirteen Sacred Jaguar, his limp body bent backward over the sacrificial altar, his chest gaping, lungs deflated, to expose the hollow where his heart had been. Pooled crimson streaked the severed diaphragm, liver, and intestines.

Thirteen Sacred Jaguar? I was sacrificing my ahau*?*

"Dead Teeth!" the bellowing call from outside the palace door brought Horn Lance fully awake. Coming to in this world, he nevertheless had to clamp his eyes shut and viciously shake the memory of Thirteen Sacred Jaguar's dead face from his head.

What did it mean? I'd never allow my ahau *to be sacrificed.*

He forced himself to sit up, recognizing the palace, its walls unfamiliar, stripped as they were of the ornaments that had once hung there.

Around him, the Natchez were rolling out of their blankets, asking each other what was happening. Horn Lance didn't need to count to realize that maybe half of them were missing along with their bedding and personal possessions.

Fled in the night. The worthless Natchez trash!

"Dead Teeth!" the voice bellowed again. "I challenge you!"

Horn Lance rubbed a hand over his face, standing. A bright shaft of morning light slanted into the room and extended past the central hearth and the smoking remains of last night's fire.

Horn Lance yanked a breechcloth over his hips as he walked to the doorway and squinted into the morning.

A black silhouette stood between the guardian posts and cast a long shadow all the way to the veranda. Blazing light bathed its outline, as if the man were something ethereal beamed from sun to earth.

He held a shield and a wide-bladed copper-bitted ax; a leather-and-wood helmet encased the man's head, and his chest was blocky with body armor.

"Who are you? What do you want?" Horn Lance was vaguely aware of the wet scent of the morning, the rising mist, the pooled water on the mound top. The terrible storm had left no trace of its anger in the crystal morning.

"I am Fire Cat, of the Red Wing Clan, in the service of Lady Night Shadow Star, of the Four Winds Clan. I come to challenge Dead Teeth to ritual combat. Man against man. I fight for Piasa and Horned Serpent. He may fight for whatever impotent Power he chooses!"

"Are you brain-addled? You are a slave of the *ahau*'s. You are his, as is all the other property belonging to your lady."

"Then you had better send Dead Teeth out with his *mac-uahuitl* and shield to see if he can reclaim your lord's 'property.'"

As Fire Cat had talked, a crowd had been growing below the stairway. Every eye fixed on the Red Wing in his battle armor. The wide-bladed copper ax, Horn Lance realized, was one of the war trophies that had been hanging on the wall before Swirling Cloud's folly.

"Get in here!" Horn Lance snarled. "That's an order."

"On command from my lady, I am forbidden from following Itza directions. If Dead Teeth will not face me, he, like all the Itza, is a *coward*!"

Fire Cat turned. The morning sun shone on the three-forked eye design he'd painted on his face. Addressing the crowd, he bellowed, "The Itza are indeed cowards! They refuse individual combat! If they so fear a bound servant, they must tremble before a Four Winds warrior! Their *kukul* must be a fraud!"

A peal of laughter rose from the crowd.

Horn Lance turned, aware that the Natchez and Itza had crowded behind him to hear. Now they were murmuring darkly to each other. Suspicious glances shot Horn Lance's way to gauge his reaction.

He smiled as the end to one of his dilemmas became clear. Maybe his day with Wooden Doll hadn't cost him as much as he'd thought. "By the White Bone Snake's breath, I spent half the night wondering how to regain momentum after the Little Sun's defeat. We needed a way to discredit the Red Wing's victory, and the stupid fool walks right up and offers himself as a sacrificial victim."

Raising his voice, he shouted, "Dead Teeth! Get dressed. Take your *macuahuitl* out there and cut that fool's head off!"

But even as he uttered the words, he had to shake off the Dream image of Thirteen Sacred Jaguar's gaping chest, the blood, and the surprised death-rictus on the *ahau*'s face.

Ninety-seven

Careful. I've got to be eternally careful.

Fire Cat had never felt so alone. He was but one man. Nor was this chunkey with rules he'd understood since youth. This was combat against an unknown foe, wielding a weapon he'd seen used only once—and then with devastating and terrible effect.

Scenes from the destruction of the Cahokian warriors had haunted him the entire night. The blurred flash of the *macuahuitl*s, the deep slices in muscle and sinew that gaped like bloody magic in the wake of what seemed the slightest touch.

The nucleus of a plan had come to mind. The value of the incredible wealth stacked on the Keeper's veranda had barely registered as he sorted through the jewelry, ceramics, fabrics, and precious stone and copper. It was the weapons and armor that drew him. In the end he chose the copper-bitted ax that had once been on Night Shadow Star's wall. The shield he strapped to his arm was a large Plains design crafted of long-dried buffalo hide. Light and maneuverable. He kept his own shin guards of dried leather, but added knee-length buffalo chaps tanned with the hair on. They'd been Traded down from the far north above the freshwater seas. Now he pinned his hopes on the shaggy buffalo wool; but for his own relief, he'd spent a hand of time cutting out most of the inside seams to provide cooling ventilation.

While he had several choices of body armor, he kept his own cuirass and shoulder cups since they fit perfectly and wouldn't impede his movement.

Movement, he hoped, would be the key.

Either he'd spotted—and could exploit—a weakness, or he'd be dead within heartbeats.

"Dead Teeth!" he roared yet again.

Behind him, the old woman was climbing the steps with agonizing slowness, the thief's dog looking up anxiously at her side. The slight breeze tousled her wispy white hair. Her age-shriveled brown face puckered with the effort.

At that moment, Dead Teeth stepped out of the palace doorway. The Itza behind him were followed by the Natchez. Dead Teeth carried his thin shield, the bark-cased *macuahuitl* resting on his shoulder. He wore only a loincloth and kilt, while a feathered leather helmet conformed to his head. He was grinning, eyes alight as he nodded his head in challenge.

The hatred and rage over what Fire Cat had done to Swirling Cloud burned in the Natchez' eyes like hot fires. Fire Cat didn't need to speak Natchez to interpret their muttered imprecations and threats.

"I challenge the Itza warrior known as Dead Teeth to single combat! My life, or his! I wager all that I own. All that I won yesterday, against his meager belongings. Does the Itza accept?"

"He does," Horn Lance cried out gleefully.

The Itza warriors were slapping Dead Teeth on the back, almost dancing in anticipation.

Fire Cat's heart began to hammer. Cold fear played its familiar havoc, tight and liquid in his abdomen. The tickling charge of adrenaline toned his muscles. Nervous sweat turned his neck and sides clammy.

"Red Wing?" the old woman's reedy voice asked as she gained the top of the steps. "How are you doing?"

"Scared as a rabbit facing a cougar, Elder."

"You should be."

Due to whatever perversity infested his souls, the dire sincerity in her voice calmed him, brought a smile to his lips.

The *kukul* emerged from the doorway before Burning Ant lifted it high. Bright morning sun reflected from the dazzling yellow, red, black, and blue designs that decorated the exotic image. The thing's snarl was more vicious than ever, the green eyes blazing.

Yes, you know, don't you, War Serpent? This day is all about you and me.

The impossibility of Fire Cat's task hit home like a fist to the stomach. This was insanity.

"You can still back out, Red Wing," the old woman hissed from behind. "You could live a long life. I could ensure that for you."

"As a slave?"

"There are worse fates."

"If I give up now, Night Shadow Star's souls will not return from the Spirit World. Life without honor and Night Shadow Star is not worth living."

"As you will."

He felt the Tortoise Bundle as it was removed from the sack. A sudden airy energy ran through his charged muscles. Throwing his head back, he screamed, *"Hoookaaiiiyaaaa!"* and charged the Itza.

The Itza swung his *macuahuitl*, slinging the bark sheath straight at him as a diversion. The bark case hissed as it passed harmlessly over Fire Cat's shoulder.

The momentum of the swing allowed Fire Cat time to close before Dead Teeth unleashed a powerful backhanded swing. The warrior's eyes were wide, startled by Fire Cat's chunkey-toned speed. Nor did Dead Teeth have room to retreat without stumbling into the massed warriors behind him.

Fire Cat caught the blow on his shield, delighted that the hard-dried leather momentarily caught and held the razor-edged obsidian blades.

The tug it cost Dead Teeth to pull it loose was all Fire Cat needed. He slammed the war ax into the hollow of Dead Teeth's upper arm where the rounded shoulder muscle dipped under the bicep.

Dead Teeth screamed. Staggered back into his crowded companions and stared stupidly at his dangling left arm. The wound hung open like a hideous red smile; jets of blood shooting from arteries. Cut two-thirds of the way through, the bone severed, it flopped lifelessly.

In shock, Dead Teeth dropped to his knees and the *macuahuitl* slipped from the man's slack right hand.

"Back away!" Fire Cat ordered as the Itza crowded around the shocked Dead Teeth. "This isn't over!"

"It's over," Horn Lance snarled, shooting him a hard look.

"Then I challenge the Itza warrior known as Split Bone to individual combat! My life against his. All that I own against all that is his! Or is the Itza a coward?"

Fire Cat saw the moment Horn Lance finally understood. The man's eyes sharpened, his incredulous glance fixing momentarily on Fire Cat, then sliding off to the side where the growing crowd was filling every empty space on the avenue and around Night Shadow Star's palace. Word of the Red Wing's challenge was burning across Cahokia like wind-blown fire.

Horn Lance straightened, ignoring Shaking Earth and Red Copal as they pulled Dead Teeth's bleeding body up onto the veranda. The two were trying desperately to stanch the spurting blood. They would not succeed.

Horn Lance stepped forward, hands raised. "You don't have to do this, Red Wing. You don't have to die and lose everything. You can't take them all."

Fire Cat knew a brief moment of hope, realization that if he just reached out, grabbed this rope to salvation . . .

Night Shadow Star will die.

He thumped his chest. "I challenge Split Bone to single combat!"

Below him, a roar went up from the crowd. By the tens and twenties, they'd started to climb the sides of the Morning Star's sacred mound to get a better view. Doing so was a potential death penalty. That they'd risk it was proof of the crowd's passion.

"Very well, die, fool!" Horn Lance spit, bellowing an order to Split Bone. The warrior shot a fiery look at Fire Cat, then ran for his weapons.

"The rest will not be so easy," the old woman called from where she stood beside Piasa's statue, the Tortoise Bundle in her hand. The dog whined, tail sagging and ears down.

When Split Bone burst from the door, he came at a run, his *macuahuitl*'s obsidian-studded blade glittering in the sun.

Ninety-eight

Blue Heron was halfway through a bowl of Dancing Sky's reheated stew when the roar of the crowd finally penetrated her muzzy thoughts. She hadn't slept well and had risen late, only to discover that the old woman, Seven Skull Shield's dog, and the Red Wing were missing.

Smooth Pebble had been laying out her dress for the day when the swell of shouting voices finally goaded Blue Heron's curiosity.

Setting her bowl aside, she walked to the veranda, packed as it was with Fire Cat's winnings. She glanced south toward Night Shadow Star's mound and shaded her eyes against the rising sun. Were those *people* climbing the side of the Morning Star's mound? Nor was that the end of it. The entire base of Night Shadow Star's mound was a seething mass of humanity, with people even scrambling up the steep slope to hang just below the palace in the attempt to see something happening in the yard.

"Get my litter," she barked to the guards. "Phlegm and spit, there's a riot out there! Squadron First, alert the Men's House. Call them out. All of them!"

"Yes, Keeper!" The man touched his forehead before shouting orders to the warriors below.

Even as he did, a Bear Clan youth holding a messenger's staff pelted up her stairs, his eyes wide, breath tearing in and out of his lungs.

"Keeper! The *tonka'tzi* sent me. The Red Wing is fighting the Itza at Lady Night Shadow Star's palace. He's killed one, and is battling another!"

"He's *battling* the Itza?" She shook her head, trying to get her sleep-numb souls around the idea. "Piss and excrement, is the man a lunatic? Smooth Pebble, get my clothes. Get them now."

Her gaze stopped as it passed over Dancing Sky. The woman looked as if she'd just swallowed a prickly pear cactus. "Oh, all right. Just get the pots off the fire so they don't burn. Yes, he's your son, but he's also a pain in my gut."

Moments later she was hurrying down her stairs to her hastily brought litter. People were pouring in streams to join the crowd. Mud and maggots, if something happened to set them off, she might not survive the short trip.

What does that maniac think he's doing? He could kill us all!

Ninety-nine

Split Bone had learned from Dead Teeth's short and bitter experience. He'd used his first charge to gain the more open ground behind the guardian posts and now leaped and thrust with his *macuahuitl*.

For the moment, Fire Cat played it safe, saving his energy, letting Split Bone charge, leap, and sidestep—his movements almost a Dance. Each time Split Bone struck, Fire Cat skillfully blocked the *macuahuitl*'s keen edge with the oversized buffalo shield. Split Bone kept darting, feinting, and circling as he sought an opening. As he did, a sheen of perspiration coated the Itza's face. The man's breathing had started to labor.

In the background, the Itza shouted advice, their effort almost drowned by the screaming Natchez who shook fists and spit anytime Fire Cat got close.

If Horn Lance doesn't keep them back, this will all be over.

That was the desperate gamble. And so far, Horn Lance had kept it, shouting orders when the Natchez started to crowd the combatants. Each time he did, his gaze went to the throngs of people perched on the Morning Star's mound, the ones peering over the mound edge, and the ones clogging the avenue.

Yes, he knew his Cahokians well. And what it would mean to his tenuous position if his side cheated.

With each attack, Fire Cat had studied his opponent. Split Bone liked to thrust, and each time Fire Cat deflected it with the shield, the Itza tried to drop the point low, snapping it back in an attempt to slice Fire Cat's leg.

Again he tried, leaping forward, thrusting low. The instant he was fully extended, Fire Cat swung. Not at Split Bone, but at the *macuahuitl*. His weight behind it, the ax struck the flat of the blade and drove the *macuahuitl* down. When the ground stopped the tip short, the blade snapped in two with a crack.

Split Bone leaped back, eyes wide, holding his handle. Panting, he backed as Fire Cat advanced.

"Hold!" Horn Lance bellowed. "He is disarmed!"

"We didn't agree to that," Fire Cat returned.

Not that it mattered. One of the Natchez leaped from the crowd, offering Split Bone a war club.

"Foul!" Fire Cat declared.

"Live with it, slave. Call it new rules." Horn Lance crossed his arms.

Split Bone wasn't good with a war club. He made a novice's mistake, figuring the stone-headed club's mass gave him an advantage. With a desperate leap, fear bright in his eyes, he used both hands to swing. The club thumped into the shield, stinging Fire Cat's arm with its impact.

As the Itza staggered to recover, both arms extended, Fire Cat's copper blade sliced into his unprotected neck at the angle of the shoulder. The keen edge lodged briefly in the vertebrae. Fire Cat wrenched it free as Split Bone fell limply to the ground.

Even as the dying Itza warrior gasped and quivered, Fire Cat bellowed, "I challenge Shaking Earth to individual combat! My life against his. All that I own against all that is his! Is the Itza a coward, or will he face me?"

A howl—as if torn from a thousand wolves—went up

from the crowd as news of both his victory and challenge was passed.

Over the roar, Fire Cat barely heard Horn Lance turn to the Natchez and say, "Kill him. Now. Make it look like you just lost your heads."

Fire Cat, throat dry, watched the Natchez warriors glance back and forth. Deadly smiles crossed their lips, but only five of them started forward, hands clenching war clubs. Their eyes had an almost dazed look, like feral and trapped beasts.

"He's killing you," Fire Cat cried. "When it's all over, he'll give you up, say that he tried to stop you! You'll hang in the squares!"

But on they came, heads lowered, grinning in anticipation. . . .

One hundred

Holding the Bundle woman's hand, Night Shadow Star's heart tore as she watched Fire Cat face the Natchez. From the moment she and the woman had grasped hands and guided Fire Cat's chunkey lance, their entire concentration had been directed toward the fiery Power radiating from Waxaklahun Kan's presence in the kukul. Countering it was like a Spirit Dance. The southern god would recede, conserve its Power, then unleash it. It might be to strengthen one of the Itza warriors, or perhaps to slow Fire Cat, or confuse his thoughts at a critical instant.

The Bundle—for Night Shadow Star had no other name for the age-shifting figure she clung to—would draw on its Power; and from Piasa Night Shadow Star would somehow channel her own. Block and parry. They had neither the time nor energy for anything else. Cunning and crafty, the War Serpent kept her from aiding Fire Cat. Her fear for him continued to grow.

Each combat had been won through his superior skill as a warrior, but for how long? When would his remarkable string of luck run out? How long could she and the Bundle continue to stymie the War Serpent's ever-more-subtle at-

tempts to alter the combat as she and Bundle had managed to affect the chunkey match?

That victory had only come as a result of the War Serpent's surprise at their use of Power. Immediately thereafter, the southern god had stunned them with its rage, diverted only by Swirling Cloud's execution.

The entire rest of the night, she, Piasa, and the Bundle had been locked in a mortal combat. Time had ceased. She existed only in the eternal moment, her senses heightened, awaiting the next thrust, the next feint. Now the Natchez were slinking forward.

"What can we do?" Night Shadow Star asked in desperation.

"We can only hold the War Serpent back, Lady. All of us, Singing together, our Song rising from a thousand throats going back to the past."

"The Natchez will kill him!" Night Shadow Star cried. "He's outnumbered! This is treachery!"

"Nothing is ever certain," Piasa's cold voice whispered from the darkness around her. "But where, we must wonder, is the Sky World's Power in this? Or has your worldly counterpart tired of playing the game?"

"If the Morning Star no longer cares," Night Shadow Star whispered in defeat, "we are all lost."

One hundred one

So this was unjust defeat. He should have been used to treachery by now. One against five, his fate would be sealed the moment the Natchez rushed him. He would have laughed, bellowed his rage at the skies. So much gained, to be lost so foully.

"Hold!" the defiant order came from the head of the stairs behind Fire Cat.

The advancing Natchez stopped short, staring past Fire Cat. Then they seemed to slink back onto the veranda.

Fire Cat turned to see Five Fists as he strode uneasily past the guardian posts. The lop-jawed old warrior gave first Piasa and then Horned Serpent a sidelong glance, touching his forehead. Behind him came no less than ten warriors, dressed for battle.

At the last moment, Five Fists shot an uneasy glance at the Morning Star's high palace, where a single individual watched from the high bastion.

You'd better take an interest, Chunkey Boy. It's your hide I'm saving along with Night Shadow Star's.

Stepping up to Fire Cat's side, Five Fists glared at Horn Lance. "A challenge has been issued. The Morning Star values the sacred nature of individual combat. He would not see it profaned by foreign perfidy and cowardice. Keep your Natchez weasels back."

A shout went up from the crowd as the old warrior's words were passed from lip to lip.

Horn Lance inclined his head, eyes smoldering. "Thank you for backing me up on that, War Leader. Sometimes, in the heat of passion, men will do unconscionable things. Your presence is appreciated."

"That's a pus-dripping lie," Fire Cat muttered.

"I'll keep things fair, Red Wing." Five Fists gave him a disdainful twitch of the lips. "Don't know who's more offensive, you or them, but orders are orders."

"Your warm concern moves me."

Five Fists barely cracked a smile before he hesitated and asked, "How do you accomplish what our best warriors couldn't?"

"They are trained to fight as teams. Move fast and distract while another strikes from the side and retreats."

"I hope you kill them all . . . and die of your wounds later." And before Fire Cat could reply, he demanded, "Where is this Shaking Earth? Is he a coward?"

Fire Cat dropped into a crouch as Shaking Earth stepped down from the veranda porch, the man's face a mixed mask of grief, rage, and vengeance. He advanced from behind a low-held *macuahuitl*, his round shield with its black-and-red concentric circles high on his arm.

A glitter lay behind Horn Lance's eyes. His mouth worked. Behind him, the *kukul* glared in what seemed to be a growing malevolence.

Unlike the others, Shaking Earth didn't make any mistakes, took his time. When he finally struck, it was to nick Fire Cat's elbow, drawing blood.

"Careful, Red Wing," the old woman called where she stood in Piasa's shadow, the Tortoise Bundle in her hands. "This one is deadly."

Then, in a blur, Shaking Earth struck again, the *macuahuitl* jabbing like a serpent's tongue to vibrate along Fire Cat's left shin protector. The man smiled, seeming to have found a weakness. His next strike shaved hair from the bison chaps, but the thick wool kept the wicked edge from Fire Cat's leg.

On the veranda porch, Red Copal was calling instructions, to which Shaking Earth replied with a nod and smile. Then he began artfully, and slowly, backing Fire Cat toward the porch.

By Piasa's balls, what are they planning?

Fire Cat ducked and bobbed, trying to circle away, only to have to leap back each time Shaking Earth's *macuahuitl* flicked and darted.

Bit by bit, Fire Cat was being maneuvered into whatever position Red Copal and Shaking Earth had decided upon. And as soon as he was there, Fire Cat had no doubt that the end would come.

Shaking Earth's victorious smile was the giveaway. With no alternative, Fire Cat pulled his arm back. Threw the ax. Blade over handle, it cut through the air. Shaking Earth froze, what had been a smile now a rictus. From instinct he ducked his head at the last instant. The copper blade made a hollow *thock* as it stuck full in the top of Shaking Earth's head.

The man's knees buckled, and he seemed to crumple, his face smacking into the rain-damp clay. The impact popped the ax loose, and it flopped on its side.

Fire Cat wasted no time skipping away from any proximity to Red Copal. Sunlight glittered on a long chert blade held low by the man's side, and a look of cunning triumph faded to dismay as he stared at the dying body of his friend.

Fire Cat was drawing breath to issue his final challenge when Horn Lance, a timber of desperation in his voice, cried, "Red Copal challenges the slave Fire Cat to personal combat. One on one. All of his possessions, against those of Fire Cat. He challenges Fire Cat to face him, naked, ax to *macuahuitl*, with no shields, no armor! Does Fire Cat accept, or is he a coward?"

"Fire Cat accepts," he shouted back over the crowd. "And he raises the stakes. Fire Cat offers to fight for Cahokia. For Piasa, Horned Serpent, and the Morning Star. Does Red Copal fight for the Itza lord, Thirteen Sacred Jaguar?"

"He does," Horn Lance said, frowning.

Yes! The moment he'd been waiting for. "Then I wager all of my belongings, the winnings, my life, and honor against the *kukul*!"

Horn Lance's mouth worked. He shot a disbelieving glance at the standard. "You can't!"

"Are the Itza cowards?" Fire Cat bellowed with all of his might, his voice reaching the crowd. "Is the *kukul* Powerless? A *false* god brought here by men who do not believe in its Power?"

He pointed toward the guardian posts, shouting, "I believe in Piasa, in Horned Serpent! I believe in Old-Woman-Who-Never-Dies! Let the gods decide which is stronger! Wager!"

The shout from the crowd was deafening.

"Wager! Wager! Wager!"

Hands curled to fists, Horn Lance faced Red Copal, explaining. The Itza glanced at the *kukul*, then out at the crowd. His mouth worked, worried gaze fixing on Fire Cat, then going back to the *kukul*. Finally he nodded and began stripping off his clothing.

Fire Cat lowered his shield, untied the stays that held his body armor, and dropped the buffalo chaps. Stepping out of his breechcloth, he picked up his ax, only to watch the once-hafted blade drop free; the bindings had loosened when it stuck in the bone, and failed when Shaking Earth's head hit the ground.

Red Copal was already approaching, his muscular body lean and agile. The *macuahuitl* seemed to dance in his practiced hands.

"Hold!" Fire Cat shouted, backing away, the worthless ax handle in his hand.

Horn Lance stood grinning, his arms crossed, saying nothing.

"It's your precedent! Split Bone received a second weapon!"

"Let him rearm, Horn Lance," Five Fists growled. "That, or we'll take a hand in this."

From his expression, Horn Lance might have been chewing rancid meat. He barked something in Itza. Red Copal's eyes narrowed as he took another step forward. Horn Lance stepped out, voice sharp as he repeated the command. Red Copal, trembling with rage, stopped short. The man almost bounced on his toes with suppressed energy.

"Where's your weapon, Red Wing?" Five Fists asked from the sideline.

"There!" Fire Cat pointed. "That *macuahuitl*. It belonged to Shaking Earth. It's now mine. Spoils of combat."

Horn Lance was translating, a sudden animation in his eyes. Red Copal chattered something in reply, nodding in anticipation as he did so.

Fire Cat tossed the ax handle to the side, warily walking forward to retrieve the *macuahuitl*. Backing away, he tested the weapon's balance, finding it lighter than he'd thought.

Naked in the morning sunlight, Red Copal flexed his muscles; the serpent tattoos on his limbs writhed as if alive. Occasional scars lined the man's brown flesh. Long, white, and thin, they could have been nothing but old wounds inflicted by *macuahuitl*s.

He is an expert, and this is the first time I've laid a finger on the weapon. The cold realization sank in that he was about to die.

The mocking *kukul* seemed to radiate anticipation, its green glare cold and hungry.

Fire Cat could feel its Power. An electric tension crackled in the air as the Bundle and *kukul* seemed to flex and shimmer. A serpent's hiss sounded just at the edge of hearing, a cry of desperation fading beneath its sibilant triumph. In that instant, Fire Cat stood alone, vulnerable, and abandoned.

He's going to kill me now.

At that instant, an eagle screamed. People gasped, looked up, and pointed. The eagle perched on the high center pole of Night Shadow Star's roof, its talons gripping the thatch. Staring down, the big bird seemed to fix on the *kukul* and screamed its fury.

In that instant, Fire Cat felt the Bundle's liquid-warm touch, like the tips of feathers running along his skin.

"You have one chance." He heard the Tortoise Bundle's soft whisper between his souls. *"Speed and agility."*

Was that Night Shadow Star's voice?

"Learn. Watch him."

He'd been hearing the same thing from Crazy Frog for the last quarter-moon. Fire Cat backed and circled. Adjusting his grip to mirror Red Copal's, he tested the long wooden blade. Found it more supple. Each time he tentatively probed with the bitted blade, Red Copal instinctively shifted his edge from contact, as if protecting the glittering obsidian.

"He's learning your moves. Notice how each time he finds it easier to avoid your thrust? Soon he'll use that against you."

Red Copal's footwork was similar to that of a trained warrior wielding a war club. A smart man, however, would expect a surprise, some technique unique to the *macuahuitl*.

Red Copal feinted, lunged, and flicked his *macuahuitl* toward Fire Cat's calf. With a half skip, Fire Cat barely avoided being maimed; a thin trickle of blood welled where the skin had been sliced open.

He'd hardly recovered when Red Copal rushed in an attempt to press his advantage. Fire Cat vaulted to the side, escaping with shallow cuts from a graze on his hip.

Red Copal's predatory grin exposed the turquoise stones inset in his teeth as he stalked in pursuit.

"Now!"

Fire Cat lunged an instant before Red Copal. Splinters of obsidian exploded from the blades as Fire Cat batted Red Copal's weapon aside. Dropping a shoulder, he would have rammed the Itza, only to have the warrior skip back.

Off balance himself, Fire Cat barely had time to recover before Red Copal planted a leg, twisted, and swung viciously at Fire Cat's head.

Reflexes saved him as he parried, more obsidian shattering as the blades met. Fire Cat leaped back and crouched, finding his balance.

Red Copal was panting, sweat beading on his skin. He charged forward. Fire Cat ducked to the side, avoided the man's quick blade, and feinted. Red Copal took the bait; his blade cut empty air where Fire Cat would have been.

"Work him. He's soft."

Of course. Red Copal had been riding in canoes, not paddling them. He'd been sitting in palaces, not practicing. He hadn't been honed by endless chunkey, nor was he used to working himself into a sweat swinging a war club.

Fire Cat darted and ducked, feinting, skipping away, forcing Red Copal to follow, to retreat.

"Careful.

"Duck right.

"Duck left.

"Duck left."

Each time, Red Copal's blade would have laid him open.

Surrendering to the voice in his head, Fire Cat danced, turned, twisted, blocked a blow, or thrust.

"He protects his blade. You've seen the flinch each time the edges touch. That's his weakness."

Fire Cat lunged for Red Copal's blade, then jabbed at the man's flexed thigh as the Itza shifted his *macuahuitl* out of harm's way.

With a cry of delight, Red Copal seemed to cock his

wrists, the *macuahuitl,* like a thing alive, darting inside Fire Cat's guard. Despite Fire Cat's quick reflexes and better footwork, the Itza's angry obsidian opened skin along Fire Cat's ribs. A couple of fingers lower and it would have cut so deep his intestines would have spilled out.

"Time is now on his side."

Fire Cat swallowed hard, the damp sheeting of blood sticky and cooling on his side and hips. The cuts in his elbow, shin and left hip continued to bleed.

He'd missed Thirteen Sacred Jaguar's arrival on the porch, but now the Itza lord appeared stunned, alternately staring down at the bleeding corpses of his dead warriors to where Red Copal closed on Fire Cat.

Red Copal began singing in Itza, dancing and swinging his *macuahuitl.* A gleam filled his eyes, reflecting that of the *kukul* as it watched from atop its pole.

Fire Cat could feel the thing as it spun its Power and sent it to Red Copal. With blood in the air, the War Serpent sensed ultimate victory, gaining in presence.

"Hunch. Act weak."

Fire Cat bent, favoring his wounded side. For the first time, he became aware of the crowd. The roar had stilled, people fixed on the terrible drama unfolding before them.

Fire Cat knew an instant before Red Copal lunged: the flexing of the man's muscles, the anticipation in his eyes.

Fire Cat barely parried in time, but the Itza's *macuahuitl* laid open another gash, this time deep in Fire Cat's left thigh.

Singing high praise to Waxaklahun Kan, Red Copal vaulted back, recovering. Following his dance step, he twirled around, expression ecstatic.

"He's done this before. Lived this moment. He knows how you will react. What your weaknesses are. He's coming for the kill."

When Red Copal's muscles tensed, his excitement bursting,

Fire Cat launched, his feet in a chunkey player's start. Red Copal couldn't have anticipated the speed, the audacity.

With a Powerful blow, Fire Cat smacked the Itza's *macuahuitl* aside with a splintering of wood. This time he hurled himself into the Itza with a thud.

To his surprise, the man didn't go down, but staggered backward. Fire Cat pressed close, howling his Red Wing war cry into the man's stunned face. The cutting edge of the Itza's *macuahuitl* slipped along the side of his leg.

Choking up on the handle, Fire Cat pulled his *macuahuitl* back and as Red Copal pulled away, jabbed it at the man's gut.

To Fire Cat's surprise, most of his blade was gone. Only a long splinter of the reddish wood and a short length of obsidian edge remained.

"Finish it."

With all of his remaining strength, Fire Cat drove the splinter into Red Copal's belly just above the navel. Grunting, he lifted the Itza warrior's body off the ground, wood cracking loudly as the remaining razor edge sliced upward through the man's intestines.

Face to face, Fire Cat stared into Red Copal's incredulous eyes, felt and smelled his explosive exhale. Hot liquid and entrails burst from the Itza's wound, running down Fire Cat's belly, around his genitals, and down his legs to sting in the cuts. The Itza blinked, seeming to hang between worlds. His mouth worked—a fish's empty gasping after it was pulled from safe waters.

With a final crack the wood gave way, allowing Red Copal's gutted body to fall. The stench rolled up around Fire Cat.

Struggling for breath, his wounds bleeding and burning, Fire Cat tossed the ruined *macuahuitl*'s handle to the side.

He blinked at the crowd, seeing Blue Heron where she stood wide-eyed beside Five Fists. His mother and sisters flanked the Keeper. The old woman remained in Piasa's shadow, standing erect, eyes closed; ancient hands cradled the Tortoise Bundle. Seven Skull Shield's dog was watching him with those odd eyes. He could feel the Morning Star's distant gaze from the high palisade.

On the veranda, Horn Lance stood rigid, eyes wide, lips clamped in a hard line. Beside him, Thirteen Sacred Jaguar had fixed his shocked and disbelieving eyes on Red Copal's corpse. His hands reached out as if in supplication to an impossibility. Then they rose, recoiling as Fire Cat hobbled toward him. The man's expression twisted as if he were seeing a monster come to life.

Thirteen Sacred Jaguar might very well take Fire Cat—bleeding, limping, the contents and stench of Red Copal's guts dripping down his front—for one of the Lords of Death escaped from his fabled Xibalba.

As Fire Cat stepped up on the veranda porch, the remaining Natchez faded away. Fire Cat reached down, picking up Dead Teeth's *macuahuitl*. His bloody fingers wrapped around the grip, and he hefted the deadly weapon. Horn Lance and Thirteen Sacred Jaguar backed away, hands out as if to ward away evil.

"I won," Fire Cat rasped. He turned. Burning Ant held the *kukul*'s staff before him as if it were a protective shield. The man's face mirrored white terror.

Shifting the *macuahuitl* to his right hand, Fire Cat laid his left on the *kukul*'s pole. "Mine!"

But only when he raised the *macuahuitl* did Burning Ant relinquish the standard.

From on high, the eagle's victorious scream split the air, and the great bird dropped from the peak, gaining speed before leveling off and jetting across the yard. People ducked as the bird passed low over their heads then seemed to vanish into thin air.

A hollow wail burst from Thirteen Sacred Jaguar's

throat, and he dropped to his knees. Pain and terror—as if his souls were consumed by fire—reflected in his tormented and protruding eyes.

"Now," Fire Cat rasped, fighting to keep from wavering on his feet. "Where's my lady?"

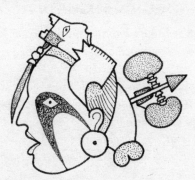

One hundred two

*T*he moment Fire Cat's fingers closed on the pole supporting the kukul, Waxaklahun Kan's brutal Power recoiled and withdrew.

"He is safe," Night Shadow Star cried with relief and sagged. She looked down where she held the ancient-looking crone's hand, and let go. As she did, the image of Fire Cat faded.

She felt rather than saw the Sky Eagle as it swooped down from her center pole, shedding its Power across her courtyard in defiance of the Piasa and Horned Serpent guardian posts at either side of her walk.

Piasa's angry hiss mixed with a cougar's rage as the Spirit Beast symbolically lifted a taloned foot and struck upward.

"If the Sky World hadn't sent the eagle when it did," Bundle—now in the form of a mature woman—reminded, "the Itza would have won. It broke the stalemate, allowed our Power to prevail."

An exhausted Night Shadow Star lowered herself to the soft mud, dropping her head into her hands. Sister Datura's strong arms tightened around her as if to suffocate her hopes and desires. She'd given everything. Poured the *essence of her souls into the shared vision with Bundle as Piasa whispered each of Red Copal's coming moves into her ear.*

I saved Fire Cat. Saved Cahokia.

"What is that worth to you, woman?" Snapping Turtle asked from where he'd burrowed into the mud, his hostile round eyes watching disdainfully.

"Anything," she whispered, exhausted and fading. "Everything."

"Your life for his?"

She couldn't summon the energy to shoot Snapping Turtle so much as a sidelong glance. "If that's what it takes to save him."

Pus and blood, she didn't want to go back. Not if it meant life with Thirteen Sacred Jaguar. In Bundle's shared vision she'd seen Fire Cat's mother and sisters in Blue Heron's company. Perhaps if Night Shadow Star were dead, the Keeper would take Fire Cat in. The man was already an overnight hero from the chunkey match. After besting the Itza warriors, he'd be legend. So popular he could dictate his own terms.

As long as he kept his mouth shut about the Morning Star and didn't precipitate his own assassination by one of the living god's agents.

If only she didn't feel so tired. "I don't care what happens to me," she said ever so softly, her souls starting to drift with Sister Datura.

"That exhausted sensation? That is your body dying back in your palace in Cahokia. For the moment, the Bundle is tying you to that last faint spark. If you choose to give up now, drift away, you will not awaken again," Piasa told her. "The Bundle will sever the last thread. Snapping Turtle will devour you as I once did, and you can float among the souls of the dead for eternity."

As if from a great distance, she heard the Bundle's voice say, "The War Serpent is only temporarily distracted. As long as the kukul exists in Cahokia, its terrible Power will continue to sow discontent and violence. You felt Waxakla-hun Kan's hunger. It feeds on blood and souls. It's weak, having only been nourished by the blood of our dead Cahokian warriors. Had it been strong, we would not have triumphed. But if it should seduce another Four Winds high chief? Perhaps Green Chunkey, War Duck, or one of the high-ranking Earth Clans chiefs? If it is allowed to strengthen, dispensing its favors to someone who feeds it ever more human beings, it will forever alter Cahokia."

"I am just so . . . tired," she whispered.

As the light began to fade into an eternal gray, she felt her chest expand, a familiar distant voice calling, "Lady? Come back to me."

"You know there is a price, Night Shadow Star," Piasa reminded. "If you heed his call, he can never go free."

One hundred three

Blue Heron stood in the doorway to Night Shadow Star's personal quarters, arms crossed. The frail-looking old woman sat at the head of Night Shadow Star's bed, her eyes closed, the Tortoise Bundle cradled in her bony hands. The crone's reedy voice rose and fell in some ancient song as she prayed for Night Shadow Star.

Blue Heron's niece lay on her back, a blanket covering her limp and cold body. Her face was slack, eyes more suggestive of a corpse's than a young woman's. Blue Heron had checked her for a pulse and found none. Nor had she seen so much as a hint of breath pass from Night Shadow Star's motionless lungs.

Only the old woman's assertion that her niece lived had kept Blue Heron from ordering the body carried to the Four Winds charnel house.

She turned, looking back into the main room.

Rides-the-Lightning was just finishing binding up Fire Cat's wounds. The old blind soul flier had unerringly stitched up the worst of the hideous and gaping cuts. At the same time two of his acolytes had reverently sponged the vile-smelling gore from the Red Wing's chest, belly, crotch, and legs.

Blood and guts everywhere. What a mess.

Thirteen Sacred Jaguar sat off to the side on one of the wall benches, gaze vacant. A man in a trance. His remaining companion, Burning Ant, knelt on the matting before him, speaking in low, reassuring tones.

The *ahau* didn't seem to be listening.

Outside, Five Fists and his men guarded the *kukul*. Other warriors were chasing spectators off the side of the Morning Star's great mound. The corpses of dead Itza warriors now littered the veranda porch. They'd have to be hauled off to be cremated. Who in their right mind would want lonely Itza souls harassing their clan ancestors in a charnel house? Patrols were ensuring that the jubilant crowd didn't let enthusiasm get the best of good sense.

And then there was . . .

She straightened. By Piasa's swinging balls, where was Horn Lance? Somehow, in the chaos following Fire Cat's victory, she'd forgotten to have her old nemesis placed under guard.

And she wanted him more than anything. Notched Cane had to be answered for, let alone what Horn Lance had intended for her. And then there was Seven Skull Shield. Deep down, she knew that whatever had befallen the thief, Horn Lance lay behind it. Once she had her one-time husband, she'd strip the man's intestines out of his body a finger-length at a time if that's what it took to find Seven Skull Shield.

She signaled War Claw where he stood by the door. "I don't care what you have to do, bring me Horn Lance."

The war leader touched his forehead, pointing to various warriors to accompany him as he hurried out.

Nor was a single Natchez left on the palace mound; the last of them had filtered away along with the crowd of spectators who'd dared to scale the slopes to see the combat.

"The Natchez? Let them go," she told herself. "And may each and every one survive the trip back to the Quigualtam Great Sun to tell the tale."

"Let me up." Fire Cat was trying to sit up.

"A moment, if you please. One last stitch." Rides-the-Lighting placed a bone-thin hand over the Red Wing's chest and pushed him down. "You have lost a lot of blood. You need to rest, heal, and drink tea. Good red meat is helpful to restore the—"

"Yes, yes." Fire Cat made a face as Rides-the-Lightning looped the last of the threads around the cactus thorns and pulled them tight to close the wound. The Red Wing barely swallowed a pained grunt.

"Expect the wounds to leak a little pus. I can't do anything about the scars."

Fire Cat ground his teeth, rolled to the side, and climbed unsteadily to his feet. Expression fixed in determination, he walked unsteadily to Night Shadow Star's door, one hand to his wounded side as if worried it would burst open. So much of his hide was stitched together he looked like he'd been assembled from parts.

"How is she?"

"Lost in the Spirit World." Blue Heron cast a glance at where the old woman continued to sing, the Bundle extended over Night Shadow Star's slack face.

"I know something that might help." Fire Cat started to shrug, only to gasp and grimace at the pain.

"Anything," Blue Heron told him.

The Red Wing eased past and lowered himself at Night Shadow Star's side. He bent down into a position that had to have pulled and shot fire through his wounds.

Blue Heron straightened in alarm, watched his chest swell. He placed his mouth over her niece's, pinching her nostrils. As he exhaled Night Shadow Star's lungs filled. When Fire Cat pulled away, breath purled from her slack lips.

Softly he whispered, "Lady? Come back to me."

Again Fire Cat took a breath, exhaling his soul into her body. And again. And again.

All the while the old woman sang, holding the Bundle against the top of Night Shadow Star's head.

For what seemed an eternity Blue Heron waited. Enough was enough. Dead was dead. The Red Wing was just fooling himself.

She stepped forward, hesitant to dash his hopes.

"Fire Cat," she whispered. "Sometimes, no matter how hard we hope, the souls just can't be . . ."

As if to mock her, Night Shadow Star sucked a breath of her own, chest rising in slow, deep breaths.

"Welcome back, Lady," Fire Cat said wearily. "It's been quite the time while you've been gone."

Night Shadow Star's eyes flickered, and she clamped them tight as if they hurt. After swallowing dryly, she said, "We came so close to losing, Fire Cat. The Waxaklahun Kan . . . I've never known such Power," she whispered. "We came so very close. You have no idea."

Fire Cat smiled. "But we won, Lady."

"What are you talking about?" Blue Heron demanded. "Pus and blood, Niece. Do I have to have you watched day and night to keep you out of the datura?"

"It was the Bundle, Aunt. It let me talk to Fire Cat. Warn him at the last instant. The War Serpent thought us weak and foolish. To it we were simple barbarians. It didn't understand."

"And where is the War Serpent now?" Blue Heron asked.

"Sulking in the *kukul.*" Night Shadow Star stared up at Fire Cat. "You know what to do?"

He nodded.

She placed a weak hand on his bare arm. "Don't let my husband interfere. We're not out of this yet."

"Of course, Lady."

"Good. Someone find a leather bag. A large one." She sat up, swayed, one hand to her stomach. Fire Cat scrambled for a ceramic pot and held it as Night Shadow Star's body was racked by dry heaves. When she recovered, her expression mirrored abject misery.

"Get my litter." Night Shadow Star turned then, staring into the old woman's fiery brown eyes. "And order a litter for the priestess Lichen, too."

At the name, Blue Heron's jaw dropped.

One hundred four

From his position in the crowd, Horn Lance watched in horror as the *kukul* was carried up the great staircase to the Morning Star's palace. The totem stood out, its bright colors radiant in the sunlight. The old lop-jawed warrior carrying it seemed wary, trying to hold the serpent carving with its bobbing feathers as far from his body as he could.

Smart man.

Behind him a litter bore Night Shadow Star. Then came another bearing an old woman followed by a dog. Blue Heron and the limping Red Wing climbed next, followed by a detachment of warriors and a collection of nobles.

They're taking their trophy to the Morning Star.

The impact of that hit him—the spiritual equivalent to a hard fist driven into his wind.

A swimming sensation left him half-staggered as the crowd pressed and surged around him. Did his barbaric countrymen understand the import of what they were doing? The *kukul* was everything: world, Power, status, and glory. The visual presence of the Spirit World in this profane existence.

The history books of the Maya were filled with stories of warrior kings losing their standards. How the legendary ruler of Copan, *Ahau* Eighteen Rabbit, lost his standard and was captured and sacrificed by *Ahau* Cauac Sky of Quirigua. As was Palenque's *ahau,* Kan Xul, when he was captured and sacrificed by his rival at Tonina, or when Tikal's Ah Cacau raided Calakmul and captured its ruler Jaguar Paw. The stories were the same whether told of Copan, Yaxchilan, Uaxactun, or even Tikal's ruler Double Bird capturing Caracol's Lord Water. In all cases, once the standard had been seized, the defeated *ahau* simply laid down his arms and surrendered to the inevitable.

I am watching that now. The slave has taken the kukul. *He now wields that great Power. We are done. Finished.*

He pressed a hand to his stomach, appalled at the gutted emptiness inside.

No sense in trying to rescue Oxlajun Chul Balam. He'd have already given up, surrendered to the only path left him by the War Serpent's desertion.

Horn Lance turned, walking aimlessly through the festive crowd. He hated them. Hated them all.

They would be searching for him now. If Blue Heron found him first, he'd hang in a square—and these selfsame barbaric fools would strip the skin from his body, slice bits of bleeding muscle from his bones, and thrust fiery torches between his legs to sear his penis and testicles into charred soot.

How then, ch'ak payal, *are you going to hurt them in return?*

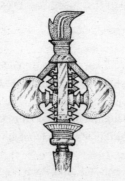

One hundred five

The sweetened tea she had drunk during her ride to the top of the Morning Star's mound eased the pain and nausea in Night Shadow Star's belly. She hurriedly washed down the last of the walnut-rich acorn bread she'd been given. Though still weak and unsteady—and with a stabbing headache—she felt remarkably good given this latest brush with death.

Afterimages of the Underworld and the desperate conflict with the War Serpent would haunt her for the rest of her life. The *kukul*'s smoldering Power still radiated from the carved effigy like heat from a white-hot rock. She glanced down at the large leather bag folded in her lap and then back at old Lichen, who rode in a litter behind her.

Who would have thought? Such an old enemy appearing as if by magic in her moment of greatest need? Cahokia's greatest need?

The Tortoise Bundle's presence was almost tangible, as if the threads that bound her to the Bundle's Power could be grasped by the hand and stroked.

So many voices—old voices—whispered just below the threshold of her hearing.

"Do you understand?" Piasa asked from behind her right ear.

She turned her head, catching a flicker as he vanished in the hot sunlight.

"Of course, Lord. I am sinking even deeper into the Spirit World. Like drowning in swamp muck, the harder I fight, the faster I am dragged down."

Disembodied laughter sounded from the air around her. Sister Datura's fading caress lingered like lines crisscrossing her souls.

She closed her eyes, taking a deep breath as she was carried through the high palace gates. To find herself, she concentrated on Fire Cat, the way his breath and souls had once again filled her lungs, swelling them with life.

The memory of his body leaning over hers, his mouth fitted against her lips, conjured an erotic tingle deep in her loins.

"He can never leave your service. That is the price of his life."

"I know."

She swiveled on the litter as she was borne past the lightning-scarred World Tree and glanced back to where Fire Cat limped along beside Blue Heron. As his eyes met hers, he smiled, belying the pain that had to scream from every cut.

Her souls seemed to melt into a warm reassurance.

He could never know the depth of her feelings for him. Were he to find out, it would destroy them both.

"Am I strong enough to make that promise?"

Unsure, she watched the *kukul* through slitted eyes. Five Fists hesitantly let it droop as he waited beside the intricately carved reliefs in the Morning Star's door.

As soon as her porters had lowered her litter, Night Shadow Star climbed wearily to her feet. Fire Cat hobbled up to help. She waved him off, granting him a conspiratorial smile. "You forgot your armor."

"Will I need it, Lady?"

"For at least this day, Red Wing, the Morning Star and I

find ourselves with allied interests. But please, see to Lichen if you would."

He considered the old woman being lifted from her litter, and shivered. "It's like a legend come alive. I still can't believe it's her."

"For a while longer." She girded herself as she picked up the large leather sack. Fragments of the Spirit Dreams conjured by Thirteen Sacred Jaguar's potions clung to her souls like old spiderweb. The world seemed to shimmer in aftereffect, the Waxaklahun Kan's angry spirit imparting a violet-and-yellow haze to the carved and painted image it inhabited.

"Yes, it knows. It awaits the moment of its release with a promise of unrestrained mayhem."

"Are you with us, Lord?" she asked Piasa.

"For the moment. My master's attentions are elsewhere."

"You will have to act at exactly the right instant."

"I know the danger better than you. Waxaklahun Kan is a Sky Being."

She led the way into the Morning Star's palace, surprised that her eyes, so recently in the Underworld, didn't need to adjust from the bright sunlight outside.

As she'd anticipated, the Morning Star sat on his altar, his dress immaculate. He studied her through knowing dark eyes surrounded by the two-forked pattern that was his calling. She could feel the three-forked design glow to life around her own eyes, though she'd not taken the time to paint it. Was it really there, visible to him, or did the lingering Dream visions in her bloodstream trick her into believing it?

She gestured, and Five Fists entered, the *kukul* held low so the terrible serpent stared at the matting with its enraged green eyes.

Fire Cat led Lichen in, holding the old woman steady on her sticklike legs. It might have been a trick of the light—the flicker of the leaping flames in the eternal fire that burned brightly in the central hearth—but for an instant Lichen looked just like Old-Woman-Who-Never-Dies. From her parchment-wrinkled face to the bone-thin arms and swollen joints of her fingers, she might have been the image Night Shadow Star had seen seated on the green-moss dais with its interwoven tie snakes.

Lichen seemed to steady as she clasped the Tortoise Bundle to her chest; First Woman's Power radiated from her eyes as she glanced Night Shadow Star's way and smiled toothlessly as if in acknowledgment.

Blue Heron and the *tonka'tzi,* with an escort of warriors, took positions in the back of the room.

The Morning Star sat regally, back straight, head erect with a soul-bundle box tied into his tightly coiled hair. He fixed his gaze on Night Shadow Star's. "Are the Spirits of the Underworld satisfied?"

"For the most part, Lord. One last thing remains to be taken care of." She turned. "Red Wing, take the *kukul* from War Leader Five Fists if you would." She handed Five Fists the sack. "Face the *kukul* at the floor so it can't see what's happening. Then have the war leader encase it in the sack."

She felt the War Serpent's rage quiet as Fire Cat, the man who'd taken it in combat, laid hands on the staff.

Five Fists was no one's fool. With a single deft motion, he slipped the heavy leather bag over the foreign Spirit Beast's head, blinding the angry green eyes.

With a trembling arm, she pointed at the fire. "Fire Cat, burn it."

He gave her a quick questioning glance, then lowered the covered totem into the snapping and crackling fire. As it dropped into the flames, Fire Cat cried out, letting loose of the staff as it if were searing hot. Jumping back, he worked his fingers the way he would if they were coated by some sticky substance.

Night Shadow Star staggered at the earth-shattering scream. Clapping hands to her head, she winced. On his high litter, the Morning Star hunched forward, his head cocked as if in searing pain. The human-head shell ear coverings seemed to grimace under the assault.

A gout of yellow flame shot up from the burning effigy. It seemed to curl, twisting into the shape of a mythical snake. The head-like tongues of flame snapped this way and that, in the manner of a striking serpent.

An instant later, smoke, in the shape of a winged panther, curled up and wrapped around it. At the same time, a cat-like wail devoured the deafening scream. Then whirling flame and smoke grayed into invisibility and vanished.

In the ensuing silence, Night Shadow Star lowered her hands, still fearful of a resumption of the scream. The Morning Star gasped in relief, straightening.

The fire now burned normally, crackled and spit sparks as it consumed the leather and ate into the *kukul*'s carved wood.

Night Shadow Star's gaze turned to Lichen. The old woman had crumpled to the matting, eyes dazed. She sat up slowly, jaw rocking as if she were clearing her hearing. Fire Cat bent to help her.

"Bring the priestess to me," the Morning Star ordered.

"No." Lichen's expression pinched, her eyes uncommonly dim.

"Very well," the Morning Star said easily. "War Leader, bring me the Bundle the old woman holds."

As if with a final effort, Lichen pushed to her feet and faced the Morning Star. "I told you only that I would bring the Tortoise Bundle to your House. It is time for another to take responsibility for the Bundle."

"You force me to—"

Lichen extended a trembling arm. "I was once asked, 'Would you give up, or would you fly for your people?' If part of you can remember that, you'll remember my answer . . . and what transpired as a result. The Bundle has found another, my wings are outspread, and the Dance awaits me."

"Do *not* cross me, Priestess, or I—"

"You'll *do* nothing! Not as you are now, bound by mortal flesh." The mass of wrinkles realigned into a mirthful grimace. "Where are your Dancers? Where's your beak, Bird Man? I dare you to reach out with your talons, locked as you are in that pitiful body. You and I both know the truth of this existence of yours."

The Morning Star partially rose, his hand outstretched. "It has to come to me, here, where it once—"

The old woman turned, her eyes burning and alive as she thrust the Bundle into Night Shadow Star's arms. "For the moment it has chosen you, daughter of the Underworld."

Night Shadow Star's flesh seemed to curl on contact with the Bundle. A thousand voices chattered at the edge of her hearing.

"Me?" she asked as she stared down at the charred and scuffed leather. Was it the aftereffects of Sister Datura and the Itza's Spirit plants, or did a golden glow suffuse the ancient leather?

Lichen's voice was almost a whisper. "You have her soul."

"Whose soul?"

"After she left with Badgertail, things just weren't the . . ."

The old woman's eyes went dull and fixed. Her relieved smile exposed pink gums and tongue. A rattling gasp uttered from deep in her throat. Fire Cat leaped forward and caught her as she collapsed. He eased her to the floor.

The thief's bearlike mongrel let out a low and mournful howl. The beast turned, shot away, and bolted out the door at a full run as if desperate to escape.

"Pus and blood," Fire Cat whispered, looking up to meet Night Shadow Star's eyes. "She's dead."

"Carry her to Rides-the-Lighting," the Morning Star ordered wearily as he stopped beside them and stared sadly down. To Night Shadow Star he said, "Out of appreciation I would have spared you the burden. But you have the Bundle now." A bitter smile turned his lips. "My deepest sympathies."

She ran her hands over the Bundle, feeling its Power.

"Are we finished here, Sky Lord?"

He considered her through pensive and gleaming brown eyes, a thousand thoughts and emotions reflected in his deep gaze. "For the moment the city is safe, the Power is balanced."

"For the moment," she agreed. The Bundle's thousand voices, like the hiss of insects, rose in warning. "It won't last." She paused. "Not for the city. Not for the two of us."

"No," he told her darkly. "It won't."

"Come, Red Wing," she snapped, turning on her heel. "A storm is rising in the distant south, and the scent of blood is on the wind."

Fire Cat limping along behind, she cast one last glance at the Morning Star. He stood as if frozen, a satisfied smile on his lips as he watched the Itzan effigy burn.

You knew how it would end all along, didn't you?

One hundred six

Mud and maggots, when would the world cease to cough up insanity? Blue Heron had been taking a report from one of her spies. Apparently some locally known rascal and suspected murderer—a man called Slick Rock—had been found that morning tied upside down from one of the River Mounds City guardian posts. Not only was it sacrilege, but the man's neck had been broken. To add to the gruesome effect, he'd been hung naked, and by the left foot, from one of the outstretched eagle's feet. The manner of the binding left his corpse dangling in the most unnatural and humiliating of positions. Speculation was running rampant about what it might mean.

Blue Heron had been pondering just that question when Night Shadow Star's runner had burst in, demanding she come at once to the lady's palace.

Now Blue Heron stared up at another hanging body—this one in the usual position. Apparently Burning Ant had tied the rope off to the rafter; and from the thick knot on the back of the Itza's neck, that, too, had been Burning Ant's handiwork. After pulling the box away from the Itza's feet, he might have given the *ahau* a sharp tug to break his neck rather than let his lord dangle and strangle. But he hadn't.

"It's apparently an action taken in response to a massive failure." Night Shadow Star stood to one side, stroking the Tortoise Bundle as if it were a puppy. "I heard Horn Lance explaining it to Swirling Cloud one night before the Spirit plants loosened my souls. According to the story, Thirteen Sacred Jaguar's uncle hung himself when my late husband was only a boy. Apparently after an unsuccessful raid on a neighboring city to capture prisoners for ritual sacrifice."

Where he hung against the wall, Thirteen Sacred Jaguar's body might have been a macabre decoration. His head was canted at an unnatural angle; purple and swollen, the man's tongue protruded obscenely between his lips. Normally bugged out, the eyes were even more gruesome now, wide-popping and death-grayed as if in disbelief.

Both his bladder and anus had let go, staining his legs, and his belly had distended in a grotesque mockery of the fit man he'd been.

Someone, probably Burning Ant, had thrown all the Itza's belongings into the fire; the remains of the gorgeous mask and quetzal cape were now but smoking ash.

For his part, Burning Ant had seated himself before his master and used an obsidian blade to open the veins of both wrists. The pool of red-black blood was now drying on the new matting.

"You found him just like this upon your return from the Morning Star's palace?"

"He ordered the staff out, told them to leave and never come back. They were waiting for me at the base of the grand staircase when Fire Cat and I came down. We found him like this."

"The key was the *kukul*," Fire Cat told Blue Heron where he sat to the side, trying to ease the strain on his wounds. "If I could just win it away, it would break his spirit. I didn't think it would be this quick."

Blue Heron shot a look back at War Claw where the war

leader and his warriors hovered uneasily in the doorway. "Cut him down. Carry him and the standard bearer out beyond the city and burn them with the rest."

She stepped back as the warriors surged forward to comply. Leaning close to Night Shadow Star, she indicated Fire Cat and whispered, "It seems we owe the Red Wing a great deal between chunkey, killing Itza, and laying claim to the *kukul*. Because of his winnings, you're now the richest woman in Cahokia. By the way, please send a party over to pack all that clutter off of my veranda. Seems that in the process you've ended up single again. Which, if I recall correctly, you planned all along. You going to do anything about it?"

Night Shadow Star's expression hardened, her eyes narrowing. "The Red Wing is bound to me. He remains that way."

At the hard tone in her voice, Fire Cat winced; then a weary smile bent his lips, as if everything were perfectly acceptable.

"You're lunatics. The two of you." Blue Heron turned, stomping out in to the daylight, headed home. "Well, who am I to care?"

Maybe she could get a full night's sleep before she tackled the distasteful task of finding Seven Skull Shield's body and whichever scoundrels had murdered him. She'd even sent a runner to Wooden Doll, who claimed not to have seen him for days.

To Blue Heron's surprise she realized that when she finally found his remains, it was going to wound her right to the quick of her souls.

One hundred seven

Long past midnight Horn Lance crept up the steep slope behind Blue Heron's palace. On bare feet he eased forward, one hand tracing the plaster, the other clutching a war club. His left arm ached, and he'd barely been up to the struggle; nevertheless, he'd managed to strangle the hapless Four Winds Clan warrior guarding the rear of the mound. Horn Lance had used an old piece of rope, then stole the guard's clothing and weapon after quietly lowering the body to the ground.

Taking a deep breath, he sniffed at the southerly breeze, smelling smoke, humans, thatch, and the ever-present humid tang of mud and wetlands. Cahokia's soul lay in the river, in the curving lakes along old channels, and her wet, rich, and fertile soil. Those were the true wealth and source of her strength.

He understood it viscerally—and perhaps in a way the Cahokians themselves didn't. Nor could they until they'd stood in his sandals at old Tikal, at Yaxchilan, and Dzibilchaltun.

But even with that hard-gained knowledge, he'd underestimated Cahokia. Dazzled by the mighty Mayan stone monuments, the elevated *sacbeob*, the sprawling cities and the gaudy costumes of their rulers, he hadn't understood Cahokia's resilient underlying bone and muscle.

The Itza—and all the legendary Nations of Maya before them—existed on a foundation built from their ancestors' bones. Their world and its gods were prescribed and uncompromising. The holy books, the *jun*, dictated the meets and bounds of belief as exactly as the sacred surveyors with their strings, sighting devices, and leveling pots measured land and space. Death, suffering, and blood—as recounted in the *jun*—balanced joy, happiness, and prosperity. The formula was rigid and fatalistic. One lacking in imagination and hope. Stagnant.

In Cahokia he had briefly known a fresh and liberating sense of wonder. Did it matter if the Morning Star were really the incarnate soul of the mythical Hero Twin from the Beginning Times? Or was he merely Chunkey Boy playing a pretend role, as the *ahau* had concluded to his own satisfaction?

What mattered was that the people marveled as they built their city. They Dreamed, and hoped, and played chunkey. All of them. Not just the high lords' groomed players in their elite subterranean Mayan ball courts. Nor were Cahokians slave to the perpetual ritual warfare he'd grown accustomed to. What a relief to be free of the constant anxiety that came with each cycle of raiding for sacrificial captives. Gone were the worries that not enough bodies had been accumulated, not enough souls dispatched, not enough *itz* or *ch'ulel* offered—each measure of blood accurately counted and credited against the desperate hope for a bit of joy, relief, and contentment.

He checked the heft and balance of the dead guard's war club. It would do. He needed only to sneak past the guard out front, charge in, and make it to Blue Heron's door. Despite the stiff pain in his arm and shoulder joints, he could do that. Even if he didn't kill her in the darkness of her bed, he'd break enough bones, cripple her with pain. And that might be the better outcome. She'd have plenty of time to live with what he'd done to her.

He rounded the stuccoed corner, peering through the night. A warrior slumped with his back to the wall, head down. Even from where he stood, Horn Lance could hear the man's deep breathing.

On cat feet, Horn Lance eased past the sentry, lifted the plank door quietly to one side, and crept into the great room.

The glowing coals in the fire pit barely illuminated the room. The door to Blue Heron's personal quarters would be through that black square in the rear wall.

He stopped short, halfway across the mat-covered floor. Was that a low growl shushed by human lips?

He glanced warily around, war club at the ready. Nothing moved among the shadows cast by the faint reddish glow. Anyone looking up would see the familiar silhouette of one of Blue Heron's guards.

Reassured by the silence, he hurried forward.

The clack of a kicked pot warned him. Spinning, he raised the war club, striking out at the dark form rushing toward him.

The club smacked flesh, eliciting a grunt.

Horn Lance ducked and evaded the grasping hands. Wheeling, he slammed the club into the assailant's side. The shadowy figure bellowed in pain, then roared, "You piece of *maggot meat*! Hit me? Sneak into the Keeper's in the middle of the night? You *pus-dripping penis*! Gonna grab you! Gonna *rip your balls off*! You piece of *shit-chewing, piss-drinking*—"

Horn Lance backhanded the club into the man's middle. The big man's breath exploded from his lungs, and he bent double, trapping the war club. The handle was ripped out of Horn Lance's grip.

Whirling, he turned and ran, only to have a dog land on his back. The impact knocked him to the floor. The beast had sunk its teeth into the stolen warrior's cloak. As the dog's full weight came to bear, the beast tore the cloak from Horn Lance's shoulders, growling and savaging the fabric.

Freed, Horn Lance scrambled to his feet. Fueled by panic and terror, he was out, pounding down the walk past the eagle guardians.

"The Keeper is attacked!" he cried. "Quickly! A big man and a dog! They're going to kill her!"

Somehow he made it down the steps without breaking his neck, and as the guard pounded up in his wake, he was running for all that he was worth.

But where to? What sanctuary could he find now?

A slow smile bent his lips. Of course. But just for a day or two until the furor died. And then he'd have to be gone. Downriver. Perhaps to the Natchez. There at least, he could be an advisor, a valued and honored man.

All Cahokia now promised was a slow and agonizing death in a square.

One hundred eight

"Did you miss me, Keeper?" Seven Skull Shield asked as Smooth Pebble inspected the darkening bruise on the meaty part of his forearm. Given how he could rotate his wrist and flex his fingers, neither of the bones had broken.

"Miss you?" Blue Heron snorted where she sat on the sleeping bench beside him. "Spit and piss, thief, we've had enough troubles while you've been off slipping into married women's beds."

"Is *that* where you think I've been?"

"What else would occupy you?"

"By Piasa's swinging balls, Keeper, I've been saving Cahokia! I had to get the Red Wing to Crazy Frog, so he could figure out what was afoul in his chunkey game, so he could beat that Natchez filth. I got sold out by a woman. Betrayed. Grabbed by a bit of walking scum named Slick Rock and—"

"The man hanging from the eagle guardian post overlooking the Avenue of the Sun outside River Mounds City?"

"Well, what do you expect? I can't have just any walking piece of vermin think he can whack me in the head and haul me off. I have a reputation to maintain. And there's still *two* left that I have to deal with. Horn Lance was next on the list.

I'd have seen to it sooner, but I got hung in a square over-night. That's where all these scabs on my wrists came from."

"Who hung you in a square, and why?"

"Um, it was payback for a good deed. And I had to be hanging there so Horn Lance could haul off and kick me smack in the old pride-and-joys, if you know what I mean. Otherwise, he'd have known it was a farce."

"A farce? Hanging in a square is a farce?"

"Isn't that how everyone gets paid back for doing a good deed?"

"But you got free?"

"That was the payback part." He narrowed his eyes, add-ing, "Like I said, some things I just can't let go. Like being kicked in the tenders, or allowing bits of slimy worm shit to poison my friends. I promised that before I dealt with that rascally woman I'd pound your husband into bloody mush."

"*Ex*-husband."

"Ex-husband. By the time I got here today, you all were up burning the War Serpent. There was no sign of Horn Lance. So I made myself look ordinary in the crowd, and started searching." He pointed a finger. "Horn Lance, Keeper, is just not the kind to let a thing go. And he hates you. So I knew it was just a matter of time."

He reached down, petting the dog's ears. "So I'm search-ing for the weasel, and people in the crowd start talking and pointing. I look up and see the dog here, racing down the grand staircase."

"So you went to meet it?"

"He found me. Sniffing through the crowd, you see. So I had to get thin for a while. Horn Lance would have known it was my dog. But your old husband, he was canny. When I heard the Itza had hung himself, I knew Horn Lance had nothing left. He'd be coming to settle with you, and he'd be seething."

"So you snuck into my palace?"

Seven Skull Shield gasped as Smooth Pebble prodded his

ribs. "Easy. Ah, pus in buckets that hurts! That's where he hit me with the club."

"It's bruising," the berdache told him. "That's going to be a beautiful black and blue tomorrow, but I don't think any ribs are broken."

"Looks like you got the worst of it," Blue Heron told him, a look of disappointment barely veiled. "Wish you could have kept him occupied until the guards could have grabbed him. They're mad enough to spit flint because he tricked them. That was Brittle Feather's cloak the dog ripped from his back. They found Brittle Feather's body, strangled, out back." She glanced away, shaking her head. "Another one we owe him for."

"It was a pot I kicked," Seven Skull Shield grumbled. "I was tired, Keeper. Been a couple of days without sleep. I was clumsy, and he heard me coming."

She nodded, reaching out and laying a comforting hand on his shoulder. "It's all right, thief. I'm just glad to have you back."

"What if he gets away?" Seven Skull Shield asked. "He might, you know. Cahokia's a big place."

"Oh, it is. But don't you worry. As big as Cahokia is, I have even bigger ears. And you never know. He might just fall into one of the traps I've set."

She stood, a fondness and relief behind her normally crafty expression. "Now, it's the middle of the night. Get some sleep, thief. Fire Cat's mother and sisters will have a fine breakfast waiting for us."

She took a step toward her personal quarters, only to turn and jab a finger. "But if that dog pisses on the floor again, he's stew!"

One hundred nine

Leave us!" Night Shadow Star commanded as she stepped
out of her personal quarters. She wore a clinging black dress
that was pinned over her left shoulder. Her hair hung free to
her buttocks and gleamed blue in the morning light.

Her household staff was busy replacing the trophies
Swirling Cloud had taken down, hanging them in their traditional places on the plastered wall above the sleeping
benches. The rest of the wealth was piled in heaps just inside the door.

"Red Wing, stay if you would," she added as he stepped
down from positioning an old Quiz Quiz war shield taken
during a great uncle's raid.

Fire Cat eased himself down, careful of the stitches
holding his wounded hide together. He made a face as he
straightened.

Clay String led the others out, casting one last look to
ensure the palace was empty.

Night Shadow Star's gaze ran over the piles of blankets;
jars of food and oil; wooden boxes, many of them inlaid, full
of every manner of possession. It had all been stacked on
the bare clay floor with its imprint of the now-missing mat.
She'd had them rip it out last night and toss it down to the

Avenue of the Sun. As she'd expected, it had been carted off by parties unknown—but welcome to it, fouled as it was by Natchez stink and Itza blood.

"Lady?" Fire Cat asked, rubbing his hands to clean the dust as he met her eyes. "Did you sleep well?"

"For the first time in a moon. I awakened clear-headed and refreshed." She gestured toward the door. "From what I've overheard this morning, Clay String, Winter Leaf, and the rest are delighted to have you running the household again." She gave him a lazy smile. "You've become their hero."

He tried to hide a sly grin. "It would appear that in their eyes even being second choice after an Itza lord is improvement."

She laid a hand on his muscular shoulder; just the touch of his warm and tanned skin kindled a desire in her breast. She met his level gaze, heart skipping. "You have become the hero of all Cahokia."

"It will fade with time, Lady. All things do."

She could feel him trembling, read the pain and desperation he tried so hard to hide behind that steady brown gaze. "Fire Cat, defeating the Itza came at a price. Piasa asked me to choose between your freedom and Cahokia. I . . . chose the city."

He nodded. "As you should have, Lady. Anything else?"

"Isn't that enough?" She felt the tearing within her. "I needed you to know that I would have chosen differently had there been any other—"

"Lady," he said gently as he placed his own hand on her shoulder, a tremble running through her at his touch. "If that's the choice Power gave us, I would rather live bound to you, emptying your chamber pot and carrying your water, than be high chief of Red Wing Town. The things I did? Swirling Cloud? The Itza warriors? They were not for Cahokia. They were for you."

At the love in his eyes, the passion in his voice, her soul

twisted, exploded. A frantic relief and terrible fear churned inside her.

"What do we do?" she whispered, pulling him close. "I am Piasa's creature. To use as he will. And now there's the Tortoise Bundle, with dangers and pitfalls of its own. My life is not mine to live, Fire Cat. I dare not allow anyone close. I have to keep parts of my soul walled off, aloof and distant. It's just . . . just . . ."

"You are like lightning that can strike at any moment. Deadly and unpredictable. I am fully aware of the danger."

She nodded, savoring the feel of his body against hers. The liquid warmth spreading through her pelvis came as a welcome surprise. She'd worried that the Itza had killed that desire in her. She could feel his male arousal through his breechcloth, and was reassured when he didn't try to pull away in embarrassment. She tightened her grip, hearing him grunt against the pain in his wounds.

"Then you know why I have to remain aloof, distant."

"I'll serve you until we are finally destroyed, Lady." She felt him tense. "And you promise me that you will never, ever, marry a man you do not cherish and respect. I really can't bear it."

At the tone in his voice, unbidden laughter came bubbling up from her exhausted core. "I do swear. You hear that, Piasa? The next mythical lord to appear, you find another woman to put in his bed."

As if in answer, she saw only the flicker of movement at the corner of her eye.

Yes, he knows.

Only then did she push back, her heart hammering, her breasts tender and sheath tingling. His face was flushed, eyes smoldering like damped fires.

"Until we're destroyed, Fire Cat," she promised. "Now, I heard you say you owed some chunkey player a debt in River Mounds City. Use whatever you need to of this to re-pay it. Oh, and send Green Stick to find us a new floor mat."

What a sense of joy to be concerned with the mundane problems of life. She would savor them. Enjoy them, knowing full well that such inconsequential pleasures would be coming to an end too soon.

"Yes," Piasa whispered behind her ear. *"Trouble coming. A fluttering of moths in the night. Soon now."*

She turned, but the terrible beast had already vanished, leaving only a shiver of fear to run down her spine.

One hundred ten

It's been three days," Horn Lance said as he lounged in Wooden Doll's bed. He'd awakened late that morning, surprised that she'd let him sleep. To his additional delight, she'd sat on the edge of the bed, a wrap around her magical hips, and spooned him a tasty broth rich in sturgeon, prairie onions, ground nuts, mulberries, and mushrooms.

Then she'd laid the horn spoon aside, pulled the wrap from her waist, and eased her long body onto his. Veils of her hair had draped around her shoulders and down to tickle his skin. She'd made slow and languid love to him, stopping, holding him inside, only to rekindle an ever-more-pounding anticipation.

When his body had finally exploded, he'd felt unusually lethargic. For whatever reason, he just couldn't summon the energy to rise.

"Three days," he repeated. "Perhaps tonight you should send that girl of yours to see if there's a Trade canoe headed south. You said that most of the Natchez got away."

He studied her as she walked over and picked up a long-toothed shell comb before he added, "You could come with me."

She laughed, returning to settle at the foot of her bed.

In long strokes she began working the tangles out of her glistening black mane. "And what would I do in Natchez?"

"Be my woman."

"Why would I do that, Horn Lance?"

"I'm an honored and revered man among the Natchez. The Great Sun and the White Woman owe me. I was the one who disposed of their predecessors and handed them the Quigualtam alliance. In the meantime, I need to outfit and dispatch a canoe to the south, along the gulf. It will take a year or two, but I can get a message to the *multepal*. Tell them that *Ahau* Oxlajun Chul Balam has become ruler of Cahokia, and that they need to send a force posthaste to reinforce him."

"But your lord is dead."

"They won't know that in Chichen Itza. When they finally arrive, it will be two or three years. I'll tell them that in the meantime, my lord was assassinated, and that his body was abused by the Cahokians. They'll hear that in Natchez, where truth is whatever I declare it to be." He smiled, feeling dreamy. "The important thing is to establish Chichen Itza's northern base on the river. After that it's just a matter of time before the whole . . ."

He frowned. "Odd. I'm so tired. It's the empire. My empire. Built among the Natchez, and then we'll come for the Morning Star and Cahokia."

"Can you even sit up?" she asked, thoughtful eyes on his as she ran the comb down the length of her hair.

"Of course." He tried, his muscles gone oddly flaccid. "Well . . . This is odd. Maybe . . ."

"How can a man who can't sit up build an outpost for Chichen Itza?"

"I just have to get word to them."

"Uh-huh," she said with a smile. Then, rising, she walked to the door and set it aside, calling, "Newe, could you come in?"

Her slave girl obediently entered, going to sit where Wooden Doll pointed. Then Wooden Doll picked up a red cloth and waved it out the door. Letting it flutter down onto the firewood, she asked, "Newe, did you see the warriors out there?"

"Yes, many."

Even as the girl said it, Five Fists ducked through the door followed by five additional warriors.

Cold terror, like a spear, seemed to cut through Horn Lance's body. He should have been on his feet, panic-driven muscles ready to fight, but his body remained supine, unwilling to move.

Then Blue Heron stepped in, followed by, of all people, Seven Skull Shield.

"Hello, Horn Lance," Blue Heron greeted with a smile. "I would have liked to have discussed things with you the night you tried to kill me yet again, but apparently you had other commitments."

"How?" he whispered, surprised that his voice still worked.

Blue Heron glanced at Wooden Doll and shrugged. "You're not the only one who can offer a fortune in Trade. Fortunately, Wooden Doll is a very pragmatic businesswoman—a Trader. She and I came to an agreement. Began negotiating clear back at the wedding, actually. We concluded our agreements a while back. I asked her to distract you, a task at which she was most effective."

"How? Why?"

Wooden Doll shrugged. "She just Traded more for you than you offered. But I had an incentive. You really shouldn't have used me, led me to betray Skull. Business is business, but that really soured my regard for you."

Meanwhile, Newe had been staring up at Seven Skull Shield with frightened eyes, her arms crossed defensively over her chest.

Blue Heron followed the thief's hard gaze to the girl. She asked Wooden Doll, "Is it all right to take her now?"

"Of course."

"My pleasure," Seven Skull Shield said, reaching down with a bruised arm to drag the girl to her feet. He shoved her back to one of the warriors. "Tie her up like a turtle for roasting."

"*Mistress!*" Newe shrieked as one of the warriors dragged her toward the door.

"Your betrayal was even worse, Newe. I can't abide that."

Screaming, the girl was dragged from the room.

Wooden Doll glanced sadly at Horn Lance. "Two shell necklaces for Seven Skull Shield? That's *all* you offered her? You cheap bit of two-legged trash. I would have demanded a cup full of that wonderful achiote spice for him."

He saw her turn and wink saucily at Seven Skull Shield, who winked back and grinned.

Then the warriors were picking Horn Lance's limp body from the bed, carrying him out into the morning sun, where a crowd was calling insults beyond a line of warriors. He glimpsed Newe, gagged and bound, being tied to a carry pole. A second, stouter pole awaited him.

"Oh, don't worry," Five Fists told him. "Rides-the-Lightning tells me the feeling will come back to your limbs in a couple of hands' time. But by then you'll be safely hanging from the Morning Star's square."

The ugly war leader grinned his lopsided grin, adding, "The Keeper says no one can torture you until the thief gives you one real good hard kick down in the tenders."

"*Waxaklahun Kan! Help me!*" The plea sounded as if it had been torn from his throat.

But no War Serpent formed in the smoke-hazed blue sky.

Epilogue

Wet Bobcat led the weary party up the wide and well-traveled creekside trail. The air shimmered with humid heat. It seemed to silver the various greens of hickory, sweet gum, red and white oak, sassafras, and beech trees. He filled his nose with the familiar scents of home: the sweet grass, the blossoms of fall flowers, and rich red earth.

Fields ripe with corn, goosefoot, knotweed, beans, and squash were ready for harvest, and greetings had been called from the farmsteads they passed.

Rounding a bend he could see the immense mound of earth. Heart of his Nation, and second in size only to the Morning Star's mound, it was topped by the Natchez confederacy's famous walls. Above them, temple roofs, the World Tree, and the Great Sun's palace speared up toward the sky.

Home.

Behind him a chorus of sighs broke from his men. They were laughing now, the sensation of elation having risen during the entire long journey down the Father Water. With each day, and Cahokia farther behind, spirits and souls had recouped.

Yes, it had been a failure. But now that the gamble for

Cahokia was lost, what an incredible story it was to tell. "Honored Men," that is what the Great Sun would make each and every one of them.

Celebrated for their attempt, they'd each marry Sun Born; their children would be the next generation of nobles. Wealth, status, honor. It was all theirs to claim. The only Natchez failure, after all, was that incredible chunkey game. Lost to the Red Wing on that fatal last cast.

"We won't mention the Little Sun's last moments," Wet Bobcat reminded. "As of now that memory is forgotten. All that matters is that he knelt, and the Red Wing struck from behind. The Little Sun died as a Sun Born lord should."

"Agreed," Bitter Wood growled, then added, "Are those warriors emerging from the gate? It looks like they're lining the approach to the city gate."

"That youth we sent as a runner from the canoe landing has surely delivered our message. He has no doubt told the Great Sun, the Great Serpent, and the White Woman of our arrival." Spearing Beak almost chortled.

"We're getting a hero's welcome," Two Throws chimed in.

"Let's look like we deserve it." Wet Bobcat stiffened his back, head held high as he strode majestically past the ranks of warriors on either side of the road.

At the great gate, he bowed his head in humility and entered, climbing the stairway to the mound top where the plaza opened to the Natchez palaces and temples. The lightning-scarred World Tree pole dominated the center of the elevated plaza.

To Wet Bobcat's delight, the warriors had formed a box around them as they approached a party of Sun Born in the plaza center. The man in front wore the Great Serpent's high headdress, carried the traditional shield and war club. He had painted his face in red and black—a curious choice since it indicated violence and death.

Only when Wet Bobcat came to a halt before the party did he realize that the Great Serpent—as the high war chief was called—was not Fire Moccasin, the man who'd sent him to Cahokia at Horn Lance and Swirling Cloud's behest, but Sky Stiletto, a cousin to the recently deceased White Woman, High Pine. Nor was the White Woman, who now stood among the Sun Born behind the Great Serpent, the same Sacred Oak who had ruled when they'd left, but a cousin who'd been named Thread Woman.

"Where is Fire Moccasin?" Wet Bobcat asked, breaking protocol.

"His name is no longer spoken," Sky Stiletto told him coldly. "Is Swirling Cloud with you?"

"He is dead. Are you truly the Great Serpent? And where is Sacred Oak?"

"I am the Great Serpent. The name of the woman to whom you refer is no longer spoken. Among true Natchez, those names, along with that of the man I asked you about, are forgotten. As if they never existed."

"I don't understand." Wet Bobcat shot a sidelong glance at the box of warriors surrounding him and his small party. The looks he got in return were hard, filled with disgust.

"It was only after you went north with the Itza and his servant that we learned the extent of their treachery. How they murdered our beloved White Woman, our Great Sun, and even in Cahokia, assassinated Nine Strikes before he even knew of his brother's heinous murder. You were part of it, confidants of that foul man whose name is forgotten. You, all of you, are loathed among the Natchez!"

Wet Bobcat's heart was hammering, a fear sweat breaking out on his body. Behind him, his men were gasping in disbelief.

"How do you know this?" he cried. "What proof do you have?"

Against the black-and-red face paint, the Great Serpent's narrowed eyes looked even more deadly. He made a motion with his hand, and an Honored Man stepped forward. With a flourish, he unrolled a familiar crimson-feathered cloak.

"But . . . No! How did you get that?" Wet Bobcat almost whimpered, tears of disbelief forming behind his eyes. "It was stolen!"

Too late, he realized what he'd said, what it implied. The feeling was like his stomach and guts had dropped out of his belly.

"A Trader from Cahokia, an Anilco man named Water Bird who is well-known among us, said he had been sent by Notched Cane, a trusted servant of the Four Winds Clan Keeper and the Morning Star himself. The Trader brought the cloak along with fine pieces of copper, exquisite fabrics, and remarkable wooden carvings. These he gifted to the Natchez people, along with the cloak, explaining that the Morning Star had presented the red eagle-feather cloak to the Little Sun Nine Strikes at the conclusion of the Busk. He said that Nine Strikes had been murdered by a man named Swirling Cloud to keep him from knowing that he had become the new Great Sun upon his brother's poisoning. Adding to our horror we heard that to hide his perfidy, Swirling Cloud placed a black feather in the dead Little Sun's mouth, seeking to blame the death on the black witch!"

People gasped, most of them making warding signs with their fingers.

"He told us the Morning Star was aggrieved that he had not been able to protect Nine Strikes, and sent the gifts to the Natchez people as a gesture of his respect and a measure of how appalled he was to discover that not only Nine Strikes, but so many beloved Natchez had been assassinated by Horn Lance, the Itza, and Swirling Cloud."

Wet Bobcat fell to his knees, words frozen in his throat.

Given Sky Stiletto's expression, something foul-tasting might have been in the man's mouth. "We investigated the Cahokian's words. And found them to be true. Sun Born murdering Sun Born. Invoking the name of the black witch! The ultimate abomination. Now you come here, the last of the abomination, marching with pride after being part of the most reprehensible act in Natchez history."

"But I . . . But we . . ." Wet Bobcat lifted his arms, a desperate emptiness in his chest.

"Take them," the Great Serpent ordered. "Escort them deep into the forest just over the Choctaw border. Bury them alive beside the corpses of those whose names we have forgotten."

"No! You don't understand! We didn't—"

But hard hands reached out to grasp him by the shoulders. He felt his weapons being torn away, along with his pack and belt. They wrenched his hands around behind his back, binding them tightly.

He cast only a single glance back as he and the rest were marched away. It seemed as if the sunlight burned more brightly red as it bathed the crimson-feathered cloak.

Read on for a preview of
MORNING STAR

Moon Hunt

W. Michael Gear and Kathleen O'Neal Gear

Available in November from Tom Doherty Associates

Prologue

Years of hardship, danger, and war had imbued War Leader Five Fists with the instinct of a forest-hunting cat. Perhaps it was just a stirring of the air that brought him awake, for the Morning Star made no sound as he padded silently from his personal quarters in the great palace's rear.

Though the eternal fire had burned down to coals it cast a faint orange glow through the gloom. Just enough illumination. Five Fists was able to recognize the living god's familiar walk and posture as he headed for the artistically carved double doors that opened out into the walled courtyard.

Wincing because it was the middle of the night, Five Fists threw back his blanket, pulled on his breechcloth, and reached for his war club.

"Wasss wrong?" Foxweed asked as she stirred and clawed her long hair back. She had been sharing his bed for more than a month now. A Panther Clan woman from one of the outlying lineages, she reveled in her newfound status, and didn't mind that Five Fists was older, ugly with his poorly healed and off-centered broken jaw, or that he had problems with his sexual abilities.

"He's up," he whispered. "Go back to sleep."

"It's the middle of the night."

"He's a living miracle. The hero of the Beginning Times brought to earth in a human body. What does he care?"

Five Fists gave his head a toss, as if to shake sleep's cobwebs from his thoughts. Then, hefting the club, he started across the mat-covered floor, his steps as silent as his master's.

Outside the night was dark: Occasional clouds blotted the starry heavens. A chill lay heavy in the air and sent a shiver down Five Fist's sun-darkened and scarred hide. He ran a hand over his tattooed cheeks.

Where was . . . ? Ah, yes.

He saw the Morning Star's shadowy form as it climbed the ladder up to the bastion that dominated the southwestern corner of the clay-covered wall. The Morning Star often retreated to the high bastion, where he could look down from his monumental mound, see his remarkable city, and perhaps touch the essence of the Sky World from which his Spirit had been called.

Five Fists, from long practice, took his position at the foot of the ladder and wished he'd brought a blanket to cut the chill.

"You need not inconvenience yourself, War Leader." The Morning Star's words carried a wistful note.

"You shouldn't be out here alone, Lord."

"She's still on the river, War Leader. I can feel her."

"Who, Lord?" Five Fists stepped out so that he could see the Morning Star's shadowy form against the midnight sky. The living god stared intently off to the southwest, the smoke-laden breeze fingering the strands of his long hair where it hung down his back.

"She's so . . ."

Five Fists waited, then couldn't stand it. "So what, Lord?"

Another silence from above, then Morning Star asked, "Do you think she understands?"

Safe in the darkness, Five Fists made a face. All these years of service to the living god, and half the time he couldn't make head nor tail of what the Morning Star was talking about. Despite knowing that any answer probably wasn't going to make sense, he asked, "Understands what, my lord?"

"That all of Creation is the One, War Leader. Life is death, creation is destruction . . . hatred is love."

"I don't . . ." He took a breath. Why bother?

The ensuing silence stretched for nearly a finger of time; then the Morning Star softly said, "I am giving you an order, War Leader. You must not execute her."

"Execute who?"

"She's only a piece in the game. But a necessary one. Poor thing hasn't a clue about what is at stake."

"Lord? If you'd give me a better idea about what—"

"The balance has to be maintained, War Leader. Lady Night Shadow Star will understand. Aid her in any way you need to."

"Yes, but, what are we talking about, Lord?"

"And the woman? Hear me, War Leader. She is to be *unharmed*! Especially afterwards."

"Afterwards? After what?"

"After she achieves my death, War Leader."

The Harrowing

I *run my fingers through damp and sandy soil and listen to
the sounds of the night. The canoes are pulled up on the
beach, and I can hear waves slapping against the sterns.
An endless blanket of stars gives the night sky a frosted
look. The whitish band running across the heavens marks
the Road of the Dead—the path taken by so many of my
ancestors after their souls traveled to the western edge of
the world and made the leap through the Seeing Hand and
into the Sky World.*

*I wonder if I will ever follow in their footsteps, or if I
even want to.*

*I reach up and rub my thin face, feeling the high cheek
bones, the triangle of my nose, and point of my chin. I force
myself to smile, and know that it makes my broad mouth
into a rictus mindful of a death mask. Some call me a
beautiful young woman. Who are they trying to fool?*

*For the moment, all that matters is my deep, burning an-
ger. Call it an inferno between my souls. A hot, roaring,
devouring kind of fire.*

*I stare out at the river, which is nothing more than an
inky darkness in the night. I hear a fish splash, the croaking
of a thousand frogs, and the whir of the night insects. Even*

through the pungent tang of the greasy puccoon-root mosquito repellent that I've slathered over my skin, I smell the musky scent of river, of willows, and cottonwoods along the bank.

I think of the Powers inherent to water—of the Tie Snakes who live in the river's depths, and Snapping Turtle, and the Underwater Panther. I think of the stories told by Albaamaha elders late at night. Of men who swam down into the depths and darkness and became Tie Snakes themselves.

Since the night I drank the nectar, I, too, have become a being of darkness. Ultimately, the nectar will be my weapon of revenge.

War Leader Strong Mussel barks a laugh—the sound of it as disturbing to me as the cracking of a wooden beam. I really hate that man. Him, and all the warriors that my father sent to "escort" me to my new home. To the husband I am promised to marry.

My father? He is White Water Moccasin of the Chief Clan. High Minko, or supreme ruler, of the Sky Hand people. My mother is Evening Oak of the Raccoon Clan, who serves the people as high matron.

It is to be my "honor." Those are my mother and father's words. The verdict and order my lineage and clan. Their ultimate betrayal after I came so close to escaping.

I still don't know how it went wrong. Just an accident of circumstance? Or Power inserting itself into my life?

Power can be such a capricious force, working for its own purposes. Changing lives. Playing with someone like me as if I were nothing but a toy dangled from a string. I'd made it. Escaped. Run away with young Straight Corn. We were free, taken in among the forest Albaamaha. For those few months, we lived the rapture of our love, sharing laughter, smiles, hopes, and exploring our bodies . . .

But I lose the thread of my thoughts. I need to concentrate on where I am and why. It's been twenty days now

*since leaving Split Sky City. I have been paddled up the
Black Warrior River, carried across the portage and through
the T'so lands, and down to the Tenasee River. From there
my seemingly inexhaustible guards raced downriver to the
Mother Water. After resting for a day at its confluence with
the Father Water—and visiting with the passing Traders—
we're heading up the great river.*

*This night we are camped below what are called the
chains, a rocky constriction in the Father Water's channel.
Immediately east and behind our small camp, a gray, moss-
covered, sandstone bluff rises. Its base is choked with brush,
its top forested with oak, maple, ash, and hickory trees.*

*Our camp is positioned on the sloping bank of the
river—a narrow, sandy strip of low-terraced beaches left
by the falling water lines. War Leader Strong Mussel has
ordered my bed to be placed between the fire and the canoes,
where it is illuminated by the crackling bonfire. The rest of
the warriors surround me in a half circle, barring any
chance of escape into the willows just up from the beach.*

*As if I could get away in the first place. Strong Mussel
has tied a rawhide leash to my right ankle. He cleverly poured
water onto the complicated knots, which caused them to
shrink so tightly I'd need a couple of hands of time and the
use of a pointed hardwood stick or a sliver of bone to work
them loose. No fool, he checks my tether every night and
again the next morning.*

*I could cut the strap with a sharp stone or a flake of bone,
but they search the ground carefully before each camp. I
never have less than three sets of eyes on me at any given
time.*

*My people are the Sky Hand Mos'kogee. Masters of the
raid and war. We are adept at taking and transporting desperate prisoners over long distances. Once upon a time, I
took pride in that, having watched our victorious warriors
returning from distant raids, parading their prisoners be-*

*fore them. Now I stare longingly at the darkness, wishing I
was just beyond the fire's gleam. Out there, where I could
vanish into the night and fade into nothingness.*

*My party of warriors might be called an "escort," and I
might be the first daughter of White Water Moccasin, of the
Chief Clan's ruling lineage. My uncle, who is mother's
brother, or* mosi, *might be the tishu minko, or second chief
of the Sky Hand people. I might indeed be the second-most
important woman in my people's world, but after what I
have done, Father, Uncle, and Mother consider me a disgrace. A scandal to be dispensed with, eliminated, and forgotten. All of which means I* am *as desperate a prisoner as
these veteran and blooded warriors have ever transported.*

*I listen to an owl hooting up on the cliff, and the war-
riors tense, gazes shifting to the night. Owls are considered
bad luck among my people. Especially when they are en-
countered by war parties. This, however, is a peaceful expedition. A fact signified by the White Arrow that Strong
Mussel carries before him.*

*White is the color of peace and tranquility, of wisdom
and restraint and harmony. None of which exists within my
storming souls. I am red inside, the color of chaos, blood,
conflict, and creation.*

*I am here because I fell in love with Straight Corn. They
knew, of course. There were never any secrets in the high
minko's palace. But they thought it a child's infatuation, as
though I was enamored of a kind of sophisticated pet. The
sort of girlish intrigue that would pass when I became a
woman.*

*I'd passed my fifteenth summer when the cramps and
bleeding started. Dutifully, they locked me away in the
Women's House for the obligatory lectures on how to behave
like a proper woman. I was told in detail how a woman's
monthly discharge had to be restricted to the Women's House.
That it would pollute a man's Power, sicken his souls, and*

contaminate his possessions. A boring and endless repetition of the things I'd grown up hearing. As if I hadn't had it pounded into me since I was a baby.

Then they'd given me my first woman's skirt with its carefully tied virgin's knot, fixed my hair, and paraded me out into public for my woman's feast. For two days my womanhood was celebrated: they dangled me before every high-ranking male in the territory as a potential wife. I was given the most lavish of gifts.

And then, the final night, as guests were leaving, and Uncle and Mother where slapping themselves on the back in celebration over the triumph, I sneaked out into the darkness, took Straight Corn by the hand, and we ran away together to start our new lives.

As I sit here by the river—surrounded by guards—and nurse the rage in my heart, I wonder where he is. Is he staring up at the same night sky? Is he, too, hearing a distant owl? Is he longing for me as much as I long for him?

I know they didn't catch him. I saw Fox Willow slip away before she was spotted. She would have warned the others, given them ample opportunity to ghost away into the forest before Uncle's warriors could be sent to comb the area.

Knowing how important Straight Corn is to the Albaamaha resistance, they'd do everything in their ability to keep him free. For that, at least, I can be thankful.

I may be promised in marriage to the Morning Star, but I am far from consigned to my fate. While I was in the forest, living with the Albaamaha and sharing Straight Corn's bed, I learned the ancient ways. Became an initiate into the ancient secrets of darkness and the dangerous arts.

For now I must bide my time. Strong Mussel understands intuitively. He knows I'm far from being defeated. Somewhere, some way, I will see my chance to get away. Can he and his warriors maintain their vigilance forever?

But eventually I will no longer be his concern. Once I become the Morning Star's wife, everything is going to change. The rage is going to burn free, and I will find my way back to Straight Corn. Assuming I can be clever enough and use the ancient arts to their fullest effect.

This one thing I swear on the blood of my ancestors: Straight Corn, I will find my way back to you no matter what the cost! And no one will stand in my way.

Willing the Power to rise within me, I close my eyes, find that place of strength deep inside. I extend my arms to either side, stretching, feeling the slight breeze on my skin.

As I touch the Power, I send my call into the night. I feel them stirring, the strengthening of wings. Around me, the night stirs.

Yes, come to me! Bring the ancient Power.

I feel the first of them as they alight on my hands, fore-arms, and shoulders. Their wings caress my cheeks.

Why haven't I done this before?

A scream jerks me back to the now, and my eyes blink open.

More screams.

At first I can't make sense of the sight. The warriors are on their feet, arms flailing at a swarm of humming moths.

Is this my chance?

I get to my feet, take a step. Only to feel the leash pull tight.

Batting at the swarm of moths around us, Cloud Tassel—eyes wide with panic—nevertheless keeps hold of my tether.

The moths vanish into the night. But I smile. It will only be a matter of time.

Forge

Award-winning authors
Compelling stories

. . . .

Please join us at the website
below for more information
about this author and other great
Forge selections, and to sign up for
our monthly newsletter!

. . . . 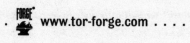 www.tor-forge.com . . . .